A ROSE AND A STAR

To Pam

A ROSE AND A STAR

A Historical Novel

Gloria West

*love
nancy ('gloria')
x*

iUniverse, Inc.

New York Lincoln Shanghai

A ROSE AND A STAR
A Historical Novel

iUniverse books may be ordered through booksellers or by contacting:

iUniverse
2021 Pine Lake Road, Suite 100
Lincoln, NE 68512
www.iuniverse.com
1-800-Authors (1-800-288-4677)

Because of the dynamic nature of the Internet, any Web addresses or links contained in this book may have changed since publication and may no longer be valid.

This is a work of fiction. All of the characters, names, incidents, places, organizations, and dialogue in this novel are either the products of the author's imagination or are used fictitiously.

ISBN: 978-0-595-47254-3 (pbk)
ISBN: 978-0-595-91530-9 (ebk)

Printed in the United States of America

PART ONE
ROSE OF THE FOREST

CHAPTER 1

▼

YEAR OF OUR LORD, 1747 A.D.

LYNDHURST—THE NEW FOREST

The room in the Verderers Court at the Queen's House was hushed and still with anticipation hanging heavily in the air.

Emotions in that room were mixed. Some of the kinder spectators wore looks of compassion while others were openly contemptuous. Some people were just curious as to the outcome of the trial. They were not particularly bothered about the defendant being found innocent or guilty.

Some, however, were possessed of one of the worst aspects of human nature, that malicious instinct which delights in misfortune befalling another. They hoped to witness the young woman in the dock being punished by a good, hearty flogging.

But all, men, women and children, were interested in what the magistrate would have to say. The jury had already pronounced their verdict and the gypsy had been found guilty of poaching on private land. The majority, of course, believed her to be guilty. It was a widely held belief that gypsies by their very nature were bound to be thieves.

The magistrate, Miles Denny, had no pretensions to nobility but he was definitely a member of the land owning gentry. He owned a large estate and was the squire of three villages. He was particularly well known in the village of Topcliffe.

Denny took a deep breath and turned to whisper to the other two magistrates sitting beside him. Then, he studied the gypsy girl in the dock. She was very thin and somewhat wan looking. Observant in such matters, Denny noticed that there was pride in her bearing and traces of beauty in her face. She was of average height for a woman but she held herself erect, with an almost arrogant tilt to her head.

The girl's dark looks contrasted with Miles' own extreme fairness. For an uncharacteristic moment, he felt mesmerised as his blue eyes wandered to the girl's small but shapely bosom. He blinked and looked up again. Suddenly, he spoke.

"Rosina Clayton, you have been found guilty of poaching in Denny Woods. A wicked deed, to be sure, but we think that to some extent you were led astray by others. We are prepared, therefore, to deal mercifully with you." He gazed haughtily around the room, almost daring the onlookers to challenge him. No-one moved or spoke.

Rosina furiously blinked the tears out of her dark eyes. She had been determined not to show these hostile strangers the inward terror that had been gripping her. So far, she had kept her body immobile, her face impassive. Her performance had been comparable to the most famous actress treading the boards on a stage. She could not be defeated now. Denny had promised mercy but she had not known if he would keep his word and compassion would be forthcoming; it was often hard to tell with his kind.

Miles Denny spoke again. "The more merciful courts, like ours, have been known to send criminals to Virginia and the sugar islands as indentured servants."

So that was what he intended her fate to be! Rosina thought. Denny paused as Rosina dug her long nails into her palms in fury.

"We did wonder about sending you to one of those far-off places, Clayton, but I had a better notion concerning your future. You will spend a day and a night in the House of Correction, then you will become a maidservant in my house on the Denny Woods where I can observe you and make sure you do not steal in future. I trust you realise that you will be expected to work hard for your keep."

A collective sigh echoed around the courtroom. Some were disappointed that they would not see the lovely gypsy whipped. Her arrogant stance invited hostility. She had shown little reaction to her merciful sentence. Surely, under the circumstances, she could at least try to *look* humble. But there were a few who admired her quiet dignity and composure in the face of adversity. Almost everybody had been surprised by the leniency of the sentence.

The squire was young, in his late twenties and he was still single. He had a reputation for being a fairly heavy drinker, a good hunter and was well known for wenching. There were some who tried to keep their female relatives out of Miles Denny's service, especially if they were young and comely. Whispers began; the squire was handsome after all and his attentions could easily turn silly maids' heads. But would even he bother with a common gypsy, even though the girl was beautiful in a scrawny, swarthy sort of way?

Denny was not generally regarded as unfair or an especially hard man but neither was he an altruist. The whisperers were rebuked and silenced.

"I trust you realise your good fortune, Clayton, and will be suitably grateful to Squire Denny," one of the other magistrates said.

Unable to speak, Rosina nodded as a sense of enormous relief began to flood through her body. Vaguely conscious of her arm being taken and being led away, she felt as if the whole trial were a dream from which she would soon awaken.

She had not been unaware of the feelings of those who had witnessed her trial. Now she felt as indifferent to them as if they had been insects flying and buzzing in the air.

Rosina cast her mind back to the events that had led up to her trial.

*   *   *   *

Sixty people lived in the camp on common land situated just outside the town of Knaresborough in Yorkshire. The Claytons lived in a large, lime green caravan. They made their living from dealing in horses they sold at markets and whenever possible, they supplemented their income with their music-making.

The head man liked them but then he caught the contagious fever which had swept through the camp, halving its population. Like so many others that year, he died from the illness. Rosina had nursed her parents through it but she and her brothers, Jacko, Arnold and Spencer, had somehow, miraculously escaped the fever This had made them unpopular with other members of the tribe.

They discussed their future, often arguing. "We'd better try our luck on the roads," Jacko said, finally. "There are ways we can make a living." He scowled at his younger brothers. "I don't want to leave the tribe any more than you do. But what else can we do? They're blaming us for the sickness."

Rosina nodded, sadly. "We know it wasn't our fault. We didn't bring the sickness to the camp. But who's going to believe that? Jacko's right. We have to leave."

The only person who had remained friendly with the Clayton family was old Esmerelda, the *cohani* or wise woman, The young girls, particularly, sought her advice on any matter under the sun. She had a special fondness for Rosina.

Esmerelda picked up her stick which she needed for walking and hobbled over to the Claytons' wagon. Nobody laughed at her awkward gait as she was well respected.

She spoke directly to Rosina who looked intently at the old woman's wrinkled, weather-beaten face.

"I 'ave always liked you Rosina, and don't wish you to come to no 'arm so I've brought you a gift which will guard you from danger. I thought it the best thing I could give you."

Esmerelda fastened a red coral necklace around Rosina's neck. The girl looked at it and fingered it, admiringly. "It's very beautiful," Rosina said and thanked Esmerelda.

"Guard it well, lass, and it will serve you right."

"I promise you I will."

Esmerelda hesitated. "I should say one other important thing before you go."

Rosina gave her a questioning look.

"Beauty can be both a blessing and a curse, girl. There are many who would take advantage of you, if you let them. Take great care not to let your beauty become your downfall."

"Tell me how I can avoid this."

Esmerelda shook her head. "I've warned you so you'll have to find out for yourself. You all go with my blessing. I've nothing further to say."

The Claytons left Yorkshire on a bright morning in early Spring. Before their parents' illness, the Claytons had been musicians of some note. Jacko was a good fiddler, Arnold played the flute, Spencer banged a tambourine. Rosina, a graceful dancer, packed her best crimson skirt, together with the castanets and tiny cymbals she used for her performance.

Travelling the lanes and by-ways, they sometimes played at fairs where there were other gypsy entertainers like fortune tellers, knife swallowers, tattooed jugglers and bare-knuckled fighters. There were also taverns where Rosina, wearing her crimson skirt, stamped, leaped and twirled. Silver coins were sometimes thrown her way. The more generous landlords provided the gypsies with a substantial meal.

Rosina's brothers, however, always kept careful watch. If any patrons tried to become too friendly with her, she would be hustled away.

On a few occasions their vigilance led to arguments which had nearly resulted in brawls. Some *gorgio* or non-gypsy men were of the opinion that a gypsy dancing girl was fair game. Rosina always managed, somehow, to persuade her brothers to leave before any physical violence took place.

"Maybe we'll find another Romany tribe who'll make us welcome," Arnold said.

"If we're that lucky, I'll look for a suitable 'usband for you, Rosie," said Jacko.

The night before, they had almost been involved in another tavern brawl and Rosina knew her brothers were becoming a little weary of constantly trying to protect her.

She nodded and closed her eyes for a second. She was not sure that she wanted to have a husband chosen for her, although she knew Jacko was concerned for her safety. But her constant dream was of herself wearing fine clothes in a very large *gorgio* house set in its own grounds, not a gypsy camp. She was not a *dukkerer* or fortune teller but now and again, she knew she had flashes of second sight. She did not mention this vision to her brothers, instinctively feeling it would be unwise.

When they were not being fed in the taverns, the Clayton brothers trapped and killed hares, rabbits, hedgehogs and pigeons. Rosina carefully removed the prickles from the hedgehogs, plucked feathers from birds and skinned hares and rabbits. They all took fish from the streams, which Rosina cleaned. She collected wood to light fires and cooked on them, also gathering herbs to flavour the food. They slept in barns or huts when it was very cold or wet, creeping out at dawn. When the weather was fine, they slept in ditches or under hedges, huddling closely together for warmth.

The Clayton family eventually wandered into the New Forest. In this ancient hunting ground, they met outlaws, deserters from the armed forces, deer poachers, thieves, footpads and highwaymen.

They finally settled with another gypsy tribe on Setley Plain, an expanse of heather and gorse at the side of the high road from Brockenhurst to Lymington. The tribe were camped at the northern end of the Forest, amongst scattered trees and thickets. The golden colour of the furze vied with their red and yellow wagons, creating an impression of immense brightness that was even more brilliant when the sun shone.

CHAPTER 2

▼

Rosina earned her living by making baskets and brooms, which she sold at markets. She also picked wild flowers which she made into posies at large towns. Wishing to make themselves useful, her brothers helped to tend the horses and ponies although they had not forgotten their music. The gypsies liked to watch the Claytons play and dance by the light of a campfire.

One evening, they went to perform at an inn called 'The Seagull' in the nearby village of Topcliffe. It was a tumbledown building. The shutters were hanging from their hinges and there was a general air of neglect about the place. Inside, a haze of tobacco smoke hung in the air, staining the grey plastered walls.

Rosina took her position with her head held high. She picked up her red skirt between her finger and thumb and made a swirling motion. Then she clicked her finger cymbals.

The fiddle and flute both played a few introductory notes as Spencer lifted up the tambourine. Then he started to shake it, making the bells on it tinkle,

Rosina swayed slightly. Then she began to whirl and dart, spin and leap. She crouched and her slim hips swayed. Her crimson skirt spun around her legs as her feet traced intricate patterns. She raised her arms, remaining absolutely still for a moment, then she began to dance more seductively.

The Claytons were all aware of a sharply indrawn breath and became aware of the fair man sitting in the corner. He was dressed like a fine gentleman, incongruous in these surroundings. He had been in conversation with some other men, who looked far more likely to be the patrons of this kind of inn.

The music having reached a climax, Rosina finished her dance with a final clash of the cymbals. Her face flushed, she curtsied as many silver coins were thrown her way. But the blond gentleman tossed a whole golden guinea!

Rosina thought that she ought to thank her benefactor personally but he left 'The Seagull' quickly.

"Well done, Rosie, you've 'elped earn us suitable reward for all our 'ard work," Jacko said, patting her on the back.

Rosina felt like saying that she had not *helped* to earn the guinea. She had been given it for her own efforts. But she knew their earnings varied widely and bit back the retort.

"We're doing well this night." Arnold spoke with considerable satisfaction. "Smile sweetly at all the fine gentlemen, Rosina, and we'll make our fortune."

Jacko frowned. "Happen," he said, "But it had better be *only* for her dancing."

"I'm certain that's *all* Rosie will be rewarded for. She deserves a lot of praise for the way she moves," Spencer said.

Rosina smiled at her brothers. "I couldn't dance nearly as well without all of you playing your instruments so well." She felt a great rush of affection for them, but it was accompanied by an inexplicable moment of foreboding. Determinedly, she cast the feeling aside. The Claytons returned to the camp, singing loudly.

Two days later, four ponies were missing from the gypsy camp and the Claytons volunteered to try to find them. All day they searched with no success. It was evening when they finally wandered into Denny Woods.

"I doubt we'll find them now," Rosina said. "We'll never see them in the dark. We'd better get back to the camp."

Reluctantly, as they were all tired, her brothers agreed. They had wanted to ride to the camp in glory on the backs of the missing ponies.

"Hurry up, Rosina, try and keep up with us if you can," Jacko said, giving a curt nod. He strode on ahead with Arnold, Rosina following with Spencer.

They were almost outside the boundaries of the estate when they heard the sound of running feet.

"Quick, Rosina, we have to get out of here!" Spencer offered her his hand to help pull her along. Rosina struggled to keep up with her brothers; then, to her horror, she fell headlong into the bracken as a sharp pain seared through her ankle. She saw a ditch.

"Get away, Spencer, run for your life! I'll hide in that till it's safe again," Rosina said, pointing to the ditch.

The young boy looked uncertain. "I'll not leave you on your own, Rosina. I can't!"

Rosina felt desperate. "Don't be so stupid. You might even be hung if they catch you."

Spencer paled. He had seen men publicly hanged. Then he shook his head. "I'm no coward who leaves his sister behind."

"God grant me patience! You must see sense!" With some difficulty, Rosina stood up and gave her youngest brother an enormous push in the small of his back. "Run! And tell Jacko so that he can come back and fetch me when it's safe."

"I'll tell him 'e'll need to carry you," Spencer shouted, as he ran on at last. Rosina half walked, half crawled over to the ditch.

She waited, terrified, as she heard the sounds of men talking and dogs barking as they drew nearer and nearer to the ditch. A few of the dogs started to sniff at the ditch.

"See what's down there." Rosina heard the abrupt order as her heart sank.

"God in Heavens, what 'ave we here?" the burly gamekeeper exclaimed. His underlings were hovering around, interested in the proceedings.

Rosina's voice came out in almost a croak. "I meant no harm, sir, honest, I was looking for some ponies which went missing from our camp. I thought they might have wandered round here."

"It's you, maid, who's been wandering about in places where you 'ave no business to be. This is Squire Denny's land. What have you been trying to steal?"

Rosina was indignant. "Nothing, I wasn't stealing. I was looking for ponies which are ours by right."

The gamekeeper snorted. "A likely tale! Do you take me for a fool, girl?" Without waiting for her reply, he said, "I believe you to be a thieving gypsy wench, probably trying to do some poaching."

"I was doing no such things! I've already told you this."

The gamekeeper slapped her hard across the face. "Hold your lying tongue. It's unusual for women to be horse thieves but that's what I think you intended when you came here tonight. I 'ope you know that stealing horses is a hanging offence."

"They can' t hang me for something I haven't done."

"I believe you tried to steal valuable horses from this estate. My master, the Squire, is away from home so I shall be handing you over to the night watchman in Lyndhurst and he can deal with you." The burly man called to one of his assistants to bring a rope and a horse.

Rosina began to weep silent tears, her ankle hurting more than ever. The rope was used to tie her hands behind her back and she was lifted up on to the horse in front of the gamekeeper.

The ride into Lyndhurst was bumpy. Rosina was extremely uncomfortable. To her horror, the gamekeeper placed his hand on her breast and began to fondle it.

She managed to bend her head far enough to bite his hand. With an oath, he drew it away but he did not try to interfere with her again.

Rosina was taken to the unkempt night watchman who flung her into a cold, dark cell. She could not sleep at all on her straw pallet as she was much too frightened of the rats that scuttled around, scratching, and the human screams that echoed around the building.

Early the following morning, the tall, blond man strode into her cell. Rosina's eyes were now accustomed to the light; she stopped blinking and noticed every detail concerning her unexpected visitor.

She knew that he must be a gentleman because he was dressed in clothes she considered to be finery and she stared at him in surprise. There was something vaguely familiar about the stern face and tight lips.

"Squire Miles Denny has come to speak with you, woman," the night watchman said, with obvious surprise.

The squire removed his black tricorne hat and she observed that he wore no wig, his golden hair being tied back with a satin ribbon. His blue eyes met her dark gaze and he gave a start.

"Were you the gypsy dancer in the Seagull in Topcliffe two nights ago?"

"Yes, sir."

"You are somewhat dirtier now." Miles Denny looked at the black ringlets, now dishevelled. Her tightly laced, low-necked yellow bodice was dusty and the long, black skirt had been torn. He looked down at the calloused bare feet.

"It's hardly my fault, sir. It's the sorry circumstances I find myself in." She hoped to see some compassion in his face but his expression did not alter, He patted the dark blue silk coat he wore over an embroidered waistcoat and re-adjusted the flounce of his white cravat. Suddenly, he spoke again.

"I see your spirit has not yet been broken."

Rosina gave him a hostile glare, but he ignored it.

"My steward had some garbled tale from my gamekeeper about a young gypsy woman trespassing on my land and attempting to steal my horses. What do you have to say about that?"

"I didn't mean to trespass on your land or to steal your horses, but your gamekeeper wouldn't listen to me."

He frowned. "I have a lot of trouble with poachers, but they're not usually women. But what *were* you doing on my land?"

"I'd come with my brothers to look for ponies which had gone missing from our camp. We didn't know the woods belonged to you."

"I only have your word against that of my gamekeeper who for all his faults, is no liar."

Rosina grimaced as her ankle gave another twinge.

"Where do you ache?" the squire asked. He spoke kindly but the abruptness of the question took Rosina by surprise.

"My wrists and ankle hurt and my feet ache horribly."

Squire Denny nodded. "I cannot say I am surprised. What is your name, girl?"

"Rosina Clayton. What is going to happen to me, sir?" she asked, fearfully.

Denny sighed, wearily. "Oh, this is a most tiresome business. If I had found you myself, I could have dealt with the matter in my own way. As things are, you will have to stand trial. Don't worry, it will only be a formality. I am one of the magistrates and the others will heed me."

Rosina did not know what a 'formality' was. She sensed that things were not going to be quite as bad as they had seemed and she began to feel the first stirrings of relief.

"And my brothers, sir, will—will they also be tried?"

Squire Denny waved a dismissive, well-manicured hand. "No, even though they had the temerity to look for you. My gamekeeper chased them away with his gun and my dogs and warned them never to come back again or else they will hang."

"They will be worried about me."

"Don't fret, Rosina. They will find out soon enough that you've come to no harm."

Rosina wondered how the squire knew this but made no comment.

Denny studied her a little longer. "How old are you?"

"Seventeen, I think."

"Ah, are you married?"

"No, sir."

"Unusual. Most gypsy girls are wedded young."

"My eldest brother wished to find me a husband but as yet he says he has not found one who was suitable for me."

"He will not need to look much further."

Rosina looked at the squire, puzzled, not understanding what he meant but he did not elaborate upon his remark.

"Listen, Rosina, and mark my words, " Denny continued. "At your trial look contrite and humble, but do not weep. You will have to spend one night in the

House of Correction which will be uncomfortable but not unbearably so. After that, you will be brought to my house the following morning."

"For what purpose, sir?" Rosina asked although she already had a very shrewd suspicion about the squire's intentions. She had lived too close to nature to be unaware of the facts of life. There was also a certain look in men' s eyes when they looked at her, which she recognised in the squire's.

She was resigned to her fate. Being seduced by this gentleman would certainly be better than being executed or brutally whipped. At least he was clean and personable. There might even be some who would envy her!

Nevertheless, once she had been seduced by Squire Miles Denny, she doubted that it would still be possible for Jacko to arrange a suitable marriage for her. She wondered if she would ever see her brothers again. She knew her thoughts were rambling.

Rosina came out of her reverie, vaguely aware of what the squire was saying.

"You will be set to work as a sewing maid. I have need of one because the last silly wench got herself with child by a footman and had to be turned off. You will save me the expense of hiring a new girl in the usual ways. In the meantime, I shall send a woman to bring you food, drink and blankets. She will also clean you up and attend to you with healing salves."

"You're being kind to me and I'm very grateful."

Denny smiled. "Maybe. I'm sure there will be many ways in which you can repay my kindness."

"I'll work hard for you, sir."

"I know you will—I shall tell you so in Court. You have no choice, because my housekeeper will not allow you to spend your days in idleness." He hesitated, then went on. "There is one more thing I must say to you, Rosina."

"Yes, sir?"

"Above all else, I wish to see you dance again. I have spared your life for this purpose."

Squire Miles Denny turned swiftly on the heels of his black leather boots, leaving the astonished Rosina staring after his tall figure.

CHAPTER 3

▼

In the narrow building of the House of Correction with its high windows, Rosina was led to a room where the other inmates paused from beating hemp to stare at her. There were rough looking men, ragged women and dirty children.

"I wonder what she's in for," one of the women said.

"Same as us I s'pose. Sellin' her fine young body."

The speaker was fat, middle aged and plain, so there was a loud shout of raucous laughter from both men and women.

"I'd sell my soul for a drink with her," one of the men said.

"It's because you was too often in your cups you're in here, you silly old devil."

"I'm 'ere just because I was poor and had to beg to live," another male voice said, bitterly.

The jailer swore at them to hold their tongues and get on with their work. He was a wiry old man without teeth who spat when he spoke but he was adept at aiming the heavy cudgel he carried at those who offended him.

To Rosina's surprise, she was given a tiny cell of her own although she had to sleep on straw like the others. The jailer left her there returning with two dry crusts of bread and a cup of water.

Later that evening, he unlocked the cell door to admit a respectably dressed, rosy cheeked, middle-aged woman who was carrying a bundle. Rosina thought the bundle looked heavy and wondered what was in it. The Jailer locked the door again as he left.

"Squire sent me to tend to you, maid. I have to say I'm 'mazed myself that you're to work in our household but it's not for the likes of me to ask him about his reasons. I'm his upper-parlourmaid. My name's Lydia Maynard," the woman said.

Rosina did not reply. She felt as if she were in a complete daze.

"Eat and drink first. You must be famished." Lydia produced bread, cheese and a flask of cider from her bundle and took apples from her apron pocket.

"Thank you," said Rosina. "I'm very grateful to you."

"It's Squire you should thank. I'm only obeying his orders."

Rosina proceeded to eat and drink voraciously while the older woman watched. When she had finished, Lydia said, "I'm known to have a certain touch with healing matters. If I'd been born a boy, I might even have become an apothecary but as things are—" she shrugged, "I'm used a lot to treat the servants' ailments."

"It must be most useful to have this knowledge, ma'am," Rosina said, trying to appear courteous.

"Oh it is, I assure you. At least in some ways." Lydia seemed pleased, then her manner became more brisk. "I'll see if the water I've brought is still hot." Gingerly, she took a jug and a cake of soap out of her bundle, testing the water with her elbow. "It's just about warm enough. Wash yourself. You'll have a proper bath tomorrow. I know Mrs Webb will make you." She handed the jug and soap to Rosina who obediently washed her hands and face.

"And your feet, they badly need it," Lydia said.

"I shall have to pour the water over my feet, it might make a puddle on the floor."

"No matter. The jailer can see to its being cleared up."

Rosina poured the water over her feet. She wriggled her toes, liking the feeling.

"Now lie down on the floor and lift up your skirts so that I can see your legs properly. I was told you had some bruises and cuts, but nothing too serious."

Hesitantly, Rosina did as she was told.

"No need to be feared, girl. I'm not going to hurt you. In fact, you'll be as right as rain when I'm done with you." Lydia took some ointment from her apron pockets and proceeded to rub it over Rosina's legs, arms and chest. It felt comforting.

"I feel a lot better now," Rosina said, trying to hide her surprise.

Lydia nodded with satisfaction. "Try and sleep as best you can. I'm sure you need it." She brought two thick blankets out of her bundle and placed them on top of Rosina who thanked Lydia for all her help.

Lydia smiled. "It was nothing much, really." She banged on the cell door and shouted for the jailer, who hurriedly came to open it. Rosina was pleased to see he seemed to have some respect for Lydia. The woman pointed to the water on the floor and left without a backward glance. The jailer called for his assistant who brought a cloth to wipe up the water. Then they both left the cell.

Rosina lay down in her tattered shift, closed her eyes and fell asleep.

Early, the following morning, one of Squire Denny's grooms arrived to collect her.

"Squire's 'orse waits outside, maid," the man said "You're to ride behind me. I'll help you mount if you can't manage."

"I'm used to horses and ponies," Rosina said, proudly.

The groom shrugged. "Come on, then," he said, brusquely. "Follow me."

Miles Denny's house was the finest Rosina had ever seen. The glistening white panels on the front door had a large brass knocker in the centre. Long windows gleamed at each side of the door, behind sturdy pillars. Rosina considered it to be very grand and wondered how it would feel to live there.

The groom reluctantly helped her to dismount. She sensed that he did not approve of her. He tied the horse to a post.

"I'll take you to the kitchen," he said. "Here be the gypsy maid you was expecting, Mrs Webb."

The housekeeper nodded. "Ah yes, Rosina Clayton."

When the groom had left, however, she looked Rosina up and down.

"I know Lydia Maynard tended to you last night as well as she could. But you'll have a real bath now and given some decent clothing. I expect you're somewhat dirty in your habits."

Rosina bit back the retort that she had always bathed in streams and lakes. She thinks I'm nothing but a dirty, thieving, gypsy brat, she thought. I'll have to prove her wrong.

Mrs Webb sent the menservants out of the room. "Undress yourself," she said, curtly.

"Yes, ma'am, " said Rosina.

The housekeeper rang a bell and a tin bath was brought in by a young maid-servant who gave Rosina a curious glance. Other maids started filling it with jugs of hot water.

"That's enough gawking," Mrs Webb snapped and they hastily assumed modest expressions.

"Where shall I put my old clothes, ma'am?"

"Leave them on the floor." Mrs Webb looked as if she found the subject highly distasteful. She gazed disdainfully at the brightly coloured skirt and shawl. "They are much too outlandish for a servant in this household." She noticed that she had kept her coral necklace on.

"Take that necklace off at once. Fripperies and gewgaws are not seemly for servants either."

Although she did not want to offend the housekeeper, Rosina felt she must make a stand. She had great faith in the necklace's powers for good fortune. She fingered it, protectively. "I'm afraid it's impossible to remove, ma' am."

Mrs Webb frowned. "A likely tale. Take it off this very minute or I shall do it for you."

"I have already told you, Mrs Webb. I can't."

The housekeeper moved forward. But something about the look in Rosina's eyes made her draw back, almost fearfully.

"I suppose there's not much harm in one small item of jewellery. It was only a cheap fairing I suppose," she muttered.

"This is no fairing, ma'am. It was a precious gift," Rosina said.

Mrs Webb ignored her comment. "Be quick now, girl, and get into that bath before the water gets cold."

Rosina stepped gingerly into the steaming tub, catching her breath as the hot water swirled around her body. One of the maids handed her a cake of soap and a washcloth. Sinking beneath the water, Rosina abandoned herself to the luxury of the bath, closed her eyes and lay back.

"Get on with it, girl!" Mrs Webb's sharp voice made her jump and she sat up, so quickly that the water splashed over the side of the bath. "And you can clear that up when you've done," the housekeeper told her, tartly.

By the time she had finished washing herself, her body was pink from the heat of the bath and little creases were appearing on her hands. She took a deep breath and plunged her head beneath the water, using the soap to work up a lather all over her dark hair.

"Here—dry yourself and make haste about it!" ordered Mrs Webb, shoving a coarse towel into her hands

A young girl entered the kitchen with women's clothes over her arm. "Hurry up and get dressed, Clayton," Mrs Webb snapped. The girl handed the clothes to Rosina.

Rosina put the clean white shift on first, then the grey homespun gown with the linsey woolsey petticoat. She tied the striped linen apron around her waist and put the mob cap on her head. She felt strange in them, as if she had suddenly acquired a totally different identity.

"And now your shoes. We cannot have you going around like a ragamuffin," the housekeeper said.

Mrs Webb sent the girl to fetch a pair of plain leather shoes which Rosina found a little too large but she did not argue about wearing them.

"Do you know what your duties here will be, Clayton?"

Rosina shook her head. She thought it prudent to deny any knowledge of the squire's expectations. "I have no idea, ma'am."

Mrs Webb pursed her thin lips. "The Master says you are to become a sewing maid. I presume you can sew well."

"Of course I can."

"I would have said we already have enough sewing maids. Now *if* this matter had been left to me—" Her manner left no doubt in Rosina's mind that in her opinion, the housekeeper ought to have been the one to decide—"I would have engaged you as a scullery maid. However, you will be sharing a bedroom with two scullery maids and our kitchen maid. Have your supper now and then you will be shown where you are to sleep."

Rosina was told to sit at the stick back chair at the smaller table in the kitchen. Mrs Webb gave instructions to one of the maids to burn her old clothes. Reluctantly, Rosina watched the girl take them away.

The housekeeper took her place for her own meal with the rest of the upper servants at the refectory table.

After Rosina had eaten, the kitchen maid showed Rosina the attic bedroom where she would sleep. They passed Lydia Maynard in the corridor. She smiled cordially at Rosina who warmed to her even more, relieved to think there was at least one kindly servant in the squire's employment.

The kitchen maid pointed out a room where the under-parlourmaid slept. "She's lucky enough to sleep on her own," the girl said with a sly wink at Rosina who did not respond.

Rosina had no desire to gossip and jeopardise her new position or to talk about a possible friend of Lydia's.

CHAPTER 4

▼

The next morning Rosina was taken to the sewing room by Polly Davis, the under-parlourmaid. She was a pretty, blonde girl with a slightly affected manner. Without actually saying anything uncomplimentary, she appeared to look down on the other girl.

Rosina thought Polly gave herself airs and graces. It was not long before she knew why. She heard rumours from the other servants about Polly providing certain favours for the Master. So that was why she had a room to herself, to provide easy access for the squire! Well, she did not care, if it kept his attentions away from herself.

There were three other sewing maids, Annie Duke, Eliza Collins and Susan Williams. All the girls were supervised by Mrs Johnson. The head sewing maid was a widow whose late husband had been one of Squire Denny's tenants. Like Mrs Webb, Mrs Johnson showed little surprise at the sight of Rosina. Very briefly, she introduced Rosina to the other sewing maids.

"Right, Clayton, follow me, I'll show you where you have to sit and give you your first piece of work."

"Yes, ma'am." Rosina followed Mrs Johnson to a small table on which needles and thread had been placed.

"I'll bring the cloth over to you," Mrs Johnson said. "You'll be making a shirt." She paused, with an air of having a piece of important news to impart. "Let me make one thing clear, Clayton, on no account do my maids talk to each other while they are working."

Rosina shook her head. "I won't, Mrs Johnson."

"You'd better not. Now sit down on that chair." Mrs Johnson brought some white lawn over to Rosina and handed it to her. "See you make a neat job of it." The head-sewing maid bustled away.

Rosina bent her head to her task and plied her needle industriously, determined not to let any faults be found in her work. She noticed that when Mrs Johnson' s back was turned for a second, the girls whispered to each other although they ignored Rosina. Susan, however, gave her a tentative smile. Rosina decided that the other girl was probably timid.

On her second day, Rosina saw Annie Duke knock Susan's arm as she walked past her table. Susan put her hand on the table to steady herself.

"Oh dear," said Annie, "I'm so clumsy at times. I don't mean to be."

"She did mean it," Susan, nearly in tears, whispered to Rosina.

"Is she Mrs Johnson's favourite?" Rosina asked. Susan looked startled. "Yes, how did you know?"

"I guessed."

"I've pricked my finger now and will be in trouble for spillin' blood all over the squire's shirt."

Rosina saw Annie Duke speak to Mrs Johnson but did not hear what was said. Eliza Collins looked in Rosina's and Susan's direction. Her expression was fearful.

Angrily, Mrs Johnson strode up to Susan's table. "Another garment you've ruined with your carelessness, Williams. I ought to turn you off."

"Ma'am, please don't do that!" Susan pleaded, choking back a sob.

Mrs Johnson hesitated for a moment, then sighed before she spoke again. "I'm too soft hearted for my own good, sometimes. Very well, Williams, I'll give you one more chance but you can work late tonight and your wages will be docked."

"Excuse me, ma'am, but I don't think you're being fair," Rosina said.

"And who asked for your opinion, Clayton?"

"Nobody, but I saw what happened."

"Really, what was that?"

"Annie knocked Susan's arm. She probably didn't do it on purpose but she made Susan prick herself with the needle."

Mrs Johnson frowned. "Is this true, Williams?"

For a split second, Susan seemed about to deny it. She caught Rosina's eye, then looked at Mrs Johnson, her manner much more bold and said, "Yes, it is, ma'am."

Mrs Johnson pursed her lips. "All right, I'll believe you both this time. There'll be no punishment for an accident. Go and wash your hands, Williams, then come straight back." She turned her head. "Stop gawking as if you're at a freak show, Collins. All of you get on with your work."

When she had the opportunity, Susan whispered to Rosina. "Thank you for speakin' up for me, I'm really grateful."

"It was the least I could do in the circumstances. You didn't deserve to get into trouble."

Eliza Collins crept over to Rosina's table when Mrs Johnson had left the room for a few minutes. "That was a brave thing you done, Rosie, speakin' up for poor Sue like that. Annie Duke's always tryin' to cause trouble for her."

"I hope she won't in future."

Annie Duke rushed over to Rosina's table, her face crimson with rage. "You tryin' to call me a liar, Clayton, tryin' to make me look a fool in front of Mrs Johnson?"

Rosina met the other girl's furious gaze, calmly. "No, I said it was an accident that Susan's shirt got spoilt."

Annie was about to make a further heated retort but she quailed at the hard look in Rosina's eyes and said nothing more. She drew back as Mrs Johnson returned.

"Maids!" Mrs Johnson said, furiously. "There's been far too much gossiping and idling already today. I don't expect to hear another sound from any of you. Get back to work this instant and look sharp about it!" The rest of the day passed uneventfully.

Rosina felt that Mrs Johnson, like Polly, secretly despised her. She tried to please the older woman who neither favoured or bullied her more than the other sewing maids in her charge. Rosina was wary yet polite with Annie. She had made friends with the other two girls, which had pleased her.

She had not been sure at first if the other servants would readily accept her or if they would openly despise her for her gypsy blood. Among the indoor staff there were a butler, a cook and many footmen. On the whole they were reasonably friendly as far as this was possible with all the work they had to do which kept them fully occupied.

Rosina was often puzzled by the fact that the staff never seemed to make even a casual remark about the Romanies. Once the initial surprises of her new life had been overcome, Rosina settled down. Although she had to work hard with long hours spent plying her needle, she did not find her tasks especially arduous

She learned that the squire had brothers and sisters. They were all married and lived in different parts of the country.

There were, however, aspects of her old life, which Rosina missed badly. She missed watching the sun rise and the brilliant glow of its setting. The dawn chorus of the birds was now fainter to her ears. She missed the company of the tribe, where she felt she was accepted and not a stranger. She longed to hear of her brothers' welfare but knew this was highly unlikely.

But there were compensations. Rosina was better fed, eating more substantial meals with more varied fare than she had ever had before. Even the small attic bedroom offered better shelter and more comfort than a tent or wagon. As for the house itself, it was certainly more luxurious than anywhere else she had known. She was not allowed to go into the squire's rooms. Having merely glimpsed them, her favourite was the ballroom. Oh, how her feet itched to dance again!

One morning, Mrs Johnson thrust two lengths of silk into Rosina's hands, one purple and one yellow.

"The squire especially asked that you should make yourself a bodice with the yellow silk and a skirt with the purple, Clayton. The skirt should reach just above your ankles."

Mrs Johnson gave a disapproving sniff as the other sewing maids stared.

"For myself, ma'am? It's not usual, surely?"

Mrs Johnson shrugged "The squire has given instructions."

"An order we are not to question, I believe? I have often heard you say the gentry can be somewhat strange in their whims."

Rosina was being more daring and facetious than usual. For some reason, she felt an inner excitement, an emotion she had not experienced for a long time.

For once, the head-sewing maid was flustered. "Quite so, Clayton. There is much for you to do, so do not waste the day in idle gossip about matters which do not concern you."

Rosina bent her dark head, hiding a smile.

Mrs Johnson marched to the table on the other side of the room and brought back some tiny silver bells. "Squire has also instructed that you are to sew these to the hem." She turned to rebuke the other girls for staring. "Clayton, these garments are to be finished for tomorrow evening, so hurry up."

Rosina worked hard on the garments and was grateful when the time came at last to eat her supper. When she went to bed, she passed Polly Davis on the staircase and wondered why the other girl gave her a look of dislike. Rosina did not sleep well; she was disturbed by strange dreams.

*   *   *   *

"I trust you have finished the garments Mrs Johnson instructed you to make for yourself, Clayton," Mrs Webb said the following evening.

Rosina nodded. "Yes, I have."

The housekeeper cleared her throat. She looked as if she were about to disclose distasteful news.

"You are to put them on immediately, then, as he wants to see you. Go to the Master in the saloon. He has come back from his hunting trip and finished dining."

Rosina stared at her, not daring to ask why the squire wanted to see her.

"Go on girl! Don't keep him waiting."

"Yes, ina'am."

Rosina left the room with her head held high. She ignored the pointed looks, sly nudges and whispers that followed her.

CHAPTER 5

▼

Timidly, Rosina ventured into the saloon where Squire Denny and his three friends, all around the same age, were seated at a mahogany table. A deck of cards and empty wine and brandy glasses stood on the table.

Denny looked up and smiled as Rosina entered. The tiny bells stitched on the hem of her purple skirt tinkled as she moved.

She took a deep breath and bobbed a small curtsy. "I was told you wished to see me, sir." He gave a slight inclination of his head.

Startled, Rosina noticed the stockily built parson, Sebastian Coleman, was present. She had known the squire had company but not who his guests were.

Mrs Webb always ushered the servants into the parson's presence in the private chapel for a service early on Sunday mornings. Rosina had never liked the parson. His sermons often tended to be sanctimonious and he seemed to enjoy talking about hellfire.

The schoolmaster, Robert Elms, was tall and thin with a long featured face. Rosina did not care for the way he was ogling her. There was also a new acquaintance of the squire's, a sea captain called Charles Mountjoy. The captain was aged thirty but he looked younger. He was tall with broad shoulders and his complexion was weather-beaten. His thick, dark hair was tied back in a pigtail. He was not quite conventionally handsome as his features were a little on the large side but Rosina thought he had a very pleasant face. She felt attracted to him yet nervous in his presence.

"This is my wild, gypsy rose, Mistress Rosina Clayton," Denny said, placing a proprietary arm around Rosina's shoulders. "Rosina, this is Captain Charles Mountjoy; we met quite recently as we did some business together."

Charles inclined his head. "I am honoured to make your acquaintance ma'am." The captain had a deep, resonant voice and as he bowed over her hand, making her feel that he was treating her as if she were an important lady, Rosina flushed with pleasure.

She was forced to turn her head away, however, as Miles spoke to his other companions. "I also told you two gentlemen about the gypsy wench. What do you think of her?"

"A fine filly, to be sure, if a little coarse complexioned. But that's only a minor blemish," said Elms. "One which can easily be overlooked if the maid pleases in other ways."

Rosina blushed; she was embarrassed by Elms' words in front of Captain Mountjoy. She glanced at the captain whose face was impassive."

"I have seen the girl before," Coleman said, "at my services. The way you have dressed her now, Miles, is certainly an improvement upon her dull servants' gowns."

"I am glad you approve of her," Denny smiled.

Rosina clenched her teeth and waited in trepidation for his next words. What did these men want of her? She was frightened that she might be raped by all four men and possibly murdered afterwards. Instinct told her that Captain Mountjoy was not a rapist and murderer but perhaps he would be egged on by the others. She decided he would be the one she would appeal to should she seem to be in any sort of danger.

"Then, what do you say to my suggestion that we have a wager? Whoever wins, will enjoy the gippo's favours?"

"Why don't we all take it in turns to enjoy her? I should like that very much, indeed," Elms said, almost licking his lips.

Rosina repressed a shudder, watching them with wide, frightened eyes.

"I strongly object," Captain Mountjoy protested. "I don't wish to take part in such a distasteful bet."

"Come on, Mountjoy, don't change your name to 'Killjoy'," Coleman said. The others laughed and Rosina disliked them for doing so. "You're Miles' guest after all, so why spoil his game?"

The captain looked as if he were about to make a heated retort; then Denny swiftly whispered into his ear. Mountjoy said nothing more although he looked uncomfortable. "As a clergyman," Coleman continued, "I could not allow this matter to become widely known but I should definitely savour every minute of it."

Rosina decided that she hated Squire Miles Denny. She would have hated him if he had merely wished to seduce her himself, then turned her off. But to enjoy taking part in her rape with three other men—he was a dreadful villain.

The squire glanced at her. For a moment, she saw a vague hint of compassion in his blue eyes. She saw Captain Mountjoy's sympathetic gaze and his clear grey eyes locked and held with hers. Rosina turned away, feeling like crying.

Denny shook his head. "I think it will be more fun if one of us wins her. Let's play a hand of whist with Rosina as the prize."

All of the men looked at each other, doubtfully.

"What do you say, Robert?"

Elms hesitated. The squire clapped him on the shoulder. "Come now, you're normally a good sport."

"Yes, I suppose I am. Very well, we'll do as you say."

"I'm game," Coleman said.

"And you, Captain, what do you say?" Denny asked Mountjoy.

Mountjoy paused, looking uneasy. "I am your guest, I suppose," he said, stiffly.

"Good, I'm glad we're all in agreement," Denny said. He turned to Rosina. "Go and sit in that corner while we play." He pointed to a walnut chair at the other side of the room. Rosina obediently walked over to it and sat down, watching the men, carefully.

She guessed that the clergyman had had mixed feelings about seducing her. She prayed that he would not win the game. Neither did she want Elms to win. She disliked Miles Denny for suggesting it, therefore she very much hoped that Captain Mountjoy would be the winner.

Rosina closed her eyes and clasped her hands tightly together while the whist game was in progress. She saw herself standing on the top of a barrel. A crowd stood around her and their expressions were malevolent. She fingered her coral necklace, opened her eyes and the vision disappeared.

Deliberately, she studied the portraits of the squire's relations and ancestors, and the tapestries of hunting scenes hanging on the walls.

The hand of cards came to an end with a triumphant yell from Denny. "I have won the wager, Rosina! Come over here. You are my prize."

She stood up slowly, disappointed that Mountjoy had not won. She knew she must not show this, and walked over to the squire. He put a possessive hand upon her shoulder.

"Accept my condolences, gentlemen, that you are the losers. But I have a little compensation for you. You have not seen Rosina dance. Believe me, it's well worth watching."

"Shall we be watching this in the ballroom, Miles?" the clergyman asked.

"Yes, if Robert will kindly play the spinet for us."

Elms agreed that he would and they all went to the large, gilded ballroom where the squire sent for more wine.

The schoolmaster played a few bars of music while Rosina climbed steps that led on to a small stage. Denny and Mountjoy sat down where they would have the best view of her.

Rosina was more used to dancing to the music of a fiddle than a spinet but she knew that she danced just as well.

Her dance described the flight of birds and the ripple of streams and towards the end, it became frenzied. Miles Denny held up his hand to call a halt.

"Enough!" he said, harshly. He handed Rosina a glass of white wine which she drank, thirstily.

"I have never seen such an exciting performance before," Mountjoy said. "Thank you for letting me watch it, Squire Denny, but I fear I must go now. I hope you will excuse me."

"Yes, of course."

"Goodnight gentlemen, goodnight Mistress Clayton."

"Goodnight, sir," Rosina said, disappointed that he was leaving early. "I hope you will return soon." Denny gave her a sharp glance and she forced herself not to watch Mountjoy's departing hack as he strode out of the room as if he were in a great hurry and with a face like thunder.

"Bravo, gypsy," Sebastian Coleman said. "The best dancing I have seen in many a long day."

"You did not think it was a little—well, *sinful*, sir?" Rosina asked.

The clergyman looked uncomfortable. "Er no, not in these circumstances. Servants should always strive to please their masters."

The squire coughed in order to smother a laugh.

"I wish I had won you from your master's service, wench," the schoolmaster said.

Rosina wondered why she disliked him. He had not, after all, done her any harm. Her intuition told her that he was probably a little over-severe with his pupils so possibly he would be the same with his women if he had any. She did not think he was married.

"I trust you will be leaving now, gentlemen. The hour grows late." Denny's tone implied that he very much wished them to depart.

"We knew you had a special trick up your sleeve, tonight, Miles, you sly dog," Robert Elms said.

"It was most entertaining," said Sebastian Coleman.

With some reluctance, they took their leave. Rosina was vastly relieved to see them go. The squire turned to her and winked. He held out his hand and Rosina took it, no longer caring what would happen to her. She expected the squire would take his pleasure then send her away. If he did so, she would appeal to Captain Mountjoy to employ her as his servant.

"I should not have cared for Mr Coleman or Mr Elms to have won the game, sir," she said, shyly.

"Or the captain?" Denny asked.

"He would have been preferable to the other two," Rosina said, carefully.

Denny smiled. "It was always my intention to win you, Rosina. I did not want the others to put their greedy hands upon you. My cards were marked." He took her hand and led her through the saloon and the withdrawing room behind it, to the bedroom.

Until now, Rosina had been forbidden to enter the squire's rooms so she was unprepared for the apartment they entered. It was a large room, beautifully furnished with green japanned chairs and lacquer chests. Heavy gold brocade curtains were drawn across the huge windows, and in the ornate grate a fire burned and crackled. The only light came from a candelabra, holding six tall candles, which stood on a table beside the huge canopied bed.

Rosina had never seen such an enormous bed before. It was covered with a glowing crimson damask counterpane and piled high with an assortment of velvet cushions.

For a moment, she swayed, almost overcome by the heat of the room and the scented air. It smelt almost like a church, she thought.

Beside her, Miles slipped an arm around her waist to steady her, aware that she was trembling.

"Are you unwell?" He sounded impatient and Rosina flinched at his tone.

"No, no—it's just so warm—and the perfume ..."

He urged her towards the bed. "Come, I'll help you remove your charming clothes; you will feel cooler and I shall delight in warming you up again."

Rosina blushed and looked down at the floor, biting her lip. There was an aura of masculinity about Squire Miles Denny which she found appealing in spite of herself.

Denny picked her up, placed her on the bed and began to slowly undress her. Rosina was experiencing an unknown sensation all over her body and knew she had never felt like this in any other man's company.

She knew she was acting against all her family's and the church's teaching by experiencing forbidden desires of the flesh. Rosina felt, however, that she was as powerless to resist her longing to come to know Miles Denny's body intimately, as she was to command the waves of the sea to stop foaming.

His tone more gentle, Miles said, "I know it's your first time so I'll try not to hurt you." He took her in his arms and stroked her face. "You've developed some pleasing curves while you've been living here—you're not as thin as you used to be. Your looks have definitely improved."

Rosina was delighted by his compliment and thanked him warmly.

They kissed, a completely sensuous kiss that aroused her responses and her lips gradually opened under his. She felt as if she were in a seventh heaven; nevertheless, she was nervous of disappointing him.

"Miles, I'm not sure what to do to please you."

He laughed. "I'll soon show you, sweetheart, just trust me now." He cupped her breasts in his hands and kissed them. Rosina began to relax in the tight grip of his arms as his hands caressed her with an expert touch and she discovered feelings she had never known existed. The golden glow of the candlelight illuminated her face.

"Rosie, my love, you're beautiful," Miles whispered.

Rosina felt a sharp pain that made her cry out as Miles entered her but afterwards she felt as if she had been swept away on passionate wings of love. They gave a mutual sigh of contentment as fulfilment came.

Denny turned back the bed covers. "I think we should spend the rest of the night inside the bed." Happily, Rosina nodded in agreement. Miles shouted for a footman to bring two glasses of wine. When the manservant came, his face was impassive; he did not look at the gypsy girl lying in his master's bed.

The golden wine glowed through the crystal. Denny and Rosina drank and when she had finished she toyed with her glass. The squire gently removed it from her fingers and placed it on the floor beside his own.

He pulled her head on to his shoulder. "Go to sleep now, Rosina." He smiled down at her. "My dear, I may wake you up again later." Rosina gave him a warm smile in return. "I shall not object in the least."

He laughed and gave her bottom a light slap. "You're already becoming a wanton."

"Only with you, Miles."

"I warn you, it had better be only with me!"

Drifting off to sleep in a state of complete happiness, Rosina thought of what a gypsy wedding would have entailed—matrons entering the bridal tent to examine the deflowered bride and emerging with a handkerchief soaked in her blood which they would show to other members of the tribe. At least, she had been spared that humiliation.

She knew that gypsy men expected virgin brides and terrible punishments existed for gypsy women who lay with *gorgio* men. Severe beatings or even mutilations could take place. She had seen old women who had been mutilated and the sight had struck terror into her heart.

Rosina gazed at Miles' sleeping form. She now had faith in him not to send her away and to protect her from such suffering.

CHAPTER 6

▼

Rosina woke early in the morning, Squire Denny had made love to her twice more during the late night hours and she had felt happy and fulfilled.

He woke not long after her and curtly told her to dress herself quickly. Trying to hide her disappointment that he wished to send her back so soon, she did so and began to leave the room.

"Rosina, where are you going, girl?"

"To the sewing room when I have changed my clothes."

"Stay here. Come and sit on the bed. I have an announcement to make to all the household which you, above all, should hear."

Puzzled but unquestioning, she did as she was told.

Denny rang a bell and a sleepy footman appeared, carrying a breakfast tray with two plates which the squire took from him.

Rosina looked hesitantly at the food.

"Eat with me, Rosie. You must be hungry."

The footman returned to say that all the staff had been assembled in the saloon.

"Come, Rosina. I need you beside me," Miles said, offering her his hand. She felt as if she were experiencing a dream from which she would soon awaken.

The servants all stared when the squire entered the saloon with Rosina by his side.

"What a brazen hussy, flaunting herself like that! I *never* behaved in such an improper fashion, I was most discreet," Rosina heard Polly Davis speak softly to Lydia Maynard, who frowned.

Squire Denny held up his hand for silence. "The reason I have sent for you all is to inform you that Mistress Rosina Clayton is no longer my servant. She is your new mistress."

There was a general shuffling of feet, a sullen murmur although Susan Williams was grinning and Eliza Collins was smiling slightly. Mrs Webb and Mrs Johnson looked horrified. Polly made no effort to disguise her look of pure venom at Rosina.

"She is at all times to be obeyed and treated with the greatest respect," Denny continued.

There was more shuffling of feet, twitching of skirts and clearings of throats. Polly's face had turned white. She clenched her teeth and stared down at the floor as if she would like to summon a devil from it.

"I trust I have made my wishes quite clear," Miles said, firmly.

"With all due respect to *you*, sir," Mrs Webb said, "I don't feel I can stay in your service. I should like to retire and live with my widowed brother."

"As you wish," Miles said, abruptly. Mrs Webb gasped; she had thought he would try to persuade her to stay in his employment.

"May I leave now, sir?"

"Yes, immediately. Does anyone else wish to do the same? Say so now, I'll not try to stop you."

Some of the servants looked uncomfortable but none of them spoke. Mrs Webb made what she hoped was a dignified exit from the room although she was almost running.

Rosina, while understanding how the staff felt, could not help a sense of elation. She would soon be empowered to order around some of the very people who had looked down upon her as a common gypsy when she had first come to the household. They had resented her presence amongst them. Now they would regret it! She had decided, however, to try to help three particular servants.

She wondered at her daring but steeled herself and whispered into the squire's ear. He nodded and spoke to the assembled company.

"From today, Lydia Maynard is the new housekeeper. Eliza Collins, a sewing maid, will become Head Parlourmaid and Susan Williams will become Mistress Clayton's lady's maid. You will need to engage two more sewing maids, Mrs Johnson."

"Yes, sir," Mrs Johnson said through clenched teeth.

Lydia looked amazed and Susan was beaming. "You can look mighty pleased with yourself, Sue Williams but you ain't workin' for no lady!" Polly Davis hissed. Susan ignored her.

"Come, Rosina." The squire offered her his arm. She took it, but could not resist a beaming smile at the staff as she swept out of the room.

"You have done me a great honour sir," Rosina said. "I don't know how to thank you."

He smiled. "I shall soon be going out hunting again but in the meantime, we will return to the bedroom where I shall show you how you can thank me properly."

Denny winked at her, making Rosina feel as if her heart had turned over.

As Rosina lay in her new lover's arms, Miles said, "I shall instruct a dressmaker to call, but in the meantime they will be making two new dresses for you in the sewing room."

"They need two new maids," Rosina said, smiling.

"Don't worry, Mrs Johnson will soon find them. I have to leave you soon, love, but I'll hurry back."

She started to sit up, but he gently pushed her back on to the pillows.

"Stay there and rest. I'll send Lydia to you. I shall be back as soon as I can to enjoy your company." He kissed her again.

Denny rose, dressed quickly and departed. Rosina watched him go with a fond, drowsy smile.

She had almost fallen asleep again when there was a loud knock on the door. Lydia Maynard and Polly Davis entered.

Rosina frowned. "I was told you were coming to see me, Lydia, but why is Polly here?"

Polly glared at Rosina as Lydia said, "Squire told me to ask you what sort of dresses you would like made for you. Polly's going to help in the sewing room till Mrs Johnson has her new maids."

"I see. Well, Polly, go and fetch me a pencil and paper and I'll draw what I want."

Polly gave Rosina another look of dislike and stalked out of the room.

"Will you have Polly dismissed, Rose—I mean, ma'am?" Lydia asked, stiffly.

"I don't think it's in my power."

"You could have a word in the squire's ear."

"I shall not do so if she keeps a civil tongue in her head."

"You are generous, ma'am, and I can't thank you enough for what you have done for me."

Rosina waved the older woman's thanks aside. "Think nothing of it."

"But I do, I'm very grateful to you, only I have to say, ma'am, that I think you should be careful while Polly's around. She said you had put a spell on the squire."

Rosina sighed. "I expect all the servants believe this even though it's not true. Some of us gypsies do have knowledge of magic lore. I know you have some healing knowledge. Do you also have magic powers?"

Lydia looked uncomfortable. "My mother, like her grandmother before her, was considered to be a witch."

Rosina leaned forward, fascinated.

"Tell me about them."

"My grandmother was a herb woman who lived in her own cottage. She sold herbs and flowers at markets, but she also made tinctures and special honey for fevers, cough syrups and healing salves. She taught my mother who passed her knowledge on to me."

"Did she also know how to make love potions?" Rosina asked, with a smile.

Lydia looked sheepish. "Some thought so. I don't."

"So we shall never know."

"No. Other people thought worse things about my mother. One of the charcoal burners who lived nearby was a simpleton and one day he tried to drown her in a stream because he had heard the parson preach against witches."

"Oh, poor woman, how unfortunate! Did she drown?"

"No. The squire rescued her. He pulled her out of the water."

"That was very brave of him." Rosina began to see Squire Denny as a knight in shining armour.

"It was, but she died soon afterwards from a fever which could not be cured. That was when the squire took me into his service. He's always been kind to me."

"And I'm sure you've repaid his kindness by being a loyal servant."

"I've always tried to be one, ma'am. As I shall be to you."

There was an impatient knock at the door then Polly entered with the pencil and paper.

"Lydia, I confess I'm uncommon thirsty," Rosina said. "Please have a cup of hot chocolate sent to me from the kitchen."

"Of course, ma'am, I'll see to it at once." Lydia went out with obvious relief.

Rosina made a couple of sketches of dresses of a simple line and showed them to Polly.

"You should be able to manage these, won't you?"

"Naturally," Polly scowled. "You may think you can queen it over us all now because the squire's lost his wits and took some strange fancy to you." She placed her hands on her hips. "I warn you, he'll come back to me soon and then it will be the worse for you. You'll get your comeuppance."

"You are an impertinent slut." Rosina spoke contemptuously. "I shall overlook your impertinence this time. See that you treat me with respect in future."

"Respect a common gypsy wench who's wormed her slimy way into her master's favours?"

Rosina resisted the impulse to strike the other girl.

"I know you're disappointed that you're no longer warming the squire's bed and you're jealous of me because I have taken your place. I understand this. But speak to me like that again and I shall have you dismissed."

"You've no say in the matter. It would be the squire's decision. I've already told you, he'll return to me when he tires of you. We all—all the servants believe that Lydia has 'elped you put a spell on him. He's bewitched now, but such spells can be broke by a greater power."

A knock at the door heralded Lydia with the cup of hot chocolate.

"Had you better not look sharp and be about your duties, Polly?" Lydia said coldly as she handed the cup to Rosina. Polly gave Rosina another look of dislike and stalked out of the room.

"I don't know what to do after I'm dressed, Lydia," Rosina said.

"He says you're to sit in the parlour with some embroidery or whatever else pleases you until his return."

"Embroidery would please me better than sitting in that sewing room, stitching till my fingers ache. Mrs Johnson and the others will probably be stabbing pins into her material, pretending it's my heart."

Both women laughed although Lydia still looked a little wary.

"I'll send Susan to you to help you dress, ma'am."

"Thank you."

By the time Miles returned, the early autumn evening was chilly. Rosina had already ordered a fire to be lit.

"I'm so glad you're back, Miles," she said.

"I'm glad to be back," he replied. "I find you entrancing." Miles put his arm around Rosina's shoulders and drew her closer to him. She noticed that he smelt of the sea and salt.

"I must have your portrait painted, sweetheart. It will hang on the wall for all our guests to admire. I wish you to wear a white robe which they will make for you in the sewing room."

Rosina hid a grimace as she thought of Polly sewing this garment. Aloud, she said, "Are you sure it's a wise idea? Many of our visitors would probably disapprove."

Miles frowned. "Let them, I do what I like in my own household." Then he smiled. "I need a drink to warm me."

He took a flask of brandy from his hidden pocket and took a swig of it, offering a sip to Rosina who refused.

"Wise girl to remain sober," he said.

Miles unpinned Rosina's hair and wound a strand of it round his hand. She moved into his arms as he kissed her. At first, she shivered as his cold hands began to stroke her soft skin, then began to relax in his embrace. Slowly, he undressed her, then himself, and lowered her to the floor.

"You understand now, Rosie, why I'm so pleased to be home."

"I'm delighted you are."

"I've already told you, you've become a wanton very quickly."

"Does that displease you?"

"On the contrary, but you still have things to learn."

"I'll be a good pupil."

"I know you will."

Miles taught Rosina new thrills which left her exhilarated as the flames flickered, illuminating their entwined bodies.

CHAPTER 7

▼

The dressmaker called, bringing silks, brocades and laces, petticoats, and stockings. Miles told Rosina to choose what she wanted and he would buy her anything she wanted. She was thrilled to sort through them and decide what she wanted. Susan gave advice on what would suit her. In the sewing room, her white quilted satin robe was completed. It covered her from the top of her breasts although showing a tantalising glimpse of them. It had very short sleeves and only reached her calves.

"I wished you to wear this because it clings to your body and shows off your curves," Miles said.

Rosina sat in a high backed mahogany chair in the centre of the saloon. Miles had said the portrait was to hang on the wall above the place where she was sitting.

The artist was a small, ugly man who walked with a slight limp and bore the marks of smallpox on his face. Rosina did not like the way he stared at her. "Don't worry, mistress, I do my best to see you from all angles," he said. "That's why I have to look at you so hard. Squire will be angry if I don't capture a true likeness." His voice was gentle and reassuring and she gradually began to feel more at ease in his company. She pushed back a lock of her long, loose, black hair.

When the portrait was completed, the squire came to look at it. He studied it intently before he spoke. "Very good! I'm impressed and will treasure this picture."

Rosina flushed with pleasure. "I like it very much, myself," she said, shyly.

Miles paid the artist who was delighted his work had been so well received. Then, the squire commanded his servants to hang the portrait carefully in the place of his choosing.

"Dance for me now, Rosie," the squire said, after the artist had departed.

Rosina started to dance seductively. The squire leaned forward, then stood up and moved over towards her. She hesitated.

"Don't stop," Denny said. Deftly, he managed to remove her satin robe. "Your movements have been especially sensuous—they have excited me!"

Rosina shivered with cold but obeyed him, making her actions even more provocative.

"That's enough now," he said, sharply, after a few moments. "You're too cold, I must make you warm again." He picked her up and carried her to bed.

The sewing maids were ordered to make her one red and one violet skirt, both embroidered with tiny bells. She wore them only when she was dancing.

Squire Denny invited Sebastian Coleman, the parson and Robert Elms, the schoolmaster, to watch Rosina dance in the ballroom again. At those times, country fiddlers were engaged to accompany her. She was afraid that Miles would expect her to strip naked in front of them and begged him to spare her this humiliation. He reassured her that he had no intention of making this request of her; when she danced naked, it was for the squire's own pleasure and for his alone.

"Robert, you'll teach Rosina to read, write and cipher, won't you?" Denny asked Elms one evening after she had danced. "I feel she should have this knowledge."

Elms looked startled then said, "Yes, I will, with great pleasure."

"Good, I'll arrange for you to come twice a week."

Rosina had mixed feelings. She wanted desperately to learn to read but she was not sure that she wanted to be taught by Elms. However, she assumed a bland expression and thanked him for his willingness to educate her.

When Elms came, she studied hard. "You're a good pupil, Rosina," he said, obviously surprised. "You learn quickly and you're very fast at reckoning."

"It's because I used to sell baskets of flowers and suchlike to customers."

Elms frowned and cleared his throat. "Yes, well, let's get on with some more reading."

Rosina hid a smile, knowing he was embarrassed by her allusion to her former life. When he was in one of his impatient moods, she tried to not to be upset by his bad temper. One day he said to Miles, "I think Rosina should be instructed in etiquette."

Miles looked thoughtful. "Yes, I agree. I know an ex-governess I'll engage. She's an elderly widow now; her name's Mrs Wharton."

Mrs Wharton was small and stooped with a somewhat bird-like face but she was certainly mentally alert. "Well, Rosina, you're graceful enough," Mrs Wharton said. "I don't need to teach you much about deportment. You should learn, however, how to be a good hostess. The correct way to treat guests at a ball, for instance—listen carefully."

"I will," Mrs Wharton.

"And so you should, it'll do you a power of good." Mrs Wharton verbally issued a list of instructions which made Rosina's head reel.

"Can I write all this down, Mrs Wharton?"

"By all means. Learn it by heart."

"When guests come to dine, this is what you must do." Another long list of what Rosina absolutely must do and definitely must not, on any account do, followed so she wrote it all down again.

"The right way to treat servants is to be firm but fair and never tolerate insolence."

"I think I already know the right way to treat servants," Rosina said. "I have been one."

Mrs Wharton looked uneasy. "Yes, I know." She brightened. "Ah, but when taking tea with other ladies, you must—" Here we go again, thought Rosina, another list as long as my arm! Aloud, she said, "Mrs Wharton, I'm afraid I shall have to write this down as well."

"It's quite an accomplishment that you can read and write, my dear."

"I'm happy that I can do so," Rosina said.

She had been living with the squire for nearly six months now. The notorious style in which Miles was keeping Rosina had caused some scandal and gossip in the district. Surely, the squire could have been more discreet than to openly flaunt a gypsy woman on his arm and treat her like a wellborn lady! Some of the more straight-laced members of society shunned him but he did not care a fig for their opinions. Others were somewhat amused by his daring defiance of convention.

One evening, as dusk was falling, she was walking in the garden, wrapped up warmly against the cold when she heard a crackling of twigs. She turned around to see her brother, Spencer, leaning against a tree. She dismissed Susan and beckoned to him. After a good look around to ensure nobody was watching him, he crept forward.

"It's good to see you—you seem to be livin' in high style. Whoever would have thought our Rosie would end up such a fine lady!"

"I'm glad to see you, Spencer. Jacko, Arnold, the rest of the tribe, how are they all?"

"As well as can be expected. Jacko told me off good and proper when you got caught but the way you've gone up in the world since then, well, I'll be damned and no mistake!" He gave his sister an admiring glance.

Rosina gave him a gentle tap with her gloved hand. "Get away with you, Spencer. You can't see me properly in this light."

"I've got sharper eyes than you realise."

"It's cold out here. Come into the kitchen, have a drink and a bite to eat."

He shook his head. "Happen it's better I don't. I'll be off now. I'll be able to tell Jacko and the others you're bein' took good care of."

Rosina laughed. "Really good care. Give them all my love and tell them not to worry about me. Tell them I hope to see them all soon."

"Well, maybe," Spencer said. Rosina noted the hesitation in his voice.

"Why should they not want to see me?"

"There are reasons but I'll tell you some other time. I must go now. Jacko's waitin' for me."

"Goodbye Spencer, promise me you will take care of yourself."

"I will." He began to run, turning to wave to his sister who watched him until he was out of sight.

"Where have you been, Rosina?" Denny asked, when she went back into the house.

Her intuition told her not to mention Spencer. "In the garden for a breath of fresh air."

He raised his eyebrows. "A little late and cold for that, I should have thought."

"I know," Rosina said. "I just felt a longing to be outside."

Denny shrugged. "A strange fancy, to be sure. I'll take you for a ride tomorrow, if you like."

"I would like it very much indeed." She loved her rides with him even more than their long, leisurely walks, when the weather permitted, along the seashore at Christchurch and Topcliffe.

The following morning, Miles took her for a ride in the beautiful woodland and moorland which surrounded Lyndhurst.

Miles was pleased that Rosina was already quite an accomplished horsewoman even if her style of riding was a little unconventional.

On their ride, they met Captain Mountjoy who was on foot. Miles shouted to Rosina to stop. After they had greeted each other, Rosina wondered if she had imagined that the captain's eyes, as grey as the sea on a stormy day, lit up when he saw her, but had clouded slightly when he had seen Miles. She felt excitement in the pit of her stomach.

"I hope you will dine with us one night next week, Mountjoy," Denny said. "I wish to discuss an investment of mine in your new vessel."

"I should be honoured to do so," the captain replied. "Will next Friday be convenient?"

"Yes, come at eight o'clock," said Denny.

Mountjoy looked directly at Rosina. "I hope you will dance for us again."

"Yes, she will," Denny answered for her.

"I shall look forward to watching you again, Mistress Clayton."

"Thank you." Rosina, knowing it was Tuesday, also began to look forward to Friday.

Turning to Denny, the captain said, "Could you come to Mudeford Quay where my ship, the *Susan Jane* is moored, as soon as it's convenient?"

"Yes, I shall, this very day. See you later. Come, Rosina." As she and Miles resumed their journey, he began to gallop. Following him, Rosina wondered why the squire was in such a hurry. She thought she could make a shrewd guess.

Rosina had long suspected that the squire had clandestine dealings with the smugglers. While she lived in the Forest she had become familiar with these "gentlemen of the road". There were whispers among the villagers that Parson Coleman, too, passed the bottle in the parlour with the free traders. It was also common knowledge that he kept hounds to maintain a supply of hares for his table. She prayed that Miles did not place himself in any danger.

Suddenly, he took an unexpected turn.

"Where are we going?" Rosina yelled.

"You'll soon find out."

They rode to a cottage in the New Forest where Miles knocked on the door to be answered by a countrywoman who smiled and curtsied when she saw the squire.

"Good day to you, Mistress Hart."

"Please enter, sir." She looked at Rosina. "And ma'am," she added, hastily.

Mistress Hart was a farm labourer's widow who lived with her spinster sister, Anne Marston. They brewed a dish of tea for the squire and Rosina.

"What can we do for you, sir?" Mistress Hart asked.

"Captain Mountjoy brought you the goods, I presume."

Mistress Hart nodded.

"Then, be so kind as to show them to this young lady and let her choose a length. Rosina, I have to go now. I'll send a groom to fetch you from here."

Rosina looked at him in surprise but Mistress Hart beckoned the girl to follow her. She took her to her bedroom and opened a cupboard door. "I'll open this chest and you can have a good look at what's inside." She fished a key out of her dress.

There were bolts of bright silks, rich satins in all colours of the rainbow and frothy lace. Rosina looked at them admiringly, feeling overcome with wonder.

"Go on, you can touch them," Mistress Hart said. Rosina fingered them, fascinated by their luxurious feel.

"Which bolt would you like? Squire says you can have any of them to be made into a gown."

"They're all so lovely, it's hard to pick one out," Rosina said, delighted. Finally, she chose a bolt of cherry red silk.

"Me and Anne will arrange to have it sent to Squire's house. If you don't mind me sayin' so, maid, I think you've made a good choice. That colour will suit you."

The women made her some more tea and chatted to her about village affairs. Although they were polite, she was not sorry to leave the cottage when the groom arrived, sensing that the women did not approve of her relationship with the squire.

CHAPTER 8

▼

Two days later, Squire Denny strode into the parlour where Rosina was examining her length of red silk and deciding what style of dress the sewing room maids should make for her.

"Stand up and close your eyes, Rosina," he said.

She did so, puzzled. He removed her coral necklace and placed a new one around her throat. He led her over to the mirror and when she opened her eyes, she saw that it was a circlet, of seed pearls in a pattern of roses. She fingered it admiringly.

"It's very beautiful."

"I chose the design myself. It becomes you because you are a rose." She flung her arms around his neck and kissed him.

"Even so," she said, tentatively. "I should like to keep my coral necklace."

"Why? It's only a bauble of little value, such as the village girls wear."

"It. was a gift and I am still fond of it for that reason."

Denny shrugged and handed it back to her. "My necklace is intended to be a wedding gift."

Rosina stared at him. "Surely, you don't mean to marry *me?*"

"Who else?"

"But—but you should marry a lady. If you wed me, think of all the scandal it will cause. There will be even more wagging tongues than there are already."

The squire snapped his fingers in the air. "That is how much I care for wagging tongues. I think we should be married as soon as possible."

Rosina shook her head in wonder. "I am overwhelmed. I don't know what to say."

"You don't have to say anything. Come here." He took her in his arms and kissed her, tenderly. Rosina felt as if she were in a seventh heaven.

*   *   *   *

When Friday night at last arrived Squire Denny, Captain Mountjoy and Rosina all enjoyed a substantial dinner. When it was over, Rosina stood up to leave the room so that the men could enjoy their port. Denny put out an arm to detain her.

"Stay here, Rosie, we'll want you to dance for us in a little while." Rosina saw the captain's eyes light up.

"Do you have the materials from the cottage?" Denny asked Mountjoy.

"Yes, they were delivered to my house last night. The gentlemen will know where to sell them without too many questions being asked."

"Good, I believe the women were beginning to be suspected, or so I heard."

"They have been useful to us. I shouldn't like to see them get into trouble," Mountjoy said.

"I agree. I have some other news for you which might come as a surprise."

"What's that?"

"Rosina and I are to be married next Wednesday. You are invited to the wedding of course."

Rosina thought she saw Captain Mountjoy frown. She wondered if he disapproved of the squire marrying a common gypsy. The next moment he was all smiles. "That's marvellous news. Allow me to congratulate you. It's quite a coincidence because it will not be so very long before I am wed, myself."

Rosina could not understand why his words came as a disappointment.

"Right, Rosie," Denny said. "Now is the time for you to dance. Let's go to the saloon."

Unusually, Rosina would have preferred not to perform; she would rather have sat quietly in the parlour and made conversation. Not wishing to disappoint either of the men, however, she obliged them but felt that her dancing was not up to its usual standard.

The captain was, as usual, complimentary about her performance although she thought he was probably just being polite. He left not long afterwards, promising he would be a guest at the wedding. Rosina felt a mixture of relief and sadness at his departure. Miles seemed especially attentive to her that night.

The following morning, Susan chatted to Rosina about her wedding dress. "They're workin' really 'ard in the sewing room to get the dress finished in time, ma'am. I'm glad I'm still not in there though I've promised to put finishin' touches on it." With Susan's advice, Rosina had had a low cut gown fashioned from her length of red silk. It was embroidered with tiny white satin rosebuds, trimmed with ribbon bows and the sleeves were overlaid with lace ruffles. The small hoop underneath it made the skirt stand out.

"You'll look lovely in it, ma'am."

Rosina smiled. "They say every bride's beautiful on her wedding day."

Susan pursed her lips. "I wouldn't say that, ma'am."

Thursday dawned bright and clear. Miles had slept in a different bedroom the night before, saying Rosina needed a good night's rest. She had, however, been far too excited to sleep soundly so she was up well before dawn.

Rosina donned her dressing gown and slipped down to the kitchen where not even the scullery maids were about. She had asked Miles if the servants and estate tenants could have their own feast that day when they had finished their work and he had willingly agreed.

She brewed herself some tea to calm her nerves but could not eat. Lydia entered the kitchen, amazed to see Rosina. "You shouldn't be in here ma'am. I would have sent you some tea if you'd asked for it."

"I couldn't sleep, Lydia. You're up early, yourself."

"There's a lot to do, today, ma' am." She smiled, shyly. "Might I say I'm thrilled for you, ma'am? I have a little gift for you." She handed Rosina a finely embroidered handkerchief. "I worked on it, myself."

Rosina was touched. "Thank you so much. I do hope you enjoy your own feast. I'll go back to my room now."

"I'll send Susan to you this minute."

Susan helped Rosina to put on her wedding dress.

"Oh, Sue," Rosina said, I can hardly believe this is really happening to me."

"We all know it is, ma'am, and I'm so happy for you, I could sing at the top of my voice."

"Perhaps you'll be able to sing at your feast."

Susan laughed. "I don't think so; have you ever heard me sing, ma'am?"

Rosina smiled. "No, I haven't."

"If you did, you'd never want to, again."

"You're probably too modest." She hesitated. "Sue, could you find the red coral necklace for me?"

Susan fastened it around her mistress's neck.

"Me and Eliza have bought you a wedding present, ma'am."

Tears threatened Rosina as Susan presented her with a pair of white stockings.

"They're gorgeous, Sue! Thank you so much. Will you help me put them on?"

"Of course, ma'am."

Rosina sat down on the bed, careful not to crease her gown while Susan brushed and dressed her hair. When the girl had finished, Rosina stood up and looked at her reflection in the mirror. She felt as if she were looking at a stranger.

"You'll be the loveliest bride in the whole world, today, ma'am."

Rosina laughed. "You exaggerate. I'm sure I don't deserve such a compliment even though I feel as if I'm the happiest bride in the world today."

Parson Coleman came to escort Rosina to the private chapel where she was to be married to Squire Miles Denny.

Rosina thought how handsome Miles looked in his amber velvet coat curved back to show the waistcoat of green watered silk trimmed with silver lace. His cambric stock was perfectly tied and there were gold buckles on his shoes.

As he wanted a quiet wedding, the only witnesses present were Robert Elms, the schoolmaster and Captain Mountjoy, looking unusually fine in a blue velvet suit with an intricately embroidered waistcoat.

The parson looked embarrassed, mumbling the service, but as she took her vows, Rosina felt an overwhelming rush of love for Miles, although she was apprehensive, knowing how many people would disapprove of her marriage.

After the ceremony a breakfast was held in the dining room. There was rump of roasted beef and an apple tart with cream. Wine and port flowed freely and as she was still feeling nervous, Rosina drank far more than she normally did.

"Well, gentlemen," Miles said, when the meal was at last over. "Our entertainment, tonight, is my new wife dancing for you. I have engaged a country fiddler."

"We are not trying to win her, this time?" Elms asked slyly and Rosina felt as if she could have knifed him.

"Of course not," Miles snapped. "She has just married me."

"And a beautiful bride she is, too," said Mountjoy.

"We had better go to the saloon, now," Miles said, curtly. He stood up and offered Rosina his arm. The others followed.

Rosina began to mount the steps to the stage but slipped on the top one and lost her balance. She was caught by Captain Mountjoy who grasped her.

"Have you hurt yourself, Rosina?"

"No, captain, not at all, thank you for your timely help."

"It was nothing." He tried to draw her into an embrace. "As she is the bride, Squire Denny, may I kiss her?"

"No, Mountjoy, you may not," Denny snarled. "Let go of her at once."

Reluctantly, with a startled expression, Mountjoy released Rosina

"She will not be dancing now. We will merely listen to the fiddler play some country tunes." All the men looked disappointed although Rosina was relieved.

"I think I had better leave, now," Mountjoy said.

"As you wish," Denny said, stiffly. Rosina was sorry to see him go but said nothing.

Denny signalled to the fiddler to begin playing. Rosina found that the tunes although well played, grated on her ears, as she was very tense. After the man had finished playing three tunes, Denny told him to stop.

"But I thought you wanted more, sir," the fiddler said. "I 'ope you wasn't disappointed."

"Not at all, man. I've just had enough for tonight, that's all." He paid the fiddler, waving the man aside, then turned to the parson and the schoolmaster.

"I trust you two gentlemen are also leaving now."

They both looked taken aback by his bluntness but agreed that they were, indeed, leaving.

After they had gone, Miles looked annoyed. "You are my wife now, Rosina. I expect you to act modestly, not like a coquette."

"I did act properly," Rosina protested, stung.

"You shouldn't encourage the attentions of other men. I don't know how far Mountjoy would have gone if I hadn't stopped him."

"I wouldn't have let him, you should know that. I couldn't help falling. I didn't do it on purpose."

He sighed. "I suppose we all had too much to drink so I'll make allowances. Remember, in future, your behaviour should be above reproach."

"I'm determined to be a good wife to you." Rosina felt like crying. Her wedding day should have been the happiest in her whole life. It had started off well and now seemed to be turning sour with her new husband unfairly suspecting her of flirting.

Miles' expression softened and his tone became gentler. "I can understand why Mountjoy was tempted but don't encourage him. You're looking particularly beautiful tonight, sweetheart."

He picked her up and carried her to their bedroom.

CHAPTER 9

$\blacktriangledown$

One early summer morning after Rosina had been married for a few months, she decided to go for a ride on Topcliffe Beach. Miles had gone out early on some mysterious errand of his own.

When she returned, she realised that her coral necklace was missing from the carved box in which she kept it. She summoned all the servants to question them; they all denied any knowledge of its whereabouts.

"I think I've seen it in Polly's bedroom, ma'am, " Lydia said.

Polly gave Lydia a look of pure hatred.

"I shall come to your bedroom, myself, to look for it, Polly," Rosina said.

"I did not take it," Polly protested vehemently, yet it was found under her bed.

"You are dismissed from my service, Davis," Rosina said. "I should have done this long ago."

"Somebody has done this to get me into trouble!" Polly screamed.

"Get out of my sight once and for all," Rosina snapped. She left the room in her most regal manner.

"I'm glad Polly Davis has gone, ma'am," Susan said. "I always thought that girl was nothing but trouble."

"I'll have to reward Lydia. How did she know Polly had stolen my necklace?"

"She overheard Polly sayin' she liked it very much and knew it would suit her."

"I don't know what will become of her now, Susan, but I'm not sorry she's gone."

Rosina was amazed when her husband returned quite late that evening, accompanied by a tearful Polly.

"I hear you dismissed Polly, Rosina," the squire said, frowning.

"Naturally, when I discovered she had stolen my coral necklace. I hardly think it's a good idea to keep dishonest servants in the house."

Polly looked down at the floor.

"I employ the servants. You have no real proof that Polly took your trinket."

"It was found under her bed! That was proof enough for me and everyone else."

"She suspects that some spiteful female servant did this on purpose to bring her name into disrepute."

"Anyone can say that!"

"Come my dear," the squire said, firmly. "I think you should give Polly another chance to prove her honesty and loyalty."

"Loyalty and honesty be damned!" Rosina snapped. "I don't want her under my roof."

"I would remind you, Rosina, that it is my roof and I insist that Polly remains as a servant in my employment."

"In that case, there is nothing more to be said." Rosina walked out of the room, noticing the triumphant gleam in the other woman's eyes. She went to her bedroom and cried with humiliation. She decided to retire early and sent for Susan to help her undress.

"It's a real shame that Polly Davis has been allowed back here, ma'am."

"You know already, then," Rosina said, dully. "I don't understand how she knew where to find Miles."

Susan twisted her hands together. "Some believe she helps the free traders. I expect the master met her in the village."

Rosina gave a rueful smile. "No, I believe she probably met him while he was assisting the gentlemen. I may not be a servant myself, nowadays, Sue, but that doesn't mean I no longer overhear their gossip."

Susan blushed.

"Please ask Lydia to make me a sleeping draught. I don't want to stay awake very long."

"Are you sure it's wise, ma'am?"

"I wouldn't ask for it if I didn't want it, you silly girl!"

Rosina awoke with a headache the following morning to find that she was alone in the bed.

She decided to go for a walk along Topcliffe Beach to clear her head. Before she went, she put on the coral necklace.

As she was walking on the sands, she put her hand to her throat and realised with horror that the necklace was missing. She burst into tears. Then she saw Miles Denny riding towards her. He dismounted from his pony.

"Rosina, what are you doing here on your own?"

"I had a headache so I decided to come for a walk. What are you doing here?"

Denny looked displeased. "I had business to attend to." He looked at her closely and said, more gently. "Why are you distressed? Surely, you're not still sulking about Polly Davis."

"It's nothing to do with her. Are you visiting her bed?"

He moved a little closer to her and Rosina could see that he was highly displeased. For a moment she thought he was going to hit her. She tensed herself for the blow which did not come.

"I shall treat that question with the contempt it deserves."

Rosina was not reassured but decided not to press the point.

"I have lost my coral necklace. I put it on before I came out."

Denny sighed. "I cannot for the life of me understand why you prize that bauble so highly. I have given you far more expensive jewellery."

"And I am very grateful. But I have told you before that one piece was special to me because I had it from a dear friend. Please try to understand what it means to me."

He sighed again. "I do not, but if it keeps you happy, we'll look for it."

They searched thoroughly in the sand but there was no trace of the necklace. Rosina was very upset. Denny finally lost his temper with her and told her they should go home.

Rosina was haunted by the feeling that the loss of her coral necklace was a portent of misfortune. She tried to shake off her misgivings with very little success.

*   *   *   *

"Captain Mountjoy is coming to dine with us again next Monday," Denny said at breakfast a week later.

Rosina looked up in surprise. "Is he?"

"Yes. Oh, I know I spoke a little harshly to him at our wedding because he tried to take liberties. I met him in the village recently, and though his manner towards me was cool at first, we have many interests in common."

"Will you expect me to dance?"

"No." Miles' tone was curt. Rosina felt a mixture of relief and regret yet she found herself once more looking forward to Charles' visit.

When Mountjoy came, his manner with Rosina was courteous yet restrained. In her presence, his conversation with the squire was of his forthcoming marriage, the weather and village affairs. Rosina sensed that the men wished to be rid of her so she left the table as soon as she had finished eating. Charles studiously avoided watching her leave the room.

As she had guessed, her husband wished to discuss business matters. Rosina pleaded a headache and went to bed early.

Polly Davis came into the saloon when the men were on their own.

"Excuse me intrudin', sir," she said. "There's a man called to see you—says it's really important."

The squire looked annoyed. "Surely, you could have told him I have a guest with me at present."

"With respect, sir, he says it's a matter of life or death."

"You'd better go and see him, then, Squire Denny. I'll go now," Mountjoy said.

"No, stay until I find out what's happened." He poured Mountjoy another drink.

The squire returned after about twenty minutes.

"As I suspected, it was an exaggeration that it was a matter of life and death. One of the gang has been injured in a chase with the Revenue. I've agreed to pay the doctor's fees."

"Will he survive, do you think?"

"Yes. The others will have to keep their heads low for the time being. They did suspect there was an informer amongst them but the fellow, a newcomer, has left these parts."

Mountjoy looked thoughtful. "H'm. I suppose we always run that risk. It's hard to know what to do for the best in circumstances like that."

"Yes, I know. For the time being, however, let's see the plans for your proposed new ship."

When the captain was due to leave, his tricorne hat was missing. Miles told all the servants to search for it in every nook and cranny.

Eventually, Polly came in. "Might I have a private word with you, sir?" she said to Denny. Without waiting for his reply, she whispered into his ear.

The squire coloured. "Are you sure, girl?"

"Yes, sir, definitely."

"I'll come and have a look there, myself."

As Denny left the saloon with a face like thunder he did not see Polly holding her hand over her mouth to suppress her laughter.

In the bedroom, he swore as he found Mountjoy's hat on Rosina's dressing table. She was asleep and he shook her awake. He held the hat up. "What's the meaning of Mountjoy's hat being found here?"

Rosina shook her head in bewilderment. She was still drowsy. "I don't know."

Miles looked furious. "Don't play the innocent with me, madam. When Mountjoy crept in here, he forgot to take his hat back, didn't he?"

Rosina stared at him, her own anger mounting. "Don't be stupid! He's been with you all night. How could he have come in here?"

"Polly told me I had a caller insisting upon seeing me. I was detained for about twenty minutes. He could have come to see you, then."

Alarm bells rang in Rosina's mind that Polly Davis was deliberately causing mischief.

"I assure you the captain hasn't been here at all. I think Polly deliberately put his hat where you found it."

"Why on earth should she do that?"

"She doesn't like me. She wants to make you dislike me, too, whether you believe me or not." Rosina began to cry.

Denny's expression of anger was replaced by a perplexed look. Finally, he spoke. "Maybe I'm a fool but I'll give you the benefit of the doubt this time and I'll dismiss Polly Davis." He sighed. "It's high time the captain had his hat back."

Rosina smiled through her tears.

Denny walked to the door with the hat in his hand. Then he turned. "For your own sake, Rosina, you'd better be telling me the truth."

CHAPTER 10

▼

Squire Miles Denny, his wife, Rosina, Robert Elms and Sebastian Coleman sat in a private parlour of 'The Boat' Inn in the village of Bucklers Hard.

Rosina was pleased that her husband had seen fit to bring her with him. They had been married for a year and he had often been absent from home lately. She had not danced for him for a long time.

In his best schoolmaster's manner, Robert Elms explained to her that this village had originally been called Montagu Town. It was created by the second Duke of Montagu. He had sent an expedition to St Lucia to found sugar plantations. His intention was to import sugar through the new port to be built on the Beaulieu River. This venture had failed and, as a result, Montagu Town had developed into Bucklers Hard.

The evening before, the party had been entertained by the master builder in the village's wooden banqueting hall.

"I hope you are all ready for the launching, gentlemen," Charles said after he had joined them. Rosina knew he had recently married Catherine Barnes. She was the eldest daughter of John Barnes, a prosperous ship owner, timber merchant and maltster.

The captain was generally thought to have made a good match but Rosina had mixed feelings when she heard about his marriage. She and the squire had been guests at the wedding. Charles danced with her once, squeezing her hand quite warmly.

In an effort to be completely respectable, Captain Mountjoy had given up his occasional bouts of smuggling. Rosina suspected that her husband was still involved. She still wondered if the captain felt attraction towards her but dismissed it as whimsy. His new wife was young and pretty in addition to her large dowry.

"I'm sure we are all looking forward to watching the launching of our ship, the *Katie Barnes*," Charles said. "I can't wait to become a shipowner of some importance now that I have resigned my commission in His Majesty's Navy."

"Let's drink another toast to her prosperity," Squire Denny agreed. "We all have a great interest because we all have shares in her."

"Excellent idea," said the parson, raising his glass.

"I quite agree," said the schoolmaster. "I hope she's going to make us all rich beyond our wildest dreams."

They all drank another toast to the ship's prosperity.

The keel of the ship had been made from some of the great elms in Denny Woods. Oaks had also been used and the inside walls of the Katie Barnes were filled in with beech.

Rosina shared some of the men's excited anticipation. They were all hoping to make their fortunes from the new ship. But she also felt a sense of foreboding. She closed her eyes briefly and thought she saw an image of a man falling and screaming. Then, the picture faded as quickly as it had come.

Finally, they all went outside to join the shipwrights, sailors, fishermen and agricultural workers who had gathered to watch the launch of the *Katie Barnes*. Some of them stared at Rosina with open curiosity, others whispered. She tried to ignore them. With an uneasy jolt, she saw Polly Davis standing beside a sailor.

The day was dull although not particularly cold. Rosina felt a chill sweeping over her body. She shivered and her husband put his arm around her. Gratefully, she drew warmth from his touch.

The launching of the *Katie Barnes* was planned to take place one hour before high water. At the preceding low water, the sliding ways had been greased with melted tallow and soap.

The squire's party watched strong men gradually transferring the weight of the ship from the blocks on which it had been built to the bilgeways. They drove wooden edges under the keel starting at the stern. The bilgeways were then inserted between the keel and building blocks.

It was a long process as the men holding the bilgeways had to stand in water and mud in the early stages.

There was a sudden shout as one of the men slipped in the mud and slid below the water. Rosina recalled him having stared at her more boldly and for longer than any of the others. Some of his companions pulled him up. He coughed and spluttered and he was slapped hard on the back. After a cursory examination by a sailor with a rudimentary medical knowledge, it was not thought that any real harm had come to him.

"It's a bad omen," Rosina whispered to herself, horrified.

"You grow over-fanciful, Rosina," Denny said, coldly. "The man is safe, is he not?"

Rosina agreed that he was, but the horrible feeling of foreboding had not completely left her.

To the accompaniment of loud cheers, Captain Charles Mountjoy broke a bottle of red wine on the bows of the vessel. "I name this ship the *Katie Barnes!*" he shouted. "God bless her and all who sail in her. There will be entertainment at the Boat Inn next Saturday evening for all who helped to build her. You all deserve to enjoy yourselves."

The ship began to slide into the water.

"Look!" a sailor called out in horror. "It's Peter Cooper. He'll be 'urt bad if he has no 'elp."

The crowd followed the direction of his pointing finger. Rosina recognised him as the stocky man who had fallen earlier.

Drag chains and ropes weighted with heavy timber had been used to brake the speed of the vessel as it ran down the greased launchways. One of the workmen had become entangled in the chains. He was screaming as the squire was chatting to Robert Elms and Sebastian Coleman. Captain Mountjoy ran forward and Rosina followed. Denny tried to restrain her but she pulled herself away from him. She heard both Elms and Coleman snigger and decided she disliked them both even more than formerly.

Charles turned to her. "Should you not rejoin your husband, Rosina? I'm not sure what you will be able to do, here." His tone was not unkind.

Rosina shook her head. "No, I shall stay here. I may be able to help as I have some knowledge of healing."

The captain shrugged. "Very well. But before he is healed, he must be freed." He began to bark out orders to others who had gathered around.

Between them, they managed to free Peter Cooper. As soon as he was released, he fainted. The apothecary who examined him stated that one of his legs would have to be amputated. Rosina shuddered.

A dark shadow was cast over the day which had started with such high hopes. The unfortunate man was taken back to his cottage. Captain Mountjoy also went. Some of the crowd drifted away but others stayed.

Rosina returned to her husband's side to find him pale and tight-lipped. Elms and Coleman had disappeared.

"I'm sorry if I have displeased you, Miles, but I had to do something to help."

He looked at her in exasperation. "You might have fallen and been hurt yourself, or caught a fever from the injured man."

"I doubt it. I'm healthy and I'm sure Captain Mountjoy would have helped me if I had fallen."

Denny scowled. "You are over-friendly with him for my liking."

"Once again, you're being unjust and you know it! There is nothing between us. There never has been."

"Be careful to give him no sign of encouragement whatsoever in the future."

Rosina sighed, despairingly. "Shall we go home now?" she asked, in a small voice.

Denny shook his head. "No, we will stay to watch the rest of the proceedings. You seem to have forgotten how much interest I have in this vessel."

The *Katie Barnes* came to rest in midstream. The men on the deck threw ropes to the riggers awaiting them in small boats. The ship was then towed to Fiddlers Reach where the hulls of newly-launched ships were anchored en-route for Portsmouth.

"What will happen now?" Rosina asked.

"The ship will be towed by men in rowing boats in Beaulieu River to the Solent, then at Portsmouth where it will be fitted out with masts, rigging and fittings—the bilge pumps and anchors," Denny explained.

"I do try to take an interest in your affairs, Miles," Rosina said.

"Not all of my affairs concern you, Rosina," Denny snapped. She flushed and bit her lip.

More gently, he said, "You probably knew I was involved in smuggling."

Rosina nodded. "I had suspected."

"I'm giving it up. I admit I used to receive goods and turned a blind eye to the free traders' activities because I knew some of them would live in dire poverty if they didn't take part. But this latest event sickened me."

"What did they do?"

"The smugglers suspected an informer. The man had escaped from them but they traced him and when they caught him, they threw him down a well."

Rosina shuddered. "I had heard rumours. I'm very relieved you're finishing with it all."

Denny smiled at her. "We will go home now."

＊   ＊   ＊   ＊

"Ma'am," Susan said to Rosina the following morning. They were seated in the parlour. Rosina was embroidering a handkerchief and Susan was turning up a hem of one of Rosina's dresses. The squire had gone out on a morning visit to Robert Elms. "Did you know that Polly Davis is in thick with the gentlemen?"

Despite her dislike of Polly, Rosina was interested. "Is she?"

"Yes. She stands on Verely Hill and wears a really bright red cape to warn about the Customs men bein' around."

"I know Verely Hill. It's near Picket Post. Polly Davis will get herself into deep trouble one day, the silly girl. Anyway, Sue, how do you know so much about what she gets up to?"

Susan blushed, looking embarrassed. "We're both friends of Mistress Mountjoy's personal maid, Connie Wilkins. I have warned Connie that Polly's no good but she won't listen to me."

"You can't always make people see things like that, Sue. This Connie will have to find out for herself."

Susan breathed a sigh of relief. "You don't mind me bein' friends with Connie, ma'am?"

Rosina smiled at her. "I've no wish to choose your friends for you, Susan." She hesitated. "As long as they don't include Polly Davis. I don't want you warning about Customs men. You can have one for a sweetheart if you like." She caught Susan's eye and they both laughed.

There was a sudden knock at the door and Lydia appeared, looking flustered. "Ma'am, I'm sorry to disturb you but a Connie Wilkins, Mistress Mountjoy's maid's here. She says it's really important she speaks to you." She looked at Susan. "Alone."

Susan gasped. "Talk of the Devil!" Rosina motioned her to silence

She sighed. "All right, Lydia, show her in. I'll ring for you when I want you again, Susan."

Constance Wilkins was a tall, thin girl with a dramatic way of moving and talking. "Mistress Denny," she said, "I believe you have a brother called Jacko?"

"Yes, that's right," Rosina said, alarmed. "Is he in danger?"

"I'm afraid he could be, ma'am. He's been working as a gardener for my master."

"I don't see how that should cause him to be in peril." Constance made a great performance of looking around the room and at the door, to make sure no-one was listening. She leaned forward and whispered into Rosina's ear. "I think he's in love with my mistress."

Rosina was disturbed. "Has he—"

"Bedded her? Forgive me for speaking bluntly, ma'am but. I think so." Constance looked scandalised.

Rosina studied her, wondering if she were telling the truth or merely trying to stir up trouble. "How am I to believe this is not all spiteful gossip? You have probably come running to me with foolish tales."

"No, I'm not, ma' am. The captain's gone out this morning but when he comes back, I know he'll have a gentleman with him and this gentleman has a grudge against Jacko."

"A gentleman! Don't you mean a free trader?"

"Yes, I do, the one who killed the other fellow."

"But why should he want to harm Jacko?"

"Jacko was friendly with the informer. So you see, ma'am, if the captain comes back and finds him with my mistress ..." Connie noisily cleared her throat. "The captain would be angry and it would give the other gentleman an excuse to murder Jacko."

Rosina turned pale. "Thank you for telling me. I'll have to come with you to warn Jacko he must flee."

Rosina sent for the carriage and it was soon racing towards the Mountjoys' house. When the two young women dismounted, however, Constance said, "That's where you'll find the head gardener, ma'am." Rosina followed the direction of her pointing finger.

"Excuse me if I don't come with you, only I've been allowed to have today off. I've got to meet somebody." Constance picked up her skirts and ran away from the house as fast as her legs would carry her. For a moment, Rosina stared after her in astonishment, then gave a mental shrug and went in search of the head gardener.

"Jacko Clayton?" the head gardener said. "Aye, he's given us a hand now and again but not for a long time now."

"Thank you," Rosina said, bewildered. She was about to walk back to the carriage when she saw her husband and Robert Elms approach.

Denny's face was like thunder when he saw Rosina. "What are you doing here?" She opened her mouth to explain but before she could do so, he added, "Don't bother to tell me, I can guess." He turned to Elms. "Go on, Robert, I'll join you later."

With a little reluctance, Elms did so.

The squire slapped Rosina hard across the face. "You've come running to Mountjoy behind my back because you knew his wife has gone on a family visit."

"I knew no such thing!" Rosina shouted. "I came here because Mistress Mountjoy's maid told me my brother, Jacko, was in danger."

"Don't tell me ridiculous lies, I don't want to hear another word from you."

"If you were fair, you'd listen to me and let me explain the true situation," Rosina protested. She was frustrated that he would not listen to reason.

He grasped her arm. "I told you, not another word. If you dare to utter one more, I swear I'll not be responsible for my actions." Denny marched her back to the carriage and bundled her into it. "I'm going to see Mountjoy now. You're going home. When I come back, I'll deal with you."

"You won't hurt the captain?"

Denny gave Rosina a look full of scorn. "I suppose you're afraid I'll call him out." His blue eyes were cold. "I don't think you're worth it, my dear."

He gave orders to the groom before striding away. After he had helped her to dismount, Rosina saw that the groom looked worried. "I'm truly sorry, Mistress Denny," the man said, "but it's squire's orders that I'm to lock you in your bedroom."

Rosina felt angry and humiliated although she understood the groom's position.

"You'd better do so, then," she said, dully.

In her bedroom she lay on the bed, too dispirited even to cry. She did not eat or drink for the rest of the day although both Lydia and Susan tried to urge her to do so.

The squire did not return until late that evening. He went straight to the bedroom. Rosina thought she could smell alcohol on his breath.

"Are you going to beat me?"

He gave a harsh laugh. "You deserve it. I married you, Rosina, because I loved you. The way you have repaid me is to be unfaithful with a close acquaintance of mine, making me a laughing stock."

"I know you did me great honour by marrying me and many people disapproved of your choice. So I always tried to be a good wife to you. I was never unfaithful, whatever you think."

Denny held up his hand. "Enough!" he said, harshly. "I will not listen to your Banbury tales." He moved a little closer to her. Rosina could not help but flinch at the expression on his face.

He laughed again, the sound ugly in the quiet room. "I shall not spoil your looks, Rosina. You can continue your love affair with Captain Precious Mountjoy. I intend to sell you to him at auction."

CHAPTER 11

▼

When the squire's words had finally registered upon Rosina's horrified mind she exclaimed, "I cannot believe you are serious. I cannot bear it. Please tell me you are only joking."

Denny shook his head. "My mind is made up, nothing will change it."

"I cannot be sold like a slave!"

Denny spoke with extreme coolness. "Not as a slave, my dear, as a wife. There will be other offers for you to begin with. However, Captain Mountjoy will buy you in the end. I've made arrangements with him."

"How can he? Captain Mountjoy is already married."

Denny shrugged. "It's still possible for him to buy you, even it it's really for a mistress instead of a wife,"

"I won't let you do this, either of you. I'll leave here this minute."

Rosina began to rise from the bed but the squire quickly rang a bell and then caught hold of her. He pinned her arms behind her back, forced her back on the bed and held her down.

She struggled, tried to butt him with her head, kicked and spat at him and even managed to bite his hand but he was too strong for her.

The more she tried to pull away from him the tighter his grasp became. She heard herself screaming with mingled fear and frustration.

Susan came in answer to the bell. She looked horrified when she saw that Rosina was being physically restrained.

"Tell Lydia to prepare a sleeping draught. She's to come here and give it to your mistress by her own hand. And fetch some cords."

"Don't go, Susan!" Rosina yelled. "Ignore him."

Susan looked at Rosina, then at Denny.

"But sir, I can't do this."

"You can and you will, girl! Jump to it!" Denny snapped. Frightened by his tone and looking back at Rosina with a muffled sob, Susan fled from the room.

Lydia entered the bedroom, looking worried. To Rosina's surprise, Annie Duke accompanied her, holding some strong cords.

"I've come because your maid, Susan Williams, the milksop, is too lily-livered to do this but I'm goin' to enjoy it," Annie Duke said, vindictively.

"Hold your tongue and get on with it," the squire barked. He looked at Annie Duke with an expression which Rosina, for a fleeting moment, imagined was dislike.

Rosina said nothing. She merely stared at the other young woman with loathing. Something in Rosina's eyes made Annie look away in spite of herself.

Between them, Denny, Annie Duke and Lydia bound the still struggling Rosina's hands and ankles.

"Lydia, why are you doing this?" Rosina cried out in anguish.

Shamefaced, Lydia looked at Rosina. "I pity you, Rosina and I truly wish this wasn't happening but Squire saved my mother."

Lydia forced as much of a strong tasting cordial down Rosina's throat as she could. Then Annie pushed a gag into her mouth. Against her will, Rosina realised she was drifting into sleep.

"She is nearly asleep," Denny said to the two women. "Untie her wrists and place her inside the bed."

"But sir, we thought that she should be—" Rosina recognised Annie Duke's hateful voice.

"Do not question my orders." Denny spoke with barely concealed fury. Rosina heard him turn on his heel and leave the room.

The women placed her in the bed. Rosina heard them speak to each other but she did not hear what they said. As she finally fell asleep, she heard Annie Duke laughing.

$$* \qquad * \qquad * \qquad *$$

The following morning, Lydia and Annie Duke aroused Rosina from her drugged sleep and forced her to eat. She was still feeling dazed and muddled and she had a bad headache. The women dressed her in a bright yellow bodice and her purple skirt with the bells sewn around the hem. They thrust wooden shoes on to her feet and a halter was placed around her neck.

The groom who had first escorted Rosina to the squire's house now arrived, grinning broadly. He announced in a grand manner that he had been commanded to take her to Squire Denny's waiting carriage. Annie Duke smiled. Rosina looked over his head as if to pretend he was not there.

Accompanied by the three servants, Rosina walked to the carriage, which was waiting in the grounds. She kept her head high and looked straight ahead, knowing it would be useless to try to escape.

Squire Denny and his steward were waiting in the carriage. Denny seemed uneasy once Rosina was inside although neither of them spoke.

Wild thyme and broom were flourishing in the honeysuckle-wreathed, foxglove clustered thickets of the New Forest. Dragonflies flew and the sun shone warmly overhead.

Notices had been posted on trees in the Forest. They advertised the sale of a wife outside the 'Queens Head' Inn in the small village of Burley. The posters stated the wife was a lovely young gypsy woman whose beauty was praised in glowing terms. Most of the local farmers and tradesmen had given permission for their apprentices, servants and labourers to attend the sale. Schoolchildren had also been given the day off, much to their delight.

Early in the morning, a large crowd had gathered outside the Queen's Head Inn to see the wife sale.

The crowd was mainly good-natured, in the mood to enjoy an extra holiday. There was a general air of interest to see a spectacle although there was some jostling and petty quarrelling for the best positions.

Many had brought glasses of ale, porter and cider from the inn. Some had brought food with them, bread, cheese and apples. Sweetmeats for the children had been eaten in profusion. Others had bought food from the inn. The staff had agreed amongst themselves to take it in turns to run outside to gain glimpses of the proceedings.

"This is what 'appens when maids get above themselves," a farmer's wife warned her eldest daughter.

"I wouldn't have minded gettin' above meself if I'd been in her shoes," her daughter replied, pertly. "Squire's handsome."

"That's quite enough foolish prattle on your part, you silly goose. This one had airs and graces and ideas well above her station and her a common gypsy wench into the bargain."

"She's a bargain herself now," a shipwright said and there was a general laugh.

"I reckon she put a spell on Squire, but now it's worn off with Christian prayers and blessings," said an old fisherman.

"Parson's here today, look. He'll probably tell her to pray for a kind new 'usband," the farmer's daughter said.

"I wouldn't have thought this was the sort of place a parson would come. It's not seemly, a poor example to his flock." The farmer's wife clucked her tongue.

"Maybe he'll be prayin' he can afford to buy her," a joiner said and his friends laughed with him.

Not long afterwards, Captain Charles Mountjoy arrived. Although he gave Elms and Coleman a curt nod, he chose a place in the crowd well away from them.

"I wouldn't mind buyin' her if she's as comely as they say," a young sailor said. One of his companions was about to make a more ribald retort when a farm labourer shouted and pointed. "Look, look, the maid's coming!"

All the spectators turned to look in the general direction of the squire's carriage which was just arriving. As they were about to dismount from the carriage, Denny touched Rosina's hand. "We did have some good times together. I shall miss you a little." He sounded wistful.

Rosina did not reply. She merely looked at him with utter contempt, almost making him recoil from her.

"Come on," he said, curtly. "We've no time to waste."

Rosina shrugged her shoulders. Despite the pleasantness of the weather, the chill in her heart felt colder than the worst snows of winter.

The crowd began to cheer and jeer as the landlord brought out a barrel. Rosina felt several pairs of hands lifting her onto it. Denny left her to stand beside Elms and Coleman.

"The lady's pretty," Rosina heard a child say. She could not help smiling at this tiny crumb of comfort in an apparently hostile world.

Denny's steward stood beside the barrel.

"What is the first offer for this gypsy woman, formerly married to Squire Denny, who is, today, on a sale as a wife?" His voice, loud in normal conversation became almost a bellow.

"Sixpence!" an old fisherman shouted, to the accompaniment of much mirth.

"One and six," said a farm labourer. "More than I can afford, really, but I think she'd be worth it."

Rosina saw the tall figure of Robert Elms speak to Coleman. Both men were laughing. She decided she hated them both and fervently hoped neither of them would offer for her. She thought she saw her brother, Spencer, in the crowd and her heart ached for him witnessing her humiliation. Angrily, she blinked the tears out of her eyes. She must show this rabble that dignity was on her side, not theirs, whatever they believed about her. She would not break down in front of them.

Her hopes were dashed when Elms shouted: "Five shillings!" He appeared to be gloating.

"Five and six," another voice said. Rosina was surprised to see the artist who had painted her portrait.

"Any advance upon five and six?" the steward asked.

"Six shillings! I can't really afford that but she was kind to me that day when I lost my leg. It's the least I can do for her." It was Peter Cooper, leaning heavily on his sound limb.

"Five pounds!" Parson Sebastian Coleman shouted.

"Any advance upon five pounds?" the steward shouted. There was no further offer. Rosina experienced a few moments of mental panic. She tried desperately not to show it. "Right, sold to—" the steward began. He was speaking very slowly indeed.

"Ten pounds, I offer ten pounds," another male voice called loudly from the back of the crowd. Rosina recognised it as that of Captain Charles Mountjoy.

The steward looked around him. "Any further offers?"" He hesitated for a split second. "The gypsy woman has been sold to Captain Mountjoy for ten pounds! The sale is concluded. You may all return to your homes."

The assembled crowd began to drift away, still chattering to each other.

Rosina saw Mountjoy thrust sovereigns into Denny's hands. The parson and the schoolmaster joined them.

"Thank you for carrying out our bargain," Rosina overheard the squire say to Mountjoy.

"I kept my word. Please leave us now, gentlemen, as I wish to be alone with Rosina."

All three men departed without a backward glance.

The landlord went inside the inn rubbing his hands. He was well satisfied with the extra trade he had had that day.

Charles and Rosina were alone.

CHAPTER 12

▼

Charles lifted Rosina down from the barrel. "Down you come, Rosina, that nightmare's all over."

She looked at him, almost handsome in his dark blue cloth coat ornamented with silver buttons worn over an ivory waistcoat, with a sour expression. "I heard the squire thank you for buying me. If this arrangement had already been made between you, why couldn't you have arranged it all privately instead of putting me up for public auction like a slave?"

Charles sighed. "I agree it was a most unpleasant business but Denny insisted it was the best thing to do in the circumstances even though he found it somewhat distasteful himself."

"He did not!" Rosina was indignant. "He unfairly believed I had been unfaithful to him, so because he believed I had brought shame on him, he wanted to be rid of me." Rosina could not hide her bitterness and, to her horror, she began to sob.

Charles took her in his arms and pulled her head gently against his chest. She made a feeble attempt to push him away but in an odd way, she found his presence comforting. He stroked her dishevelled black hair.

When she had stopped crying, he offered her his arm. They strolled amongst the beech woods of Ridley Wood where they were at the highest point of the Forest which offered a panoramic view of the coast.

They finally sat down under a beech tree. "Do you wish to return to the Romanies?" Charles asked.

Rosina laughed, mirthlessly. "If you intend to send me back to them, you may do so. You have bought me fair and square."

He smiled. "I think you were quite a bargain when all is said and done."

Relaxing a little, Rosina returned his smile. "And I am glad I was not forced into the hands of the parson or the schoolmaster." She shuddered.

"I understand how you felt about them. Denny did, too, I think. But what is your answer to my question? Do you want to go back to your own people?"

Rosina shook her head. "I admit there are times when I miss them and my old way of life. But I have been away from them for a long time now. They also know that I have lain with a *gorgio*. They might not accept me back."

"It's difficult to know what to do with you. As you know, I'm married so I can't wed you."

"I know, you couldn't become a—what is it called, a bigamist?"

"Quite," Charles said, wryly. "I should love to set you up in a house of your own where you could live under my protection. Then I could visit you at my leisure. But I cannot really afford to do this just yet. You will have to earn your own keep."

"Could you take me into your house as a servant?"

Charles shook his head. "My wife, understandably, would be somewhat suspicious of my intentions."

"Perhaps I could find work on a farm or leave these parts and go into service elsewhere?"

"I should much prefer you to be nearby." Charles clapped his hand to his head. "I have the solution! Why did I not think of it before?"

"What is it? What am I about to become?"

"The landlord of the 'Seagull' in Topcliffe died recently. He was an old widower who had outlived all of his own children. I bought his inn. I do not have the time to run it myself so I have appointed Peter Cooper to look after it for me. You could live there, working as a barmaid and I shall be able to make the occasional visit to your bedroom."

"Are you taking me there now?" Rosina was not too sure that she was exactly thrilled by the prospect of her new employment. But it was preferable to taking chances amongst strangers in a new district.

She also knew, if she were honest, that she wanted to be reasonably near to Charles.

Charles shook his head. "Not today. I think you deserve an outing before you start work. We will go and dine in Lymington. Wait here while I fetch my coach."

At the half timbered and thatched inn in Lymington where Charles hired a private parlour, they ate well-cooked roast chicken and plum pudding, washed down with wine. It was the first meal Rosina had eaten that day. She was hungrier than she realised.

"Smuggling still takes place at the Seagull," Charles said. "You should know what goes on. Sometimes when there's too many goods to be stored at the Cat and Fiddle, some of the smaller things are taken to the Seagull."

Rosina knew that the ancient Cat and Piddle Inn, situated on the very edge of the Forest, was the smugglers' first paying customer. The town of Christchurch lay at the confluence of the Rivers Avon and Stour. The extensive shallow water of Christchurch Harbour was sheltered by Hengistbury Head, which curved around the southern flank and was a favourite place for the free traders to rendezvous.

"What sort of things do you mean?" Rosina asked.

"Tea, tobacco, coins, straw hats, that sort of thing mostly. I turn a blind eye to it although I have given up dabbling in smuggling otherwise."

"It's strange. The squire said he no longer had the heart for it. Did you also not like the way the informer was murdered?"

"No, I didn't. The free traders' old leader disappeared one night with a lot of spoils. He'll be a marked man if they ever find him. They suspected the informer knew his whereabouts but there's still no trace of him."

"Just as well. I suppose they must have a new leader."

"Yes, a far more ruthless one. It's not only dislike of him that's made me stop dealing in contraband. It's because I also have a wife and children to consider."

"Polly Davis, our—I mean the squire's—old servant, has been seen standing on Verely Hill to warn of Customs men."

"I know. She also rides a pack pony and rides astride with her skirts tucked up with flagons of spirits flung across its back."

"As I said to my old maid, she will be caught one day."

"I think so. Be careful, yourself."

"Thank you for the warning but I shan't become involved."

"Wise girl. Now you've finished eating, I'm taking you to the dressmaker's."

The dressmaker's establishment was situated in a medium sized building with a large sign outside the door and wooden floors. There was a long marble counter behind which the dressmaker served them herself rather than leaving it to her assistant, as she normally did. Her apprentices were working at their benches in the back room. The dressmaker was very anxious to please a fine gentleman.

"What do you require for your lady, sir?" she asked. "Just name it and it will be attended to at once."

"Well, Rosina," Charles said. "I think you will need two working dresses."

"Yes," Rosina said, without a great deal of enthusiasm.

"What do you think you will need? The decision is yours."

She chose a striped orange, brown and black linsey-woolsey dress with a white lawn apron and a light grey homespun gown with a blue cotton kerchief to fasten around her neck and tuck into the front fastening of her bodice and a white muslin cap.

"Now it's my turn to pick out your party clothes," Charles said.

"I doubt I shall be going to many parties," Rosina said, sharply.

"I shall make sure you attend at least one." He turned to the dressmaker and arranged for her to make a cream damask gown trimmed with ivory lace and another dress, a pale pink silk with the bodice trimmed with blue satin bows.

"You can't buy me these gowns, Captain," Rosina protested. "They're far too expensive and I don't know when I would be able to wear them."

"I can afford them. I wouldn't have brought you here if I couldn't. I'll make sure you have occasion to wear them."

Rosina was thrilled by his words.

The dressmaker's eyes lit up. "Is there anything else you would especially like, sir?"

"Is there, Rosina? You make the final decision."

"No, you have bought me more than enough already."

"You must have one more item. I insist."

"Do you have any scarves?" Rosina asked the dressmaker.

"Yes, mistress, the very one. I'll fetch it for you."

The woman brought a rose coloured gauze scarf trimmed with gold fringe and gold tissue flowers from the workroom.

Rosina fingered it. "I didn't mean one like this. I expected something plainer. This is beautiful."

"Like yourself, Rosie," Charles said. "I'll definitely buy this one," he said to the overjoyed dressmaker.

He draped it around Rosina's shoulders as careful as a lady's maid but with much more tenderness than a lady's maid would have shown.

"Come for a drive with me before we go to Topcliffe," Charles said. "You should like that."

They walked back to his coach where his coachman awaited them. Charles instructed the man to drive back to Burley. Once there, he wandered with Rosina under some ancient oaks.

"These trees are called the 'Twelve Apostles'," Charles said. "An interesting name, don't you think?"

Rosina nodded. "I should like to go back into the woods again," she said.
"Very well, if that is your wish."
"Oh, it is, most definitely it is!"
Charles' exploring touch discovered the sweetness of Rosina' s shapely young body. As they came together and became entwined as one with a telepathy between them which went beyond passion, they were illuminated by the silvery light of the full moon.

Rosina knew Charles felt no guilt about his wife, as she did not feel ashamed either. Their lovemaking seemed right, and entirely natural, almost pre-ordained.

This strange day had started so badly but now she did not want the magical night to end.

*   *   *   *

Rosina worked long, hard hours as a barmaid, in contrast to the ease of her previous life with the squire who she knew she missed dreadfully. It annoyed her that she missed him but she had the consolation of knowing that he never visited the Seagull nowadays.

She knew many of the free traders and always treated them with great respect.

Peter Cooper initially tried to fondle her. She pushed him aside, informing him that Captain Mountjoy would soon be visiting her and she knew he was jealous. She mentally crossed her fingers that the captain would keep his promise in this respect. Peter accepted this, and a rough and ready companionship gradually developed between them.

Rosina did not mind the hard work as much as being considered an object of ridicule in the area. The news of the wife sale had spread far and wide.

Captain Mountjoy, however, kept his word and visited her as often as he could. Rosina was most contented at these times. She had become very fond of the captain.

No-one laughed at her openly because of Captain Mountjoy's influence There were still knowing looks and sly innuendoes which Rosina hated. At these times, she gritted her teeth and thought of her lover. Then, she received some devastating news.

CHAPTER 13

▼

Captain Charles Mountjoy had taken his wife and two small twin daughters on a short visit to London.

"I've missed you very much while you've been away," Rosina said. "I couldn't wait for you to come back."

Charles looked uneasy. "I'm afraid I have to go away again soon, Rosie, on a very long and important journey. We'll have to make the most of our time together before I leave."

Rosina was crestfallen. "Where do you have to go and why is it so very important?"

"I'm sailing to the West Indies, my love. To visit a sugar plantation."

"What's it like there, the West Indies?"

"It's very beautiful, with tall mountains, clear springs, very bright vegetation, blue sea and white beaches."

"I wish I could come with you."

"So do I but as you know, it's not possible. I have to go myself as I have important business to attend to. The plantation owner supplies the molasses from which my crews' rum is made."

"When I was living with the squire, I seem to remember Lydia telling me it was also used in jams and medicines." Rosina feared she was prattling about nothing. She was not really interested in what molasses were used for.

She had just said the first thing that had come into her head. She could hardly order a ship owner not to embark upon a journey because it was against her wishes.

"Will you be taking your wife with you?"

Mountjoy stiffened. He did not like discussing his family with Rosina. He felt that the two women were two separate parts of his life.

"No, I will not. She might have come if the children were not so young but we felt at their age, it might be too hazardous."

Rosina felt relieved. She feared that if the captain's wife had accompanied him, he might have decided not to return to his mistress.

"I shall bring you back some pretty trinkets, Rosie—such things as you will most likely not have seen before."

"It's a kind thought but I' in not bothered about them. I would rather you bring yourself back, safe and sound, as soon as you can."

"Let's make the most of the time we have left together."

He took her in his arms and kissed her, tenderly. Rosina could not prevent herself from clinging to him. She had a premonition that this would be their last night together.

Two months later, Catherine Mountjoy called at the Seagull. All the staff were amazed that a lady like her should visit such a place, riding a pony and accompanied only by a maid. She was a fair-haired young woman still of a slight build after childbirth She asked to speak to Rosina privately.

"Take me to the room where you keep the contraband," Catherine said. "Don't look so startled, I know very well it's stored here as well as at certain other inns."

Rosina took Catherine to the secret room. She was a little afraid that. Charles' wife might try to attack her. She had informed Peter Cooper to search for them if she were not back within twenty minutes.

"I believe you have been my husband's mistress," Catherine came straight to the point.

"Yes, I have and I also believe I shall be when he comes back."

A tiny smile played on the corners of Catherine's mouth.

"Do you feel no shame that you have associated with a married man? A gentleman far above your station in life?"

"I had no choice, madam," Rosina said, angrily. "The circumstances I found myself in forced me into it, though I admit I'm very fond of your husband. He has been very kind to me."

"And over-generous, I think," Catherine said, waspishly.

"You can think what you like, Mistress Mountjoy."

"I can say what I like to your sort. For your own good, however, you must listen to me."

"Why should you wish to do me good?"

"I don't, particularly. I just thought you should know what I'm about to tell you. You've been honest with me so I'll tell you the truth concerning my husband."

"What is it?"

"He wasn't a bad husband apart from his unfaithfulness with a common gypsy girl." Catherine paused, dabbing at her eyes with a lace embroidered handkerchief.

As Rosina was about to make a heated retort, Catherine spoke again. "An officer came to visit me yesterday. I fear my husband has left me a widow with two young orphan girls to care for."

Rosina felt the blood drain from her face and stared at the other woman in horror.

"Yes," Catherine continued. "His ship with all its crew sank to the bottom of the sea."

Rosina burst into heartbroken sobs. Charles had become the most important part of her existence. She wished her own life would come to an end. Rosina was distressed to think that she would never again feel his touch and hear his dear voice.

"You are most upset as indeed, I am, myself." Catherine was remarkably calm for someone in an upset frame of mind. "I shall take my leave of you now." She turned on her heel and walked away. Rosina followed, walking at half her normal speed.

"Where is Mistress Mountjoy?" Rosina asked Peter Cooper.

"She just left in a great hurry. She reminded me of a bat escapin' from Hell. Maybe she felt this wasn't a suitable place for a lady like her. You know 'ow some of 'em look down their long noses at us."

Rosina did not reply and Peter looked concerned. "Are you not feelin' well, maiden? You look as white as a ghost."

"I felt faint for a minute, Peter. Bring me a glass of water to revive me."

In the days following the news of her lover's supposed death, Rosina tried to immerse herself in her work. She felt indifferent to nearly everything else that went on around her.

As she was serving a customer one evening, a fisherman also known to be a free trader leaned over the bar.

"Did you 'ear about Polly Davis, Rosie?"

"No," Rosina said, without much interest.

"She was caught red-'anded by Ridin' Officer, carryin' loads of things."

"Things she had no right to have I suppose?"

"That's right, maid. She's bin tried. They found her guilty and she's bein' transported to West Indies as an inden—indented, some sort of servant."

"Indentured, I think it's called," Rosina said.

"You're too clever for a gypsy maid," the fisherman said.

"She is," Peter Cooper said, almost with pride. "Polly Davis, now, she'll be like a slave, not a servant, treated just like the blacks are." His ugly, monkey-like face was illuminated by a smile that was not entirely without rancour.

"I'm afraid I can't feel sorry for her," Rosina said. "She brought it on herself."

"Yes, she did, silly bitch," Peter Cooper agreed. "I don't feel sorry for Captain Mountjoy bein' drownded, neither."

Rosina glared at him. His sly grin disappeared and he was forced to look away from the hostility in her dark eyes.

*   *   *   *

Rosina was serving in the bar one evening when her brothers arrived, carrying their instruments.

"Jacko, Arnold, Spencer!" she exclaimed in delight. "I'm so glad you've come here."

"We're glad to see you, Rosie," Jacko said.

"You've been treated shameful," Spencer said. "When I found out you was to be sold, I wanted to knock squire down. I didn't come into his house that day I come to see you, Rosie, because even then, I felt I didn't trust him."

"I'm sure you would have knocked him down if you'd gone in, Spencer," Arnold said, sarcastically. "You was the one what let Rosina get caught in the first place."

"That's enough," Jacko said. "It's in the past and we can't change what's happened even though none of us liked it. As we all know, people like Squire Denny are too powerful for the likes of us."

"I've not done badly for myself," Rosina said, hastily. "I'm happy enough."

"I don't think you are, really," Jacko whispered, peering into her face as if he could read secrets there.

"I am happy," Rosina said, desperately. "It's wonderful to see you all again." She called Peter Cooper over and introduced him to her brothers.

"Peter's been good to me," Rosina said.

"Not as good as Rosie was to me," Peter said. "She almost saved my life when I had an accident. I'm looking forward to hearin' you all play. It's grand to have a bit of music now and again."

"You'll let Rosina dance Peter?" Jacko asked.

"Of course."

Rosina began to dance spontaneously. It seemed such a long time since she had danced that she had wondered if she would remember her steps, but to her immense relief, they all came back to her. She gave an inspired performance to the accompaniment of her brothers' instruments.

When she had finished, all the watchers applauded with Peter Cooper clapping his hands together, the loudest and hardest of all.

After her brothers had taken their affectionate leave of Rosina and all the other customers had left, Cooper said, "I really enjoyed watching you dance maid. It was very exciting."

"I've always liked dancing, Peter. Thank you for your compliment."

He shrugged and moved towards her, taking hold of her hands.

"There's a matter I bin givin' a lot of thought to, lately."

"What's that?"

Cooper cleared his throat and shuffled his feet slightly. "Now your captain's dead and gone, maybe I could wed you."

She stared at him with horror. Although she did not dislike him, she found the idea of physical relations with the man almost unbearable.

Rosina suppressed a shudder as he released her hands. "It's kind of you to make me this offer, Peter, but I really have to refuse it. If you're of a mind to marry, I'm certain some other woman will accept you as a husband."

I don't want no other women. You're the one who shall be my wife."

Rosina flushed and shook her head. "I have just told you, your offer is refused. In any case, I've no wish to marry again."

"There's no need for this bashful and maidenly act, woman. You opened your legs for the captain often enough so don't play games with me."

Cooper lunged towards her and managed to grab hold of her. She struggled in his grip as he forced her head back to try to kiss her. Suddenly, Jacko burst through the door.

"Rosina, I forgot to tell you that—" He broke off as he looked at his sister, taking the situation in at a glance.

"Put my sister down at once, Cooper. Leave her well alone in future if you know what's good for you."

"Don't interfere, gyppo," Cooper said. "The wench is just in a silly and stubborn mood. She will come to her senses soon enough." He tried, unsuccessfully, to kiss her again.

"Don't believe a word he says, Jacko!" Rosina shouted, looking at Cooper with loathing in her eyes.

The enraged Jacko rushed up to the couple, managed to part them and pushed Rosina aside.

Cooper began to pull a knife out of his pocket but Rosina had picked up a cudgel kept behind the bar and crept behind the two men. She swiftly handed it to Jacko who brought it down hard on Cooper's head, knocking him unconscious.

Rosina's hand flew to her mouth. "Jacko, have you killed him?"

Jacko looked down at Cooper's inert form. "No, he's still breathing. But we must get out of here at once!"

He pulled her out of the door and they began to run until they were out of breath.

"Where are you taking me?" Rosina asked.

"To a cave in the Forest where you shall sleep tonight. Don't worry if it's cold, it will only be for one night. I first came to the inn to warn you that the Customs men will most likely call there. I heard a rumour that an informer has told them where the contraband is hidden in the secret room."

"How did you know about that?"

"News travels fast around these parts. I also meant to tell you that I have been offered a position in Catherine Mountjoy's house as a gardener."

"Constance Wilkins lied to me that you were working there as a gardener. Now you really will be; it's a strange world."

"Connie Wilkins, you say. I know her; she's a free trader's doxy. I'll have a word with her some time."

"Are you going to accept this position?"

"Aye, the wage is quite high and I've a fancy to live in a real house for a while."

"And I expect she has a fancy for you. Even though you're a common gypsy like your sister, you're tolerably handsome." Jacko looked sheepish.

"To be honest, Jacko, I wish you weren't going to work for her."

"I've already accepted."

Rosina knew it would be useless to try to change his mind. After what seemed hours of walking, they crept into the cave. Jacko lent Rosina his rough jacket to put on to give her a little warmth.

"A wagon will arrive at the cave mouth to collect you in the morning. The waggoner will whistle to wake you up. He's taking apples, potatoes and turnips to the market in London and underneath there will be—" Jacko winked, "a girl."

Rosina smiled. "Me?"

Jacko nodded. "And wine, gin, brandy and suchlike from the flaskers to take to another address where rich folk live."

"I'm not at all surprised by that." Rosina knew that 'flaskers' was the name given to the smugglers who specialised in liquor. "But why must I go to London, brother?"

"I don't think the Forest will be a safe place for you, in future, sister. It's well known you worked in the inn where the Preventy men will probably arrest Cooper. London is huge You can easily hide yourself there and find some sort of work."

"Jacko, why don't you come with me? You're probably in some danger yourself. When Cooper wakes, he'll probably accuse you of attempted murder and he'll also say it was me who stored the contraband."

"It's only his word they'll have which they might not believe."

"He has a number of friends among the smugglers. They'll help him if they can. And the Revenue men will probably be pleased to arrest you."

"They won't be able to prove that I'm guilty of any crime."

"Don't be such a fool. You're a Romany. They'll trump up some charge against you if they can." She clutched at his sleeve. "I want to know you're safe and well, Jacko. I won't sleep at night if I don't know how you are faring."

Rosina had just experienced a frightening mental picture of Jacko lying on the ground, his body lifeless. It terrified her.

Jacko patted her hand. "I assure you I shall be quite safe, Rosie. I'm sure Mistress Mountjoy will protect me from any false accusations."

Rosina tried to smile but she sensed that some sort of trouble was brewing for her brother. She knew she would not be able to persuade him that this was the case. He was probably infatuated with Catherine Mountjoy.

"I shall come and visit you in London," Jacko said.

"How will you know where to find me?"

"You learned to read and write while you were in Squire's household, didn't you?"

Rosina nodded.

"I thought so. You can write me a letter sometimes. There's sure to be at least one other servant of Mistress Mountjoy's who can read 'em to me and write back to you for a small fee."

"Jacko, I wish you were coming to London with me."

"So do I, but I think it's wiser for you to go alone."

"It seems such a shame that we've only just met again after a long time. When I thought, we could see each other more often, be part of a proper family again, we have to part."

"I don't like partin' neither, Rosina, but it has to be. It won't be for ever."

"I wish I could believe that, Jacko."

"You're gettin' foolish fancies, Rosie. Try to get rid of them. When you're settled in London, I'll come and see you as soon as I can and so will Arnold and Spencer."

Rosina forced a smile. "I'll look forward to that."

"And me. Goodbye for a while, then, Rosina. Have a good journey and God go with you."

"May He go with you too, Jacko. I shall always love you."

"Me, Arnold and Spencer have always loved you, too."

Brother and sister embraced each other warmly but the dreadful foreboding that she would not see Jacko again had not left Rosina.

When Jacko had gone, she lay down, huddling into his jacket. Her dark eyes filled with the tears she could no longer suppress. Rosina felt completely alone in the heart of the hostile Forest.

CHAPTER 14

▼

The journey in the bottom of the wagon seemed to go on forever. By the time the waggoner stopped at a hostelry for refreshment, Rosina felt sick and bruised. A hasty meal of bread and cheese and ale refreshed her, but the second half of the journey seemed even worse. By the time the wagon rolled into Covent Garden, she was exhausted.

"Thank God we're here!" She scrambled down onto the cobbles, dirty and dishevelled. As the strong wind swept her tangled hair into her eyes, she pushed it back impatiently.

Rosina was overwhelmed by London. She had not been prepared for its size, noise and the unceasing activity.

There were coaches and carriages of all descriptions, sedan chairs, carts and barrows bawling peddlers and hawkers who carried goods and shouted exaggerated descriptions of their excellence. There was also a constant parade of rakes, beggars and drunks. Ladies and gentlemen of quality passed poor people without giving them a second glance.

"There's wicked women in London, maid," the waggoner said. "They'll entice you into evil ways if you let them. I'm takin' you to an inn where I know the innkeeper. He'll give you a meal and a bed for the night."

"Will there be enough room for the two of us?"

He shook his head. "I have to make haste to be about my own business. I'll fix you up with work at the tavern. You'll 'ave to work 'ard but should do well if you're careful not to fall into bad ways."

"Thank you for all you've done for me. I'm very grateful."

The waggoner shrugged. "Come, I'll take you to the inn now. "Rosina wondered why he appeared to be in such a hurry. He had been a taciturn companion on the journey but not a morose one.

Outside the Rose Tavern, ostlers and stableboys were busy. Procuresses were waiting to meet the arriving coaches and wagons in order to entice country girls into prostitution.

Inside, men and women were rolling upon the sanded floor, fighting and scratching. Drunken women, bared to the waist, wrestled together.

There were also 'Posture Girls' who Rosina later discovered specialised in perversions. Some of these girls stripped naked and mounted upon the tables; others stretched on the floor in suggestive imitations of sexual behaviour.

Glancing around, Rosina was puzzled, wondering why the waggoner had warned her against wicked London women and then brought her to a place like this.

She had already decided she would not stay here very long. Rosina was also amazed that all classes of society seemed to be gathered there.

"Here's a new girl for you," the waggoner said to the innkeeper. "If you're wantin' a waitin' maid or barmaid."

The landlord looked Rosina over so intently that she blushed. "Yes, I am, she can serve as both," he said, brusquely.

"I've said she can have her supper and sleep here tonight," the waggoner said. "Then she'll start her work in the mornin' if that suits you."

"All right," the innkeeper said. "What's her name?" he asked the waggoner as if Rosina were not there.

"Rosina Clayton. She's a gypsy and she can dance as well as serve."

Rosina wondered how the waggoner knew so much about her. She also thought he had glanced at her with a certain amount of concern but then dismissed this idea as a figment of her imagination.

The landlord nodded in approval. "We'll call her 'The Gypsy Rose'; it's the right name for this tavern." He called to his wife. "Take this new girl, Rosina, to the kitchen. Give her some supper and show her where she'll sleep. You can set her to work in the mornin'."

His wife nodded and beckoned to Rosina to follow her. Turning around, Rosina saw that the waggoner and the innkeeper were deep in discussion. They each spat on the palm of one hand and clapped it against the other's. Then the waggoner departed. Rosina guessed he had agreed to leave some liquor at the inn.

She was given a hot, reasonably well-cooked meal in the kitchen, then shown to a small, plainly furnished but comfortable room in the attic.

The innkeeper's wife pointed to a linen chest. "Put them clothes on tomorrer mornin' before you start work," she said, leaving the room swiftly.

Rosina opened the chest and saw a dark blue cotton gown, a starched white apron and a frilled white cap. She wondered how the innkeeper's wife already knew these garments would fit her.

Rosina took off her old gown, her shift and petticoats, lay down in the truckle bed and fell into an exhausted sleep.

*   *   *   *

Rosina found that she had to work hard for John Carver, the Rose's portly, balding landlord. She carried heavy trays of food and drink to his customers, morning, noon and night.

She was permanently busy and her feet often ached, but she was not resentful. In his own somewhat rough and ready way, Carver was a basically fair man.

The behaviour of the tavern's customers both fascinated and repelled Rosina. She was courteous to the Posture Girls but tried to avoid them as much as possible. She served hot suppers to the nobility and gentry who came to the Rose after attending the theatre. One earl was a rake and sportsman, who moved in the highest Court circles as well as the lowest bordellos. There was a theatre procuress who was always in the company of 'gallants' and whores. They crowded around her for advice and assistance. Her prices varied considerably. Many actresses were paid low wages apart from the money they could make from their annual benefits. Some of them took up part time prostitution.

Rosina disapproved of the licentious, sometimes violent, actions of some of the tavern's patrons. In spite of herself, she liked the general air of liveliness and jollity in her place of employment.

She never succumbed, however, to any of the men who swarmed around her, evading their grasping hands. She was reminded of the old days on the road with her brothers. Some of her admirers gave her quite generous tips, including many silver sixpences. Bets began to circulate amongst them as to who would be the first to seduce her.

Carver said that she could probably make a fortune if she permitted them to take liberties. Why not take advantage of them while she was still young and pretty? Rosina shook her head and said pertly that she intended to remain as virtuous as she could in such a place.

John Carver shrugged and laughed a little ruefully. "The waggoner what brought you 'ere said you was a good girl and he asked me to keep a special eye on you. He even paid me a bit of money to do so. I didn't know whether to believe him or not but I s'pose it must be true. You're one in a million."

Rosina felt touched by the waggoner's concern. She wondered where he was and what he was doing now. She decided he had probably returned to the Forest for which she, herself, was frequently nostalgic.

Carver's wife, Sally, practically ignored Rosina. Occasionally, she snapped a curt command to her but never engaged her in conversation although she talked to the other maids in the tavern's rare slack times.

One day, Carver said, "A girl called Mary Simpson is playin' 'ere tonight. She's an expert on the pipe and tabor and should draw in the crowds to quench their thirsts. I want you to help her all you can, Rosina."

Rosina was puzzled. "How can I help her?"

"I particularly want to see if you can dance as well as the waggoner said you could." She guessed that Carver had engaged in bets with some of his customers that she would dance for them.

"It's time you earned your keep here, properly," Carver continued. "I shall pay you a little extra."

"I have always worked very hard for you," Rosina protested. She was not sure that she wanted to dance.

Carver shrugged. "Maybe, but you will oblige me in this special way."

"And if I refuse?"

Carver wore his sternest expression. "Then, I shall put words into all the right ears to make sure that you will never again find work in this or any other inn or tavern in the Garden."

Although she would not have admitted it, Rosina believed in his power to do this. Without saying a word, she left the taproom, slamming the door hard behind her.

The next morning, much to his wife's disgust, Carver sent Rosina out with the barmaid to buy more suitable clothing for dancing. She deliberately chose garments that were brightly coloured and comfortable, of serviceable, not rich material.

The barmaid had urged her to buy more revealing styles. Rosina, however, had been adamant and the barmaid had eventually given in to the stronger will.

Mary Simpson proved to be a small, wiry girl of sixteen. She had curly red hair, blue eyes and a pale, freckled skin which, to Rosina's eyes, looked unhealthy. There were dark rings round her eyes and Rosina noticed she always held a rag in her hand, into which she frequently coughed.

Mary soon engaged Rosina in friendly conversation and the older girl warmed to her.

"You're the gypsy girl what I'm to play for tonight, ain't you? I recognised you straightaway. I think you'll be good. I'm a good judge of people. I've had to be in my life, I can tell you."

Taken aback, Rosina said, "Yes, that's right, I am."

"We should deal well together. We'll draw the right sort in—them with plenty of coins to jingle in their pockets. We'll soon winkle them out into our own 'ands."

Mary grinned infectiously and Rosina smiled in return. The younger girl was not exactly pretty but due to her vivacious manner, she had plenty of admirers.

She explained to Rosina that she was the daughter of a poor soldier who had long since died of consumption. She could not remember her mother; an older sister had brought her up.

"I hope your sister was kind to you," Rosina said. "You must be grateful to her."

"Oh, she was, in her way," Mary replied. "Could be a bit free and easy with 'er fists but she done the best she could for us."

Mary glanced around the room. "I bet George Blackwell will be here early tonight."

"Do you like him?" Rosina asked, both puzzled and curious.

Mary gave a slight grimace. "I wouldn't exactly say I like him but it's strange, I always feel as if I want to please him, to do the best I can while he's around."

"I think I know what you mean, Mary."

Rosina smiled inwardly.

✳   ✳   ✳   ✳

George Blackwell did appear at the Rose early that evening. Rosina heard a man in the audience whisper to his female companion. "That's the notorious George Blackwell. He's been a soldier, sometimes he acts, has his fingers in all sorts of pies."

The woman with him glanced at Blackwell's tall figure and brooding dark looks. "He's handsome, though," she said.

"He may not always be," her companion said. "Especially if anything should happen to that damned hunchback, Rook, who acts as his eyes and ears."

The woman shuddered. "That fellow makes my flesh creep."

Rosina knew that many people feared Rook because he was rumoured to be an expert with a knife he carried.

Blackwell shouted: "Carver, have you anything interesting for me to watch tonight or shall I be bored?"

Carver replied, "No, I shall not bore you at all, Captain Blackwell. Let's not waste our time talking. Let's get on with the entertainment. I'm certain you'll be delighted with it."

Blackwell opened his mouth but before he could speak. Rosina quickly continued, "We shall now begin our performance."

A space was cleared in the middle of the floor for the two girls where all the customers could have a good view of them. Mary looked disappointed. She had hoped to have her fortune told and be informed that Captain George Blackwell would surely become her next lover.

Mary began to play her instruments as Rosina closed her eyes for a fleeting second before beginning to dance. She was initially nervous, unsure if she had lost all of her former ability. She gained confidence after the first few moves. Finally, she was oblivious to everything apart from the rhythms of the music and her accompanying movements.

As the young women finished, there was much cheering and loud applause broke out. Many silver coins were thrown their way. Laughing, Mary picked them all up from the floor.

"We'll divide these between us," she said.

"It's most generous of you," Rosina said. "As you're much better known than me around these parts, I should have thought you would have expected the greater share."

John Carver's hand fell on her shoulder. "Hand over 'alf of that to me, Rosina. You owe it me as I'm your master."

"Don't be ridiculous, Carver, let her keep it. It was very well earned on her part and you know it. You also know you'll make a very handsome profit with your customers if you charge them to come and watch her."

"I'll thank you not to interfere with my affairs, Captain Blackwell."

Blackwell glanced, apparently casually, towards the door.

"I believe Rook is now entering your premises, Mr Carver. I think he suspects your wife shortchanged him the other night. He has let it pass this time as a mistake on her part."

Carver looked as if he were about to swear. He hesitated for a moment, then muttered, "I spoke 'astily, wivout thinkin', Captain Blackwell. Forget what I said" Red-faced and visibly sweating, Carver went back to the bar.

"Thank you, Captain Blackwell, it was most kind of you."

He smiled. "No matter, Rosina. I didn't want to see you unfairly treated."

"You didn't need to take my part. Most folk would have considered it a private matter between my master and myself."

"I am not 'most folk,' my dear. I am an individual. I have watched gypsy dancers before but yours was one of the finest performances I have ever seen."

Rosina thanked him for his compliment. The captain ran a hand through his dark hair, looking thoughtful.

"I'm sure you'll be able to do me a favour at some time in the future. In fact, you've given me an idea."

"Might I enquire what it is?" Rosina asked. In spite of her feeling of apprehension that she could neither fully comprehend nor completely suppress, she was interested.

Blackwell smiled, showing his even white teeth and shook his head. "No, I have to give it further thought before a I make a final decision."

Rosina gave a slight nod and turned away from him.

CHAPTER 15

▼

"Come and see the Wild Gypsy Rose, the wonderful new dancer at the Rose Tavern." The ugly dwarf linkboy shouted his news at every corner he turned as he led his clients towards their destination. If they complained about his raucous, unofficial advertising of a place of entertainment, he would threaten to put out his torch and leave them stranded in a dark street.

Rosina was quite happy not to serve customers with food and drink any more. She was permitted to rise late in the mornings. Carver paid her only a slightly larger wage than the one she had previously earned but she was also allowed to divide the many coins that were thrown her way between herself and Mary. Captain Blackwell usually gave the largest amount. She still did not allow any of the inn's patrons to touch her and the bets continued as to when she would finally lose her virtue although some had lost interest.

Rosina wondered whether to look for new lodgings for herself but decided against it. Her food, drink and board at the Rose were all free. She still hoped, eventually, to leave the Rose and set up her stall.

Then Mary announced that she was leaving the Rose and would be playing in the 'Shakespeare's Head' instead. She now had a new sweetheart, having long since given up the idea that Captain Blackwell would fall in love with her. Her lover, one of Rook's childhood acquaintances, was now a cook at the Shakespeare's Head. Mary explained how the inn was divided into two parts. One was a coffee house and the other sold liquors and victuals.

Officers of the East India Company met there to eat and drink and exchange information. Then they visited the brothel next door. Captain Blackwell knew several of them.

"Would I be able to come with you, do you think?" Rosina knew she would miss the younger girl, who was her only friend in London. Perhaps, too, she might earn more substantial tips from the patrons of the Shakespeare's Head. The inn was gaining a reputation for being a meeting place for men of wit and culture.

Mary looked doubtful. "I ain't too sure, Rosie."

"But you could ask, Mary."

"To be honest, Rosie, my man had the devil of a job to persuade the landlord to take me on. He said I might take his mind off his work."

"Maybe if he saw us perform together, he would be persuaded," Rosina urged.

Just then, Rosina felt a masculine hand on her shoulder and Captain Blackwell whirled her around to face him.

"No, Rosina, I have a better suggestion. I don't think you should go to the Shakespeare's Head. You will obviously be unwelcome."

"And where do you believe I should go, Captain Blackwell?" Rosina asked, peevishly.

The captain was unperturbed by her attitude. "I can find a place for you, dancing at the Haymarket Theatre. You would earn more than you do here and I could find you more suitable lodgings. What do you say?"

"You'd be a rare fool to say 'no,' Rosina," Mary said.

Rosina held her head high. She was hurt by Mary's attitude. "I'm not sure whether to accept your offer or not, Captain Blackwell. I shall have to give it a lot of thought."

Blackwell shrugged. "Suit yourself. I give you until tomorrow at noon and no later."

Rosina nodded, managing to keep her face impassive.

After a night of tossing and turning, she informed Captain George Blackwell that she had considered his offer carefully and decided to accept it. He congratulated her on having made the wisest choice. She wished she could be as sure, herself.

"My first performance at the Haymarket is at six o'clock tonight," George Blackwell said. "I shall be speaking the prologue so you will only have a few hours in which to search for lodgings. You will not be able to find somewhere else which is suitable for you in so short a time."

"But I shall not be dancing until much later than that."

Blackwell shrugged. "Perhaps, but the manager there insists upon you arriving at the same time as myself. Unless you do so, you will not set foot upon the boards there."

Rosina grudgingly conceded defeat. "Very well, I shall go with you to see this house and if I like it, I shall sleep there tonight. Otherwise, I shall take a room at an inn. And I still intend to find my own lodgings in the future."

"Of course you will, Rosina," Blackwell said, silkily. She glanced at him suspiciously but his face remained impassive. "Fetch your belongings and we'll leave now. I'll hire a couple of sedan chairs."

The brick built house with its sash windows and pantiled roof, was larger and more opulent looking than Rosina had anticipated. It was situated on a long strip of ground running back from the street. The house covered the front part of the strip. There was a courtyard in the middle part and stables at the back.

Iron railings rose on either side of the stone steps which led up to the door. "This house is jointly owned by two people," Blackwell said. "Isaac Mandleberg, a ship owner and ship broker, and is well known on the Exchange. He owns the gin shop here. The other is Elizabeth Vale, the widow who will be your new landlady."

Just then, a middle-aged woman came out of the house and greeted Blackwell effusively.

Rosina secretly studied the older woman. She was of average height and quite plump, elegantly dressed yet discreetly painted. Obviously she had been slim and attractive in her youth, but not a great beauty.

Blackwell introduced the women to each other, then asked Elizabeth to show them around the house.

"Yes, Captain Blackwell, I would be most honoured to do so," she said. Her voice was low and almost seductive but Rosina thought she simpered and was irritated by it.

Once they were inside the house, Rosina was impressed, in spite of herself, at the amount of fine mahogany furniture, statues, silverware and paintings it contained. The huge parlour had high plasterwork ceilings gilded in pink and white, with crystal chandeliers. The mantelpiece was of carved marble.

There were sofas, classical statues, Italian cabinets with many drawers and cupboards inlaid with a variety of marbles. A fiddle had been left upon one of the marquetry side tables and large oval mirrors hung along the walls. In one corner stood a harpsichord. Rosina looked around with wonder. She found the room beautiful yet strangely oppressive.

"How do you like this room, Miss Clayton?" Elizabeth Vale asked. "I believe you are impressed."

"Yes, I am," Rosina said. "It's most—" She searched for the correct word, "unusual."

Captain Blackwell hid a smile but Elizabeth showed no reaction to Rosina's words.

"I have several other young ladies staying here. Most of them use the parlour from time to time. You're welcome to use it yourself. I have to warn you, though, special guests are frequently entertained here and most of them like their privacy. It would be best if you only come in here during the daylight hours."

Rosina nodded.

"You will probably make a lot of new friends if you decide to stay, Miss Clayton. I hope you do."

"I have still not decided, Mrs Vale," Rosina said.

"I should also tell you that there is a separate entrance to Isaac's gin shop on the bottom floor," Elizabeth said.

"I doubt I would want to go there," Rosina replied.

Elizabeth Vale's manner became more brisk. "Come, I'll show you the room you will have, should you decide to stay." She led the way to a room well away from the parlour.

Rosina could not help but be impressed by the room to which she was shown. It had flowered wallpaper, satin curtains at the windows, a Turkey carpet, a large mahogany wardrobe and a rosewood and gilt dressing table, a washstand and basin. The bed was quite wide with satin sheets and a patchwork quilt. There were also a sofa and two large oval mirrors.

"They are for your use if you wish to practise your dancing," Elizabeth said. "The rent would be three and sixpence per week. Is that not fair?"

"It's more than fair," Rosina said. "It's very generous." She thought back to the Rose where her room with its whitewashed walls, was almost a quarter of the size of this one. There had been rag rugs on the floor, a tiny table, a much smaller washstand and basin, two chairs and a wooden linen chest. Yet in its own peculiar way, that room had been quite cosy. This room, however, was sheer luxury in comparison.

"I shall stay here for a little while, Mrs Vale," she said. Blackwell and Elizabeth exchanged smiles.

✳   ✳   ✳   ✳

George Blackwell always took Rosina home from the theatre, Rook lighting their way. Rosina liked him a little better now although she had no illusions about the house in which she was living. She now knew it to be a discreetly run brothel, intended for wealthy citizens and merchants of the City of London.

Virgins were available for those patrons who could afford the higher price. Two young orphan girls worked there as general maids. Elizabeth did not allow any of the men to molest them and on the whole, they were not ill-treated.

The finest wines and liquors were served by well-trained menservants. The girls had been chosen for their beauty and charm and an ability to be tactful. They were required to be well dressed, well mannered and they could all dance. Some had asked Rosina to teach them more diverse steps to add to their repertoire.

She had agreed quite willingly as she wished to be on friendly terms with them although Rosina had no intention of staying here. She was certainly not going to sell her own body to any man. When Rosina was not teaching the other girls to dance, she kept well away from the parlour.

Rosina had often wondered where Blackwell's own house was situated. She asked both Rook and Elizabeth but both said they did not know. She did not believe them.

Rosina had spoken to Isaac Mandleberg a few times. A keen businessman, he always spoke to her pleasantly and offered her a free tot of gin to warm herself when she returned from the theatre late on the cooler nights. "Have a tot of my 'Blue Ruin',—it'll warm you and do you good," he would say. At first, Rosina was not sure that she liked it but she began to like its warming effect and the fact that it gave her a little more confidence before she went on stage.

The manager of the Haymarket sent for Rosina one night. He told her that her services would no longer be required. Rosina was crestfallen. A grave faced George Blackwell stood beside the manager and she gave him a suspicious glance, wondering why he had to be informed of her dismissal.

"But the audiences like me," Rosina protested. "I know they do. I can say, without conceit, that I have many admirers. Surely I am a draw to your customers?"

"I'm sorry, Rosina, I can no longer afford to pay you."

"It's useless to argue, Rosie. Come, I'll take you home," Blackwell said, taking her arm.

Rosina shook him off and turned again to the manager. "Surely, I could be allowed to stay a little longer."

The manager shook his head. "No."

"I wouldn't expect a higher wage," Rosina persisted. "And if you let me know how long I can remain, I could search for other work, in the meantime."

Once again, the manager shook his head. "I have no choice in the matter. You must leave now."

Rosina's attitude changed from a plaintive one to a slight belligerence. "I'm not sure that you can make me do so."

"He can and well you know it, Rosina," Blackwell said, firmly. "His word is law here."

"And so, to a very large extent is yours, I believe," Rosina said, bitterly.

Blackwell said nothing, offering her his arm. This time, she took it as she left the theatre in the haughtiest manner she could muster. Inwardly, she was seething, convinced Blackwell had, somehow, had a hand in her dismissal. But she could not prove it.

Outside the house, Blackwell said, "I'll see you, tomorrow."

Rosina gave him a curt nod in reply. Once she was inside, Elizabeth Vale said, with some consternation. "I must speak to you privately, Rosina. Could we go to your bedroom?"

Rosina sighed. She was tired and dispirited. "Can't it wait till tomorrow?"

"No, it's a matter of great importance."

CHAPTER 16

▼

Squire Denny looked at the portrait of Rosina hanging on the wall. Whenever he looked at it, he was filled with an uncomfortable feeling of shame. He had tried, unsuccessfully, to take it down but at the last minute, his nerve had failed him. Although Denny had turned Rosina's face to the wall on one occasion, he found that she haunted his thoughts and dreams even more than formerly so he had turned it back again.

"Oh, Rosina, you don't know how much I wish I could see you in the flesh again. It's nearly a year now since I last saw you," Denny said, aloud.

Lydia knocked loudly on the parlour door, jerking him out of his reverie. "Captain Mountjoy and Susan Williams wish to see you, sir. They say it's most important."

Miles sighed. "Very well, Lydia. Show them in."

"We've come to see you about a personal matter," Charles said.

"Yes, sir," said Susan. "You gave me a good reference when I left your service but I ... I'm goin' to be married."

"To a ship's chandler called Dick Freeman, a fine young man," Captain Mountjoy said, smiling.

"I wish you both well, Susan," Miles said.

Susan blushed. "Thank you, sir." She twisted her hands in her apron. "What we've really come to see you about is Mistress Rosina," she blurted out.

Denny started. "What about her?"

"Excuse me speakin' so frank, sir, but I was always worried about the way she was—the way she left. Well, I've found out that Connie Wilkins tricked her into goin' to Captain Mountjoy's house. Connie run away as soon as Rosina was there to make it look like she'd come on purpose to see the captain. She knew you was a bit jealous of him."

Denny looked intently at Mountjoy. "Did I misjudge you? You were not having an affair with Rosina?"

Mountjoy shook his head, emphatically. "I liked her very much and I admit I was attracted to her. You told me she had been unfaithful but it was certainly not with me."

Denny coloured. "I owe you a most sincere apology. I should never have suspected you."

"I accept that it was a misunderstanding."

"Your attitude is noble, captain. It does you great credit."

"Thank you. When I returned from the sea, I went to the Seagull to see Rosina but the inn seems to have completely closed down. It looks like a ruin."

Denny turned to Susan. "How did you find out what Constance Wilkins had done? Do you know why she did it'?"

"She was thick as thieves with Polly Davis. I think Polly put her up to it out of spite. She 'elps the smugglers same as Polly Davis used to. Connie's sweetheart's their new leader."

"Amos Baker," Mountjoy said. "I believe Dick Freeman knows him."

Susan nodded. "Yes, he does. Baker blamed Mistress Rosina's brother, Jacko, for an earlier run what went wrong and got him arrested."

"Did he, indeed'?" Denny said, dryly.

"Yes, sir. Dick knows some of the gang though he's certainly not one of them. There's to be another run at the Cat and Fiddle, this very night."

"That's interesting news," Denny said.

"When Connie got very drunk once," Susan continued, "she boasted about what she'd done to Mistress Rosina 'cause she thought it was funny. I certainly didn't."

"Neither do I," Denny said, grimly.

"Nor I," said Captain Mountjoy.

"Are you sure there is *definitely* going to be a run tonight, Susan?" Denny asked.

"I'm as certain as can be, sir. I think Amos Baker and Constance will be there earlier than everybody else. They like to do a bit of courtin' while it's quiet before all the stuff's brought to the inn."

Denny looked thoughtful. "That's given me an idea."

"Another thing I should tell you, sir, is that Baker's the only one who has a pistol and a knife. He don't let the others have nothing like that. I think it's because he's afraid one of them might kill or wound him."

"Sooner or later, one of the gang would probably challenge him," Mountjoy said. "Although I've no doubt some keep secret weapons on them."

"More than likely," Denny said. "Susan, the captain tells me we've both made handsome profits from the *Katie Barnes*, so I'll make sure you and your Dick are well rewarded."

"Thank you sir." Susan looked uncomfortable. "But—"

"But what?" Denny prompted.

"If you tell the Customs men and it all goes wrong, Baker will name my Dick as bein' an informer."

"Don't. fret, Susan," Denny said, kindly. "I know the free traders will be taken by surprise. I shall describe my plan to the captain here."

"Before you tell me," Mountjoy said, "I want to reassure Susan about her Dick. I'll send him on a short journey and when he returns all this will have died down. There'll be no suspicion attached to his name."

"Thank you, sirs, I have to thank you both very much. I hope whatever your plan is, it will go well." Susan curtsied and left, her expression a mixture of relief and anxiety.

Denny outlined his idea to Mountjoy.

"I suppose that will work as well as anything else," the captain said.

"It will have to," Denny said, grimly. He summoned four of his strongest menservants, gave them their orders and swore them to secrecy. The squire then gave orders for his carriage to be made ready and informed the coachman to drive as fast he could.

The squire and the captain went to see the new Riding Officer, Simon Gibson, an earnest young man who lived in Topcliffe and took his responsibilities seriously. It was not usually possible to bribe him to turn a blind eye to the smugglers' activities.

"What can I do for you, gentlemen?" Simon asked.

"We have some information about a run which is to take place at the Cat and Fiddle tonight."

Mountjoy thought he saw Gibson's ears literally prick up. "Tonight? Thank you for telling me. I'll have to inform my fellow officers immediately."

"Quite," Squire Denny said, smoothly. "I expect you'll recover a lot of contraband and will be recommended for promotion."

Simon Gibson's eyes lit up.

"The only thing is," the squire continued, "the free traders' leader will have disappeared."

"Sir, I must protest if you're thinking of taking the law into your own hands, " Simon said.

"Squire Denny is a magistrate," Captain Mountjoy said.

The squire put his hand on Gibson's shoulder. "I know what you're thinking. I'm not going to secretly murder him or have another do my dirty work for me."

"Then, if I may ask, sir, what are you proposing to do?"

"Give him a friendly warning that he should be out of the way when you fellows arrive. If I had to try him, I should have to sentence him to death and I don't want to do this. The landlord of the Cat and Fiddle is also unaware that his inn is being used as a hiding place."

"I see, sir," Gibson said. His expression belied his words.

"The squire's telling the truth, Gibson," Mountjoy said. "He's a humane man, believe me. The rest of the gang aren't armed so they'll probably only be sentenced to transportation."

"And we'll have rid you of the most dangerous one who might try to harm you when you take him into custody. Don't forget that as a magistrate, I can have a word with your superiors as to how wisely you have behaved in this matter."

Gibson hesitated then he spoke. "Put like that, sir, all I can say is that I'm very grateful for your information."

"Sensible fellow," Denny said. "Come, captain, we have other business to attend to." Denny and Mountjoy rushed away, watched by a puzzled Gibson.

Simon shook his head. "First I've heard of a magistrate wanting to show such mercy to an infamous smugglers' leader," he murmured to himself. "But some say Squire Denny has a reputation fur being a little eccentric at times." His expression brightened. "I hope he keeps his word about me being promoted."

At the taproom of the Cat and Fiddle Inn, Denny said to the landlord, "Do you know when Amos Baker is likely to come in here?"

The landlord nodded. "About six o'clock, sir."

"With a woman?"

The landlord nodded again.

"Well, the captain and I would also like a little privacy ourselves." Denny ran some coins through his hands. "All these and more will be yours if you do as we ask."

The landlord leaned over the counter, looking interested. "Anything you say, sir."

Denny looked at his watch. "It's four thirty now. Do you have a private room where Captain Mountjoy and I can dine?"

"Of course, sir. Would you like two maids to keep you company?"

"No, we would not!" Mountjoy snapped.

"What we would like," Denny said, "is for you to lock all your other customers out while Baker and his woman are here."

"Yes, sir, I'll do that."

"And then you are to admit the squire's servants in by your back door but no-one else. Not one more soul."

"Yes, sir."

"We know there's a run here tonight, there's going to be a raid by the Revenue men."

The landlord looked alarmed.

"Don't worry," Mountjoy said. "The squire's word is trusted as a magistrate and he knows you had no idea your inn was being used in this way. So you won't get into trouble."

"I really didn't know they used my inn," the landlord said with an expression of wide-eyed innocence.

Denny and Mountjoy exchanged glances and turned away to hide smiles, both knowing the man was lying through his teeth. Aloud, Denny said, "Well, the captain and I have been riding like devils and wearied ourselves talking. We're both hungry and thirsty but before you show us to our private room, I'll call my men in so that you'll know who they are."

He went to the door and called to his servants who had been told to wait outside. They had ridden horses to the inn and tethered them outside.

"My men can eat in here, I hope," Denny said.

"By all means, sir," the landlord said.

"Good, here's the money for the meals plus the extra for your good service." He handed the landlord several gold sovereigns.

"Thank you, sir," the man said, looking at them greedily. He bawled orders to his wife and maidservants to prepare the food.

Just after six in the evening, a barmaid informed Denny and Mountjoy that Amos Baker had arrived with Constance Wilkins.

They thanked the girl and hurried down to the taproom where Amos Baker, a beefy looking, unkempt man with a long, straggly beard was kissing Constance Wilkins in a shadowy corner of the bar.

Mountjoy thought that Constance, herself, looked a lot scruffier than when she had been Catherine's maid. A strong feeling of dislike for her overcame him.

Stealthily, two of Denny's armed menservants crept up to the pair and discreetly drew pistols from their coats as Denny, Mountjoy and the other two menservants formed a ring around the couple.

Baker's arm was twisted behind his back and a pistol prodded into his back. The same was done to Constance who screamed but a strong hand was clamped over her mouth.

"Bloody hell! What's this?" Baker exclaimed. He looked at the landlord. "We're bein' attacked, vicious. Get them off us!"

"Sorry, Amos, but I couldn't go against Squire's orders," the landlord said.

Baker spat. "You dirty turncoat!"

"My man will not hesitate to fire if you make another sound, Baker," Denny said.

Mountjoy looked at Constance with distaste. "You ran away from my wife's service to become a smuggler's doxy," he said.

"You deserve to he punished for what you did to my wife and I," Denny said. "But what's going to happen is this. The Revenue men will be calling later on. Baker's followers will be caught like rats in a trap."

"There's horses waiting outside. You'll be put on them and escorted out of the county," Mountjoy said. "If you ever come back, we'll betray you to the Revenue."

The couple were pushed and prodded outside. "Put Amos Baker on a horse," Denny said. His men seized hold of the struggling Baker and threw him, none too gently, into the saddle.

"Take your hand away from Constance's mouth," Denny said to his servant. "I want her to talk to me." Constance looked wide-eyed and frightened. Baker watched them with hatred in his eyes.

"I won't hurt you if you don't lie to me," Denny said to Constance. "Why did you entice my wife, Rosina, to Captain Mountjoy's house?"

"Polly Davis put me up to it. She knew Rosina didn't like her and she knew you was a bit jealous of the captain."

"That fact seems to have become well known," Denny remarked, dryly. "Go on, girl."

"Polly knew Rosina would never have agreed to see her. So I'd do, instead, to get Rosina over to the captain's house."

"I see," Denny said, grimly.

"Polly told me to make sure you seen Captain Mountjoy and Rosina was lovers."

"Which I unfairly suspected. Have you any idea where Rosina is, now?"

Constance shook her head. "None at all, sir."

"You stupid bitch! You should have told him some tale and made money for us!" Baker shouted. One of Denny's servants cuffed him into silence.

"I was going to let you go free in exchange for this information."

Constance looked sly. "If you let me go on livin' around here, sir, I could find out for you."

Denny glared at her, turning to Baker. "Where is the gypsy, Jacko Clayton?" he asked. "If you tell me the truth, you'll be a free man."

"In prison in Portsmouth, waitin' for his trial," Baker said, sullenly.

"I'm glad I've found out." Denny turned to his men. "Put the woman on the other horse and escort them until they are well out of the county," he said. "Come back to my house, Charles, and we'll share a bottle of wine."

"Why did you let that pair go, squire?" Charles asked.

Denny shrugged. "I wanted information from them. I know they're unsavoury and would have deserved whatever punishment they received, but we were not blameless ourselves in our younger days."

"No, we were not," Mountjoy agreed.

"With Baker out of the way, the gang will not be so powerful."

"They'll all be caught by the Revenue."

"They may not. Word gets around quickly about these things. Someone may warn them. If not, the others will receive lighter sentences than Baker would have. In any case, I'll see Gibson gets some sort of promotion."

Mountjoy looked thoughtful. "I suppose it might not even have been possible to prove much against Constance Wilkins. I never liked her very much but I tolerated her for my wife's sake. Just now, I loathed her."

"You will probably never see her again." Denny sighed. "I wish she had been able to tell me where Rosina has gone. I owe her a thousand apologies."

"I suggest you make enquiries in the district, put notices on the trees even. Offer a reward for information."

Denny smiled. "Good idea. Yes, I'll do that."

CHAPTER 17

▼

"George Blackwell gave these to me last night. He asked me to give these to you," Elizabeth Vale said. She handed Rosina a bunch of roses.

"Thank you," Rosina said, sniffing their fragrance and sighing as she read the note attached to them. The note expressed Lionel Jarrett's admiration for the 'Wild Gypsy Rose,' as she had become known

Rosina had initially met Jarrett at the Rose but he had not appeared to take any great interest in her. Yet, since she had appeared at the theatre, be had become her most devoted admirer. She was flattered, amused and irritated by his attentions.

Lionel, a tall, fair-haired young man, was the youngest son of a baronet with numerous children. The family home was in Leicestershire. He had been sent to London to study law at the Inns of Court, which he hated. He much preferred to spend his time as a gentleman of leisure and resented the fact that he had not been sent either to university or on a grand tour like his elder brothers. But his father held the purse strings. He could not run the risk of completely deserting his studies.

The baronet allowed his son just enough money to enjoy the sort of life he desired. In Lionel's eyes, it was not enough and he often felt frustrated. He was determined to find a rich wife, but he was not ready for marriage yet.

Rosina did not dislike Lionel, though she did not want to become involved in a relationship with him or any other man at present. She wondered if he would lose interest in her when she learned she was no longer appearing at the theatre.

Rosina looked incredulously at Elizabeth. "Is this all you wanted to say to me?"

Elizabeth shook her head. "No. Come with me to see Isaac."

"It's very late. Won't he be in bed?"

"No, I've already spoken to him."

"Rosina, you must get out of here, as soon as possible," Isaac said. George Blackwell is a powerful and dangerous man. He has asked me to make you dependent on gin before he sets his other plan in motion."

"He needn't worry about that. I like a drop of the stuff now and again but I won't let it ruin my life."

"You think that now but you don't know his methods like I do. I've seen Blackwell in action with girls more than once. He will use you as a whore."

"He's right, Rosina," Elizabeth said.

"I assure you I won't become a whore. But why are you both concerned about *me* if you didn't try to stop him with the others?"

Isaac shrugged and Elizabeth looked pensive. "For some reason, we both liked you better than them."

"While we were talking to each other, we both decided we didn't want to see you dragged into the gutter," Elizabeth said. "But," she added anxiously, "we hope you will be discreet about us."

"Of course I will."

"There's another thing I should tell you, Rosie," Isaac said. "Two gentlemen came here yesterday, asking about you."

"Who were they?" Rosina thought they might have been two of her admirers from the theatre.

"One was a country squire, a handsome man, and the other was a sea captain I sometimes do business with when he's in London."

"A country squire?" Rosina said, turning pale. Her emotions were in a whirl with thoughts tumbling round and round in her head. She felt almost excited at the idea that the squire had sought to find her but could not guess what his purpose was. She guessed the waggoner had told the squire he had taken her to the Rose Tavern.

However, Rosina was not sure that she could face seeing Squire Denny again. She wondered who the sea captain was. Perhaps he was a new acquaintance of the squire's.

"A country squire as I've already said." Isaac was a little impatient. "And a sea captain. Apparently they made enquiries about your whereabouts at the Rose Tavern. The landlord there told them Blackwell might have brought you here."

"I must leave this house this very minute," Rosina said.

"No, you're not, madam," a male voice said. "I'm taking you to the parlour."

Both women stared in horror as George Blackwell, Rook and, to Rosina's surprise, Lionel Jarrett entered the gin shop.

The next minute Blackwell had picked Rosina up in his arms.

"Put me down at once!" she yelled, indignantly.

"No, I shall not," he said, coldly.

Rosina began to struggle and scream but he was too strong for her. "Hush your noise, woman!" Rook said. "Nobody here will bother to help you." Rosina hated the venomous tone in which he spoke.

"Could she not walk? Must she be carried like this?" Lionel Jarrett protested.

"Yes, she must," Blackwell said, grimly. Rosina thought that Isaac Mandleberg and Elizabeth Vale had been struck dumb.

Nevertheless, they followed Rosina and the three men to the parlour.

"Strip her, Elizabeth," Blackwell said.

"I must protest," Mandleberg said.

"If you do, I'll completely ruin your business," Blackwell said. "You know very well I *can* do so."

Isaac had the grace to look ashamed.

"Rosina, I knew they planned to do this. I just didn't know when except that it would he soon. I honestly don't want to see what's about to—"

"Stop whining like a lily livered woman!" Rook growled. He went to the door and beckoned to two of Elizabeth's menservants, who were hovering nearby. The two men forcibly threw Isaac out of the room.

"Well, Elizabeth, get on with it, woman," Blackwell said impatiently.

"I don't want to," Elizabeth said, defiantly. Rosina gave her a grateful look.

Blackwell's eyebrows rose. "Oh, don't you? I hope you realise what the consequences may be." Elizabeth looked frightened but made no move. He shouted for Elizabeth's servants who came running to do his bidding.

They forcibly undressed the struggling, screaming, weeping Rosina. When she was completely naked, Blackwell spoke as if discussing arrangements for a party. "Dance for us now, Rosina."

"I shall do no such thing," she spat out. Rook re-entered the room.

"Yes, you will, I think," he said. He drew out a knife, and held the blade to her throat. Rosina was too terrified to move or speak.

"I must protest. This is going much too far." Lionel Jarrett sounded agitated.

"Very well, we'll forget the dance and just get on with the real business." Blackwell spoke in a bored voice. "I said I would prepare her for you."

He unfastened his breeches and forced Rosina to the floor. Two of the menservants held her down, as Blackwell brutally thrust her legs wide open and opened his breeches.

"Please, sir," Lionel Jarrett said, almost weeping as he glanced at the young woman's dishevelled figure. "If I forget the money you owe me for the bet, may I spend the whole night with Rosina, in private?"

"Your bet?" Rosina asked, horrified.

Lionel blushed. "I'll explain later."

To her amazement, Blackwell nodded, fastened his breeches and stood up. None too gently, he hauled Rosina to her feet.

"You've spoilt tonight's sport, Jarrett, but I won't hold it against you this time. Come, Rookie, we'll find entertainment elsewhere where we know we'll be made welcome." Blackwell gestured to two of Elizabeth's strongest menservants. "You two can come with us."

The four men left the house.

"I'll show you where her room is. Come this way," Elizabeth said quickly to Lionel Jarrett, picking up a lantern.

Jarrett picked Rosina up in front of the disappointed, jeering servants and carried her to her room. He made a dismissive gesture to the older woman who left them alone.

Gently, Lionel placed Rosina on the bed, drawing the sheet over her, Her head was turned and her eyes were closed.

"Please look at me, Rosina. I'm not really such a devil as I must have appeared to you."

"All who set foot in this evil house are devils! I should never have been such a fool as to come here in the first place. I'd be better off in a madhouse."

He began to stroke her unkempt hair and patted her shoulder.

"Why don't you just get on with what you've come up here to do instead of taking all night about it?"

Jarrett shook his head. "It's not what you think. Blackwell had a bet with me that I would be the first to seduce you because it was well known at the Rose you would let no man touch you."

"Trust him to try to turn that fact to his advantage," Rosina said.

"He offered me a lot of money if I managed to do so. He said he would prepare you for me first, but I would be counted as your first lover."

"I see," Rosina said, bitterly. "And I suppose there were a lot of bets. And you were too greedy to refuse to take part?"

Looking remorseful, Lionel said, "I didn't think it would be rape but I did think it would be a special sort of deflowering. Blackwell told me that although you were a virgin, you had agreed to let me be the first because you liked me best out of the Rose's customers."

"Did he, really?" Rosina's tone was sardonic.

"He said you had consented to a game where it was played like a rape because you had become a good actress during your time at the theatre."

Rosina stared at him. "And you honestly believed that? I should have thought you had more sense."

Jarrett shrugged, looking sheepish. "I had wanted you for so long you see, that I was prepared to believe Blackwell. You must know, yourself, what a good actor he is and that way he has of convincing people."

"Oh, I do know that," Rosina said, beginning to laugh hysterically. "I, of all people, know that, to my great cost."

Lionel put a hand over her mouth. "Hush, we don't want them to think I am murdering you."

"I don't believe they would care if you did."

"I'm sure they would, some of them, anyway. Listen to me, I regret what I have done and I am ashamed."

"It's too late for regrets."

"I know, but listen to me, Rosina. I shall go soon if that is what you wish. Yet if you will permit me, I should like to spend the night with you."

"I cannot prevent you from doing so."

"I have no desire to hurt you in any way. Do you want me to stay or go?"

"Don't leave me on my own in a whorehouse of ruffians, " Rosina said.

Lionel took her in his arms. "Let's go to sleep now, my dear," he said.

"Before we do, would you fetch me a glass of gin from Isaac's shop? It will help me to sleep."

Lionel looked surprised at her request. "Very well, it's probably a good idea."

After he had gone, there was a light tap on the door. "Rosina, it's me, let me in," Elizabeth whispered.

Sighing, Rosina did so.

"Thank you for not trying to force me into being raped, Elizabeth. I'm very grateful."

"I didn't want to see it happen. I have had an idea or rather Lionel Jarrett has. He's just had a quick word with me."

"What did he say?"

"No man apart from him would be able to have you again. Yet you would be a lure to the other patrons if you danced for them to put them in the right mood before they—em—to put it delicately—deal with my other girls. You would be paid a handsome salary for this and well guarded from unwanted attentions."

Rosina looked perplexed. "You advised me earlier to leave here, Elizabeth. Now you speak as if I'm staying."

Elizabeth looked frightened. "I don't think it would be wise for you to leave just yet, Rosina. Wait till Blackwell is off his guard."

"No, I'm leaving in the morning."

"Rosina, don't be a fool," Elizabeth pleaded. "Blackwell will find out and have you brought back."

"I am not his property."

"Maybe not but if you leave now, he will set Rook on to you, to track you down and kill you."

"You are surely exaggerating, Elizabeth." Rosina was incredulous.

"I'm not but if you agree to Lionel's suggestion, it will be more bearable for you to live here. He's offered a much higher fee than usual if we keep you exclusively for him. You will not even have to dance naked. You will be permitted to keep your clothes on."

"I am highly honoured," Rosina said sarcastically. "If you have finished what you came to tell me, please leave me in peace now because I am very tired."

"I hope you come to your senses after falling asleep," Elizabeth said as she crept out of the room.

Rosina did not answer her and climbed into the bed.

Lionel returned with a bottle of gin and two glasses and put them on the small table by Rosina's bed. She picked her glass up and threw it at his head. He ducked. It narrowly missed him and fell on to the carpet where it broke into small fragments.

"How could you have given Elizabeth Vale orders to have me kept a prisoner, you cunning swine?" Rosina asked.

Lionel looked puzzled. "I gave no such orders."

"Don't act the innocent with me, Lionel Jarrett, trying to tell me you know nothing about it!"

He gently took hold of her shoulders and looked into her furious dark eyes. "I swear I do not. The last thing I should ever want to do is keep you a prisoner."

Rosina shook her head despairingly. "I wish I could believe you," she said bitterly. "She told me you had requested to keep me for yourself for a higher fee."

Lionel looked worried. "Yes, I agree I did ask for this favour but only with your consent."

"And she said she wants me to dance in the parlour for her clients."

Lionel looked even more concerned. "I did also ask her to request that you would do so because I wanted so much to see you dance again."

"I could have danced for you privately. I want to leave this place, go far away from that evil Blackwell and the horrible Rook and even Elizabeth, the whorem-istress though she's been kind to me and never see any of then again."

"It may not be necessary for you to leave in order not to see them again. I have—"

There was another light tap on the door. "What the devil is this?" Jarrett exclaimed.

"Rosina," Isaac said in a loud whisper, "I have the two gentlemen here who were asking about you. I beg you to let them enter."

"Ignore them," Jarrett commanded.

Rosina stood up and hastily threw a wrapper around herself.

"I have to see who they are." She brushed past Jarrett and opened the door

When she saw Squire Denny and Captain Mountjoy, she fainted.

CHAPTER 18

▼

"Elizabeth, come at once!" Jarrett shouted. "Rosina has fainted."

The men stared at each other. Denny's face grew dark. "I know what this place is. Are you one of Rosina's clients? Have you mistreated her, causing her to faint?"

Lionel made a dismissive gesture. "I understand that the situation must look like this, sir. But it's not true."

"No, it's not," Isaac said. "Mr Jarrett is an honourable gentleman, not like a lot of others who visit this house."

"I'm glad to hear it," Denny said.

Isaac introduced the men to each other, then turned to Denny and Mountjoy. "I brought you both here because I thought Rosina was in danger and you two might be able to help get her away from here." He introduced the men to each other.

"I hope we're not endangering her further," Captain Mountjoy said.

"I'm sure you're not. She was nearly raped tonight but fortunately it was avoided."

"Nearly raped?" Denny asked, horrified.

"Fortunately, she was not," Lionel said. He saw that Rosina's eyes were beginning to open. "I can't explain yet."

"I hope you will be able to explain properly soon enough," Denny snapped.

Lionel could not help feeling irritated. "I have already told you, sir, I can't explain now but will do so as soon as I can."

Mountjoy made an impatient gesture. "Gentlemen, don't start arguing, please. Look, Miles, Rosina is coming round, that's surely more important."

Rosina looked over in their direction. "Lionel," she said, "you're real, aren't you?"

Lionel moved to her bedside. "Of course I am, Rosie."

"Oh good, I am awake. I have had some strange dreams. Even now, I think I can see two gentlemen I used to know some time ago. I do hope I'm not losing my mind, seeing phantoms."

Charles Mountjoy walked over to the bed and took Rosina's hand. "No, Rosina," he said, gently. "We're not ghosts, we're two real flesh and blood men." He looked around the room. "And we're heartily sorry to find you in such circumstances."

"I was told you were dead," said Rosina.

As Denny moved to the bed, Charles and Lionel walked a discreet few steps away.

Denny cleared his throat. "Rosina, I know you may have found what I did to you unforgivable. I should not have done such a despicable thing to you. I found afterwards that I was missing you terribly, that I did love you after all."

Rosina gave a faint smile.

"Then, when I found you had gone away, I determined to find you. Charles, here, kindly agreed to help in my search and to cut a long story short we have succeeded. I will understand if you no longer wish to have anything to do with me but at least I have been able to apologise." He hesitated and bit his lip; then he said, "If you can find it in your heart to forgive me, I should like to take you home to Topcliffe."

Rosina smiled graciously. "I know you're a proud man, Miles. It must have been an effort for you to say you're sorry for what you did to me."

"It was the least I could do," Denny said, stiffly. The squire looked at Jarrett. "But I must admit, however, it's a shock to find you in this sort of house with a—"

"I am not Rosina's lover," Lionel protested, hotly. "I'm her friend."

Denny and Mountjoy both looked sceptical.

"Listen to me, all of you. I've been betrothed to a young lady. She's an heiress in Leicestershire where I come from."

Rosina stared at him. "I didn't know that, Lionel."

"I was going to tell you, Rosie, honestly. My father is pressing me to marry soon."

"You don't love her, though, do you?"

"Truthfully, no. She's a quiet sort of girl and I like her well enough."

Rosina looked intently at Denny. "Miles, I should love to return to Topcliffe."

The squire beamed, then he frowned. "Who, exactly, are you in danger from, Rosina?"

"From George Blackwell," Elizabeth answered for her. "A black hearted villain who more or less controls this house."

"Please," Rosina said. "Will all of you, except Elizabeth, leave my room while I dress?"

"I'll call you back when she's ready, gentlemen," Elizabeth said.

"I want a word with Mr Jarrett, anyway," Squire Denny said.

"Come to my gin shop," Isaac said.

Elizabeth helped Rosina put on a serviceable blue linsey-woolsey gown before she re-admitted the men.

"You should put a cloak on for travelling," Isaac said.

"But where will I go?" Rosina asked.

"You must come to the inn where the squire and I are staying," Captain Mountjoy said. "It's a comfortable place."

"I'm not sure that I should."

Denny placed a hand on Rosina's arm. To his surprise, she did not try to shake it off. "Don't argue. You must come with us—you can't stay here. My carriage is outside."

"We'll make sure you have a room to yourself, Rosina, and ask the landlord to watch over you. You will have a good rest and not be disturbed," Mountjoy said.

Rosina was still hesitant. She felt dazed and confused, as if she would soon awaken from a dream. "Well, I—"

"Go on, girl, hurry up!" Isaac Mandleberg said, giving her a push in the small of her back.

"I'll help you pack your things," Elizabeth said.

"You needn't take everything," Denny said. "Just essentials. I'll send a servant to fetch the rest, tomorrow."

When the women had finished packing, the squire turned to Elizabeth. "Will you take Rosina to my carriage, please? The captain and I wish to have a little more discussion with Mr Jarrett before we come down, ourselves."

"Yes, of course."

Rosina threw a red cloak around herself and as Elizabeth linked arms with her, she felt like a sleepwalker.

Rosina kissed Elizabeth's cheek. "Elizabeth, I have so much to thank you for, I don't know where to start."

"Don't try. I'm glad to have helped another woman for once in my life. It's also nice to have played a trick on Blackwell. You remember you used to tell me you would like to have a coffee house, eventually?"

Rosina nodded.

"When I come there, you can let me have free coffee and cakes."

They both laughed.

Denny's coachman helped Rosina into the carriage. She sank back against the velvet seat. She closed her eyes and was dozing when Denny and Mountjoy joined her.

"You've been through a lot, Rosina," Mountjoy said.

"We'll make it up to you," Denny said, grimly.

Rosina nodded. She felt that whatever happened to her now was in the hands of fate and there was nothing she could do about it.

When they reached the large inn in Marylebone, a pearly dawn was breaking. Both men linked arms with Rosina.

When they went indoors, apart from a few sleepy servants, hardly anyone was about. Denny ordered one of them to fetch the landlady. "We're sorry to disturb you at this hour, mistress."

The plump landlady simpered. "It's no trouble, sir. You had said you would probably be back late and we like to oblige our customers."

"Thank you. Show this young lady to her room and serve her a hearty breakfast in the morning, but serve it at noon as she needs a good sleep. She should have a glass of wine before she goes to bed. And could one of your maids attend her?"

"Certainly, sir. Come this way, miss."

Denny turned to Rosina. "Have a good rest."

"Thank you. I feel I need it."

"I'm sure you do," Mountjoy said.

"We'll, see you tomorrow," said Denny. "Goodnight, Rosina."

"Goodnight, gentlemen."

The room Rosina was shown to was big with satin wallpaper and rosewood furniture. The good-sized bed had a goose feather mattress and silk sheets.

"I'll send a maid to you," the landlady said.

Rosina shook her head. "There's no need to disturb them. I can manage perfectly well on my own."

The landlady looked doubtful.

"Please fetch me my wine," Rosina said. "A large glass of white wine."

"Yes, miss, at once."

When the landlady returned, Rosina had undressed and was in bed. She was almost asleep.

"You got into bed mighty quick, miss."

"It's because I'm tired. I had a troublesome night."

"I'm sorry to hear that," the landlady said, obviously hoping to hear what had happened.

"Thank you for bringing the wine," Rosina said, firmly. "I look forward to seeing you again tomorrow."

The disappointed landlady left the room. She consoled herself with the thought that Rosina might be more forthcoming the following day.

Rosina closed her eyes. She was asleep as soon as the landlady closed her door. She dreamed of her brother, Jacko. They were sailing in a boat together and reached a small Island. But he had fallen into the water and was drowning. She made futile attempts to rescue him. She thought he had drowned but then he reached land. He was holding his hands out to her but she could not reach him.

She awoke in a cold sweat with tears springing to her dark eyes. She clutched her pillow. "You're in trouble, Jacko, I know it," she whispered. "I have to find out where you are and help you if I can." Rosina hoped for a vision which would tell her what had happened to Jacko but none came. "I must be able rescue you from whatever pickle you're in." She began to pray.

After a lot of worrying about Jacko, she eventually fell into a deep, dreamless sleep.

✳   ✳   ✳   ✳

At midday the next day, Rosina ate a hearty breakfast in her bed. Afterwards, she wondered what to do as there had been no sign of either Denny or Mountjoy. She dressed and decided to go out for a walk It had been raining earlier but the weather was now fine.

In the inn's courtyard, she saw Denny and Mountjoy walking towards her.

"Where are you going, Rosina?" Denny asked, looking displeased

"For a walk."

"I think that would be a stupid thing to do on your own."

Rosina was irritated. "I just felt like a breath of fresh air."

"After everything that has happened to you?"

"How do you know about everything that has happened to me? I don't really understand why you should care, anyway."

Denny flushed. "There are reasons why I care. The captain and I had a long talk to Mr Jarrett."

Rosina pursed her full lips. "I see."

"I think we should continue this conversation, indoors," Mountjoy said, noting the listening ostlers. "I'll order some coffee for us."

"How did you know where to find me?" Rosina asked over the rim of her coffee cup. The three of them were seated in a private parlour.

"The waggoner who brought you to London took us to the Rose Tavern," Mountjoy said.

"Then," said Denny, "when we couldn't find you there, we asked the landlord if he had any idea where you might be and he said a fellow called George Blackwell knew you."

"He guessed," said Charles, "that Blackwell might have taken you to a woman called Elizabeth Vale's house but he couldn't be certain. I knew Isaac Mandleberg slightly, anyway."

"We were lucky to find you there." Miles said.

"Yes, we were," Mountjoy agreed. "Our talk with Jarrett was also interesting."

"How did you know the Carter I journeyed with?" Rosina asked.

"I made enquiries, posted notices on the trees. The waggoner was keen to claim his reward."

"You rewarded him for information about me?" Rosina was incredulous. At the same time she found it hard to understand why her heart seemed to give a leap of joy.

"Yes, I owed you an apology."

"I'm grateful for that and also for the fact that you now know I was never unfaithful to you when I was married to you; but it seems extraordinary that you should go to such lengths to find me."

"Rosina, we were horrified to learn that you were nearly ravished by Blackwell," Mountjoy said. "It's a pity you have no protector in London."

"I shall manage well enough without one in future," Rosina said, stiffly.

"Maybe, although I rather doubt it," Denny said, dryly. "There's another thing I should tell you, Rosie," he added. "I have challenged George Blackwell to a duel at dawn tomorrow. The captain and Mr Jarrett have agreed to be my seconds."

Rosina stared at him. "You have called him out? Are you completely mad?"

Denny shook his head. "It's a question of honour. He tricked me and shamed you. It would remain forever on my conscience if I did nothing about it."

"But I am no longer your wife. I should mean nothing to you!"

She was surprised to see Denny flinch. He shrugged. "It's a way of making up for what I did to you," he said, lamely.

"I don't want you to 'make it up to me' in this way. Blackwell is an excellent swordsman."

"And I am a very good shot. I have had plenty of practice on my estate so we will be using pistols."

He sounded confident. Rosina wished she could feel the same, although her intuition told her that Miles *would* return safely.

"Even if you kill the captain which I very much doubt, Rook will murder you in turn."

"We have found out that Rook's master has sent him with a message to an officer in a barracks stationed far away from London so he is safely out of the way. His journey will take a few days," Mountjoy said.

Rosina played her last card. "Miles, what if you are arrested and charged with murder?"

"I know enough other magistrates in London, sweetheart, to drop a quiet word in the right ears. They will understand it was caused over a matter of honour."

"The squire's right, Rosina," Mountjoy said.

"I very much hope he is!" Rosina said.

She knew instinctively that Denny was determined upon his course of action. She tried to suppress her feeling of pleasure that the squire wished to avenge an insult to her. She felt a little ashamed of herself.

Aloud, she said, "Where is this foolish duel to be held?"

"I cannot tell you that now." Denny sounded annoyed.

"Captain Mountjoy, will you tell me?"

"No. It's better that you don't know."

"I didn't mean to offend you, Squire Denny. I am flattered that you wish to defend me from the likes of Blackwell. I am just so frightened for you, that you will be badly hurt or even worse ..."

Mollified, the squire moved towards her, took her in his arms and kissed her.

Captain Mountjoy turned on his heel and left the parlour. Neither Denny nor Rosina saw him go.

CHAPTER 19

▼

Rosina worried, raged, wept and prayed while the captain and the squire were gone, having made one final, futile attempt to dissuade them from going. She could not eat. Finally, she sent for a bottle of gin and poured herself a glass, tossing the drink down her throat.

Denny returned with a slight wound to his arm. He and Mountjoy were both in a jubilant mood. Rosina was amazed and delighted to see them back.

"What happened?"

"We met at St Martins-in-the-Fields, as we had arranged. Blackwell is not dead, only injured. The ball from my pistol passed through the muscle below his shoulder. He has been taken to St Thomas's Hospital.

"Blackwell's injuries have been explained to the hospital as being caused by footpads who set about him, when he was alone, late at night."

"I'll bathe your poor arm," Rosina said. She did so with a mixture of gin and water and tore a strip off one of her petticoats which she tied around his arm. "You will have to explain your own injury by saying it was caused by a bad fall on sharp stones or some such."

"Thank you for your kind nursing care and suggesting a satisfactory explanation for my wound, but I hope you have left enough gin for us to have a drink together." Denny winked at Rosina.

*   *   *   *

Very early the next morning, Rosina donned an old cape and tied a scarf around her head. She slipped out of the inn before the squire and the captain were awake and hired a hackney coach to take her to Covent Garden in order to buy fruit. Rosina thought she would make the excuse to Denny and Mountjoy that she had gone early to obtain the choicest wares on offer.

Then, she hired another hackney to take her to the hospital in Southwark.

Blackwell looked pale but he was still handsome. "Have you come to gloat, Rosina? I'm not that badly hurt, you know."

"No. I came to give you some fruit. I've bought. God knows why but I felt a little sorry for you."

"I don't need pity, girl. You cursed me once. I hope you know that a curse always returns to the curser. You could die a terrible death."

Rosina shivered at his words. She flung an apple and an orange at him.

"You don't deserve these George Blackwell. I hope I never see you again in this life. You'll come to a bad end, yourself."

She ran out of the hospital, hearing his mocking laughter following her.

✳   ✳   ✳   ✳

When she arrived back at the inn, the landlady said, "Miss, I'm so glad you're back. The two gentlemen have been worried out of their wits about you. I'll be so pleased to tell them you're back, safe and sound."

"Tell them I'm grateful for their concern," Rosina said. "But I'm going to my room to have a rest. I don't want to see them at the moment."

"That's where you're going to be disappointed, Rosina," Squire Denny said, appearing behind her. He looked annoyed and Rosina swore under her breath.

To the landlady, Denny said, "When the captain returns, tell him the young lady's returned safely and. the three of us will be dining together, tonight."

"I would prefer to dine alone in my room," Rosina said.

"You will dine with us because I have something important to tell you and I shan't tell you until Charles returns. In the meantime, my dear, I think you have a little explaining to do."

Denny glanced at the landlady who was watching them with great interest. "I'll escort you to your room." He took hold of Rosina's arm. She tried to shake it off but his grip tightened and he marched her to her room.

His face like thunder, Denny asked, "Where have you been, Rosina? Captain Mountjoy and I were worried sick about you."

Defiantly, Rosina threw hack her head. "As I told you before, I'm no longer your wife. You cannot command my actions and you have no right to question me."

"After avenging an insult to you, I think I have some right to he told of your actions. Anything could have happened to you. You cannot blame the captain and I for being concerned. We have been taking it in turns to look around the city for you while the other stays at the inn just in case you returned here."

Rosina sighed, feeling ashamed of her thoughtlessness. "You're right, and I'm grateful to you both for caring about me though it's probably more than I deserve."

"You do deserve our caring about you." He no longer seemed angry.

Rosina was touched. "Thank you," she said, simply.

Denny smiled. "Well, can I now have your explanation?"

Rosina bit her lip. "You won't like what I have to say."

"I still want to hear it."

"I went to see George Blackwell in hospital."

Denny stared at her. "I can't believe this!"

"It's true, I went early this morning because I thought if I saw either you or the captain, you would both try to stop me going."

Denny shook his head. "But why? That blackguard has done you nothing but harm. Even tried to rape you."

"I know, but he didn't succeed."

Denny scowled. "Perhaps it was some sort of trick between the two of you. I'm beginning to wish I hadn't bothered to challenge him."

Rosina flinched at the bitterness of his tone. She laid a hand on his arm but he shook it off.

"You don't understand, Miles. I honestly don't like the man but as I felt that. I was the cause of his being injured, I had to see for myself how badly wounded he was."

"I hope you were satisfied it wasn't serious."

"No, it wasn't. I took him some fruit to help speed his recovery but his arrogant attitude annoyed me so I threw an apple and an orange at him."

Denny threw back his head and laughed. Then he took her in his arms and kissed her.

It was not the affectionate peck she expected. It was a long, passionate kiss that left her breathless. Their eyes locked and held. "Come to—" Denny started to say when there was a loud knock on the door. "Damn!"

"It's me, Charles. I couldn't find Rosina but I hear she's back."

Breaking away from Denny, Rosina flew to the door and opened it. "Charles, I owe you an apology for my thoughtlessness. I really didn't think either of you cared for me so much. I'm sorry to have caused you so much trouble."

"I have been searching for you, Rosina, with no success, but it's a great relief to me—to us, I mean, that you've come back. We were both worried out of our wits."

"Thank you. I was explaining to the squire that. I went to see George Blackwell."

"Good God!" Charles said, startled.

"Don't misunderstand, I wanted to know if he was badly hurt."

"Considering what he tried to do to you, it was unnaturally kind of you to go to see him. Most women wouldn't have cared what became of him."

"I found out he doesn't deserve even a tiny bit of kindness."

"Well, I'm pleased you realise that."

Charles glanced at them, then smiled to himself. "I have some business to attend to in the city so I'll take my leave of you now."

"Will you dine with us tonight, Charles?" the squire asked.

Mountjoy shook his head. "No, thank you, I already have another invitation."

Denny laughed, "You haven't wasted much time since we've been here."

"I'll look you both up in Portsmouth, Miles."

Miles laughed. Rosina looked puzzled as Mountjoy hurried away.

"Why did he mention Portsmouth?"

"Because your brother, Jacko, is due to go on trial there in two weeks time."

Rosina glared at Denny. "Why didn't you tell me this before?"

"I thought you had experienced enough shock for the time being. I meant to break the news to you gently."

Mollified, Rosina said, "I wish to go to Portsmouth first thing in the morning."

"I knew you would. I'll take you there but for now, let's go to bed."

They did so and took enormous pleasure in rediscovering each other's bodies. Their loving became filled with ecstasy as they finally merged as one.

Rosina awoke from sleeping in Denny's arms with a terrific shout which startled him. "What the devil?" he exclaimed.

"I'm sorry, Miles, I had a bad dream. It was about Jacko—I've had it before." She explained the shipwreck dream.

Miles looked slightly alarmed. "I understand your concern. I know full well he's on your mind."

"I hope this hateful trial will be over quickly so that we know his fate." Rosina could not repress a shudder. Denny pulled her towards him, cuddling her.

"Oh Miles, I couldn't bear it if they sentence him to—to—" She could not bring herself to say the dreaded word.

"I'm sure they won't hang him. He should receive a lighter punishment than that."

The squire hoped he was not being over-optimistic. He wanted to keep Rosina's spirits up until the trial took place.

She managed a watery smile. "As you must know, I'll be hoping and praying for that."

*　　　*　　　*　　　*

When she had got dressed, Rosina said, "I don't want any dinner. I have to go to Portsmouth."

"I knew you would. I'll take you there first thing in the morning."

"No, I'll get the stagecoach and save you the trouble."

"I insist you come with me in my private carriage. It will be far more comfortable than the public coach."

"Thank you, but I'll still get the coach."

"Don't be a stubborn little fool, Rosina, and stop arguing. I want to be present at the trial, myself."

"All right, I'm very grateful to you but I would like you to leave me, now."

"Very well. Are you going to dine with the captain and I?"

"I've got no appetite."

"You must keep your strength up for the journey. Eat a little."

"If you'll excuse me, I'll eat on my own, off a tray."

Denny sighed. "I'll arrange for it to be sent up to you. I'll leave you to have a proper sleep now."

He gave her a gentle peck on the cheek and left the room. After he had gone, Rosina threw a wrapper around herself, walked over to the window and stared out of it with unseeing eyes.

Some time afterwards, she walked back to her bed, knelt down beside it and prayed aloud more earnestly than she had ever prayed in her life.

A knock at her door eventually disturbed her. "Ma'am, I've brought your meal up as the squire said you was feelin' a little indisposed."

"Thank you," Rosina said, listlessly, taking the tray from the other woman.

She picked at the food, leaving most of it. Then she went back to bed but, feeling sick with worry, she tossed and turned.

It was a very long time before she finally fell asleep.

CHAPTER 20

▼

In Denny's carriage, Rosina stared out of the window, biting her lip. Denny thought she looked pale and drawn.

"You look tired, Rosina," he said, gently. "Couldn't you sleep?"

"I didn't sleep well."

"I can understand that. I promise to do everything in my power to help Jacko but you might need to assist me."

Rosina frowned. "I don't really see what I can do."

"I'll explain later."

"Very well," Rosina said, listlessly.

"The captain will be travelling in his own carriage. As it's a naval town, he has many acquaintances in Portsmouth. I'm hoping he'll introduce me to some of them."

"I expect he will," Rosina said.

For the rest of the journey, she either dozed or stared out of the window, seeing nothing of the passing scenery. They stopped twice at inns for refreshment but Rosina found she had no appetite. Denny coaxed her into eating a little.

When they reached Portsmouth, Rosina, almost in a complete daze, allowed the squire to take command and arrange accommodation for them at separate but close inns.

"The captain will stay at the Boat as well as myself," Miles said. "The Anchor is smaller but I think you will find it quite cosy."

"I'm sure I will but I must go and visit Jacko before I do anything else," said Rosina.

"It's too late now," Miles said firmly. "You need to rest after travelling. I've arranged for your meals to be served in a tray in your room."

"Thank you but I'd rather see Jacko first."

Denny nodded. "I understand how you feel, Rosie, but it's better to go tomorrow when you're fresher. I'll come with you and we'll buy some food and take it to him."

Suddenly, Rosina smiled warmly at Denny. "I'm really grateful to you for all this trouble you're going to but I can easily go on my own."

Miles shook his head. "I'm definitely coming, too, Rosina. I'll see you in the morning at ten. Goodnight."

He kissed her on the cheek, turned and his heel and walked away, leaving a surprised Rosina staring after him. The inn where she was staying was not as luxuriously furnished as the one in Marylebone but it did not lack comforts.

$$* \qquad * \qquad * \qquad *$$

It was cold and wet the following morning when Miles fetched Rosina from the inn. She put her red cloak on and drew the hood up over her head. "Bring a handkerchief," Denny said. "You might need to put it over your face to hide the smell of the prisoners."

Rosina repressed a shudder, remembering her own night in the cell. She dreaded seeing Jacko with gaol fever.

"I hope Jacko has a good appetite," the squire said.

"He always used to have," said Rosina, forcing herself to appear calm.

Denny bought bread from a baker's, cheese and pies from a grocer's. He had brought a jug of ale from the inn.

"Let me pay for them," Rosina said. "I have enough money and I can't let you pay for everything."

Miles shook his head. "I wouldn't dream of allowing you to pay."

"Please, I can afford it."

"So can I. I'm quite a wealthy man now, Rosina."

"Even so, you don't need to spend your money on my brother and myself."

Denny made a dismissive gesture. "I may not need to but I choose to. So I think we should now forget the matter."

"I've so much to thank you for," Rosina said. "I don't know where to begin."

Denny shrugged. "No matter."

The prison was a grim building with grimy walls. Rosina felt quite faint when she saw it. She deliberately recovered her composure.

Denny knocked loudly on the huge iron ring which hung on the gate. The jailer looked out of a grille. He looked at Rosina first. "What do you—" When he had had a good look at the well-dressed squire, his manner changed. "Can I help you, sir?"

"Indeed you can. We wish to see Jacko Clayton, the gypsy. We've brought him some food and ale."

The amazed jailer opened the gate. Denny dropped two shillings into his almost outstretched hand. They walked along narrow corridors, hearing deafening noises from the prisoners. Rosina put her handkerchief to her nose to cover the horrible smell that hung over everything.

The jailer eventually stopped at a tiny cell.

"I'll come back for you later, Rosina," Miles said. "I guessed you'd want to be on your own with Jacko."

Rosina nodded, her thoughts in a whirl.

"Jacko Clayton, come here. There's a lady to see you." A figure moved slowly towards her from the back of the cell.

"Aye, what is it?" Jacko said.

"It's your sister," Rosina said, strangling a sob. Jacko looked filthy, scruffy, unshaven and as thin as a rake.

He stared at her. Then his dark face was illuminated by a beaming smile. "Rosina! It's good to see you, lass."

"And you, love. We've brought you some food and ale."

Jacko wolfed the food down and drained the ale at a gulp. "Bless you, Rosie." Then, he scowled. "We? Who was the man?"

"Squire Denny."

"Good God, Rosina!"

"I know it must seem strange," Rosina said, swiftly, "but he really means to help you."

"But after he sold you? I don't understand why you would see him or why he would want to help me."

Rosina sighed. "It's a long story, Jacko."

She explained her adventures in London to him.

"It's as good as a story book," Jacko said. "Do you remember some of the tales old Esmerelda used to tell, how we loved them?"

"I do. It seems a lifetime ago, now."

Jacko looked thoughtful. "I reckon Squire loves you, Rosina."

She shook her head. "I don't think so. I think he feels sorry that he sold me. When he found out I wasn't unfaithful, he tried to make it up to me."

"Even so, I don't think he'd go to all this trouble for me if he didn't love you."

"Get away with you, Jacko Clayton. This place is making you have weird fancies."

Jacko looked sombre. "If they 'ang me, Rosie, at least I know you're all right. I worried about you after you'd gone to London, wonderin' how you'd fare."

Rosina shuddered. "I don' t think you'll hang, Jacko." She spoke with more conviction than she really felt.

"No, Jacko," said a masculine voice, "we'll do our best not to let that happen." Rosina whirled around to see Squire Denny.

"I'm very grateful to you, sir," Jacko said.

"Do you forgive me for what I unfairly did to your sister?"

"I hated you at the time but now—well, I'm hardly in a position not to forgive you."

"We have a bargain then. If I decide to marry Rosina again, you will not object, physically or mentally?"

"Of course not, sir."

"Good. Let's shake hands on it."

Denny spat on his hand. Jacko did the same, then they shook hands. The squire showed no revulsion at the dirtiness of Jacko's hand.

Rosina stared at them both wondering if she had merely dreamed of the words she had heard the squire utter.

"I'll take you back, now, Rosie," Denny said.

"I'll be back to see you tomorrow, Jacko, " she said.

"Seein' you will mek my life in here worth livin' at last," Jacko said. "Even though I might not have much life left now."

"Please don't talk like that, Jacko," Rosina said, with tears in her eyes.

"I won't if it upsets you, lass. Only I have to face reality, like."

Rosina nodded, unable to speak. Jacko held his arms out to her.

Denny stood aside as brother and sister embraced each other warmly.

*   *   *   *

Every day, Rosina visited Jacko in prison, taking him food and drink. Denny escorted her to the gaol, leaving her alone with Jacko who was now much cleaner and more decently dressed.

As the jailer was now almost warm in his attitude to her, Rosina guessed that Miles had bribed him to make Jacko more comfortable. She felt so much gratitude to the squire that she thought her heart would burst with it.

Miles always left Rosina with Jacko for three hours before bringing her back to the inn. Once she was back at the inn, she ate a light meal, read a book and went to bed. Miles never attempted to stay with her.

Two days before Jacko's trial, Denny said to Rosina, "This is where you will have to help me, Rosina."

"What am I to do?"

"I wasn't idle during the times you spent with Jacko. Through the captain's introductions, I managed to meet the judge who will pass sentence on your brother."

"What's his name? What's he like?"

"His name is The Honourable Mr Justice Lightwood. He's about fifty, small and fat. I think he enjoys good living."

"Not like the poor people he sentences," Rosina said, bitterly.

Denny ignored her comment. "The Boat has a ballroom. I am entertaining Lightwood, a friend of his, Mr Colin French there. Charles will also be present. You must dance for us tomorrow evening."

Taken by surprise, Rosina said, "Of course I will, but do you really think it will make any difference to poor Jacko?"

"If you charm him enough, Rosina, yes, it will."

"Then, I shall dance as if my own life depends upon it."

Denny smiled. "Good girl. I knew you wouldn't fail me."

The following evening, Rosina took great care over her appearance. After her visit to the prison where Jacko was in reasonably good spirits, she had a long, hot bath. Afterwards, she perfumed her whole body.

Then, Rosina put on a lilac silk low cut dress with half-length sleeves ending in a froth of white lace. It. was drawn tight at the waist with a wide skirt that revealed her ankles, covered by white stockings.

She vigorously brushed her dark hair with many strokes, hoping it would shine. She twisted it into a coil on top of her head and skilfully painted her face. Rosina gave her reflection a last approving look before throwing her red cloak around herself and walking over to the Boat inn.

When Squire Denny met her, she read approval in his blue eyes when he looked at her although he said nothing. He led her to the ballroom where the three other men were waiting. Mr Colin French was as tall and thin as his companion was short and fat.

Both Denny and Mountjoy smiled warmly at Rosina.

"Here is the famous gypsy dancer I promised you, gentlemen," Miles said. "Mistress Rosina Clayton or, as she is more famously known, 'The Wild Gypsy Rose, ' fresh from the London stage."

"I hope she's as good as you said," the Honourable Mr Justice Lightwood said, curtly, making Rosina's heart sink.

"It'll be interesting to see if she is," Colin French said. "Let's get on with it, Denny."

Slightly resentful of the fact that neither Lightwood nor French had acknowledged her, deliberately keeping her face impassive, Rosina glanced at them and curtsied.

As if sensing her feelings, Mountjoy said, "It's good to see you again, Rosina."

"Thank you, captain. I hope you had a good journey down from London."

"She speaks uncommonly well for a gypsy," Lightwood said, obviously surprised.

"Rosina has always had pretty manners," said Charles.

She looked at him gratefully, a small smile playing around the corners of her mouth.

Denny led her to the small stage where she mounted the steps. With a swift movement, she threw off her cloak, letting it fall to the floor. Then she unpinned her hair, letting it fall loose. She arched her neck and made caressing movements with her hands over her body while not actually touching herself at all. She looked at the men with an innocent expression on her face, then began a dance with movements describing the sea and everything floating on it.

Finally, Rosina made a beckoning gesture with her arms as if she were a seductive sea goddess, beckoning all marine beings towards herself.

When she had finished, she sank into another deep curtsy, to the sound of loud applause.

"Magnificent!" French shouted.

"I can understand why she's the toast of London," Lightwood said to Denny.

Miles helped her down from the stage. "Well done," he whispered.

"We didn't lie to you about how good she is," Mountjoy said.

"Indeed not. I think you should dine with us, my dear." Lightwood spoke to Rosina for the first time.

"Thank you for your kind invitation, sir," she said, demurely. "But I'm not hungry, I ate earlier."

"I'd love to see her dance again soon," French said, almost leering at Rosina.

Denny scowled. "Come, Rosina, I'll take you back to your—back home. I have some business to discuss with the gentlemen. The young lady lives quite near. I'll be back in about ten minutes."

"I think I'll take my leave of you, myself, gentlemen," Charles said. "I have to rise very early tomorrow morning."

Rosina put her cloak on and took both Denny's and Mountjoy's offered arms. She left the ballroom without a backward glance.

When they came to the Boat, Charles bade Miles and Rosina good night.

At the Anchor, Miles said, "Have a good night's sleep, sweetheart. I'll take you to the court tomorrow."

With tears in her eyes, Rosina said, "Jacko might be sentenced to death tomorrow and I'll hate myself forever for dancing for the man who sends him to the gallows."

"I don't think he will be, love, Trust me."

Denny took Rosina in his arms and kissed her. For a few moments, she clung to him. Reluctantly, he gently put her aside.

"I have to return to them though I'd much rather stay with you. See you in the morning." He walked away, leaving a desolate Rosina behind him.

She decided to go to bed although she knew she would not sleep.

*   *   *   *

The street in front of the court was crowded with people all anxious to have good seats to watch the trials. Denny bought Rosina some lemonade from a man at the door.

"It'll be hot and stuffy inside," he said.

"It always is," Mountjoy said. "I hope the trial's not going to be too much of an ordeal for you, Rosina."

"I have to be here, Charles."

"Of course."

Rosina was already feeling faint and sick but hoped it would not show.

Other men were selling pasties and chestnuts indoors. "Do you want anything to eat?" Denny asked.

"I couldn't eat if I tried," Rosina said. Miles squeezed her hand in understanding. The indoor vendors were sent out at ten o'clock

Denny, Mountjoy and Rosina were shown to the seats which had been saved for them near the front of the courtroom. It was small and not well ventilated.

Rosina looked around, fearfully. There were a lot of cubicles entered by separate staircases. The room was painted a dark grey colour. Guards, jurors and witnesses filled the front of the room with a few public places behind. Some of the ladies waved fans over their faces and some gentlemen took snuff from their boxes. They ignored what they considered to be noisy rabble behind them.

Rosina started as she saw Arnold and Spencer sitting at the back of the courtroom. She wondered how they had afforded the stagecoach fare and where they had been staying.

The clerk of the court rapped with his hammer, and a court usher shouted for the court to 'be upstanding.' As Rosina stood up, she felt Denny's hand support her elbow.

The Honourable Mr Justice Lightwood entered, looking full of his own self-importance. He bowed to the court, sitting down with the sheriffs and aldermen. Rosina noticed he carried a bunch of sweet-smelling herbs. Lightwood glanced at his pile of papers.

There was a murmur of interest as Jacko was ushered in with another man and one woman. A jury was sworn in with no objections. Rosina clasped her hands together tightly. The two men were led out again.

The woman was charged with stealing a handkerchief from her former mistress. It was a first offence so she was sentenced to have her hand branded with the letter 'T' for thief before being discharged.

The man who came next was found guilty of begging. Lightwood gave a long, pompous speech about how he could have earned an honest living if he had tried hard enough. Rosina wondered what made the judge so sure of his facts. She knew he had never experienced dire poverty. The unfortunate man was sentenced to be whipped.

Now it was Jacko's turn. Rosina experienced a wave of nausea. She forced herself not to submit to it. She heard the clerk speak the hateful words.

"Jacko Clayton, a gypsy of no fixed abode. You are accused of smuggling contraband goods. You are also accused of the attempted murder of Peter Cooper."

There was a fascinated gasp from some of the watchers.

Jacko pleaded guilty to receiving contraband goods but not guilty to attempted murder. The prosecuting counsel presented the case for the Crown. He was eloquent, with an attractive voice. When the junior counsel for the Crown added his speech, he was almost as eloquent as the prosecuting counsel and Rosina felt her heart sink.

The excise man gave evidence that he had found smuggled goods on which duty was not paid at the inn on the night in question. To his credit, he did not say that Jacko was there at that time. But he knew the accused had had dealings with a smuggling gang and was known to frequent the inn.

Other witnesses were called. Some admitted they knew Jacko had done a little smuggling but he was not a ringleader. A few said he was of good character otherwise. No-one claimed they had seen him attack Cooper. Towards the end of their testimony, Rosina felt as if all their voices were merging into one.

She nearly fainted when she saw that Peter Cooper was the next witness. He saw her and gave her a baleful glare.

Cooper began to testify. He described the inn where he had formerly been employed and the night he had been attacked. "I knowed the prisoner was involved in smugglin'," he said. "He wanted all the spoils for himself."

Rosina leaned forward in horror at his next words. "His slut of a sister throwed herself at me on the night in question but I didn't want her so he tried to murder me. He didn't succeed because I'm too strong, you see."

"That's not true, you lying bastard!" Jacko shouted from the dock. "You attacked her, I was trying to save her." He was cuffed into silence.

When Cooper had finished speaking, the last witness called was Amos Baker.

The clerk looked highly embarrassed. "My lord, this witness has not appeared. He has gone missing. No-one knows where he is."

Some of the public grinned at each other, delighted to watch this exciting diversion. What would the judge do now, they wondered.

Lightwood's face almost turned purple. "He turned King's evidence. He must be found to face the charge of contempt of court amongst others." He turned to the foreman of the jury. "You might as well retire and consider your verdicts."

As Rosina waited in an agony of anticipation, Denny touched her hand. "Don't. worry, he won't hang."

"How can you be so sure?" Rosina snapped. Denny did not answer her.

The jury were back after twenty minutes. "Gentlemen, have you reached your verdict upon the attempted murder of Peter Cooper?"

"Yes, my lord," the jury foreman said. "We find him not guilty."

Rosina gave a long drawn-out sigh of relief. Denny smiled at her.

"Prisoner at the bar," Lightwood said in a bored voice. "You have been found not guilty of the attempted murder of Peter Cooper. It is my own belief you were trying to protect your sister."

There was a sudden cheer in the courtroom with the judge threatening to turn everyone out if there was any further noise He looked stern.

"Nevertheless, Clayton, you have admitted to the serious charge of smuggling contraband goods on which duty was not paid. I believe you resisted arrest. This is cheating the Crown so I could pass the death penalty."

Rosina felt herself begin to sway. Denny gripped her arm. After a dramatic pause, Lightwood said, "But I'm a merciful, God-fearing man. I have a plantation in the West Indies. You will be shipped out there to work as an indentured servant for seven years."

The judge went on to give orders for Peter Cooper to be arrested for perjury but Rosina hardly heard him.

"I'll make sure Jacko sails out on one of my ships," Charles whispered to Rosina.

"Let's get out of here," Miles said.

Tears of relief pouring down her face, Rosina allowed Denny and Mountjoy to lead her out of the courtroom.

CHAPTER 21

▼

Outside in the fresh air, Arnold and Spencer walked up to Rosina. Denny and Mountjoy moved aside to let them speak to her.

"Good news eh, Rosie?" Arnold said. "Jacko's only goin' to the Indies."

"Yes but I'm worried about his journey. It's a hell of a long way and the conditions on board might be bad."

"I don't think so, Rosie," Spencer said. "He's strong and I don't think he'll have too hard a time on one of the captain's ships."

"I hope so."

"We work for the captain now as grooms," Spencer added with not a little pride. "He's very fair to us."

"Good. I hope you work hard for him."

"Of course we do."

"I wondered how you'd managed to come to Portsmouth."

"Captain Mountjoy said we could come. He's now said we can see Jacko before he sails away," Arnold said. He frowned.

"Squire Denny's become real friendly with the captain. Squire told us he was sorry for what he done to you but I'm not sure I'm too happy about you keepin' company with him, Rosina."

Rosina flushed. "The squire couldn't have been more helpful, Arnold. I know we owe the lightness of Jacko's sentence to him so I'll thank you not to insult him."

Arnold looked uncomfortable. "I meant no offence to Squire," he said.

"I should think not."

"Arnold, I think we'd better see to the captain's 'orses now, don't you?" Spencer said.

"I suppose so," Arnold said, reluctantly following his younger brother. Rosina watched him go with a mixture of fondness and exasperation.

"Your brothers are proving to be excellent grooms, Rosina," Captain Mountjoy said.

"Thank you for employing them, Captain. I'm very grateful to you."

The captain looked at her, a little sadly, Rosina thought. She did not know that he was longing to say to her that he would have preferred her love to her gratitude.

Denny's voice broke into their thoughts. "Come back to the Boat with us, Rosina. We'll crack open a bottle of wine there to celebrate before we go back to the Forest."

"I think we should celebrate with a special dinner," Mountjoy said.

Denny looked thoughtful. "A good idea. I believe Rosina has not been eating properly while she has been awaiting Jacko's trial."

"You're right, I think, Miles, She looks as if she's lost some weight," Mountjoy agreed. "You must both come to my house when we go back to the Forest. I'll tell Catherine to order the cook to prepare something special."

Rosina was alarmed. "But I can't come to your house, Charles. Catherine dislikes me."

Charles made a dismissive gesture. "I severely reprimanded her when I found out she had lied to you about my death."

"That will hardly make her like me any better."

"I shall tell her you are the squire's guest and I cannot invite him without asking you as well."

"But I'm not the squire's guest."

Denny took hold of her hands. "Please, Rosina, when we leave Portsmouth, will you stay at my house as my guest even if it' s only for a short while."

Rosina hesitated; her feelings were mixed. She was overjoyed to know that Miles wished her to be under his roof once more. She wondered if he wished to make her his mistress for a week or two. Rosina felt she could hardly refuse after what he had done for Jacko. But she dreaded the reaction of his friends and servants.

"But your servants—they might not wish to serve me."

Denny raised his eyebrows. "They have no choice." Then, glancing at the expression on Rosina's face, his tone softened. "My old steward has left my service. I also have different sewing maids."

"Then I accept your kind offer, Miles." He kissed her hand.

Rosina turned to Charles. "Much as I should love to come to your house, I'm still concerned about Catherine. It will be horrible for her to be forced to entertain a woman she hates."

"I don't think she hated you, exactly, Rosina. I think she resented you but I shall convince her she has nothing to fear from you."

"You don't want to disappoint Charles by refusing his invitation, do you, Rosina?" Denny asked.

"No, of course I don't."

"I'm glad it's settled then," Mountjoy said.

At the Boat, the trio drank the contents of a bottle of claret with some sweet biscuits. They were talking, laughing and joking all at once.

*   *   *   *

Late that night, in a small cottage on the outskirts of Portsmouth, Amos Baker said to Constance Wilkins, "Well, Connie, did that slut, Beatrice Glaze, find out what I wanted to know?"

"Yes, Amos. She slipped out from the tavern to watch the trial. There was a great to-do when they found out you'd gone missin'.

Baker gave an ugly laugh. "I thought there would be. Silly buggers don't know I'm almost under their noses."

Constance looked worried. "All the same, you'll 'ave to be careful, Amos."

"I will, sweetheart. They won't catch me."

"I do hope not."

Baker became impatient. "What was the sentence on Jacko Clayton?"

"Not guilty of the attempted murder of Peter Cooper."

Baker swore and his face darkened.

"But guilty of smugglin'," Constance added, hastily.

"And will he swing?"

Constance shook her head. "No, he's bein' transported to the Indies for seven years."

Baker swore with more venom.

"I think his brothers will see him sail away in three days time," Constance said. "Clayton's sister was in the court. She was with Squire Denny and Captain Mountjoy."

"How do you know it was them?" Baker asked with great interest.

"Beatrice got friendly with Jacko Clayton's brothers when they was drinkin' at the new tavern where she works. She seen Mountjoy when he spoke to Arnold and Spencer Clayton. What's more, she knows a maid what works at the Boat."

"What's the Boat got to do with it?"

"Listen to me, Amos, don't interrupt. She 'eard Mountjoy mention to Arnold and Spencer Clayton that Denny would bring Jacko Clayton's sister to the trial."

Baker's expression became even more crafty than usual. "Beatrice Glaze has proved herself useful. You did well to find out she knows all the gossip of the town. I suppose I'll have to pay the slut even though I can ill afford it."

"You'll be a rich man, one day, Amos."

"I know I will. I'll be king of the Dorset smugglers again and no longer have to sweat as a woodcutter. You, Connie, my doll, won't have to slave away in taverns."

"It's a matter of pride to you, isn't it, Amos? To be known as the King of the Smugglers?"

"It is, and no bastard like Squire Denny's ever goin' to take it away from me again. What does the Claytons' sister look like, Con?"

"Like a gyppo, of course, Slim, black hair, dusky skin. She wears a red cloak."

"So do lots of other women, you silly bitch."

"Don't start on me, Amos. I wasn't there to see her for myself, was I? I found out what you wanted to know, though."

Baker nodded. "It's interestin' that Denny took Clayton's sister to the court. Perhaps he means to make her his doxy."

"What are you goin' to do, Amos?"

"Get my own back on Denny through his whore, then kill Mountjoy."

"You'll probably have to go back to the Forest to do that."

"I intend to but before I do, Connie, my love, make sure that Beatrice Glaze goes to see Jacko Clayton off because I think Denny and Mountjoy will be there, with any luck."

"What shall I tell her to do?"

"Isn't it obvious? Make sure Beatrice listens very carefully to what the Clayton brothers have to say about what their master's doing."

*   *   *   *

The day when Jacko set sail was cool and overcast. Most people wished the early spring weather would brighten soon.

Waiting at the harbour where they had already seen the regular crew and passengers, mainly planters, embark, Rosina saw her brothers speak to Beatrice Glaze. The sight made her feel uneasy.

Beatrice was a very pretty girl who knew well how to turn her looks and false charm to her own advantage. Instinctively, Rosina did not trust her.

She overhead an admiring Spencer say, "So you did manage to come, Beatrice."

Beatrice tossed her brown, curly hair back and widened her large grey eyes. "Yes, I knew I would. The landlord likes me, you see. I can usually get my own way with him." She smiled, revealing dimples.

"I'm glad you came," Arnold said. "It'd be a sad day for us, otherwise."

"Yes, I know, I'm sorry about your poor brother. You'll miss him. And I'll miss you two when you go back to the Forest."

"We go back tomorrow," Spencer said. "But perhaps if we save up some of our wages, we could come to Portsmouth and see you now and again."

Beatrice dimpled again. "The captain might keep you too busy."

"We get a night off now and again," Arnold said. "Do you know when your next one is?"

"Probably not tomorrow, but the night after," said Spencer.

"What a pity I can't share it with you, then."

"Happen there'll be other nights when you can," Arnold said, hopefully.

There was a shout from the watching crowd. "They're bringin' the prisoners now, the ones what's been indentured."

Rosina yelled, not caring who overheard her. "Arnold, Spencer, Jacko's coming!"

They turned their heads in the direction of her pointing finger where fettered men and women walked in a line, guarded by soldiers. Rosina felt like crying but knew she had to he strong for Jacko's sake.

The soldiers pushed a group of them including Jacko on to the ground. The younger Claytons all ran up to their brother.

"I'm in a sorry state," Jacko said.

"You'll feel better once you're aboard," Rosina said, with more conviction than she really felt.

"Look after Rosie while I'm away," Jacko said to Arnold and Spencer.

"We will," Spencer said. Arnold nodded in agreement.

"When you return, Jacko, you might even be a rich man," Rosina said. She thought she was probably talking nonsense but felt compelled to cheer Jacko.

"Some hopes of that, Rosie, but I intend to come back one day, safe and sound. Then I'll seek you out." He glanced towards Squire Denny who was standing well back.

"Remember what I told you, Rosie. I really do think squire loves you."

"I wish I could kiss you, Jacko."

"So do I, love. I'd even kiss Arnold and Spencer if I could." He gave a weak smile.

"We'll all remember you in our prayers all the time you're away, Jacko. God speed."

"You, there, hurry up, we don't have all day!" a soldier snapped.

Rosina turned away, unable to watch Jacko being hustled on to the ship which was to take him away from her for seven long years.

Squire Denny took her arm. "Come away, Rosina. I know it's a distressing sight for you."

Rosina nodded, blinking back unwelcome tears. She took his offered arm.

"I'll escort you back to the Anchor. Can you get ready to travel?"

"Yes. I'll be glad to get out of this town."

At the Anchor, Denny asked if one of the landlady's serving girls could act as Rosina's temporary maid for a small fee. The woman readily agreed.

As they climbed into his carriage that evening, Denny smiled at Rosina. She returned his smile although she felt as if she had butterflies in the pit of her stomach. They broke their journey for refreshment. Rosina thought she would have preferred to have gone straight to the squire's house although she ate more heartily than she had done for days. Her new maid was delighted by the diversion.

When they reached his house, Rosina was pleased to see that very little of its contents had changed. She was delighted to see that her portrait still hung on the wall. Lydia welcomed her warmly, serving her with coffee and cakes. She took Rosina' s maid to the kitchens. To Rosina's amazement, Lydia had showed no surprise whatsoever at her reappearance in the squire's household.

Denny gave his housekeeper orders that Rosina was to be shown her bedroom. "If there's anything you want, just ask, Rosie," he said.

"I think I should like to have a bath, Miles, to get rid of the dust of the journey."

"By all means. Will you take tea with me afterwards?"

"Yes, I would love to do so."

Miles seemed pleased by her reply.

After she had bathed and washed her hair, Rosina changed her travelling clothes to a jacket of lime green taffeta with a full blue skirt in the same material.

Sipping her tea, Rosina discussed London theatres and fashions with the squire as if they were old, close friends. Neither of them mentioned the trial.

"Are you looking forward to dining at the captain's house tomorrow night, Rosina?" Miles asked, taking her unawares.

"I feel as if I should be honoured that he's invited me, but I'm nervous."

"Charles will make sure Catherine treats you with the greatest courtesy."

"It's good of him, but I can't help feeling sorry for Catherine."

"After what she did, I don't really feel she deserves your pity."

Rosina suddenly felt exhausted. "If you don't mind, Miles, I should like to retire now."

"I don't mind at all. If you like, I'll take you out riding in the daytime, tomorrow."

"Thank you, that will be lovely."

Rosina's maid was sent for, After the girl had left her bedroom, she worried about the visit to Captain Mount. joy's house.

Before Rosina fell asleep, she wondered if the squire would try to join her in the bed. When he did not come, she knew she should feel relieved but she did not.

Rosina sighed with disappointment.

CHAPTER 22

▼

Rain fell early the next morning. Rosina was disappointed that she would not be able to go out riding in the Forest but it proved to be only a shower.

"I could buy a pony for you," Miles said. He had arranged for Rosina to borrow a mount from his stables.

She shook her head. "No, you mustn't throw away your money on me like that."

"It would he money well spent but I'll leave it for the time being."

They rode all day, only pausing for light refreshment. Miles insisted that Rosina should have a rest before they went to Captain Mountjoy's house. She bathed her body and washed her hair in a state of apprehension.

Mountjoy greeted Miles and Rosina, warmly. "Come for a walk in the garden," he said. "I have some new plants from foreign parts I should like to show you."

As they admired the exotic looking plants, Rosina felt as if she had tight knots in her stomach. They entered the house.

"Catherine will be with us shortly," Mountjoy said. Rosina felt more nervous than ever.

When Catherine entered the room, she welcomed Denny effusively, then turned to Rosina. "You have done very well for yourself, I hear, Rosina."

"Tolerably, Mistress Mountjoy," Rosina said, forcing herself to sound pleasant.

"I don't believe any of us would ever have thought that a real theatre would employ you?"

Rosina flushed, curbing the impulse to make a heated retort when Mountjoy spoke sharply. "She was one of the best performers in the place, Catherine. I quite understand why the theatre wanted to engage Rosina."

Catherine glared at him. "Ah well, I shall not see her dance." She looked intently at. Rosina, making the other woman feel even more uncomfortable. Rosina wondered if Catherine intended to go to bed after her meal.

"There will be two other gentlemen joining us soon. I believe you have met them. They are Mr Lightwood and Mr French."

Rosina felt herself begin to sway. Denny placed a supportive hand under her elbow. "May we sit down, Mistress Mountjoy?" he asked, his tone cold.

Catherine's hand flew to her mouth. "I have been so rude allowing you to stand for so long."

Giving Denny a grateful look, Rosina lowered herself gracefully onto a satin covered armchair.

"Our dinner will be ready in one hour precisely," Catherine said. "The other gentlemen should be with us soon."

Rosina felt her heart sink.

"After I have eaten," Catherine continued, "I shall be paying a visit to my cousins."

Mountjoy frowned but said nothing. Rosina felt a wave of relief sweep over her.

"The reason I'm not staying at home," Catherine continued, "is because with four gentlemen present, there will be no other lady present to keep me company." She paused, significantly. "Except yourself, of course, Rosina, and you will be too busy to he able to pay me much attention."

"I'm sure your cousins will welcome your company, Catherine," Denny said.

Catherine pursed her lips in annoyance at the squire's implication that *he* would not enjoy being in her presence.

Further conversation was, however, halted by the arrival of Lightwood and French. They greeted everyone, including Rosina, courteously and she murmured a polite response.

Catherine announced that their meal was now ready. She took her husband's arm and led everyone to the dining room.

The dinner was well cooked but as course followed course, Rosina picked at her food. She did not speak unless spoken to and when a remark was addressed to her, she answered mechanically. Rosina was unable to give her full attention to the conversation going on around her as she was still apprehensive about her dance.

When the meal at last drew to a close, Catherine took her leave of the company. Her maid brought her outdoor clothes to her including a red cloak.

"I leave you to this evening's entertainment, gentlemen," she said, stiffly. "I hope you enjoy it."

"I know we will," said Denny.

As Catherine stalked out of the room, Rosina breathed a heartfelt sigh of relief.

"It's now time for Rosina's dance," Charles said, smiling at her. "We've all been looking forward to it."

"Indeed we have," said Lightwood, almost licking his lips.

"Excellent though your table was, Mountjoy, this is the high spot of the evening," French said.

Charles looked pleased but Denny's face was impassive.

"Come through to the drawing room as Catherine has no need of it at present," the captain said. "I have arranged for all the furniture to be moved to one side. The fiddler I have engaged is also waiting there for you, Rosie."

Rosina took a very deep breath before she began dancing. Then, as she began to listen to the music, she forgot Catherine, the Mountjoy's house, even the men watching her.

She repeated her sea dance with a few variations in the steps and movements, trying to give the impression she was a swirling wave as she finished. She gave a deep curtsey to the sound of loud applause.

*   *   *   *

Catherine drew her red cloak more tightly around herself to protect herself from the cooling night air. When she reached the stables, she gave an exclamation of annoyance as she saw two naked figures huddled together in the shadows.

"Who's there? What are you doing?"

Arnold stood up, naked and blushing. He moved forward, making no attempt to cover himself although he looked shamefaced.

"Pardon me, ma'am. It was my night off and—"

"And I can see what has been going on behind our backs!" Catherine snapped. "Bring the girl forward."

"Beg pardon, ma'am, but it was my fault and—"

"Do you mean you ravished her?"

Arnold looked uncomfortable, "No."

Beatrice Glaze walked forward. She had hastily pulled on a brown skirt but she was naked to the waist. Beatrice held her head high.

"Arnold didn't rape me, I was willin'."

"Who the hell are you and why are you on our property?" Catherine asked, furiously.

"My name's Beatrice Glaze. I met Arnold and Spencer in Portsmouth. Arnold invited me to visit him on his night off so I'm his guest."

"His whore more likely! You are impudent describing yourself as a guest!" Catherine shouted.

Beatrice did not reply.

"Where the hell is Parker?" Catherine asked Arnold. Parker was the head groom.

Arnold looked even more uneasy. "None of us thought you'd need us tonight as you 'ad visitors. Mr Parker's gone with Spencer to the gypsy camp to have a look at some ponies."

Catherine clenched her fists by her sides. She jerked her head towards Beatrice Glaze. "Cover yourself and get out of here before I tell my husband to have you arrested for unlawful trespass."

Beatrice left without a word.

"Make yourself decent at once," Catherine snapped at Arnold. "I'm going to visit my cousins. Saddle up two horses. I can't be bothered to wait for the carriage and I can ride well enough."

"Yes ma'am."

"This is the last journey you will ever take me on. After I've spoken to my husband about you, you're sure to be dismissed. And your brother."

"I can understand you riddin' yourselves of me, Mistress Mountjoy, but it's 'ardly fair on our Spencer," Arnold said, resentfully.

"We were fools to trust gypsies," Catherine said, coldly.

Arnold bit back an angry retort, merely saying, "If you won't listen to reason, ma'am, there's nothing more to say."

"You've said and done more than enough already. I don't want to hear another word from you. Hurry up, I don't want to be all night making this journey."

"Yes, ma'am," Arnold said, sullenly.

Beatrice Glaze had almost reached the large oak tree behind which Amos Baker and Constance Wilkins were hiding. "Here's Beatrice," Constance whispered.

"Hold your tongue!" Baker snapped. He was watching the woman walking ten paces in front of the man leading the two horses. "You told me the squire's doxy wore a red cloak?"

"Yes, Amos."

"We'll rid the world of her, then." Baker produced a pistol and took aim.

Catherine fell to the ground.

*   *   *   *

Inside the house, Rosina said, "I thought I heard a noise outside. Is it thundering?"

Captain Mountjoy pulled back the curtain to look out of the window. "I don't think so. It's not raining."

The next moment Arnold ran into the room with Catherine's inert body in his arms. When they saw her, everyone else gave a horrified exclamation.

"Excuse me bustin' in on you like this, sir. Mistress Mountjoy's bin shot but I think she's still alive."

Gently, Charles took Catherine from Arnold, carried her upstairs to her bed, called for her maids to attend her and sent a manservant to fetch a doctor. When he went back downstairs, everyone was talking at once.

Miles shouted over the tops of all their voices.

"Quiet, please, everyone!" To Arnold, he said, "Did you see who shot Mistress Mountjoy?"

"No, sir. I seen three people ridin' away on horseback though. There was two horses, a man on one and two women on the other."

"Which way did they go?"

"Towards Denny Woods, I think."

"We must go after them, gentlemen," Denny said. "You stay here with the captain, Rosina."

"But I want to come with you."

"Don't argue, Rosie. Do as squire says," Arnold said, sharply.

"You're a fine one to tell me what to do. From what you've told us, you're the one who got Mistress Mountjoy in danger."

"Enough!" Denny said. "We're wasting time. We'll follow them in my carriage. Arnold and I will ride on the roof. You see what the doctor says, Rosina."

"If you're waiting to hear the doctor's words, Rosina, I'll ride with the others," Mountjoy said. "I'll also take several able bodied menservants."

Rosina waited for the doctor in trepidation. He was a middle-aged man of average height and build, neither handsome nor ugly, yet he had an aura about him which made his presence felt as soon as he entered the house.

"What happened, mistress?" he asked Rosina.

"I don't rightly know everything that happened, sir. I only know that my brother said Mistress Mountjoy has been shot. We don't know who did it but the gentlemen who were here have chased after who my brother thought it was."

"Thank you for your somewhat garbled explanation. I expect it's shock which has made you inarticulate. A bullet, that's the most important piece of information you've given me."

Rosina felt humiliated. "If there's anything I can do to help you, sir, please let me know."

"I'm sure there will be. For a start you can bring me some hot water, a bowl and bandages."

"I'll do that right away." Rosina hurried to the kitchens.

When she took the hot water and bandages to Catherine's bedroom, the doctor looked up. "Fortunately, the bullet missed the lady's heart. I have managed to extract it. Pass me the bowl. On second thoughts, could you hold it for me? I'm going to bleed her."

Rosina bit her lip, unsure of the efficacy of this treatment. But she was hardly in a position to argue with the doctor. She held the bowl to catch the drops of Catherine's blood.

After the doctor had finished, he said, "Mistress Mountjoy has a fever. She must be kept warm and given plenty of liquid. If the fever breaks after three days, she will live."

"Thank you for all you've done, sir."

"I'm grateful to you for assisting me. You've been a good nurse. I'll leave now."

"I think Captain Mountjoy will wish to speak to you."

The doctor shook his head. "I'll come to see him in three days time to see if his wife's fever has broken."

As soon as he had gone, to Rosina's immense relief, Miles, Charles and Arnold returned. They looked dirty and dishevelled with minor cuts and bruises but were otherwise unharmed.

"We did it, we caught them!" Arnold said, triumphantly. "Who were they?" Rosina asked.

"Amos Baker, the would-be 'King of the Smugglers', Constance Wilkins, his whore, and Beatrice Glaze, their friend," Squire Denny said, quietly. "Arnold and

I jumped from the carriage roof after Charles had knocked Baker's pistol out of his hand. Then, Charles' men came running to help us."

"Where are they now?"

"In the custody of Justice Lightwood. Charles has left three of his men to keep watch over them. Simon Gibson, the old Riding Officer who was promoted to Surveyor, will give evidence against Baker about earlier crimes. Beatrice Glaze has also offered to turn King's evidence."

"Enough of them, " Mountjoy snapped. "What of Catherine, Rosina? What did the doctor say?"

Charles looked grave as Rosina repeated the doctor's words.

"But why should Baker want to hurt Catherine?" Rosina asked, puzzled.

"Do you remember me telling you how the captain and I escorted Baker and Constance Wilkins out of the county, Rosie?"

"Yes I do. I thought you were merciful and Baker proved not to have deserved it."

"Hurting a woman was his cowardly way of gaining revenge on us."

A horrible suspicion swept over Rosina. "I think Baker mistook Catherine for me."

Charles shook his head. "He had as much reason to hate me as he had to hate Miles."

"Maybe," Rosina said. "But he would hate me even more because I'm Jacko's sister." She covered her face with her hands. "Oh, God, I have been the cause of Catherine being wounded."

"You mustn't talk like that, Rosina," Charles said. "It wasn't your fault."

Denny placed a hand on Mountjoy's shoulder. "We'd better leave you, now, Charles. We'll pray for Catherine's recovery. Arnold, you and Spencer can escort us."

Arnold looked sheepish. "I'm not sure if Spencer's back yet, sir."

"Then go and find out this instant." Shortly afterwards, Arnold returned with an excited looking Spencer in tow.

When they reached the squire's house, Arnold and Spencer were shown to the servants' quarters.

Before Rosina went to bed, Denny said, "I felt it best that your brothers should leave the captain's service so I shall be buying them their own stables in Portsmouth where they can hire out horses."

Rosina looked at him in wonder. "You are extremely generous to my family, Miles."

"I have my reasons, Rosina. I'll explain them later. We've both had an extremely tiring night so we should go to bed now."

Rosina nodded. "You're right."

The next morning, Rosina was up and about before even the scullery maid had risen. She slipped out of the house and made her way to the stables. The sleepy new groom was amazed to see her

"Excuse me, ma'am, I've only just dressed."

"No matter. Could you saddle up the pony the squire has very kindly loaned to me?"

The groom looked doubtful. "Is Squire not ridin' with you, mistress?"

Rosina curbed her impatience. "No, he' s not."

The groom scratched his head. "Well, I'm not sure that—"

"I am sure that he said I could use a pony whenever I liked." Rosina was haughty.

"Of course, ma'am. I'll saddle the pony up right away." Rosina breathed a sigh of relief.

She rode into the heart of the Forest and collected the herbs she wanted, placing them in her skirt pocket. Then, Rosina rode to a secluded part of the beach. She tethered the pony, collected some seashells and arranged them in a wide circle. Kneeling in the centre of the circle, Rosina lit a blue candle. She held her hands together in a praying position but raised high. She uttered an incantation she vaguely remembered having overheard Esmerelda make years before when the old woman had been performing a healing spell. Afterwards, Rosina prayed hard to Saint Sarah, the patron saint of gypsies for Catherine's recovery.

As she stood up, Rosina felt her hand touch the outline of an object in the sand. She pushed her hand further into the sand and drew out her red coral necklace.

CHAPTER 23

▼

When Rosina stood up, she walked to the post to which she had tied the pony. Squire Denny was standing beside two animals, his face, contrasting with the pleasant sunny day, was a black cloud of thunder.

"What on earth do you think you are doing, Rosina? Why did you go out so early without telling me?"

"I know I should have asked your permission to borrow the pony but I have been performing a healing spell for Catherine Mountjoy. I had to be alone to do this."

"Surely that's a lot of old gypsy nonsense."

Rosina was stung. "It won't be when it works," she flashed back at Denny. I'll believe it works when it happens."

"I know it will no matter how much you doubt me. I need to brew a potion from the herbs I have collected to cure Catherine. Will you let me do this in your house?"

Denny frowned. "I'll think about it."

"If you won't, I'll do it somewhere else."

The squire shrugged. "Do what you like but I think it will take more than superstition to bring about Catherine's recovery."

Rosina looked at him a little shyly. "I have found my coral necklace. I'm really happy about that."

Denny smiled, his anger seeming to disappear in an instant.

"Good, and I'm glad I've found you. I asked my groom which direction you had taken. When I saw the pony, I was afraid you might have come to some harm."

Suddenly, he took her in his arms and kissed her long and passionately.

When she drew breath, Rosina was reluctant to break away but forced herself to do so. "I must prepare the potion now."

Denny sighed. "Very well but there's an important matter I must talk to you about. We'll go back now and then I'll send the potion over to Mountjoy's house with a servant."

"Please, Miles. I'd rather take it, myself."

Denny shrugged. "All right, but I insist upon coming with you this time."

"I'd be grateful if you would."

"And I'd be thankful if, in future, you promise not to sneak out of my house without informing me first."

"I won't, you have my word of honour."

"Good, I'll hold you to that." Denny smiled again. "Come on then, Rosie, we'd better go back home so that you can concoct your witch's brew."

"I'm no witch."

"I'm not sure I believe you. You have enchanted me in many ways."

Rosina felt a thrill of pleasure at Denny's words but her slight embarrassment made her brisk. "Could we hurry do you think, Miles, I want this potion made with fresh herbs."

Miles nodded.

*   *   *   *

At the Mountjoys' house Rosina said to Charles who was looking weary and careworn, "I have prepared a potion for Catherine which I hope will cure her."

Mountjoy looked dubious but tried not to show it. "That's very kind of you, Rosina."

"Charles, please will you promise me to make sure Catherine takes it. It should be given to her a small dose at a time, but often. You will see she takes it?"

"As you're asking me so earnestly, Rosina, yes, I will administer it to her with my own hands."

"I'm glad to hear it."

"May I offer you two refreshment?"

Denny shook his head. "No thank you, we'll take our leave of you now. It goes without saying that we hope Catherine is well again, soon."

Charles tried not to show his relief that they were leaving. "I hope you will both visit us again soon."

"I'm sure we will on a happier occasion," Denny said.

"I hope so," Charles said, a resigned note in his voice.

*   *   *   *

Late that evening, after Denny and Rosina had dined, Lydia announced that Captain Mountjoy had arrived. "Damn!" Denny exclaimed.

Rosina frowned. Denny waved a dismissive hand in the air.

"I know you're thinking I'm callous, Rosina. I want to know how Catherine is as much as you do. But I was just about to speak to you on the matter I mentioned this morning."

"Surely it can wait till tomorrow."

"I suppose it will have to wait until the morning now."

Lydia admitted Captain Mountjoy to the parlour. He took hold of Rosina's hands and covered them with kisses as Denny attempted to hide a frown. "Rosina, I cannot thank you enough," the captain said. "Catherine's fever broke after she had drunk the potion you gave me. So I sent for the doctor but she rallied before he arrived. The doctor gave us advice but I'm certain it was you, Rosie, who really made her survive."

Denny looked astonished.

"I did what I could," Rosina said. "But it was probably the doctor who saved her." Inwardly, Rosina was elated. 'I know I cured her,' she thought.

"We must celebrate Catherine's return to health," Miles said. "I'll open another bottle of claret."

"I'd be delighted to share it with you," Charles replied. "But I don't want to stay too long as I feel I should get back to Catherine. She's still a little weak."

"I think I'll go to bed now," Rosina said.

Denny put out a detaining hand. "No, you're the healer. We can't leave you out. We'll all drink a toast to Catherine's continued good health. You don' t object, do you, Charles?"

"Of course not. I'd only object if Rosina didn't join in the toast with us."

Denny smiled. "That's settled, then. We'll have some ratafia biscuits as well. Rosina likes them very much."

*   *   *   *

The following morning, after they had breakfasted, following a lengthy spell in their respective beds, Rosina said to Denny, "Wasn't it good news that Catherine is better now?"

"H'm, yes," Denny said, vaguely.

Rosina peered at him wondering if the amount he had drunk the night before was making him absent-minded.

Miles looked down at the table and cleared his throat. "Rosina, this matter I wanted to talk to you about, yesterday. It was—" He hesitated, then his words came out in a rush. "Will you marry me again?"

Rosina closed her eyes. She was very much tempted by the offer knowing she still loved the squire. But then she thought about their different stations in life. Rosina realised Miles might be despised by the rest of his class if he married her again. She did not want him to be the object of ridicule.

"Miles," she said, carefully. "You are doing me a great honour by proposing to me. I won't pretend I'm not flattered by it. But have you thought about the consequences? You could be laughed at in drawing rooms up and down the county."

Miles snapped his fingers in the air. "That's all I care for gossip."

Rosina sighed. "You think that now, but it might not last. You should marry a young lady with a good dowry."

"I don't need to marry for money."

"Perhaps not but I think you should marry a lady of your own station in life so you will not be scorned by your own sort."

"I don't want my own sort as you call it. Please believe me, Rosina, please accept me because I both love and need you."

Rosina blinked back the unwelcome tears from her dark eyes. She took a deep breath. "Miles, you are very dear to me. You always were. But I need time to think this over. I can't stay here now. I'll go back to London but I'll let you have my address so you can write to me there. There's no reason why we can't be friends."

Rosina thought that if she allowed Miles a little time, he would meet a young woman who would make him a suitable wife. Then he would forget his gypsy woman. She considered that this would be best for him, But she also felt as if her decision was breaking her heart and she must not show it.

Denny took hold of her hands and stared deeply into her eyes. She could not look away. "Are you sure you can't say 'yes,' straightaway?"

For a moment, Rosina could not speak. Finally, she said, "No, I can't. I want to return to London and go back on the stage."

Abruptly, Denny dropped her hands. "If that's really what you want," he said, gruffly.

Rosina did not reply.

*   *   *   *

The next day the squire's carriage took Rosina to Southampton to catch the London stagecoach. Denny did not come with her but before she left, he gave her a purse full of money.

"I can't take this," Rosina protested.

"I'll he most offended if you don't. Let's not argue before you leave."

Rosina hesitated. "I'll take it on condition you let me return it to you when I've earned this much from appearing on the stage." She spoke with more confidence than she felt, wondering if she would actually obtain work with a theatre.

"Very well. Guard it well and keep it hidden from prying eyes."

"I shall." She tucked the purse into a secret corner of her bundle.

"There's something else I have to say, Rosina. If you should change your mind about my offer, let me know. Do you promise?"

Rosina nodded, feeling that if she spoke, she would break down.

"I want you to make me another promise."

"What's that?" Rosina asked in a small voice.

"Write to me, let me know how you are and what you're doing."

"I'll be pleased to do so. Thank you very much indeed for all your help and hospitality. I shall always remember it and be grateful to you." Rosina knew her manner was stiff and that she sounded more formal than she would have liked. But she also thought that under the circumstances, she would not trust herself to say anything more personal without becoming emotional.

Denny looked resigned. "It was nothing much. Have a good journey. I wish you God speed."

He kissed her cheek and then told his driver to whip up the horses. Rosina leant her head against a cushion with a heavy heart. She fell into an uneasy sleep for most of the journey on the stagecoach.

*   *   *   *

When Rosina had at last reached London she spent the first night at a respectable inn. Her room was clean and comfortable but she cried herself to sleep, remembering the times she had recently spent with Denny. She knew she would miss him dreadfully.

The following day she found lodgings near Drury Lane. Her room was on the top floor of a four-storey building. It contained a bed, a chest of drawers, a table and a sofa. A smaller bedroom led from the larger one.

There was a red and yellow carpet on the floor and red curtains at the windows. There were shops opposite including a grocer's, a milliner's, a baker's and a pastrycook's. Rosina thought they would all be very convenient.

The landlady, Mrs Hall, was a tall, statuesque looking woman in her early middle age. Rosina took an instinctive liking to her. "I'm hoping to become a dancer," she said.

Mrs Hall looked thoughtful. "Are you now? I believe I could help you there. I know the manager of a small theatre nearby. He's my friend. I'll give you a letter of introduction to him. I should get in there, quick. You can go tomorrow."

"Thank you for helping me."

The landlady shrugged. "I like to do favours for theatricals, dear," she said. "I was on the stage myself some time back. I was an actress in a small way, you understand."

Rosina smiled. "I do understand."

"Nowadays, I keep a decent boarding house as you'll have seen. I'll charge you twelve shillings a week with two meals a day plus a cup of tea." She beamed as if expecting Rosina to be overwhelmed by her generosity. "Washing's a bit extra, dear. Will you want it, do you think?"

Rosina was about to refuse then she remembered the money in her purse. "Yes, I'd like you to do my washing."

"Lord above, Miss Clayton, I don't do it myself. I pay a washerwoman."

"Silly of me to suggest it," Rosina said, glancing down. "Your hands are too soft to do a lot of washing."

"Quite," Mrs Hall said, looking pleased by the compliment. "Now let's have a cup of coffee and a slice of cake. I can afford cakes from the pastrycook's over the road, you know. They're delicious."

"You were right about these cakes, Mrs Hall," Rosina said, as she bit into her slice.

∗   ∗   ∗   ∗

The following day it was raining but the weather did not dampen Rosina's spirits as she made her way to the Angel Theatre converted from a warehouse and situated in a side street near her lodgings.

The box bookkeeper glanced at her letter of introduction. "I'll see the manager for you," he said, looking dubious. "Wait here. I'll be back in a minute."

The man returned about ten minutes later, looking surprised. "You're to go to the auditorium. Mr Heaven will see you there."

Mr Heaven was a middle-aged man of medium height and build, neither handsome nor ugly but he had a very upright posture. Rosina felt he had a presence about him which was immediately noticeable.

"You're a gypsy dancer?" he asked, glancing at the letter in his hand.

"Yes sir, I am."

"And you've had some experience on the stage, it says here."

"I have, sir. As it states in the letter, my new landlady, Mrs Hall, very kindly recommended me to you."

Mr Heaven looked astounded. "Can you read?"

Rosina nodded. "Yes, I can, sir."

Mr Heaven hesitated for a little while. This young woman seemed too refined for a gypsy. Perhaps she had some Spanish blood in her and was calling herself a gypsy to make herself sound exotic. He dragged his thoughts to the business in hand.

"My goodness, you do surprise me. Well, it's not your ability to read you're here for. I'll play the violin for you while you dance."

Rosina was nervous but as usual, when she began to dance, she lost her fears and immersed herself in her performance.

Mr Heaven stopped her before she had finished. "I've seen enough, Miss Clayton, to know you're a natural performer. You have a part in my pantomime."

Rosina was delighted and thanked Mr Heaven warmly. He shrugged her thanks aside and gruffly told her to present herself at the theatre the following evening at eight o'clock sharp.

Back at the boarding house, Mrs Hall and Rosina shared another cake and coffee. "I told you he'd like you, love," Mrs Hall said. "Well done."

*   *   *   *

Rosina had been appearing at the Angel Theatre for two weeks when Isaac Mandleberg and Elizabeth Vale came to the theatre. When they recognised Rosina, they went backstage to see her.

"We were thrilled to see you again, Rosina," Isaac said. "You're looking lovelier than ever."

"I couldn't believe it was you up there on the stage," Elizabeth said. "I'm delighted it was, though."

"And I'm thrilled to see both of you again," Rosina said. "I like meeting old friends. Will you two come with me to the May Day celebrations in ten days time?"

"Of course we will," Isaac said.

"We'll look forward to it," Elizabeth agreed.

They chatted for a long time about what had happened to them all since they had last seen each other. Finally, Isaac and Elizabeth took an affectionate leave of Rosina.

As Isaac and Elizabeth entered the Rose Inn, Elizabeth remarked, "I think we'll enjoy May Day."

"Yes, we will," Isaac agreed. "It was lovely to find Rosina at the Angel."

Sitting at a corner table, in the shadows, George Blackwell beckoned Rook over to his side. "Well now, Rookie, it's most interesting don't you think, that Rosina's appearing at the Angel and attending the May Day celebrations," he said in an undertone.

Rook's small eyes gleamed. "What are we going to do with her?"

Blackwell smiled. "You're going to catch her and bring her to me."

"With pleasure, sir."

"And this time," Blackwell added, grimly, "we're going to keep her with us."

CHAPTER 24

▼

After having given the matter much thought, Rosina sent her letter to Squire Denny. She sent him a ticket for one of her performances at the theatre and promised that when she saw him, she would repay the money he had given her for her journey. Rosina waited for the night in an agony of suspense. She was glad that the daytime activities would occupy her mind until the evening.

Rosina watched the May Day procession with Isaac. Elizabeth was not attending because she was suffering from a heavy cold.

Milkmen, milkmaids and chimney sweeps held a masquerade. The women trundled a huge pyramid of flowers festooned with kettles, salvers and pieces of silver through the streets while the sweeps, their faces whitened with meal and beads framed in periwigs, banged brushes and scrapers.

Rook, disguised as a sweep, detached himself from the thick of the crowd. He stood as close to Isaac as he could in order to overhear the other man's words.

"Let's go to the fair on the green, Rosie," Isaac said.

"I'd like that," Rosina replied.

"And we'll have some tea in the tea garden afterwards."

"Lovely idea," said Rosina.

"We'll have some supper in Spring Garden tonight before you go to the theatre."

Rosina smiled warmly. "That'll be a perfect ending to the day."

"Won't it just, my lovely," Rook muttered to himself.

*   *   *   *

When Squire Denny arrived in London, he went straight to Rosina's lodgings where Mrs Hall received him graciously. She asked him to wait in her parlour.

After she had served him refreshment Mrs Hall said, "Rosina has gone to the May Day junketings in Islington."

Miles scowled. "I doubt I'll find her in all the crowds." He sighed. "I'll have to wait until later when I go to the theatre. Do you know where I could get a good supper beforehand?"

"I should try Spring Garden, sir."

"Thank you for your hospitality and the recommendation. I'll leave you now."

"I hope to see you again soon, sir."

"I'm sure you will do, Mrs Hall."

In the streets of Islington, an elegant young man approached the squire.

"I don't know if you remember me, sir."

Denny looked at him more closely. "I think I do. You're Lionel Jarrett, aren't you?"

"Yes. I think it's a stroke of great good fortune that I've met you again. I wonder if I could ask you to give me some information."

"What did you want to know?"

Jarrett looked around. "I'd rather not talk about it in the street. Could we go somewhere more private?"

Denny nodded. "Came and sup with me at. Spring Garden. You can tell me everything there."

"Thank you, I'm very grateful," Lionel said. "I've brought a pistol with me," he added in an undertone. "To guard against footpads and the like. I can honestly say that I'm an excellent marksman."

"I don't think you'll need it if there's two of us."

"I hope not but it's best to be on one's guard."

"In certain circumstances," Denny agreed. Idly, he wondered whether Jarrett had a lot of enemies in London.

When they were seated at their table, Denny said, "What did you want to ask me?"

"I've married since the last time I saw you. I love my wife in my own way but I come down to London from Leicestershire quite a lot and—" Miles raised an eyebrow while he waited for Lionel to speak again. "I wondered if you had any news of Rosina?"

The squire stiffened. "What did you want to know about her?" He very much hoped Jarrett was not having a love affair with Rosina.

"All I was hoping—" Jarrett shrugged. "No matter, I'll go now. I didn't mean to offend you."

Denny put a restraining hand on the other man's sleeve. "No, tell me what you were hoping."

Jarrett looked reluctant. He hesitated, then reached his decision. "Very well." He glanced around. "It's threatening rain. I'm glad there's not many people about."

"In that case, tell me now what you intended to say."

"I haven't been able to stop thinking about Rosina," Jarrett blurted out.

"I know exactly what you mean," Denny said, almost grimly.

"I thought if I could find Rosina, I'd ask her to become my mistress."

Denny stiffened. Although relieved that Lionel and Rosina were not actually having an affair, he felt his hackles rise.

"Really? Didn't you think that was a somewhat vain hope?"

Jarrett shrugged. "Possibly, but I wanted to find out. I don't know where she is, now. When I went to the Rose to enquire, I was told she had left there some time ago. Elizabeth Vale, however, told me she was attending the May Day festivities. It was, as you said, maybe a vain hope, but—"

"My God!" Denny said, no longer listening to what Jarrett was saying. "It's as if you've summoned her! Rosina has just arrived with Isaac Mandleberg." He pointed to them.

Both men stood up in order to walk over to the table where Isaac and Rosina had just sat down. Suddenly, George Blackwell and Rook appeared. Rook darted forward and Rosina gave a piercing scream as Isaac fell forwards.

"Murder!" she yelled. "My friend has just been stabbed. Help me!"

Some people began to gather around the table. "My wife is making a devil of a fuss!" Blackwell shouted. "She has run away from me with her would-be lover and now I'm taking her back home as is my right."

Rosina stared at him in horror, unable to believe what she was hearing.

"Her lover is not dead, only wounded, he will recover," Blackwell added.

As Blackwell grabbed Rosina's wrist, a few of the onlookers drifted away, not wishing to become involved in what they thought was a marital dispute. Others stayed to see if anything more exciting would happen.

Denny and Jarrett pushed their way through the small crowd.

Miles shouted, "This man is a liar! The lady is my own wife."

"Get that interfering squire, too, Rook!" Blackwell snapped.

There was a half-horrified, half delighted gasp from the watchers as Rook once again pulled out his knife. The next moment, Jarrett pulled the pistol from his deep pocket. Taking quick, deliberate aim, he shot both Blackwell and Rook with a bullet through the heart.

Pandemonium broke out with men yelling and some of the women screaming. Denny shouted above them all: "All of you except the lady at the table, get out of here or the same thing will happen to you." They onlookers needed no second bidding. They flew in all directions.

"You can turn me over to the authorities, if you like," Jarrett said to Denny. "I've rid the world of scum so if it now wishes to get rid of me, so be it." He shrugged and Denny marvelled at his coolness.

Miles shook his head. "You've just saved my life so I wouldn't dream of betraying you. But we must get out of here at once." The two men walked over to the almost paralysed Rosina.

"Miles and Lionel," she said in a dazed voice. "What a surprise to see you both together. Please tell me you're real, not part of my dream. I think I'm in the middle of a nightmare."

"We're real, all right," Lionel said. "Definitely flesh and blood at present."

"Why are you both here?"

"We'll save the explanations until later, Rosina," Denny said, briskly. "You certainly were in the middle of a waking nightmare, my love, but it's all over now."

Rosina breathed a huge sigh of relief.

"For Heaven's sake, stand up!" Miles added, his voice sharpening considerably. "We have to run for our lives, now, this very minute!"

Rosina stood up, still in a daze. Denny and Jarrett both took hold of her arms and half dragged her to a back way out of the garden.

When they were once again in the street, Denny said, "We have to walk as if nothing has happened."

They reached Denny's carriage. "Come with us, Jarrett," Denny said. "We'll drop you off in Wiltshire. I know it's a long way from there to Leicestershire but will you be able to get back on your own?"

Jarrett nodded. "Yes, I have some money with me. I can get the stagecoach."

"Good," Denny said, crisply. He turned to his coachman. "My plans have changed. Drop this gentleman off in Wiltshire when we reach a suitable inn. Then take the lady and myself back to my house in the Forest."

"Yes, sir," the coachman said, with great interest.

"Don' t stand there gawping, man! " Denny snapped. "Make all haste to speed us on our way."

The coachman snapped to attention, "Very good, sir."

Inside the carriage, Denny said to Rosina, "You'll have to marry me, now, Rosina. I said you were my wife and I'm not a liar. You need my protection so you're not going to refuse me, now, are you?"

Rosina shook her head, unable to speak.

"This time it won't be a quiet wedding. We'll have a big celebration and invite lots of people, of all stations of life."

Rosina nodded, happily.

Jarrett looked disappointed for a moment; then he looked out of the window.

Denny pulled Rosina's head on to his shoulder. "Go to sleep, now, Rosie. You've left all the horror behind you, now."

Rosina smiled up at him. "I feel in my gypsy bones that this is the start of a perfect new life for both of us."

Denny nodded. "You're right. You're no longer the Gypsy Rose. You're my Rose of the Forest." He kissed her, tenderly.

Sitting in the corner of the coach, a bitter-sweet smile on his face, Jarrett felt as if he had become invisible. He stared out of the window, seeing nothing.

"The squire deserves his Rose," he thought. "They obviously are very much in love with each other."

The coach increased its speed.

CHAPTER 25

▼

The weather was beautiful the day Squire Denny married Rosina Clayton for the second time. The golden sun shone warmly but not oppressively out of a clear blue sky. Birds were singing in the trees.

They were married in the squire's chapel, Miles most handsome in his lilac satin suit while his bride wore a white dress of Spitalfields brocade with a background of a delicate pink floral design. The sleeves were trimmed with ivory lace.

The bride was given away by her brother, Arnold. Spencer watched his brother and sister with great pride. The only thing that marred the day for Rosina was the absence of her brother Jacko. She fingered her red coral necklace, willing it to bring him luck wherever he was.

Catherine Mountjoy did miss the look of longing on Charles' face when Denny and Rosina exchanged their vows. She bit her lip. Some of Rosina's old companions from the theatre, including Mrs Hall, also attended the wedding.

Lionel Jarrett and his small, quiet wife, Dorcas, were guests. Rosina had begged Miles to invite Jarrett. Reluctantly, Miles had finally agreed.

"Don't they make the most 'andsome couple you've ever seen?" a village woman said, admiringly. Several of the other villagers agreed with her. A feast had been arranged for them which they were to share with the squire's servants. He was very popular with them all that day.

At the wedding breakfast, after the meal, Rosina said to Jarrett, "We were very pleased to see you, Lionel." She smiled at Dorcas. "Please introduce us to your wife."

When Lionel introduced Dorcas to the squire and his wife, she hardly spoke above a whisper.

"I'm delighted to see you again," Jarrett said. "It's been so boring in Leicester-shire. We need a little excitement now and again."

"Not too much, though, I hope," Rosina laughed.

"I've been forced into a quiet life for a while though. I shall return to London soon. Are you going to dance for us, Rosie?"

Denny frowned. Dorcas's small eyes grew wide with disapproval and Rosina flushed. "Not on her own," Denny said, sharply.

"How disappointing for us all," Jarrett said. Dorcas gave her husband a reproachful look. She had formerly looked at Rosina with curiosity; now her gaze became more hostile.

A tight-lipped Denny held his hand out to Rosina who took it. He squeezed her fingers. "Come and meet my brothers and sisters at last."

As Jarrett watched Rosina's every move, Dorcas felt alternatively like crying and like hitting him. "I think we should go, Lionel," she said. "We have a long drive to where we' re staying."

"It wouldn't be polite to leave just yet," Jarrett said. Dorcas sighed.

"My lovely wife, Rosina," Denny announced to his brothers and sisters, with obvious pride. They warily exchanged glances. He placed a proprietorial arm around Rosina's shoulders. They reacted with faultless courtesy if not exactly warmth.

Denny returned to speak to Jarrett. "I think your wife is tired. Are you, Mistress Jarrett?"

Dorcas gave him a grateful smile. "Very much so," she said in a loud voice. "Oh, please don't think we haven't enjoyed ourselves, sir," she said, her tone becoming simpering.

"I'm glad you have but I suppose you have a long journey."

"It's not that far," Jarrett began to protest.

"Even so, I believe it's probably far enough for your wife to want to leave now."

Jarrett looked disappointed. "I suppose so," he conceded. "Thank you for your hospitality."

As he watched them leave, with a smile on his face, Squire Denny wondered whether Jarrett and Dorcas would argue on their way home.

Catherine Mountjoy drew Rosina aside as soon as she had the opportunity.

"Rosina, I have to confess I didn't approve of you at first but both myself and my husband believe you saved my life. Therefore, I think you will make a suitable wife for the squire in temperament even though you were low born."

"Thank you," Rosina said, simply but with dignity.

"I do hope you will he allowed at least one dance with me, Rosie," Mountjoy said.

Rosina gave him a warm smile. She did not care that Catherine was watching her intently. "Naturally, I would be honoured to do so, Charles."

The celebration seemed to go on forever. Although both Miles and Rosina enjoyed every minute, they both longed for the moment they would at last be alone together.

When the time for them to retire finally arrived, they were both weary yet excited. "I've been waiting patiently for them all to go," Miles said, smiling.

"And me," Rosina agreed. "Mind you," she added. "It's been a marvellous day altogether."

He took hold of her hand. "We'll have to experience a wonderful night to follow it."

As they lay together in bed, Rosina thought how long she had been yearning for Denny's touch. She could hardly believe this moment was here.

"I'm never going to he so stupid as to let you go again, Rosie," Miles whispered. Rosina felt as if her heart might burst with the love she felt for him.

The squire kissed her gently at first, then far more passionately. He took his time, caressing the shapely curves of her body, stroking her soft skin. At last their climax was reached together in a glow of glorious fulfilment.

$$* \qquad * \qquad * \qquad *$$

Three months later, on a lovely day when Miles was out on urgent estate business, Rosina went out for a short ride on her pony. The pony, however, stumbled on a stone and Rosina was thrown. Fortunately, she was only shaken and bruised with no bones broken.

The servants said afterwards that it was also a marvel Rosina and her groom were so near the house when the incident occurred.

Rosina was carried indoors and put to bed immediately. Lydia brought her a soothing drink. She bit her lip. "Ma'am, I'm so sorry this has 'appened. I don't know what squire will say."

Lydia immediately regretted her words because Rosina turned her head on the pillow, closing her eyes and not saying a word. Her olive skin seemed to have turned completely pale.

The entire household fussed over her but that night Rosina miscarried the baby she had been expecting.

After she had recovered from all the pain and depression of her miscarriage, Miles took her to task, not having wanted to upset her further after she had been ill. He felt she was now well enough to be scolded.

"You were silly to go out, riding, Rosina. Very silly indeed. I was most annoyed by your behaviour."

Rosina lowered her head, feeling ashamed. "I know I was. It was just that it was such a lovely day and I was tired of being cooped up indoors. I thought it would do no harm to go just a little distance."

"Next time, you can walk outdoors but not far. You will be accompanied by a female servant even for the shortest distance. And there will be no riding at all. Do I make myself clear?"

"Yes." Tears came to Rosina's eyes. "I'm sorry I've failed you."

The squire's tone softened. "No, you didn't, there's plenty of time yet. Just make sure you don't act like a fool in future."

"I promise I won't," Rosina said, quietly.

"Good girl," Denny said.

Rosina looked up at him. "Miles, even though I've been such au idiot, can I ask you a favour?"

"Yes, what is it?"

"Next time I'm pregnant, could the village children be allowed to have rides on my pony?"

Miles considered. "I think that could be arranged." He smiled. "I'm sure they'll love it and their mothers will be able to discourage them from bad behaviour by threatening they won't get a ride."

Rosina laughed.

"That's the loudest I've heard you laugh since—" Miles checked himself.

Rosina looked at him. "I'm sure I shall being doing plenty of laughing in future. I've done more than enough crying. I expect you grew weary of me."

Miles shook his head. "Not at all. I'm only glad you've completely recovered from all your distress."

"You're the best husband in the world."

"Let me return that beautiful compliment. Come to bed with me and prove you're the best wife in the world." He picked her up and carried her to their bedroom.

*   *   *   *

Six months later, Rosina was embroidering a baby dress when she experienced a cramp-like feeling in her stomach. The cramp eased itself away, then Rosina caught her breath as another gripped her. There was also a pain in her back. The cramp went on all day, sweeping over her in waves. Then, early that evening, the cramp appeared to leap from the small of her back and surround her.

Rosina called for Lydia. "My baby's coming early, I know it," she said.

Lydia became calm efficiency itself. She immediately ordered a maid to send a groom to fetch the squire from the Mountjoys to whom he was paying a visit.

She gently took hold of Rosina's hand. Rosina gripped it hard. "Excuse my familiarity, ma'am, but we must get you to bed straightaway. We don't want the same thing happening as before."

Rosina became anxious. "Oh, Lydia, I couldn't bear to miscarry again. All that pain and disappointment. I don't think I could stand it all over again!"

Lydia bit her lip. "Madam, do excuse me. My tongue runs away with me sometimes. It was a stupid thing to say."

"I don't blame you, I know I acted foolishly last night. I just didn't expect anything would happen. Do you remember how cross Miles was?"

Lydia nodded. "Yes, that's why he's made sure you've had every care this time round."

"He was very kind after he was annoyed. He's made sure I've rested a lot and been given the choicest foods."

"Squire's a good man at heart, Madam."

"I know he is. I've loved to see the children's little faces light up when they've ridden my pony. It's been good for the beast as well. He needed the exercise."

"Very soon, ma'am, you'll be needin' to exercise and then you'll see your own little one's smiling face."

"You're a wise woman, Lydia."

Lydia looked pleased as Rosina clutched her red coral necklace.

*   *   *   *

Rosina lay in the big double bed, completely worn out but happy. She looked at the coral necklace hanging over the bed, reaching up and touching it.

"You watched over me," she whispered. "I feel old Esmerelda's spirit is living on in you. I'm giving you my daughter so that you can guard her while she grows up."

"Madam," Lydia said, anxiously. Rosina held the tiny, perfectly formed infant in her arms and kissed the downy cheek.

"We're both fine, Lydia. Baby and myself," she said. Lydia breathed an enormous sigh of relief.

Rosina's labour had been long and hard. Her life had almost been despaired of, but she had fought back and both mother and child had managed to survive.

She had prayed for a son but Rosina wondered if her prayers had not been answered because of her stupidity the last time she had been pregnant. Then, she mentally chided herself for being over-fanciful.

Rosina looked up at her husband's handsome, concerned face. "You must rest now, Rosie," he said. "I've just been on my knees thanking God you're still with me even though I'm not a religious man."

She sighed. "I hope you're not too disappointed I haven't borne you a son and heir, Miles." Rosina became pensive. "You don't think I've failed you, yet again?"

She touched the new born baby's downy cheek tenderly but her husband did not miss the nervous look on her face. He smiled, shaking his head and looking at their daughter.

"No, love, we're still young enough to have more children. And I'm sure she'll grow up to be as beautiful as her mother."

Rosina smiled, contentedly. Then, hesitantly, she said, "As she was born on a full moon, starry kind of night, do you think we could call her Starella?"

Miles nodded in agreement. "You're the Rose of the Forest. She will be its star."

PART TWO
STAR OF THE FOREST

CHAPTER 1

▼

ESTATE OUTSIDE TOPCLIFFE VILLAGE. HAMPSHIRE—1766

The ten-year-old girl stared at her visitors out of large, clear, green eyes. They were making her head ache with their constant bickering. She also resented the fact that they were discussing her as if she were not there.

"Such a shame our poor brother, Miles, died so tragically in that hunting accident. And for his wife to follow him to the grave with a fever so soon afterwards," Amanda Collett said, dabbing at her eyes with a handkerchief.

The child felt her own eyes begin to fill up as she thought about her parents who had both always treated her so tenderly.

"Amanda, that must be the tenth time you've said that, for Heaven's sake!" her brother, David, snapped.

"Don't speak to my wife like that. I'll thank you to keep a civil tongue in your head," Amanda's husband, John, said, heatedly.

"Come now," said Verity Adams, glancing at the child. "We all know our brother made a somewhat—" She hesitated, "—unusual marriage."

"I think his wits had been addled," Amanda said.

"It's true he lived very quietly with his wife and daughter in his latter years," Robin, Verity's husband, said.

"I can quite understand why, under the circumstances," Paul Denny, the late squire's younger brother, said.

"His estate was entailed, was it not so?" Angela, David's wife, said. "It will naturally pass to David as the older brother." There was an avaricious glint in her eye as she looked out of the window at the trees blowing in the strong Autumn wind.

"We know that already," Paul snapped.

"Don't worry, I will see that you receive a generous portion of his inheritance," said David.

Amanda looked at the girl. "Surely Starella is also entitled to something."

"Yes, yes," David said, testily. "We do realise that."

"We're now back to the question of where she's going to live and what is to be done with her," Verity said. "I can't possibly take her into my own household. We have far too many children of our own to even consider another mouth to feed."

"The same applies to ourselves," Amanda said. She turned to David. "As the estate is now apparently yours, do you not think you could keep the girl here with you?"

"I suppose I must do my duty by her," David said, with obvious reluctance. "It may be hard to make a good match for her with her gypsy mother's blood in her."

"There's a few years yet before you have to face that problem," Verity said, her tone crisp.

Starella wanted to scream at them all to go away and leave her alone. She did not like any of them. It was hard to believe her beloved father had such horrible relatives who all seemed to resent her.

David was about to make another remark when the butler came in. "Do excuse me for interrupting your conversation, ladies and gentlemen, but Captain Mountjoy, the master builder from Bucklers Hard, is here. He wishes to see you all."

"Mountjoy? Ah yes, I remember he did write to me and I agreed to see him some time, today. Show him in."

Starella's spirits began to lift slightly. She liked her Uncle Charles.

After introducing himself to the assembled company, Charles said, "I do hope you will forgive me for mentioning the subject but may I be blunt, Mr Denny?" He corrected himself, quickly. "I'm sorry, I shouldn't have addressed you that way now you're about to become the new squire."

"Of course, Captain Mountjoy, please tell us what you're concerned about," David said, pleased with Charles' use of his new title.

"Will Starella be living with you? I believe you have other children."

David sighed. "Yes, I have. But I can hardly turn my own brother's orphan out of doors."

'So that's the way the land lies, as I had feared,' Charles thought. Aloud he said, "I may be presumptuous to make this suggestion as she is not my own kin after all. But I could offer Starella a home with myself, my wife and our two daughters. We have plenty of room for her."

There were relieved exchanged glances all round. Captain Mountjoy did not miss them and momentarily disliked the late Squire Denny's relatives as much as Starella did.

"I'm surprised at your suggestion, yet I must say it's a very kind one," said David. Speaking directly to the late squire's daughter for the first time that day, he said, "Starella, would you like to go and live in this nice captain's house? I think you'll love it there. You'll be away from the unhappy memories of your parents' deaths."

Starella looked at him almost with contempt, hesitating for a split second. "Yes, I would like to live with Uncle Chares," she said, clearly.

An audible sigh of relief echoed throughout the room; then Starella added, "Better than living with any of you."

In the shocked silence that followed, Charles turned away to hide a smile. David found his voice. "I hope you won't be so impertinent to the captain, in future, Starella. If you were my daughter, I should box your ears for such a wicked remark; but I make allowances because you're still grieving."

"I'm sure she'll be a good girl and behave herself with us," Charles said, hastily.

"Of course I shall, Uncle Charles."

"I know you will," Charles said, ruffling the girl's bright chestnut waves of hair.

David frowned. "Make sure she's suitably grateful to you for bringing her up as your own. I'll send you regular sums of money to pay for her upkeep."

"There's no need. I can well afford to see Starella lacks for nothing."

"Noble of you, Mountjoy, but I must insist you take at least one sum from us all to cover the cost of her clothes and such like." He looked around the room. "Surely we can all give a generous donation."

Looking both embarrassed and resentful, all the men in the room gave the captain a gold coin. He thanked them in a slightly stiff manner. To Starella, he said, "Come upstairs now and we'll sort out which belongings you'll be taking with you. I'm sure your kinsfolk have much to discuss."

He offered her his hand. Starella grasped it and clung to him with all her might.

CHAPTER 2

▼

BUCKLERS HARD—
1773

Starella looked up from her seemingly endless embroidery. She was not even embroidering her own garments but those of the twins. The winter fire illuminated her chestnut hair as Catherine Mountjoy spoke decisively to her.

"The captain and I have been discussing your future, Starella."

Starella groaned inwardly. She was sure that Catherine's views would not be in accordance with her own.

"We are thinking of apprenticing you to a mantua-maker or a milliner in either Salisbury or Southampton."

"With all due respect, Aunt Catherine, this would waste the education Uncle Charles kindly provided for me, along with Augusta and Allegra." She hid a smile as Catherine never tired of reminding her of this fact.

Starella had been expected to admire and respect the twins at all times which she had not always done in reality. As she grew up, she had become a sort of unofficial companion and lady's maid to them both.

The twins were not identical although they were of the same height and slim build. Allegra, the fair one, was her mother's favourite and Allegra, the dark one, was Captain Mountjoy's pet.

Generally, they both treated Starella reasonably well although she found each of them friendlier when the other was not present. The twins were both soon to be married to two brothers, sons of a shipwright friend of their father's so there was to be a double wedding.

Catherine had bluntly informed Starella that her assistance would be required for the twins' wedding preparations. After that she would have to make her own way in the world. She would not be able to accompany either Augusta or Allegra to their new homes because they would both have more than sufficient servants.

"But I'm not a servant," Starella had protested, indignantly.

"No, but if you remain in our household, you'll be an extra mouth to feed. Hardly necessary when you're well past the age to be capable to earn your own living. You know very well that my husband and I aren't the callous sort who'd turn you out on to the streets, without a penny—"

"I know, Aunt Catherine. But I—"

"Starella, we'll ensure you're settled into a suitable post with appropriate living quarters. We'll even give you some money to buy yourself some material and trinkets before you leave us. I'll help you if you can't make up your mind about what you want."

"Thank you, but I'm sure I shall be able to make my own decisions," Starella said, dryly, secretly resenting the fact that she was expected to leave the household although she had always felt her presence in it had never been welcomed by Catherine. Starella thought she had been treated like a cross between a poor relation and an upper servant. In a way, she decided, it would be pleasant to have a little independence.

Secrets have never been easily kept in villages. Starella knew her mother had been a gypsy dancer before her marriage. Privately, the girl considered this rather exciting. Amongst her favourite toys as a child had been an old pair of castanets of her mother's. Starella had loved clicking them together, loudly.

Once, when the dancing master had been more complimentary about Starella's ability than the twins', making the girl glow with pride, Catherine had overheard. She had drawn Starella aside, warning her that she was becoming too frivolous and if she did not pay more attention to her other lessons, she would probably come to a bad end.

Starella looked Catherine in the eyes. "I should prefer to become a governess rather than a dressmaker. I like children and feel there is much I could teach them."

Catherine frowned. "I doubt if there would be a suitable family we could place you with. Even though you are a squire's daughter, you're not an heiress and were disowned by his relatives. But we will look to them for a cash gift when you marry, of course."

Starella's tone was bitter. "They might well refuse."

"We'll sort it out at the right time," Catherine said, briskly. "Our problem with you becoming a governess is that some of the respectable folk might object to the fact that their children are being educated by a—"

"Half-gypsy," Starella finished the other woman's sentence.

Catherine had the grace to look shamefaced. "Well, yes."

"I couldn't help the circumstances of my birth."

"Do you think I don't know that, girl? Even so, we can't change the way people feel about such matters. Accept the world as it is, Starella. Don't expect it to be as you would order it."

Starella sighed inwardly. Captain Mountjoy had always treated her kindly and she knew he loved her almost as much as his own daughters. But he was often away from home when she missed him. His wife, on the other hand, treated her with courtesy but no warmth or affection. Starella believed Catherine merely tolerated her for her husband's sake. She wished she and the older woman could have become closer over the years but knew it was a vain hope.

Although she knew all the villagers and liked playing with the children, Starella had always felt herself to be something of an outsider. She knew she would not be allowed to marry a sailor, fisherman or farm labourer. Conversely, it had also been impressed upon her that she should not expect anyone of too high a station for a husband.

The twins, Starella had been informed, would be bound to make much better matches. With Starella's privileged background and education, however, she could possibly wed a prosperous gentleman farmer, a tutor or maybe a parson. If she chose wisely, she would receive a generous marriage portion.

Starella thought that Catherine's ideas about choosing wisely would probably conflict with her own.

Jerking Starella out of her reverie, Catherine said, "If you complete your apprenticeship and do well, you might become a personal maid in a good household, possibly even a nobleman's."

"Afterwards, you might even be able to marry a butler or a steward or some other such person in his household, Starella," Allegra said, as if she were personally arranging this great honour.

"I'd rather marry the nobleman," Starella said, sweetly.

Catherine frowned. "Such talk is foolish and well you know it."

"If you didn't become a lady's maid," said Augusta, "maybe you could have your own establishment, a dressmaker's or a milliner's. We would be sure to place orders with you."

Starella smiled at her. "I think I should like that very much. It would be pleasant to be my own mistress. You and Allegra would be my most valued customers."

"Come now," said Catherine. "Starella has not even become an apprentice yet. How can any of us know what the future holds for her?"

*   *   *   *

The three young women were seated in satin covered armchairs in the library as the afternoon's heavy rain beat against the lead windowpanes. The twins were reading. Starella would also have liked to read a book but she was occupied with her sewing.

Allegra looked up from her page. "Father has decided to hold a reception next Friday night," she said. "I'm very pleased about that."

"So am I," said Augusta. "I enjoy meeting visitors."

Allegra sighed. "I've noticed you're often very quiet in their presence, especially with new acquaintances. They must sometimes mistake you for a field mouse. You should try to be more lively and witty and,—well, sparkle a little more."

"Like yourself, Augusta?" The question was not sarcastic.

Augusta nodded as Starella stabbed her needle quite viciously into the material she was holding. She wished Allegra would not be quite so self-effacing in her sister's presence.

"I am the one who should sparkle," she said. "I have the right name for such an activity. I may even twinkle as well."

Augusta bridled. She did not believe that the beneficiaries of charity ought to display quite so much levity in the presence of their benefactors. Allegra smiled at Starella.

"I think you'll enjoy it, Ella. There is sure to be music and dancing. I know you have always liked both."

Starella returned the other girl's smile. "So I have, very much. And I believe that some of the guests will more appreciate a good listener rather than a foolish prattler."

Allegra flushed as a furious Augusta said, "You are indeed fortunate, are you not, Starella, that you are to attend this reception instead of just watching from a doorway?"

"The only time I ever watched you from a doorway, Augusta, was when we played hide and seek as children. There's no reason why I should do so again. I am not one of the maids."

Augusta tugged furiously at a blonde curl, enraged by what she saw as Starella's insolence. Her intended tirade was prevented as her mother bustled into the room. She began to feel a little easier. Mamma had some experience of curbing Starella's outbursts.

"Girls, come on now! What are you doing, gossiping in here when your future husbands have called? They're waiting for you in the drawing room because they wish to take you out for a ride in the Forest in their carriage. The rain has stopped at last, thank goodness."

With squeals of delight, the twins rushed eagerly out of the room. Starella was startled when Catherine stayed behind to speak to her. "My husband wishes to speak privately with you in the study."

Starella nodded, put her work down and rose. She was very fond of the captain but also a little apprehensive about what he might have to say to her.

Apart from a few wrinkles, and some grey streaks in his thinning hair, Charles Mountjoy had not aged very much. He had never been truly handsome but he now had a distinguished look. He smiled at Starella with genuine affection, motioning her to be seated.

"I believe Catherine has mentioned our possible plan for you."

"Yes. I believe I am to be packed away to either Southampton or Salisbury to become an ill-used apprentice mantua-maker or maybe a milliner."

Charles winced. "I have no desire to 'pack you away' as you put it, to anywhere and I would never see you ill-used."

"It's the common lot of apprentices. You might not be able to prevent it."

He held up his hand. "I assure you I would. I know Catherine's not always—shall we say—discreet, when she talks to you. But believe me, I have always wanted what is best for you."

Starella leaned forward slightly, clasping her hands tightly together. "I've always thought that, myself. Yet, you now seem prepared to send me away upon her whim."

Charles sighed. "When your poor mother died and your father's relatives seemed reluctant to take responsibility for you, I made a bargain with Catherine to take you into our home. To care for you at least until our own daughters were wed. Not all women would have agreed to do so."

"Especially when the brat in question, even if the squire's daughter, is also a half-gypsy—'diddecoy'—I believe the Romanies themselves, call us."

Charles bit his lip as he studied her. "I understand your bitterness, Starella. You've inherited Rosina's high cheekbones but not her dark colouring. Rosina was unusual—exotic looking, almost. She was a beauty but you are more beautiful still."

Starella flushed with pleasure. "Thank you for the lovely compliment." She felt unwelcome tears spring to her eyes. "I wish my mother could have had a longer life. She was always so loving towards me."

"I know she was. I completely share your feelings." Mountjoy looked down at the floor. "Although your father's accident was also a great tragedy, of course. At the time, I wished I could have helped your mother a lot more than I did."

"You did what you could, behaving like the good friend you were. You visited her, bringing her fresh fruit. I was trying to nurse her the best that I could at that age but it was you who arranged for her to see a doctor."

Charles sighed again. "I hoped for a miracle cure but unfortunately none was forthcoming." He stared over Starella's head at the opposite window. "I remember when Rosina first went into Miles Denny's household as a servant maid. When we saw her dance, it was wonderful. Then he married her—it was the talk of the district."

Starella looked at him, shrewdly. "Excuse me for being so frank with you, Uncle Charles. But you sound almost as if you were in love with my mother, yourself."

"I was." Charles' tone was blunt. "I remember when your father sold her—" Starella stared at Mountjoy in horror. "Sold her?"

Charles clenched his fists together. "I shouldn't have mentioned it to you."

"No, I have a right to know. Why did my father sell her and to whom? How could he have done such a thing?"

"He unfairly thought Rosina had been unfaithful to him with me. So he sold her to me at auction. I couldn't marry her as I was already wedded to Catherine."

"So, what did you do with her?" Starella's tone was indignant.

"I arranged for her to work in a tavern, seeing her whenever I could."

Starella's voice softened. "I don't suppose it was always easy."

"No, it wasn't. Anyway, when I went to sea, your mother went to London and danced on the stage there."

"Yes, I was told that, myself. My father found her in London, brought her back here and married her, was what I understood. But I didn't realise it was for the second time. I'm surprised my mother agreed to marry him again."

"Don't be too harsh on your father, Starella. I think when Miles sold Rosina at the wife auction, he was half mad with jealousy. He repaid his debt to her by saving her from villains in a bawdy house. He also helped to save her brother, Jacko, from the gallows."

"I've never met my Uncle Jacko who lives in the West Indies even though I've heard a lot about him. I should love to meet him one day."

"And I'm sure you will."

"I think I'm beginning to understand why Aunt Catherine has never liked me, why she wishes me well away from here. She thinks I come from a bad lot that does your reputation no good. My father's relatives would also like me to disappear as I'm an embarrassment to them."

Charles shook his head. "You're mistaken on both counts. I agree the squire's kinsfolk could have shown a lot more Christian charity towards you than they did. They gave money for you but in my opinion, they could have done more." He shrugged.

"I swear I shall never ask them for anything at all."

"Hopefully, you'll never need to. But Catherine does not dislike you. Rosina once saved her life by making her a healing potion when she was wounded. Catherine, however, has repaid Rosina by looking after her daughter."

Starella sighed. "I suppose, Uncle Charles, you think I'm very ungrateful for what has been done for me."

"No, I don't, Ellie. But I wish I could make you see that I'm not casting you out. Instead, I'm trying to help you find the right path in life."

Starella dug her nails into her palms. "You're not helping me at all by your choice of occupation for me. I should like to become a governess."

Mountjoy cleared his throat. "Ellie, you may feel that this would be a suitable position for you. Yet with your looks, you might become prey to an unscrupulous father or elder brother of the children you're teaching."

"I should never allow them to become over-familiar with me."

Charles smiled at her confidence; then he looked more grave. "There could be instances, my dear, where you might not be able to prevent them from doing so. Do you have any admired youth in mind that you would like to marry if you could?"

Starella was startled. Then she shook her head. "Nobody I know at present is suitable."

Charles smiled again. "There are sure to be some interesting guests at our reception. Maybe some suitable young man will meet you there."

"I very much doubt it." Starella's tone was a little haughty. She did not like to think this was another convenient way of removing her presence from the household.

"Martin Alders will be there."

"Who the devil is he?"

Mountjoy frowned. "I wish you would watch your language, Starella."

"I could swear much more, if I had a mind to."

Charles sighed, half-amused, half exasperated. "You are incorrigible at times, Starella. Don't be too forward—young men don't all like it. Martin Alders is our new Riding Officer who is replacing Edwin Randall."

"Is he?" Starella asked, without much interest.

"I'm sure there are many young men you will enchant at the reception although you think otherwise. Martin Alders will most likely be one of them."

"I'm not a witch or a fairy who can put spells on men."

The captain smiled again. "No, just a little fey, like your mother. You're not in danger of being burnt at the stake for it, nowadays."

Starella could not repress a shudder. She remembered some of the gruesome tales she had been told in her childhood by some of the villagers.

"I'm sorry," said Charles. "I shouldn't have mentioned such an unpleasant topic. I think we're both now in need of some refreshment to drink to the future, whatever it may hold."

Starella knew she would welcome a drink. She waited eagerly for it as Captain Mountjoy rang a bell for a servant to bring them two glasses of his best wine.

CHAPTER 3

▼

Lights from the crystal chandeliers which had been cleaned by the servants in the early morning, shone from the windows of the master ship builder's house. Carriages arrived and the guests, mostly of the minor gentry and some of the "middling sort" poured out of them, to be swallowed up by the house.

In the ballroom, a small orchestra was assembled, and the musicians were tuning up their instruments. The bright colours and rich materials of the guests' clothes together with the women's jewellery sparkled in the candlelight.

The servants watched from the doorway, chattering quietly about the guests in a way that the visitors would not all have found flattering. The staff had been promised any leftover food from the meal they would serve later in the evening. They would eat after the guests' dishes had been cleared away. A gypsy fiddler had been engaged to play for the servants in the kitchen. Captain Mountjoy had also given his permission for them all to rise an hour later than usual the next day although his wife disapproved. He had, however, gained in popularity with his staff.

The twins did not usually dress in an identical manner now they were grown women but tonight they both wore blue silk polonaise gowns. The only difference was that Augusta's dress was a slightly darker shade of blue. Starella had helped to embroider the panniers of the gowns. Catherine, for once, had praised her work. In an unusual fit of generosity, she had allowed the modiste's assistants to make a new dress of green lutestring for Starella. Usually, the girl adapted the twins' cast-off dresses to fit herself.

With some justification, all three young women had admired themselves in their mirrors, thinking they looked very fine.

"Look at him, what a fop!" Starella said, amused, indicating a young man who had just arrived. The dandy's powdered wig with long curls stood really high on his head and his face was well rouged and a red Spanish leather patch had been carefully placed on his cheek. There were large buttons on his scarlet satin coat.

"He's what they call a 'Macaroni,'" said Allegra. "I believe they're more common in London."

"I know him," Augusta said, frostily. "His is the first name on your dance card, Starella."

Starella felt her spirits sink.

The orchestra began to play with the conductor announcing that the first dance would be a cotillion. Starella, partnered by the Macaroni, joined the captain, Catherine, Allegra and Augusta with their respective fiancés, in a square. Starella wondered if the Macaroni's buckles on his thin leather shoes might tear her pale green stockings. His linen was scented and his body heavily perfumed.

"You're very graceful," he said, in a high-pitched voice.

"Thank you," Starella replied, tempted to tell him her mother had been a dancer. She deliberately bit the words back.

"The colour of your gown matches your lovely eyes."

"I thank you once again, sir." Starella could not quite bring herself to return a compliment about his own appearance.

"Quite a sight for sore eyes, was he not, Ellie?" Charles said, trying hard to hide his own amusement although his eyes were twinkling. Then he looked sly. "You might have an admirer there."

Starella shook her head. "I don't think he's quite to my liking, Uncle Charles. I should probably find it difficult to perfume his linen adequately."

Charles smothered a laugh.

Then, the captain announced that it was time for supper in the dining room. Afterwards, although the dancing would continue in the large parlour, anyone who felt inclined to do so, could play cards in one of the drawing rooms. A long, very large mahogany as well as a few small tables had been set up by the servants especially for this purpose.

Some people appeared to be cheered by this news; others did not seem particularly interested. Starella was relieved to see that the Macaroni was one of those who seemed attracted to the idea of gaming.

Two more guests, both young and male, arrived, apologising to Captain Mountjoy for being late. They both said they had been delayed by pressing urgent business.

Both of the newcomers were tall and slim although the Salt Officer dwarfed the Riding Officer when they stood side by side. They were introduced respectively to the assembled company as Roland Chivers and Martin Alders.

"You are just in time for supper, gentlemen," Charles announced. He gestured to his wife and daughters to come nearer, then sent a servant to fetch Starella who was on the other side of the room.

"This is my—er—" He searched for the correct word. "My ward, Miss Starella Denny."

Both servants of the Crown said that they were pleased to make her acquaintance. They appeared to be staring at her but she did not mind. She dipped a slight curtsey and studied them discreetly.

Roland Chivers was dark haired with dark eyes and a light olive complexion. He looked away from her to survey the room, squaring his shoulders and raising his head a fraction. He was handsome but observing his stance and expression, Starella wondered if, on occasion, he was a little arrogant.

Martin Alders was grinning at the sight of the Macaroni. Starella warmed to him as she had already decided he had a most pleasant face. She was not, however, prepared for Mountjoy's next words.

"You will be seated next to Starella at supper, Mr Alders. Will you show him the way to the dining room if you please, Starella."

Martin Alders offered her his arm. "It's a pleasure to have so lovely a companion." To her annoyance, Starella felt herself dimpling as she thanked him.

In the dining room, she discovered that Roland Chivers would be seated on her other side. She was not at all displeased to sit next to two such attractive young gentlemen.

"I believe you hail from the West Indies, Mr Chivers," said a young lady seated nearby. "Are any of your family planters? I have heard some of them are very wealthy."

Roland shook his head. "You're quite right, ma'am. Some of them are rich but my own father is not. He owns a shipyard where he builds and repairs boats. He also supplies rum to seamen who pull in and out of the harbour."

"Oh, I see," the girl said, obviously disappointed.

"My father traded with our host, Captain Mountjoy who, I might add, very kindly helped me to obtain my present post as a Salt Officer."

"I should love to see the West Indies," Starella exclaimed. "I have an uncle there whom I have never met." She saw Charles and Catherine both frown but was determined to tell the truth about her uncle's situation, if she were asked.

Roland turned to her, smiling. She suddenly felt an incomprehensible shyness in his presence. "I used to help with my father's business but as he now has a capable assistant, I asked if I could leave for a little while and he said I could."

"That was generous of him," Starella murmured.

"Yes, it was. My father was of mixed parentage; he had an English father and a French mother. My own mother was English and I wished to see the land of her birth."

"I hope you are finding it to your liking, apart from the cold."

"I assure you I am, especially now."

Roland looked at Starella intently. She was annoyed with herself for blushing slightly.

"I hope you will have a lot more success in catching the smugglers than our last Riding Officer, Mr Alders," Charles said. "He was a local man and I have to say, he could be a little corrupt. He was prepared now and again to accept bribes from the gangs to turn a blind eye to their affairs."

Martin nodded. "You can be assured, sir that I have no intention of ignoring their actions for any reason whatsoever."

There were a few discreetly exchanged looks between people who had no aversion whatsoever to receiving contraband goods.

"I admire your integrity, Mr Alders," Roland said. He looked thoughtful. "I must admit, however, that I always turned a blind eye to knowing the whereabouts of runaway slaves who escaped from the plantations."

"Did you think that was—er—wise?" Mountjoy asked. "Maybe they could have murdered their previous owners."

A few of the ladies enjoyed a delicious shiver so that they could be comforted by their admirers.

"With respect, sir, that could happen. But their fate was so terrible when they were re-captured that I did not have the heart to consign them to it."

"I'm sure blackamoors do not feel pain as much as us, Mr Chivers. After all, they're not much higher than animals," the Macaroni said.

Roland looked annoyed. "Have you ever seen or spoken to a negro?"

The dandy smoothed his cuffs, looking a little uncomfortable. "I must confess I have not, Mr Chivers."

"I saw a black coachboy in Southampton once. I nearly mistook him for a human being," Starella said, deliberately keeping her face straight. Charles and Catherine frowned once again. She saw Martin Alders glance at her and smile and Roland Chivers hid a smile.

"Surely you're not one of these mad, radical reformers who would abolish slavery altogether, Mr Chivers," another gentleman said. "It would impoverish so many."

Roland gave an extremely slight shrug. "I feel it's an evil in many ways but unfortunately, almost a necessary one. I have to admit many of the slaves were captives who might well have been killed or enslaved anyway, in Africa. They came from tribes which have been conquered. The chiefs sold them on to the white traders."

"Poor things," Starella whispered. She was startled when Roland managed to squeeze her hand under cover of the table.

Later, Starella danced a minuet with Martin Alders. He pushed back a lock of his brown hair as he led her on to the floor; then he glanced behind him giving Starella the impression that there was a hint of amusement in his grey eyes.

"The fop seems to be rather annoyed with me for partnering you so he's stalking off to play cards. I hope he plays a favourable hand. I shall be terrified he might call me out otherwise."

He winked, making Starella laugh aloud. Quite a few heads, including Catherine's, turned in her direction so she tried to look demure. Roland Chivers appeared to be frowning slightly. She hoped she had not given him a bad impression, then wondered why she was bothered about what he thought of her when she was enjoying having an admirer pay attention to her. The conductor announced that the next dance would be a country one called 'Split the Willow' which pleased quite a lot of people.

As Starella danced with Roland, she decided he was quite the most handsome young man she had ever seen although he did not make much conversation, seeming to be a little distracted. Starella wondered if he liked her; she very much hoped he did.

When she retired to bed, tired yet happy, she was hoping she would see Martin Alders again, soon. He had been attentive to her all evening in a most flattering way. Yet, after falling asleep, all her dreams were of Roland Chivers.

CHAPTER 4

▼

Late the following morning, Martin Alders rode to Captain Mountjoy's house. Starella remembered having seen Charles draw Martin aside for a brief, quiet word at the reception. She wondered what had been said to him.

"I have brought you some flowers, Miss Starella," he said, shyly.

She was touched. "They're beautiful. Thank you very much for giving them to me. They have a lovely scent, too. I'll fetch a vase and arrange the flowers in it."

When she had done this, Charles said, "I have invited Mr Alders to come for a picnic with us in the Forest. Fortunately, the weather is fine."

Starella was delighted.

Ainsworth, the groom, carried the food hamper and spread its contents out upon the grass. After they had eaten, Starella said she would like to go for a walk.

"I'm afraid I'm too tired to come with you," said Charles.

"So am I," Catherine agreed.

"I'm too comfortable to move," Allegra said.

Augusta was apologetic. "And me, I'm afraid."

"I'll go on my own, then," Starella said. "As nobody else wants to come."

"Might I accompany Miss Starella?" Martin asked Charles.

Mountjoy hesitated. "Very well, but only for ten minutes. You go, too, Ainsworth."

Martin looked disappointed.

They strolled in an old wood of pollard beeches, Ainsworth a discreet few paces behind them. "I start work this evening," Martin said. "It's most pleasant to spend the day outdoors."

"I'm very glad you came out with us today, Mr Alders," said Starella.

He smiled at her warmly, then sighed after glancing at his watch. "I'm afraid we must rejoin the others because our time is up. But I do hope we can have other times we can walk together."

Starella hoped so, too, but said nothing.

"Let's go to the 'Barleycorn' for some more refreshment," Charles said. "This warm day's making me really thirsty. Do you all agree?"

Everyone said they did. "It's part of my duties to examine inns and taverns," said Martin.

"Surely you can forget about your work for a little while, Mr Alders," Catherine said, ignoring her husband's frown.

"Yes, I can. Please forgive me for talking about it," said Martin, looking embarrassed. Starella felt sorry for him.

"I expect your work can be fascinating, Mr Alders," she said.

"It can be—interesting," Martin replied, with a wry smile.

As the company were crossing the threshold of the ancient inn, the 'Sir John Barleycorn', before going to their private parlour, they saw a tall man engaged in the supervision of the weighing and recording of goods a carrier had brought in. The little crowd standing around him seemed to be on the sullen side.

"I believe that's Mr Chivers, the new Salt Officer, who came to our reception," Allegra said, with great interest. Catherine and Augusta glanced at him briefly, then looked away while Starella gazed closely at the young man. She thought he was returning her look, then dismissed it as probably a figment of her imagination.

"I want a private word with Mr Chivers," said Mountjoy. "Mr Alders, would you kindly escort the ladies upstairs?"

Somewhat reluctantly, Starella allowed herself to be led to the private parlour.

*   *   *   *

The next morning, Charles said to Starella, "Go to the stables. You'll find a surprise gift there."

Excited, she hurried to the stables.

"The captain decided you was to 'ave a pony of your own, Miss Starella," Ainsworth said.

Starella gasped with delight. Catherine had ensured her own daughters had been taught to ride but had felt that riding was an unnecessary accomplishment for Starella.

"It's the chestnut mare what's yours. Do you want to stroke her?"

"Of course I do. Isn't she lovely, Ainsworth?"

Ainsworth checked a desire to shrug. "Yes, she is."

"I shall call her 'Russet' because of her colour."

"As you like, Miss."

"I do like, very much indeed! I'll be back for a ride soon."

Starella picked up her skirts and ran back into the house. She flung her arms around Mountjoy's neck, causing Catherine and Allegra to frown. Augusta smiled.

"I can't thank you enough for my beautiful pony, Uncle Charles."

"You're welcome, Starella."

"But Starella cannot ride as Mama did not believe it necessary for her to learn. I'm sure she's never even been seated on a horse's back in her entire life," Allegra protested.

Starella was indignant. "I assure you you're mistaken, Allegra. The grooms often used to let me sit on the horses' backs for a few moments when I was small, after you and Augusta had gone for your ride."

"Ainsworth will teach you how to ride properly, Starella," Charles said, firmly, anxious to avoid a quarrel.

"You'll need a riding habit before you start," Catherine said, her disapproval obvious.

"I have an old habit you can borrow if you like," Augusta said.

"Thank you so much, you're very kind." Augusta sent her maid to fetch it.

The maid brought Starella the green velvet riding habit. She tried it on, relieved to find it was a good fit.

"It suits you," Augusta said.

Starella thanked her again.

*   *   *   *

Starella threw herself into her riding with eager enthusiasm. Ainsworth told the captain she was making excellent progress. She often liked to ride to Topcliffe Beach.

Catherine and her daughters said nothing about it but Mountjoy commented, "I wouldn't say this in Catherine's hearing, Starella, but I truly believe it's your gypsy blood which has made you take so naturally to the saddle. I now wish you had been taught to ride as a child."

Starella nodded, giving him a wistful smile. "No matter. I am now learning what I missed when I was younger and loving every minute of it."

Looking a little embarrassed, Charles deliberately changed the subject.

*   *   *   *

Martin Alders was often invited to take tea at the Mountjoy home where he was always made welcome. He took an interest in Starella's riding progress and often discussed horses with her. Martin was invited to be a guest at the twins' wedding. He accepted the invitation gratefully.

"I think we should encourage young Alders' attentions to Starella," Charles said to Catherine, as they were lying in bed one night.

"Yes, I agree. She could do a lot worse especially as she was so wayward over our other plans for her. He's about the correct station in life for her."

Charles smiled in the darkness, knowing a riding officer would not have been considered a good match for their own daughters. "He'd be doing well for himself. We often tend to forget Starella is a squire's daughter."

"And a gypsy wench's." Catherine's tone was tart.

Charles sighed quietly as memories of Starella's mother, Rosina, swept over him. He closed his eyes, pretending to sleep.

*   *   *   *

The twins' wedding day was dry but cool. Allegra and Augusta wore matching dresses of ivory brocade embroidered by Starella with small flowers in pink, blue and green. Their bridegrooms were adorned in blue satin coats and white shirts embroidered in silver with lace ruffles.

"They look so fine and handsome," Catherine said, wiping a tear from her eye.

"Indeed, they do," her husband agreed. He looked at Starella with approval. "And you are also looking beautiful."

Catherine tried hard not to frown as Starella beamed and thanked the captain warmly for his kind words. She had made herself a cream satin gown with a matching spotted satin cloak from lengths of material Catherine had given her.

Roland Chivers asked Starella to dance. She could see that Martin Alders was reluctant about the idea but could do nothing about it without causing an unwelcome scene.

"I hope you are enjoying the wedding, Mr Chivers."

"Very much. I believe I may be dancing at yours shortly."

Startled, she looked up at him in bewilderment. "Mine?! I know nothing of this."

"Do forgive me if I have spoken out of turn, Miss Denny. I was under the impression that there was some sort of an understanding between yourself and Mr Alders."

To her horror, Starella was blushing. "I—I am not quite sure how Mr Alders feels about such a matter. It's maybe a little early to be thinking about such things."

"Please forgive my indiscretion. Captain Mountjoy dropped some hints that you might become betrothed."

Starella laid her hand on Chivers' arm in a pleading gesture. "I should prefer you not to repeat this conversation to Mr Alders."

"I assure you my lips will be sealed." Roland lifted her hand to his lips and kissed it, causing her to draw back a little. She thanked him in a slightly stammering way of which she was a little ashamed. Then, she rejoined Martin Alders.

Starella enjoyed the rest of the celebrations. Although she tried, she could not quite dismiss Roland's words from her mind. She was honest enough to know she had found them slightly disturbing.

Deliberately, she flicked her fan and engaged in light banter with Martin.

CHAPTER 5

▼

When the twins visited their parents a month later, their father said, with a twinkle in his eye, "I do believe the next marriage we see will be between Mr Martin Alders and Miss Starella Denny."

Allegra raised her eyebrows. "Really, Papa? Has he asked you for her hand?"

Her father shook his head. "Not yet but I very much hope he will do so."

"Do you think you should—well—speak to him about it?" Augusta asked.

"Surely it's still a little early," said Starella, her tone sharper than she intended. She had been hoping for a proposal from Martin but was concerned about her hopes being dashed to the ground.

"You'd be very lucky if you made such a match, Starella. I should not like the matter to be delayed for too long."

'She's still anxious to be rid of me,' Starella thought, bitterly.

"Starella should outgrow her hoydenish ways before she marries instead of tearing about all over the place on her pony like she does," said Allegra.

Glaring at her, Starella was about to retort when Augusta spoke quickly. "I should love you to marry Mr Alders, Ellie. It would be romantic to dance at your wedding." She gave her sister a hostile look then glanced more timidly in her parents' direction.

Starella felt a lump in her throat. "Thank you Gussie. I'll always be grateful to you for your kind words."

A maid announced that Mr Alders had just called. After refreshments had been served, he said, "Might Mrs Augusta and Mrs Allegra and Miss Starella and I all go for a ride, Captain Mountjoy?"

Charles smiled. "My daughters will shortly be returning to their husbands' houses. They were only making a morning call."

Martin's face fell.

"But," Charles added. "You may go out for a ride with Starella for no longer than half an hour, providing our groom, Ainsworth, accompanies you."

"Will you not be coming as well, uncle?" Starella asked.

Mountjoy shook his head. "No, I'll leave it to you young people."

"Thank you very much, sir," said Martin.

"Thank you, uncle."

Martin and Starella exchanged delighted smiles.

*   *   *   *

Martin watched the late autumn sun shine on Starella's chestnut hair. It also brought a glow to the high cheekbones of her smooth apricot skin. He felt a surge of affection for her. Her voice cut in on his thoughts.

"Where are you taking me, Mr Alders?"

"To the Forest, if you're agreeable."

"Of course, I don't mind where I go. But I love the Forest."

"I know."

Ainsworth's eyebrows rose; then he deliberately made his face impassive.

Martin helped Starella dismount and offered her his arm. "Let's go for a stroll." He gave Ainsworth a pointed look.

"Ainsworth, could you leave us on our own for a few minutes?" Starella asked.

Ainsworth shook his head. "Sorry, Miss, but I'm under very strict orders not to let you out of my sight, even for a moment."

"Miss Starella needn't be out of your sight, Ainsworth," Martin said, desperately. "But I do have something private to say to her so I shouldn't like it to be overheard by anyone else."

"All right, sir," Ainsworth said, after initial reluctance. He stepped aside so that he was out of hearing range of their voices although he ensured that he still had a clear view of them both.

Martin took Starella's hand. "Miss Starella, you must know I have become very fond of you. In fact—I—" He began to stammer.

Starella felt a thrill of pleasure. "Please don't be nervous with me, Mr Alders," she said, gently.

Martin blushed. "I think I can truthfully say I love you."

"Are you sure you've known me long enough to believe that?"

"Indeed, I have, almost from the first day I saw you. Therefore, I am asking you to do me the great honour of becoming my wife."

"You have honoured me by asking. But surely asking Uncle Charles first would be the proper thing to do."

Martin almost looked coy. "I have already asked his permission. He's agreeable provided you are."

"Yes, I am. I should love to become your wife."

Martin beamed. "You have made me the happiest man alive."

He took her in his arms and began to rain passionate kisses upon her. Starella felt as if all the breath would be knocked out of her slim body when Ainsworth almost ran over to them.

"Beg pardon sir and ma'am, but we really must get back now. Captain's orders, you understand."

Martin was crestfallen but Starella said, brightly, "Uncle Charles will be so happy for us when we tell him our news. Aunt Catherine, Augusta and even that sourpuss, Allegra, will probably also be pleased." She wanted to sing and dance for joy but restrained the impulse.

On the way back, they passed Roland Chivers. After greeting them, Martin told Roland of their news. Starella felt he really should have waited until he had told her adoptive family before informing anybody else but she was too happy to protest. She was not sure if she saw a shadow pass across Chivers' face. Nevertheless, he spoke pleasantly.

"You have my congratulations, Alders."

"Thank you. I know I'm one of the luckiest fellows, alive."

Roland turned to Starella. "And of course, Miss Denny, I hope that you'll be very happy. Though I'm sure you will be."

Starella smiled at him. "You're too kind, Mr Chivers."

"Not at all. Good day to you both."

He rode away with a farewell wave.

$$* \qquad * \qquad * \qquad *$$

A maid admitted Martin Alders to Starella's presence. She offered him refreshment, which he gratefully accepted. "Martin," she said, "Uncle Charles has gone to Portsmouth on business and Aunt Catherine has gone to visit a farm labourer's wife whose husband was killed by a mad bull."

Martin's eyes lit up. "So we're on our own."

Starella laid a pleading hand on his sleeve. "Please may we ride to Topcliffe Beach before the afternoon is over. I have a strong fancy to go there. I don't know why."

Martin looked surprised but agreed. Starella sent for the maid, telling the girl to instruct Ainsworth to saddle up Russet and to tell him he would be required to come on a ride as the maid would be coming herself. She could ride pillion behind Ainsworth. The girl looked pleased, excited at the thought of a ride.

"H'm," the maid muttered to herself as she hurried to the stables. "I wonder if you realise Marcus Rose will most likely be abroad tonight, Mr stuck up ridin' officer."

Martin led Starella behind some cliffs where they sheltered, Ainsworth and maid a discreet distance away.

As they were sitting in a companionable silence, with Martin's arm around Starella's shoulders, they watched the ships just before dusk was falling. Martin looked away from the sea and down at the sand. "I think I can see something down there. It's probably not of much interest but I'll look, anyway." He stretched down to pick the object up. Starella looked at it.

"It's a red, coral necklace," she said, with some excitement. "I remember my mother saying she had one she loved but it was unfortunately lost."

Martin smiled. "I'll get it cleaned up for you; then you can wear it at our betrothal ball."

Starella beamed. "Uncle Charles was so kind to suggest it. Aunt Catherine and I have been busy making arrangements for the ball. She's been more pleasant to me than ever before in her life."

"I'm glad to hear it but I should like to give you real jewels."

"No, they cost too much money," she said, gently. "Anyway, I assure you, this necklace will mean as much and more to me."

Dusk was beginning to fall. Martin gave Ainsworth a small bribe to make himself scarce. He did the same with the maid, asking her to search for seashells so that they could decorate a jewellery box for Starella.

Martin took Starella in his arms and kissed her, caressing the smooth skin of her face. He lifted her down from the cliff and gently laid her on the sand. "I know we should wait until we're married. But you're so lovely, I can't wait any longer to make you mine, my love. You do understand?"

Starella nodded. "Do what you like with me."

He undressed her, slowly and carefully. Then he unbuttoned his own breeches. He cupped her breasts in his hands, kissing them while she ran her hands over his back and shoulders.

"You'll have to help me," she murmured. "I've never lain with a man before."
She saw the lovelight shining in his eyes and was warmed by it.

"I know you haven't, sweetheart. Don't worry, I'll try not to hurt you." He moved his hand down to her thighs. "Open your legs a bit more, darling. Don't be afraid to." He kissed her gently to make her more relaxed; then his kisses grew more passionate.

Starella felt a sharp pain when Martin first entered her. She cried out but when he took her again immediately afterwards, she felt as if she were almost melting in his arms, giving a cry of pleasure as they reached a mutual climax.

"I know it's most improper of me to say this," Starella said. "But I'm glad we didn't wait until we were married."

"We'll have many nights of pleasure, then," said Martin. "I suppose I shouldn't say this but I don't have the slightest objection to you being improper." They smiled warmly at each other.

"There's a lot of stars in the sky tonight," Starella said, looking up with a contented sigh after they had dressed.

Martin smiled. "You're my favourite star. My 'Star of the Forest'."

"That's the loveliest name I've ever been called. My mother said she called me after the stars she'd seen the night I was born."

"She made a wise choice. Oh, damn, here is Ainsworth." Martin was visibly irritated. The groom was rushing up to them in a state of panic.

"Mr Alders, haven't you seen what's happening out at sea?" Ainsworth looked slyly at Starella. "No, I suppose you have not."

Martin followed the direction of the groom's pointing finger. Groups of men were disembarking from a cutter and a lugger into rowing boats. "I expect they're well armed," Ainsworth said.

Martin looked worried. "Quick, Ainsworth, we've no time to waste. We must take Miss Starella home. I'll come back here, later."

When they reached Captain Mountjoy's house, Starella clutched Martin's sleeve. "Please, Martin, you say you love me. So please don't go back to the beach, for my sake."

"I'm going to get others to help me, my love. Just go to bed now and don't worry about me."

"How can I help but worry about you when you could be in great danger?" Starella snapped.

He disengaged her, giving her a little push into the house. "Do as I say. You have to understand, Starella, that I have to do my duty when it's necessary."

Starella bit her lip, determined not to let him see her weep.

CHAPTER 6

▼

Starella was frantic. "I must help Martin."

"With respect, Miss Starella," the maid said, "I think it was the Marcus Rose gang on their way to the beach this night. What can a maid like you do against such as them?'

Starella's suspicions were aroused. "They were too far away to see clearly, Janet Clark. Were you told smuggling would take place tonight? If so, by whom?"

Janet looked scared. "No, ma'am. It was just that there was such a lot of them. I thought it must be the Marcus Rose gang."

Starella had heard of Marcus Rose and knew his tall figure by sight. He was known to have bought land and farms upon which he had built cellars and tunnels.

"You'd better be telling the truth for your own sake, Janet. Is it true that Rose exacts revenge upon any farmer who refuses to lend his gang a horse or let them store contraband?"

"It's true, Miss Starella. They can get their crops burned or I've even 'eard in one or two cases, Marcus Rose has been known to murder people. They say there's a trapdoor in the floor of the dining room in his own 'ouse. It leads to a cellar where him and his gang can escape from all the secret doors and passages."

Starella put her head in her hands. "And poor Martin will be riding straight into a viper's nest."

"Please, Miss Starella, please go to bed like Mr Alders told you to. There's nothing you can do."

Starella sighed. "I suppose you're right, Janet."

Janet Clark went to the servants' quarters. She whispered to her lover, a foot-man. "The long nose may get it tonight, at last."

The footman looked around, cautiously. "Good, with a bit of luck, we'll get another one we can bribe once we're rid of him."

"Then, maybe you'll get me some silk and lace."

"I might, if you're a good girl." Janet Clark giggled.

"Hush, you silly bitch. Don't let the others hear us."

Starella tossed and turned, unable to sleep. Then she decided upon a plan of action; foolish or not, she would undertake it. She felt frustrated when she heard Catherine returning. Starella waited until she was sure Catherine was in bed her-self. She mentally crossed her fingers that Catherine had fallen asleep.

As quietly as she could, Starella rose, putting on a warm dressing gown and picking up a pair of riding boots. Over her arm, she carried a long, red cloak. She crept down the stairs in her bare feet. When she reached the bottom, she put the riding boots on. Then, Starella found a purse of money in a drawer. She took three gold sovereigns out of it.

Wrapping her cloak around her, Starella ran over to the stables. "Ainsworth, I'll give you a gold sovereign if you find me a groom's clothes to put on. Then, take me to Topcliffe Beach and bring any weapons you have. Any guns, knives, anything."

Ainsworth was astonished, as were his open mouthed grooms. "Miss Starella, I cannot let you do this. The captain would never forgive me if I put your life in danger."

Starella held out the other gold sovereign. "If you do as I ask and take me there, I'll give you one gold sovereign now and the other when we get to the beach."

Ainsworth hesitated, sorely tempted. Finally, he said, "Miss Starella, do you promise to take the blame if anything goes wrong? Will you explain to the cap-tain that I was merely actin' on your orders?"

"Of course."

Ainsworth whispered to a groom, a youth of slender build.

"Turn your backs, all of you while I'm putting these clothes on," said Starella.

*   *   *   *

The smugglers were swarming on to the beach. Some carried flaming torches. Others carried clubs of holly or ash. "They're the 'batmen'," Ainsworth whispered, from behind the shelter of the cliff where he and Starella were watching. Starella tried to see Martin. "They'll swing if they're found with barkin' irons."

Starella shuddered. She knew Ainsworth was referring to guns. He had brought a blunderbuss and a knife. "When I was a child, I once saw some smugglers and highwaymen hanging from the 'Wilverley Oak.' The sight haunted me for quite a while afterwards and gave me nightmares."

"I know the tree you speak of, miss. It's near Burley. They'll probably put some of their goods in the 'Queen's Head' Inn, there." Ainsworth put a finger to his lips. "We must be as quiet as we can. They're gettin' nearer."

They saw bales of silk and lace being loaded on to ponies' backs. Tobacco and tea were put in pouches and tied to their sides, then cloth was tied to their feet.

Then Starella saw Martin Alders arrive with the sheriff and a posse of men. They began to arrest the smugglers but a few managed to escape to the rowing boats. One drew out a pistol, aiming it at Martin.

Without thinking, Starella snatched the blunderbuss off Ainsworth and rushed to the beach, ready to fire it at Martin's assailant even though she had never used such a weapon before.

Starella heard a shot ring out and raced in its direction. "Damn her bloody eyes!" Ainsworth swore under his breath. "She got away before I could stop her. And the stupid slut didn't give me my extra guinea." He decided to make himself scarce.

Starella was about to fire the blunderbuss when another shot rang out and she saw Martin Alders fall. Screaming, she began to run over to his side. The next sight she saw almost unhinged her mind. Two men appeared from behind a cliff. They picked up Martin Alders' inert body, raced with it to the sea, dodging the Revenue men's bullets. But just before they were about to board a rowing boat, two of the Revenue men caught up with them and they were arrested. One of them hurriedly threw Martin's body into the salt water.

Starella ran to the water's edge where she could just about see the smuggler who had fired at Martin rowing away. Another man was in the boat with him. She fired the blunderbuss in a clumsy way and it missed its mark. She tried to fire a second shot, but another male hand grabbed her around the neck. Starella tried to free herself but the man's grasp was too strong for her.

"You idiotic lad, you're running straight into the line of fire. Do you want to get yourself killed? One death's enough, surely. I've never seen such a bad shot. You should leave these matters to the Revenue men who know what they're doing." Angry as the man's tone was, there was something familiar about his voice.

He pulled her head back and her hat fell off. The next minute, her hair lost its confining pins and swirled around her shoulders.

"Good God, I'd know that hair anywhere. Miss Starella Denny!"

"Mr Chivers!"

"I'm sorry I handled you so roughly, Miss Denny. I thought you were some stupid boy trying to take part in men's business."

"No," Starella said, choking back sobs. "I'm a stupid woman trying to interfere in men's business. But I was so worried about Martin being in danger, you see. I felt I needed to help him but I probably made things much worse. Oh, I shall never forgive myself."

"Well, Miss Denny, your action was somewhat—what shall we say?—foolhardy to say the least. But you were very brave. I must get you home, away from here."

"Please don't bother about me. I have only myself to blame for my foolishness. I'll walk home."

"You'll do no such thing. It would be much too dangerous." He called to a boy. "Tell the sheriff I have to take a young lady home but don't say you heard me call her by name. Here's sixpence for you if you run as fast as you can." The youth sped away on gangling legs.

"I was called out as one of the sheriff's posse," said Chivers. "I think he's had a fairly successful night, managing to arrest most of the Marcus Rose gang although not Rose himself. I'm sorry about Mr Alders, of course."

Starella bit her lip, hoping she would not disgrace herself further by breaking into noisy sobs.

Roland offered her his arm; she took it, finding comfort in it. Then he escorted her to a closed carriage waiting near the beach. He told the coachman not to spare the horses because they must reach Captain Mountjoy's house as fast as they could. "But my pony, Russet. I don't know what's happened to her!" Starella exclaimed. "The smugglers must have her. They will probably ill treat her as they did poor Martin!" She turned away to hide her tears.

Roland put his hand on top of hers. "I know this has been a terrible night for you, Miss Denny. Believe me, I do understand how you must be feeling. Don't worry, I know what your pony looks like. I'll search for her later and get her back for you."

"Mr Chivers, I really don't know how to thank you."

Roland gave a rueful smile. "Don't try to, at the moment."

"I shall be forever in your debt."

"I'm sure others would have done the same had they found you in the plight you were in."

"Not everybody would have been as kind as you, Mr Chivers."

"Ah, here we are at Captain Mountjoy's house, Miss Denny. I'll help you dismount."

"Starella!" Charles and Catherine both exclaimed in horror when they saw her tear-ravaged face, the way she was dressed and her dishevelled state.

"We have been worried half out of our minds about you. I think you owe us an explanation," the captain said, sternly.

"Please, sir," said Roland. "Miss Denny has suffered a terrible shock tonight. I really think she should be in bed with a hot brick and a sleeping draught. If I might have a private word with you, Captain Mountjoy, I'll let you know what's happened."

Mountjoy looked dubious for a minute. "Very well, Mr Chivers, come to my study with me. Catherine, can you send a lad for the doctor and a maid to attend to Starella."

Catherine rang the bell rope. The housekeeper came into the parlour. "Send Janet Clark to help Miss Starella to bed."

The housekeeper looked worried. "With respect, ma'am, Janet Clark is nowhere to be found."

"Send another girl then!" Catherine snapped.

Starella began to sway. "Let us help you sit down, Starella, before you faint away on us," Catherine said, her tone uncharacteristically gentle. She and the housekeeper gently pushed the exhausted girl into an armchair. As the housekeeper was about to depart, she added, "And make doubly sure whoever you send is not the gossiping kind."

Intrigued, the woman hurried away.

CHAPTER 7

▼

Starella was allowed to stay in bed for three days. She had her meals sent up to her on a tray but had little appetite. She had sunk into an apathy, her sleep disturbed by frightening dreams.

On the fourth day, Starella was encouraged to rise and dress herself although she was allowed to rise late. After she had breakfasted, picking at her food, she was summoned to Captain Mountjoy's presence in the study.

"Starella, I'm very sorry about what happened to Martin Alders. I know how upset you are and it's quite understandable. But—" Mountjoy threw his hands up in the air. "Whatever possessed you to ride to the beach like that? You should have known a slip of a girl like you would have no chance against a ruthless gang like Marcus Rose's!"

"Martin was in danger. I wanted to help him."

"I thought you had enough common sense to know you would only make matters worse. Obviously you had not."

Starella, flushing with shame, looked down at the floor. "A lot of Rose's gang have been caught and will be executed or transported. But Rose himself is still free, I hear."

Mountjoy sighed. "But I'm worried about your reputation, Starella. If news of your madcap actions are spread abroad, it will be hard to settle you into a decent marriage."

"But I don't want to marry anybody else, Uncle Charles!"

Starella!" Charles snapped. "I've come to the conclusion you need a man to control you. I shall be making discreet enquiries about a suitable husband. But not yet. You had better live very quietly for a while until the rumours about you die down. But Catherine and I will be keeping a close eye on you in future. You may go now."

Feeling that she had been dismissed like a servant, Starella left Mountjoy's presence without a word.

*   *   *   *

Two days later it was cold and wet. Captain Mountjoy had unexpectedly received a visitor and had gone with the other man to his house, to discuss a ship building contract as his guest had forgotten to bring his hand drawn designs with him to the Mountjoys' house. He was anxious for the captain to see them.

Allegra's sister-in-law had given birth to a son. Catherine had been invited to a party at the house after the christening. She put on her red cloak, similar to Starella's. The two women were practically the same height.

"I should be back reasonably early," Catherine said. "So I'll just take a groom rather than travel back in the carriage."

Starella was delighted to have the house to herself apart from the servants. She settled down in a soft armchair, with a contented sigh, to read a novel. Engrossed in her book, Starella suddenly heard screams and shouts. She rushed to the window and looked out.

There were three figures standing in a ring in the distance and she could vaguely make out another man and a woman. One of the men lifted a heavy cudgel, bringing it down over the woman's head. She fell to the ground and as the man standing by her turned, he was also struck with it.

Starella screamed, running outside. "Help, help, murder is taking place!" Servants came running out of the house. Starella faintly heard one of the attacker's say, "Look bloody sharp now, before they start to pry into our business."

"Quick, catch those men!" Starella yelled to the servants.

But they were too late. The felons had leaped on to fast horses and galloped away into the depths of the Forest.

A footman took Starella's arm. "We'd better go and see who's been hurt, miss. Let one of the women take you into the house, Miss Starella."

"No, I'll come with you. I want to see who those poor people are."

The footman looked doubtful, then gave in.

"My God!" said Starella when she was close enough to see the victims. "It's Aunt Catherine and that new young groom!" She looked at the men, a pleading expression in her green eyes. "You must take them inside."

"Of course we will, miss, right away."

As Starella fainted into the nearby footman's arms, he picked her up and carried her into the house. When she came round, the housekeeper and a maid helped her to bed. Blindly, still in shock, she obeyed their orders.

Captain Mountjoy and the surgeon were sent for. After a lot of hard work, the surgeon managed to save the groom but Catherine died a few minutes before her husband returned. The surgeon prescribed plenty of rest for Starella as she had experienced a great shock. He gave her another sleeping draught.

"The second fright she's had in only a little while, poor young lady," said the housekeeper.

*   *   *   *

The morning after Catherine's funeral Captain Mountjoy once again stated that he wished to have a private word with Starella in his study. She went there in great trepidation.

Charles looked grave. "Sit down, Starella and compose yourself, I beg you. The news I have is truly frightening."

"What is it?"

"Have patience while I explain, girl. Janet Clark came to me in distress, confessing that she knows some of Rose's gang well. She believes the man who saw you in your red cloak mistook Catherine for you."

Starella gasped. "How you must hate me, Uncle Charles!"

Mountjoy's tone softened. "No, of course I don't. But I am concerned about your safety. It may just be bravado on the smuggler's part yet Janet says he means to kill anybody who might be able to give evidence against him."

"What should I do? I don't want to put you in danger as well as myself."

"You must be confined to the house. Don't go outdoors at all. The servants will be told to keep a vigilant eye on you. I know it's a harsh decision for a young person but it won't be for long. Do you promise on your honour not to do anything foolish?"

Starella looked down at the floor. "Yes, Uncle Charles."

Charles hesitated. "However, I have been giving the matter some thought. To be on the safe side, it would be best to get you well away from here for a while. I have second cousins in Exeter who own a coffee house. I shall be travelling there to make arrangements for you to live with them."

"Won't they expect payment for my board?"

Mountjoy looked a little embarrassed. "I shall naturally be giving them an initial payment for your keep. But a new venture I'm engaged in is going to cost me a great deal of cash. Therefore, I hope you will be prepared to help them by working for them in the coffee house."

"I vow I'll work hard for them."

Charles looked relieved. "Good girl. Now, as for Janet Clark, she's worried about what Rose's ruffians may do to her if they find out you've escaped them. So I promised her she could come with you, travelling as your maid. Once we have reached the city, however, she'll have to make her own way in it."

The butler suddenly arrived, apologising for intruding. "But Captain Mountjoy, sir, Mr Chivers insists he wants to speak with you and Miss Starella now this minute."

"Very well, we have finished our conversation so we'll see him."

"Forgive me for being so impatient, Captain Mountjoy, Miss Denny. But I don't have much time as I have to report to my superiors soon. I just wanted to let you know I've managed to find Miss Starella's pony, Russet. The poor beast was wandering around the Forest, looking forlorn. I've taken her to your stables."

Starella was delighted. "Mr Chivers, I can't thank you enough." Then her face fell when she remembered she could no longer go outdoors.

"Mr Chivers, we are greatly in your debt," said Charles. "The sheriff praised your courage in helping to catch some of the free traders."

Roland gave a wry smile. "I only tried to do my duty as most men would."

"No, Mr Chivers, as I understand it, you were very brave. Are you able to take some refreshment?"

"I'm sorry, Captain Mountjoy. I'd love a drink. But, unfortunately, I really must go now."

As Roland took his leave of them, he cast a lingering look in Starella's direction. She wished he could have stayed longer.

*   *   *   *

Three weeks later, on a clear morning, Starella and Janet Clark travelled with the captain in his carriage to catch the stagecoach to Exeter.

The coach arrived with all the usual hustle and bustle of passengers dismounting and boarding the vehicle. Most of the other passengers were farmers and their wives with an odd small child in tow. Charles guessed that they would be selling produce at the Friday markets held in Exeter. He also shrewdly surmised that underneath some of the butter, cheese and eggs in the larger baskets would be contraband such as brandy kegs, tobacco, tea and lace.

Starella took a tearful, farewell leave of the captain. "I'll come and see you when I can and you can come back here as soon as things are quieter."

Once she was seated, Starella clutched a doll dressed in Paris fashions which had been given to her by her mother as a birthday present when she was a child. She had also taken her mother's old castanets. "I know you probably think I'm foolish, Janet, acting like a child, bringing these old toys with me. But they remind me of my mother, you see. I wanted something to remind me of her because I'm going to a strange place."

"I don't think you're silly at all, Miss Starella. The doll will probably come in useful."

Starella was not sure if she saw a sly smile play about the corners of Janet's mouth. "What do you mean?"

"Only that it will remind you of your mother, as you said."

Starella fell into a light doze. She was awakened by the jolting of the coach which seemed to be going faster as well as swaying from side to side. As she grasped a leather strap, she looked out of the window, realising they were in the countryside, some miles past Poole.

Starella heard shouting over the furious drumming of horses' hooves. Then a shot rang out and the coach came to a halt.

"Stand and deliver! Your money or your lives!" It was the age-old cry of the highwayman.

"Don't try to fire. There's a gang of us with pistols in the spinneys." As if to confirm the truth of the highwayman's words, more shots rang into the air.

The horses stamped, reared and neighed as commotion broke out within the coach. The coachman and the postillion swore horrible oaths, after deciding that their blunderbusses and small clubs were useless in the prevailing conditions. They cursed the inefficiency of the weapons they had been provided with which were no match for the highwayman's. They were also furious that they were being held up in broad daylight.

Some of the men inside the vehicle swore. One hid under the seat. Some of the women screamed. Sensing the distress of their elders, most of the children cried. Starella was curious but fearful.

The highwayman was heavily masked. He wore a long black cloak and black boots. He sat astride a large brown mare. He was armed with a horse pistol and carried a small leather bag.

The man curtly ordered all of the passengers to alight from the coach, saying they would come to no harm if they surrendered their valuables. To Starella there was something oddly familiar about his voice.

She was startled when he said, "You've done well, Janet. Sammy's over there if you want to join him." He waved towards the spinneys. With a triumphant look at Starella, Janet picked up her skirts and ran in the direction the highwayman had indicated.

The other passengers reluctantly climbed out of the vehicle as with an obviously practised hand, the highwayman took the cumbersome blunderbusses from the coachman and postillion, afterwards commanding them to lie on the ground, face downwards. Then, with his pistol aimed directly at the other men's hearts, he ordered a journeyman to tie their hands behind their backs.

"But I ain't got no rope."

One of the farmer's wives produced some cords and some lace and helped to tie the two men's hands. The coachman began to protest loudly.

"Hold your tongue, you dratted fool. I've got no choice but to do as I'm bid. Keep your mouth shut else you might get all the rest of us killed!"

The highwayman shook his head. "I won't kill none of you as long as you're all sensible." He then relieved the passengers of odd items like coins, pieces of jewellery, brandy kegs, tea, tobacco and lace.

"I'm certain sure none of us is wealthy," a farmer said.

"No matter," the highwayman replied.

"All I can give you is a coral necklace, a doll called Rose and a pair of castanets," said Starella.

"And clothes and trinkets, miss. I've seen all your luggage and I know it belongs to you." The highwayman's tone was sarcastic.

Starella was indignant, in spite of her fear. "How do you know it's mine?"

"I have ways of knowing certain things." He beckoned to a farmer. "Get all her stuff off the coach." The man obeyed with alacrity.

When all Starellas luggage had been unloaded, the highwayman said to the passengers, "Get on your way now, I've done with you."

There was a unanimous sigh of relief. "Except for this maid whose baggage we've just took down. She comes with me."

CHAPTER 8

▼

"You won't come to no 'arm, Starella, as long as you do what you're told. And don't try to run away. Most of the country folk around these parts are in our pay. They don't listen to gossip about what's none of their business."

The familiar use of her name lit the spark of recognition in Starella's mind.

"It is you, is it not? I should never have believed you would have come to this!"

"Never mind what I've come to, Starella. You needn't start to queen it over me like before, madam, 'cause now you're at my beck and call."

"Maybe I am. But you could be caught and hanged for what you are doing."

"I'll not be caught so don't start worryin' your pretty little 'ead on that account."

"Don't be so sure. I know very well that highwaymen can be hanged from high trees in front of gaping crowds. Then, their bodies are cut down to rot and the crows peck out their eyes."

"Damn your own eyes!" Ainsworth slapped Starella hard across the face, causing her to recoil. "I warned you to remember I'm not your groom now."

"Please let me go. I'll give you any money I have and any jewellery. I promise I won't report you to the authorities. I'll tell the next coachman that I fell off the coach I was previously travelling on."

Ainsworth laughed. "You'll do no such thing, maid. I've got other plans for you." He grabbed her arm tightly and half dragged, half carried her over to some thickets. She was still clutching her doll tightly, not knowing why.

Ainsworth whistled and two other men jumped up from a crouching position. Both were swarthy complexioned and dressed in farm labourers' clothing. The pair strongly resembled each other although one was nearly a head taller. Starella correctly guessed they were brothers. They stared at her and she stared back at them, feeling like a rabbit mesmerised by three vicious stoats.

"You've picked a comely 'un, Jack, this dolly you've got with you," the taller one said to Ainsworth. Starella did not like the way he was leering at her. He began to unfasten his breeches, then stepped towards her, placing his hand on her shoulder. Starella flinched. Ainsworth frowned and pushed the other man's hand away. His brother looked puzzled. "Not yet, Billy, leave her alone for now. I might be 'andin' over to Sammy, I ain't decided yet. If I do, he won't want no damaged goods."

The man addressed as Billy looked as if he were about to argue, then reluctantly moved aside.

"You said she was a dolly," said his younger brother. "I can see she's carryin' a baby dolly in her arms. She loves it." He began to laugh at his own weak joke.

"That's enough, Harry!" his brother snapped.

"What you going to do with her now, Jack?" Billy nodded contemptuously in Starella's direction.

"She can 'elp us on the runs by actin' as a decoy."

"What's a decoy, Jack?" Harry asked.

"She'll stop the coaches by pretendin' she wants food or milk for her babe which is really that doll she's bin' clingin' to for some stupid reason."

Starella glared at Ainsworth, about to protest it had sentimental value, but she decided it would be safer to say nothing. He ignored her. "She'll look to see if the coachmen 'ave guns. If they don't, then we'll take over."

Starella listened to his words with horror. She had no wish to lure innocent passengers into a trap. She began to protest but Ainsworth threatened to beat her if she did not agree. Sure he would have no hesitation in doing so, she said nothing more.

"She'll live with your ma to begin with," Ainsworth said. "Show her the way to the wagon, Harry."

Starella was hopeful that she might be able to escape from this wagon, wherever it was, especially if there were only an old woman and herself living there.

"'Arry, whatever else you do, don't let her escape."

"Of course I won't, Jack."

"Did you bring me other clothes?"

"Yes, I did, Jack." Harry was proud. He pointed to a sack. Ainsworth nodded in satisfaction, opened the sack, took the doll out of Starella's hands and handed it to Harry. He then drew out a cord from the sack with which he tied Starella's hands behind her back.

"There's no need to bind me, for Heaven's sake!" she protested.

Ainsworth shrugged. "I have to take precautions." To Harry, he said. "Me and Billy are goin' to the inn after I've changed. You can join us there later when you've took Starella to your mother."

Harry linked his arm through Starella's and began to pull her along. In spite of her predicament, she could not help laughing when she saw that he held her dirty doll under his other arm.

"I knows you likes this doll like it's your own babe," Harry said.

Starella shook her head. "Well, not quite."

"I don't likes to force you but Jack and even Billy would kill me if I didn't do what they say."

"Yes, I can quite believe that," Starella said, grimly.

"We're half-gypsies," Harry said, with not a little pride. "Our mother married a *gorgio* sailor but he was drownded."

Starella almost found herself feeling kinship with Harry. "My mother was a gypsy, too."

"But I thought you was a lady."

Starella smiled. "My father was a gentleman and I was brought up by another gentleman, his friend, after my father died."

"So you was a by …—I forget what they're called."

"No, I'm not a by-blow or a bastard as some call them. My mother and father were married to each other."

Harry looked impressed. "Some say our ma's a witch because she knows 'ow to heal with herbs and such."

"Do you think she's a witch, Harry?"

"No, I don't. And you mustn't, neither."

Starella sighed. "Very well. I believe you. She's not a witch."

"She's known as Mother Maynard. Billy's always bin a bit wilder than me."

'And nastier, too, I expect,' Starella thought but she did not say this to Harry.

"Ma and Jack are the only people what can control Billy," Harry said.

'Oh my God! What condition have I been brought to?' Starella thought. Aloud, she said, "Your mother sounds to be a most interesting lady."

The wagon was brightly painted and much larger than Starella had expected. She had imagined a primitive, hut-sized building. It was situated on the edge of a field which was on the edge of some waste ground outlying a village. At the back of the field was a small wood.

"Show your infant to Ma," said Harry.

Starella smiled, joining in the game. "Her name is Rose, after my mother who was 'Rosina'."

"A nice name."

Starella mounted the wagon's steps. Harry gently pushed her inside.

The interior contained colourful rugs, pictures, cushions. There were two small beds covered with shawls and blankets. Brassware and copper pots shone on the shelves. Billy and Harry's mother sat bolt upright in the exact centre of one of the beds. Starella looked around in great surprise.

"Not quite what you expected, maid, I can tell," Harry said, with a note of pride in his voice. To his mother, he said, "Her name is Ella."

"My true name is Starella."

Harry's mother nodded, saying, "Bring the maiden over 'ere, Harry, a bit nearer so I can see her more plain. My eyes ain't so good as they used to be."

"I'll untie her hands first, Ma." He found a pocketknife and cut the cords binding Starella's wrists, which were red and sore.

"You are beautiful, child. I remember your mother was, too, though she was much darker than you. I think you've lovelier."

"You knew my mother, ma'am?" Starella was startled, almost out of her wits.

"Don't call me ma'am. Call me 'Mother Maynard' like everybody else. Yes, I knew your ma when I was in Squire Denny's service many years ago."

Starella felt as if she had been struck dumb. She studied the older woman whose hair was grey and her complexion lined but she had a pleasant face.

"Your wrists must be painin' you. I'll put some soothin' lotion on 'em so's they'll soon feel better. I knows a lot about healing and I'll try to learn you what I know."

"My mother had knowledge of herbs and suchlike."

"I know, but I have more." Mother Maynard turned to her son. "Leave us now, Harry."

Harry started to depart like an obedient child; then he handed Starella her doll. "Here's your doll." Starella thanked him, strangely touched by his gesture.

Mother Maynard took a tin bowl down from the shelf. Then she gingerly lifted down a tankard of water. "There's some leftover stew in the pot outside. I'll get another fire going and heat it up," Mother Maynard said.

Starella shook her head. "I'm not hungry."

"You must eat to keep your strength up. Come on."

Mother Maynard led Starella a few yards away from the wagon. She picked up a pot from a boulder, indicating to Starella that she should collect twigs. The older woman lit a fire, heating the pot over it, then poured the contents of the pot into the bowl, handing it to Starella. Mother Maynard put the fire out with the water from the tankard.

Starella managed to eat all of the stew.

"Follow me to the stream where you can wash, Ella. But don't, whatever else you do, try to run away. They'll soon catch you and most everybody round these parts, knows me."

The day had become warm as the two women walked to the wood. "For your own good, maid, don't anger Sam Hill."

"Who's Sam Hill?"

"He's kingpin of the 'Gentlemen of the Road'. He's a gentleman what first took to the road to clear his gamblin' debts. But he found he liked it too much to stop." Mother Maynard laughed.

"I believe I heard Ainsworth say 'Sammy's over there,' to Janet Clark."

"Oh yes, Janet Clark's his current doxy. But he'll probably grow tired of her after a while. He runs a lot of whores. They come in useful for sellin' lace neck-cloths and fripperies as well as their other purpose."

Mother Maynard cackled again as Starella felt herself growing cold despite the heat of the day. 'So Janet Clark led me into a trap,' she thought, bitterly.

"You've gone very white, girl."

"I knew Janet Clark, she was our servant."

"And now, you feel betrayed, is that it?"

"Well, yes. I was tricked."

"Look, Ella," Mother Maynard said, "I know today's bin a shock to you, like. But just try to get used to our world and take my advice, then you won't come to no 'arm."

"Please, mother, can you tell me why I've been brought here? Why didn't Ainsworth just kill me and have done with it?"

"You're more use to him alive. Sammy might have plans for you, too. Jack Ainsworth and my sons, especially Billy, might all end up shot or with their necks stretched. They all realise this though they'll never say so."

"Maybe I'll also end up killed or hanged!"

Mother Maynard shook her head. "I don't think so, maid. I've a feeling in my bones you won't. My thoughts usually prove true. You'll be able to aid me with my tasks while you're with me. And if I lose my sons, you'll be company for me, a daughter of sorts, if Sammy lets you."

"Couldn't you persuade your sons to follow honest occupations?"

"Might as well try and tell the wind to stop blowin', Ella, for all the notice they'd take."

The wood was thick with trees and full of wild flowers. Small animals made rustling noises in the undergrowth. The sun made diamond patterns on the small stream where Starella bathed. She liked the feeling of its coolness on her skin. She wondered if she had been dreaming and was now in an enchanted forest. But Mother Maynard's words brought her back to reality.

"Get dressed again now, we'd best not stay too long. There's a well nearby where the free traders 'ides their spoils at times."

Starella guessed that they must ride their ponies through the stream and wondered if she might be able to steal one and ride away to freedom. It was a wild thought but stranger things had been known to happen.

When they returned to the wagon, Mother Maynard took two curtains from off the top of her bed. She asked Starella to help her drape them around the other bed.

Mother Maynard pointed to the bed. "You can lie down now if you like. I expect you're tired by now. I rise early, so will you."

Gratefully, Starella crept behind the curtains, undressed and climbed between the covers. After this strange and eventful day, she expected to remain awake throughout the whole night but she fell asleep immediately.

CHAPTER 9

▼

"I've two wenches come to see me this morn, Starella. Stay in your bed and don't stir while they're 'ere," Mother Maynard said very early one morning, two weeks after Starella had been living with her.

Starella had been given the clothes of a young gypsy woman with long, bright skirts and a scarf covering her head.

"What happened to my clothes that were taken off the coach?" she had indignantly asked Mother Maynard.

"Sammy will have decided what to do with 'em. They probably fetched him a pretty penny."

"Or maybe he gave them to Janet Clark," Starella said, bitterly. Mother Maynard had shrugged. "One dress or cloak p'r'aps. But I doubt there'd be more for her 'cause he'd know very well he can get money for them elsewhere."

Starella helped the older woman with the cooking, also assisting with sewing, collecting herbs for potions and making baskets.

Ainsworth had once come to the wagon and when Mother Maynard had gone outside, he pulled her towards him. Starella tried to push him away but he was too strong for her. He had tried to kiss her but she had twisted away. "Leave me alone!"

"Don't play the fine lady with me, Starella, when you ain't one no more." As he pulled her head round, she gave a loud scream.

He had clapped his hand over her mouth. "That's enough! Just let me do what I want and I won't 'urt you. I shall if you don't so be sensible."

Starella had managed to pull herself away from his grasp. She drew her hand back and slapped his face hard. "Right, I've warned you!" As he had stepped towards her with a threatening expression on his face, Mother Maynard had appeared. She was panting and out of breath. She frowned. "That's enough from you, Jack Ainsworth! Leave the maid be and get out. While she's with me, there'll be none of that sort of thing from you or the others. Or I'll tell Sam."

Starella had noticed that Ainsworth had drawn back with an almost frightened expression on his face. She wondered if he feared Mother Maynard for some reason.

Then, the scared look had gone and he was scowling. "It's about time she come out with us at night."

"She'll do that soon enough. Now leave us."

Starella had been surprised to see Ainsworth obey without question.

"Thank you, Mother," she had gratefully breathed after Ainsworth had gone. "You saved me from a nasty situation, then."

Mother Maynard had shaken her head, looking grave. "I can stop the likes of my boys and Jack Ainsworth from maulin' you. But Sam Hill, now, he's another matter."

"But maybe I'll never meet this Sam Hill."

"You will, maid, count on it."

Starella had not replied, impatiently turning away and busying herself with some sewing.

*   *   *   *

"So, my dear, your master forced you so you say and now you're with child?" Starella heard the voice of a young girl from a nearby village.

"Yes, Mother Maynard, that's right. My pa will kill me if I birth a bastard. He's already beat me because I've been turned off from my post. My old master denies it was him what's the father and after him rapin' me and all!"

"Not fair, I know. But the law won't take no action against a gentleman."

"I know." The girl let out a despairing wail. "What shall I do, mother? I ain't got no reference to go into service again."

"I'll make a brew for you with pennyroyal in it. That'll get rid of the babe."

"Thank you, Mother Maynard. And how shall I find work?"

Starella at first was horrified then she began to consider the girl's plight and to understand how she felt.

"You could try the farms."

"I have. They don't want me, not even for breakin' stones. The old 'ousekeeper's blackened my name."

"Then come to the livery stables at Poole not next Friday night but the one after. Sam Hill might find some use for you."

"Sam Hill? Oh, I don't think I could."

Starella burst out from her hiding place. "Mother Maynard, why not let this girl take my place?"

Roughly, Mother Maynard pushed her back in, pulling the curtain across the bed once more. Starella was taken aback by the older woman's strength. "Do that again, maid, and I'll beat you really 'ard with my broom!" Mother Maynard said. "You two, you've seen nothin in 'ere. There's no other maiden 'ere. If you tell, I'll set my boys and Jack Ainsworth and Sam Hill's own gang on you. Do you understand?"

"Yes, Mother Maynard," they both said in perfect chorus.

"Well now," said Mother Maynard. "If you don't want to work for Sammy, you could go to the next Hiring Fair."

"But I can't wait that long, not till September."

"I'm afraid there's nothing else I can do except to tell you to go and see Sam." Starella heard a long drawn out sigh.

"Now, as for you, my lovely. You say as young Tommy Arnold don't return your love but looks at all the other maids instead. Well, I'll make you a potion but you must understand that it might make Tom mad for you in a way. He'll think about you day and night and want you in his bed. But I can't really promise he'll love you as such. Do you still want it?"

"Oh yes, I do."

"Very well, then. Have you both brought your eggs, cheese, ale and meat for me?"

Again, there was a perfect chorus of "Yes, Mother Maynard."

"And do you both promise you'll never say you seen a young woman in 'ere to a livin' soul?"

"Of course, Mother."

"The Devil himself wouldn't drag it out of me, Mother Maynard."

Mother Maynard laughed. "Old Nick knows me already."

"Do you have the potion, Mother Maynard?" The girl's voice was impatient.

"Here it is. Find an excuse to give it to Tommy to drink."

"I will. Thank you, Mother."

"I'll tell you the recipe just in case you needs more though you probably won't. Take two pints of ale, two teaspoonsful of dried borage, a teaspoon of dried woodruff and one teaspoon of dried chervil. Pour the ale into a jug and stir in the herbs. Then leave it to cool for two hours before strainin' it."

The girl repeated the love potion ingredients to herself before leaving.

"Come on, Jenny. It's time you went, too. Your mixture should do the trick but if it don't, come back and we'll try with a knittin' needle. Don't forget to see Sam Hill about work now." With a reluctant sniff, the girl left the wagon.

"Starella come out and we'll eat now. You're to go on a raid tonight," Mother Maynard said. Her tone was frosty.

Starella emerged from her bed looking anxious. No words passed between the two women as they ate. Mother Maynard ate heartily but Starella had little appetite.

$$*\qquad*\qquad*\qquad*$$

Under cover of darkness, Starella reluctantly accompanied Jack Ainsworth and the Maynard brothers on to the highway. She almost hated them all, even Harry who smiled at her, in order to encourage her.

Starella had her doll, Rose, covered in a shawl, clutched in her arms like a sleeping baby. A coach approached the four cloaked and hooded figures. The three men faded into the background but not before Billy pushed Starella hard in the small of her back.

"Go on maid." His voice hissed into her ear. "Prove your worth."

"No need to be so rough, Billy," said Harry. "I know she'll do her best."

She stepped into the road, held up her hand and in a loud, clear voice called to the coachman to stop.

"Do you, coachman or any of your kind lady passengers have any food to spare for my poor, hungry infant?" she asked. "May I board your coach to find out?"

"Just for one minute and no longer, woman," the coachman said, brusquely.

Starella boarded the coach and gratefully accepted the food a couple of the more kindly women passengers gave to her. She quickly checked to make sure none of the men were armed or had already drawn swords or pistols. As she hastily climbed down from the coach, she waved a white scarf around her head, the agreed signal for the highwaymen. She ran to a nearby tree where she sat on the lowest branch.

'Maybe I should have tried to steal a horse from the coach and ridden away, back to Uncle Charles,' Starella thought. 'But would he take me back, now? And everybody knows there's more danger at night than in the daytime. Mother Maynard watches me like a hawk during the day, never letting me out of her sight except for tonight. Oh, I've been such a fool to let that coach go! I could have asked the coachman to take me on board. But how would I have paid him when they've taken all my money and clothes from me?' She felt the cold hand of despair beginning to creep over her.

Ainsworth and the Maynard brothers had galloped to the coach on the horses they had tied up in the nearby thicket. "Stand and deliver!" they all yelled in unison. Harry cut the leather at the back of the vehicle.

"Right, my good ladies and gentlemen, your money and your gew-gaws if you pleases. It probably don't but it pleases us three, very much it does," Ainsworth said, laughing at his own weak joke.

"Been caught by that old trick of sendin' a bloody wench to delay us!" the coachman complained bitterly. But he was powerless to stop the thieves.

"Give us your pretty baubles, ladies," said Harry. Some of them screamed. One fainted. "Look what you've done to my wife, man!" her husband protested indignantly.

"She'll come round soon enough," Harry said bluntly, proceeding to take her necklace from round her neck and a bracelet from her wrist.

"What a ruffian you are!" the man said. "No sympathy for a sick lady."

"Hold your tongue if you don't want a bullet through your guts!" The man looked angry but said nothing more. His wife came round, looking very pale. The other women all gave Billy their jewellery without protest. Ainsworth took sovereigns and smaller value coins from the men. Some of them looked indignant but none of them spoke as both Ainsworth and Billy were both managing to steal with one hand while they pointed their guns at the passengers with the other.

"Let's have your wigs, gentlemen," said Harry. "You've got a nice, curly one," he said to an elderly merchant. The man almost turned puce but handed his wig to Billy without a word.

Billy picked up a small hand mirror one of the women who had no jewellery had given him. He examined his reflection with admiration. "It suits me very well. I like it so I'll keep it. Now, let's have the rest to see if they suit me, too." The other men handed their wigs to him.

Ainsworth and the Maynard brothers rejoined Starella. Ainsworth lifted her on to his horse so that she could ride pillion.

"Well done, Starella. We had some rich pickin's from that coach," he whispered. She did not reply.

There were three more such ventures in a short space of time after this. By the third one, Starella found, to her horror, that she was almost looking forward to the robbery for the excitement it provided.

Then, the next night, the coach did not stop and the gang were splashed with mud, all of them becoming bad tempered. Starella knew the men blamed her and resented their attitude as unfair.

In a way, however, she was relieved, as she dreaded the consequences of being caught red-handed.

CHAPTER 10

▼

"Sam Hill wants to meet you, Starella," said Ainsworth, the next night a raid was due, a week later. "He's 'eard about how good you've become at 'elpin' us with our hold-ups."

"I certainly don't want to meet him!" Starella protested. "Everybody seems scared of him. He sounds nasty."

"You ain't got no choice, maid!" Ainsworth almost spat. "We'll be takin' you to the stables what we use, first thing tomorrow morning. You don't have to be frit of him as long as you do what you're told. I admit he don't stand for no nonsense and don't like to be crossed. So don't try it. We'll be takin' you to the stables what we use first thing in the mornin'."

"In that case, I don't want to come on this raid with you. I'll go back to the wagon and have a good night's rest."

Ainsworth grabbed hold of her shoulders and shook her. "As if we'd let you do that on your own, you'd only try to run away and probably get killed."

"Please, Jack, don't hurt the poor maid," Harry said, anxiously.

"She'd deserve it if we beat her," Billy said, sullenly.

Ainsworth shrugged. "We ain't got the time now. Besides, I don't want her to be marked before Sammy sees her. He should see her at her best."

A thrill of fear swept over Starella. Why should Ainsworth be concerned about her looks in the presence of the mysterious Sam Hill? His voice cut in on her thoughts. "Look sharp, all of you, the coach is comin' this way."

That night's raid was highly successful. The men managed to steal many valuables. Starella had very much hoped that it would prove to be an abortive venture.

*   *   *   *

"So this is the girl who caused so much trouble for my friend, Marcus Rose."

The man speaking was Samuel Hill and his deep, cultured voice was that of a gentleman. He was tall and broad shouldered, his body almost but not quite running to fat. His long hair was light brown and worn naturally with no wig tied back with a black satin ribbon. His complexion was florid. He wore a knee-length leather jacket over a white lace ruffled shirt and beige coloured breeches. His feet were encased in high black leather boots. Starella guessed he was probably in his mid thirties and had been handsome when he was younger. There were other men standing in a knot around him.

She had ridden pillion behind Ainsworth to the livery stables. After protesting that she did not want to go, Mother Maynard had slapped her face and pulled her hair. Starella had been startled, as the older woman had never physically assaulted her before although she had made verbal threats. Enraged, she had been about to strike the other woman in retaliation even though she thought she was no match for the older woman in strength.

Ainsworth had caught her hand and twisted her arms behind her back, making her scream out loud. Mother Maynard had made no attempt to stop him. Between them, he and Billy Maynard had carried the struggling girl to Ainsworth's horse where they had practically thrown her astride it.

Ainsworth had seen the tears on her face. "It was your own fault," he had said, brusquely. "We'd already told you we'd be takin' you to see Sammy and he don't expect refusals from you or nobody else. He uses this stable as his 'snack'."

"What's that?"

"It's a place what Sammy and others uses for fresh 'orses. He pays the owner a bit of what we makes so's we can use the stables. I come in useful because I can groom the 'orses. We've 'id there, sometimes, when we've had to run away from constables and such like, them what's tryin' to catch us."

"I hope you all get caught!"

"That's enough! You seem to forget, my fine lady, that you could swing as well as us, if they catches you."

Starella had shuddered. Now, she was hardly registering what Samuel Hill was saying because she was staring at another girl. She saw that Janet Clark was standing proudly by Hill's side, wearing an old, pink silk dress of Starella's.

Ignoring Hill, she managed to shrug off Ainsworth's restraining arm and sprang forward. "How dare you stand here so brazenly, wearing my dress, Janet?"

Janet flushed with anger, placing her hands on her hips. "Don't forget I'm no longer in your service, no more bowin' and scrapin' to the likes of you, Mistress Gypsy's Brat!"

In a calm, quiet voice which nevertheless held a menacing tone and was heard by everyone present, Starella said, "You can insult me but don't do so to my mother's memory or it will be the worse for you."

Janet tossed her head in a contemptuous gesture. She looked Starella up and down. "I ain't scared of you, you silly bitch. I'm the one what's dressed fine now and look at you. You look like the gypsy slut you really are."

"You seem to forget my father was the squire."

"Well, he ain't now, is he? Sammy here's our squire now, you might say."

There was a general shout of laughter.

"I still think you are impertinent and will pay for your attitude," Starella said, with all the contempt she could muster.

"Impertinent, am I?" Janet said, mimicking Starella's voice. "I'll soon show you how much."

Clenching her fists, she was about to punch the other girl's nose, when Samuel Hill suddenly pushed her aside, none too gently. "That's enough! I don't want a catfight between you two. There's enough to do as it is."

He pulled Starella towards him by her arms, almost bruising them. Then, he looked her up and down almost as if he were examining a prize mare. Without loosening his grip on Starella's arms, he turned his head in Janet's direction. "Get out and be about your business. Come back when you've finished it."

Janet tried to place a pleading hand on his arm but removed it when she saw the warning look he gave her. "Sammy," she said, desperately. "You should know about her. You want to send me out as a decoy. Well, I'd be better doin' what you got planned for her."

"I've already made my decision about that," Hill said, testily. "So hold your tongue, girl, if you know what's good for you."

"Sammy, just let me say this. I must for your sake. She ain't no virgin. I seen her on the beach with the old Ridin' Officer. I seen her bein' bedded by him."

Hills face darkened. "Is this true?" he asked Starella, quietly. "Don't lie to me or I'll find out by force."

She bit her lip and whispered. "Yes," feeling her face turn flame coloured. She was terrified he was going to kill her.

"Get out of here!' he shouted at Janet who left quickly but not before casting a triumphant look in Starella's direction.

After she had gone, Hill turned to Ainsworth. "You made a mistake there, Jack. Maybe if she hadn't been deflowered, we could have asked her guardian for a ransom."

Ainsworth looked frightened.

"Don't worry," Hill said, not trying to hide his contempt for the other man's fear. "I'll not hold it against you this time. Look to the horses now, man."

He turned back to Starella. "Well, my dear, you've shown you have spirit. You'll need it with what I have in mind for you. It's a pity you're not a virgin but even so, I think my idea will still work."

Starella felt as if she had lost her wits, wondering what was going to happen to her. She was certain whatever it was, it would hardly be pleasant.

"You have the manners and the speech of a lady. That's a good thing. You see, sweetheart, I'm going to set you up as an expensive whore."

"You mean this," Starella whispered in horror. It was a statement, not a question. Hill smiled but his smile was more self-satisfied than pleasant.

The stable door opened and a dark haired, plainly dressed girl, walked in. "Ah, Jenny's here," Hill said. "Come over here, girl."

The girl looked sullen but obeyed him. "Miss Jenny Lane, make the acquaintance of Miss Starella Denny because you two are going to be working together for me in future."

"I saw you at Mother Maynard's," Jenny exclaimed in surprise.

"I know," Starella replied. "She didn't want you to. Did her potion work?" Jenny looked angry for a minute then her features relaxed. "Yes, thank God." Then she looked as if she were in despair. "But I seem to have jumped out of the fryin' pan into the fire." She glared at Hill. "I seem to be in a worse coil than ever with this bas—"

He clapped his hand over her mouth. "That's more than enough! Stop gossiping and listen hard to what I have to tell you, both of you."

"Please, Mr Hill," said Starella. "Do what you like with me but this poor girl's done you no harm. Why don't you let her go?"

"I don't have to explain myself to you, Starella, not unless I'm telling you what I want done. Remember that in future."

"Now," Hill said, "I intend setting Starella up as the mistress of a fine house."

"I think you mean a brothel," she snapped.

"We don't use words like that to describe our business, my dear," Hill said patiently, as if he were explaining matters of etiquette to a child.

"She's right, that's exactly what it will be!" said Jenny. Hill ignored her.

"I could maybe have earned a bit more money from her if she'd still been a virgin. But I've been told she's not and she's admitted as much, herself." He studied her. "All the same, she can still be kept as the dearest whore for the young gallants who can afford to pay the most money."

He turned to Jenny. "As for you, you can have any of the others who might ask for you. But another thing I want you to do, is prove your worth as a thief."

"But I've always been honest!" Jenny protested.

Hill smiled again. "In your past. Your future's that of a 'Buttock and File.'" Jenny's mouth fell open. She looked horrified.

"What's that?" asked Starella.

"They're young ladies who whore and steal. They take purses, lace neck cloths, wigs and such like from pockets after they've let the gentlemen take their pleasure. A good trick is to replace the coins in the purses with lead. I've a good man in mind, to work as a 'twang,' Jenny. He'll break into the houses with his file."

Starella flushed but decided against answering him back.

"While I'm keepin' the so-called 'gentlemen' busy, I suppose," Jenny said, bitterly.

Hill nodded. "You understand me perfectly. You'll arrange a signal between you. The man I've chosen to work with you will knock the 'cull' down and—"

"What's a 'cull'?" Starella asked, her horror growing by the minute.

"What you'd call a victim," Hill said, pleasantly. "Then, Jenny, the pair of you will bring the goods back to the house which is looked after beautifully by Starella. I'll arrange for them to be sold from there."

"You'll bring us all to the gallows," Starella whispered, feeling as if she were already in a nest of vipers.

Hill shook his head. "I'm too clever and powerful for that to happen. Now, Starella, as I've already said, you have the looks and voice of a lady. So you can preside over any entertainments the gallants might wish to be amused by. I've a woman working for me who visits prisons for suitable girls and sometimes parish apprentices. She'll bring the best ones to you."

Starella stared at him, the thought 'I must escape, I must escape from here!' echoing like a wild mantra in her mind. Aloud, she said, "I've no wish to corrupt poor, innocent children!"

Hill laughed. "They might be poor. They're by no means all innocent."

"There ain't nothin' bad he wouldn't do," Jenny said, contemptuously, to Starella.

Hill's good-natured expression changed to one of anger as he gave Jenny's ear a hard cuff. "I've warned you already to hold your tongue! Just do what you're told and keep your mouth shut. Jack, fetch the carriage."

As Ainsworth rushed out of the stables, Billy Maynard swaggered into the stables. Hill turned to the two girls. "Now, my dears, we're taking a ride to Salisbury in a fine carriage we've borrowed from a friend. I'm looking at some houses to see which will make the best whorehouse. We'll also visit a mantua makers to arrange to have some grander clothes made for Starella."

He moved away to talk to some of the men.

"You're as happy as me in this situation," Starella said to Jenny. "Let's make a run for the door."

As if by magic, Hill called out, imperiously. "Jenny, come and meet the man you're to work with."

With an apologetic look at Starella, Jenny walked over to him. Starella picked up her skirts and started to run for the door. A male boot deliberately tripped her up and she fell face downwards into the straw.

CHAPTER 11

▼

Starella experienced the shock of a jug of water being thrown into her face. "You fainted," Samuel Hill said, without sympathy.

Billy Maynard's rough hands hauled her to her feet. "It's me what stopped her gettin' out," he said proudly. Then, with one hand clutching her arm, he drew his free hand back as if to strike her. Hill pushed it aside. "No, not this time, Billy."

He looked coldly at the girl. "I know you were trying to escape me. Don't even think of attempting it again. Because if you do, I'll flog you to within an inch of your life. And I'll do it in front of several others." Hill's voice was quiet but menacing.

Hill took hold of Starella's other arm and beckoned Jenny to follow them.

They climbed aboard the waiting carriage. Ainsworth was in the driving seat.

"Did you bring the pen and paper, Jack, like I asked you to?"

"Yes, I did, Sammy. Here they are."

Hill drew two pictures of stars, giving them a title. He showed them to Starella. "See, I've named you the 'Star of the Forest.' Jack and the others will be throwing this piece into the next coach. And the other picture, it'll be given to your best paying customer, probably a nobleman, once I've set you up in style in the house we're going to. Jack can have the one; put the other in your pocket for now."

Ainsworth drove to Poole. "We'll stop outside this tavern," Hill said. "I've some goods to collect which can be sold in Salisbury." Starella and Jenny exchanged glances, both hoping they would be able to climb down from the coach and run away while the men were inside the tavern.

Their hopes were dashed, however, when Hill said, "You two girls, you come in with us. I understand you might have been considering silly ideas about getting away. Well, forget them, both of you and make haste. Jenny, you can try your hand at picking pockets. We'll see how good you are at it." Jenny gave him a baleful glare but said nothing.

After they had entered the tavern, Hill bought ale for all of them including the two young women. The landlord treated him as if he were a very popular customer; he seemed to be well known to the other patrons of the tavern.

"Is the contraband all brought in, John?" Hill asked the landlord in a low voice.

The landlord nodded. "See them two over there." He pointed to the corner where two rough looking men were deep in conversation. "See them about it."

Hill nodded and walked over to them. He told Billy and another of his henchmen to keep an eye on Starella. Jenny began to wander around the room. But the henchman was telling Harry a lewd story so they were not fully concentrating on guarding Starella who rose with almost cat-like quietness and wandered over to where Jenny was standing.

Then, Starella gasped in horror as she saw Roland Chivers enter the tavern. They exchanged glances, Roland looking extremely startled but he said nothing and looked away the next minute.

'I suppose he thinks I'm now a disgraced, ruined woman so he cannot possibly acknowledge me,' she thought, with a certain amount of bitterness.

Then she had a wild idea. She made sure that Hill was still fully engrossed with the men in the opposite corner. She glanced at Harry. He was still laughing and asking for another tale from his companion. Starella whispered to Jenny who produced a pencil, handing it over to her.

Starella removed the drawing of the star from her pocket, quickly checking there was enough room to write on the paper. She swiftly wrote: "We two females are being kept prisoner."

Deliberately, Jenny took Roland's arm. He looked as if he were about to shake it off but she clung to him with all her might, laughing loudly into his face. Then, she slipped him the piece of paper.

Billy came over. He grabbed Starella by the nape of her neck. "Let me go!" she said, indignantly. "I'll come back to my old seat with you, I don't need to be dragged there." Hiding her distaste, she linked her arm through Billy's.

Out of the corner of her eye, Starella saw Roland hand the drawing back to Jenny. He then left the tavern, giving a quick glance at her over his shoulder. She could not read his expression.

"We'll be on our way, now," Hill said to Billy. "I've arranged for quite a goodly bit of stuff to be brought over to the stables."

When they had all boarded the carriage where Ainsworth was waiting for them, once more, Hill said to Jenny, "And what did you manage to filch, sweetheart?"

Jenny looked down at the floor. "Not much, Sam." She put her hands in her skirt pocket, taking out a cheap ring, a few coins of small value and the pencil.

Hill nodded. "Not too bad for a first effort. You'll get better, no doubt." Then his face darkened, his tone became more threatening. "And why did you show that well dressed fellow my drawing?"

Jenny blushed and stammered. "Well, Mr Hill, I thought as he was smart dressed, he might be more on his guard than the others that he'd have things took off him. So, because I wanted to take his attention away from what I was doin', I thought I'd show him the picture."

"I see," Hill said, grimly. "Well, take my warning not to do that again without me telling you to, first. Did you get anything valuable from him?"

"The—the pencil," Jenny said, desperately.

Hill's eyebrows rose. "A pencil. They're worth a great deal, I must say." Jenny looked scared by his sarcasm.

"You took that golden guinea from him, didn't you, Jen?" Starella prompted. "I think you forgot to mention it."

Jenny gulped and nodded, giving Starella a grateful look.

"Well," said Hill, with an air of great satisfaction. "You'll certainly be able to steal many more sovereigns in the future, I hope. That is, if you want to please me which I'm sure you do, don't you?" His voice was mild yet his look was threatening.

"Yes, of course, Mr Hill," Jenny replied. She was subdued for the rest of the journey. Starella was also silent but her thoughts were racing madly.

When they reached Salisbury, they stopped near the Cathedral. "You stay in the coach, Jenny. Starella, you get down with me," Hill said.

Escorted by Hill, Billy Maynard and another man, Starella walked down a street at the back of the Cathedral. They arrived at a large imposing looking house. Hill rapped loudly on the door. A tall, burly manservant answered it.

"Is your mistress in?"

"Yes, Mr Hill, come this way, if you please." Starella noted the apparent respect in the servant's voice.

In a daze, she followed Hill and the other men into the house. Inside, it was well furnished with thick carpets, mahogany and rosewood furniture and many highly polished mirrors. As they walked through the corridors, they heard the sound of young, feminine voices with an occasional deeper male voice coming from the adjoining rooms where the doors were firmly locked.

They were admitted to a salon where another burly man stood outside guarding it. A middle-aged woman sat on a sofa covered in red satin in the centre of the room. Starella was surprised that she was alone. The woman's blue dress was simply styled with no fashionable hoop, but was made of a costly silk. She wore a high, well-powdered wig over her own dark but greying hair and her face was highly painted. This did not make her look attractive in Starella's opinion. On the other hand, her face did not look ravaged as Starella had expected; neither was her expression hard or calculating. "Samuel, this is a pleasure," she said, extending her hand. Starella was surprised that her voice was quite cultured.

"And for me, Caroline."

The woman looked intently at Starella, looking her up and down. Starella deliberately looked away.

"May I present Miss Starella Denny to you, Mistress Caroline Turner," Hill said, as if he were introducing two ladies to each other in a society drawing room.

Both women stared at each other but neither spoke.

Hill frowned. "Come now, ladies, this isn't very friendly."

"Samuel," Caroline Turner said. "Could you leave us for two minutes so that I might speak to Starella alone?"

Hill looked reluctant, then shrugged. "Very well, but no longer than two minutes!" He left the room.

Caroline patted Starella's hand. "I know you've been brought here by force. I admit I find parish apprentices and street urchins myself, but they're poor. You have a look of breeding about you despite the gypsyish clothes you're wearing." She hesitated. "You'll find this hard to believe but I was a governess once. The master of the house seduced me and kept me as his mistress but then he married me after his wife died. We lived in some style but after he died I found out he had debts so I sold the house and bought this one with the profit after paying his creditors." She sighed. "But there was very little money left once this house had been furnished. I certainly didn't want to marry again or become an impoverished governess at some family's beck and call."

"Then, you don't really like what you do," Starella said, with some hesitation, trying to fight the liking she was beginning to feel for the older woman.

Caroline shrugged. "I've become accustomed to it. It has its compensations."

"But don't you feel guilty about corrupting children?"

Caroline gave her a shrewd look. "Some of the apprentices, my dear, are treated little better than slaves by their masters and mistresses. Some of the urchins are near starving or gallows meat before I take them in. At least, they are well fed here."

Starella still looked doubtful. "You seem to have already guessed a lot about me. Did you know I would be coming here?"

Caroline gave a rueful half-smile. "Sam Hill has many spies and messengers. I was told he would be bringing a young lady here. I wasn't told for what purpose though I made a pretty shrewd guess. I expect you've already learned it's most unwise to cross him."

Hill came back into the room. "Starella and I have been discussing the fashions we shall have made up for her at the mantua-makers," Caroline said to him. "I thought you might be bored by such a feminine topic."

"Caroline is an excellent Madam, Starella, and I want you to learn from her before I set you up in your own establishment of a similar nature where she'll receive goods as she sometimes does. It'll be a smaller house, though. For the present, Caroline, Starella is to be kept for your richest clients, young noblemen and so forth. I shall also take my own turns with her."

Caroline nodded in agreement. Starella was horrified at Hill's last words but tried hard not to show it.

"We should go to the mantua-makers now," Hill said, after young girls had served them with food and drink.

"I'll tell my coachman to make the carriage ready for us," said Caroline, picking up a handbell and ringing it. A young maid dressed in white came in and was despatched to inform the coachman.

When they left, Hill insisted upon two strong looking manservants accompanying them. It had begun to rain and the carriage was stuck in a muddy rut for a few minutes but the coachman managed to extricate it. Starella had hoped they would not be able to go any further.

At the dressmaker's premises, Hill said he had urgent business to attend to. He positioned the two male servants outside the shop, stating he would return to Caroline's house at the end of the week. "I want first turn with Starella so don't let anybody else have her before me and make sure she is well guarded at all times," he admonished Caroline.

"Yes, I'll do that, Samuel," she replied.

Starella felt as if she were in the middle of a waking nightmare that was gradually holding more and more terrors.

"This is a milliner's shop as well," Caroline said, as the two women entered the premises. "While we're waiting for Samuel to visit you, I'll engage a dancing master to teach you special ways of dancing to entertain gentlemen. Maybe you could be taught a few notes on the spinet. And I've got some books you can read which have interesting drawings in them. They'll show you different ways to entice men."

Starella registered her words with trepidation.

"Ah, Madam Turner," the proprietress said in a fawning manner because Caroline's house brought her a lot of trade. "Now, what can I do for your good self?"

"I wish to purchase some pretty clothing for this young lady."

"Of course. I'll bring out my very best finery."

As they examined materials, arranging for gowns to be made, looking also at hats, cloaks, scarves, shawls, handkerchiefs and ribbons, Starella began to laugh hysterically.

Caroline slapped her face but not very hard. "Hush, girl, don't draw too much attention to us."

"I was just thinking," said Starella, still laughing at the irony of the situation. "My guardian's wife wished me to become an apprentice to a mantua-maker, such as this. She never thought much of me. I can imagine what she would say, seeing me come to this, being fitted out at one to become a whore to rich men!"

CHAPTER 12

▼

Two nights after Starella had been taken to Caroline Turner's house, Ainsworth and the Maynard brothers had gone out on an unsuccessful raid. Rain had been falling hard all night. They had only seen one coach and it had not stopped even when Billy had fired a gunshot at it. When they returned, their mother was missing. Janet Clark was in the wagon. She had not gone out on that night's raid because she had been nursing Mother Maynard who had a cold.

"Where's Ma?" Billy asked, the expression on his face matching the thundercloud outside.

Janet looked scared. "She insisted on goin' out, Billy. She wanted to see somebody in the village because she'd been scryin'."

"That's when she looks into the future," Harry said, unnecessarily.

"Said it was important because she didn't trust that Jenny Lane," Janet continued. "Sammy needed warnin' about her and the man in the village knows him well so she had to see him."

"Why didn't you stop her, you silly bitch?" Billy asked.

Janet looked even more frightened. "I couldn't stop her, Billy—honest!"

Billy Maynard put his hands around the terrified girl's throat and began to squeeze it. Ainsworth pulled him off her. "Leave her be for now, Billy. We'd best all go out and look for your ma."

They searched thoroughly, finally finding the prone body of Mother Maynard under an oak tree in the small wood. "She never reached the village, then," said Ainsworth. He examined the woman. "She's still alive but she's very hot so I think she's got a fever. Looks like she's fell over, probably tripped up by a branch and sprained her ankle so she couldn't get no further."

The men carried her back to the wagon between them. Janet undressed her, replacing her wet clothes with a clean, dry shift. She put the older woman to bed, heating a brick to put at her feet and preparing a hot drink which they all forced down her throat.

"I'll have to make sure she's kept warm until the fever breaks," Janet said, unable to keep the anxiety from her voice.

"She'll be right as the rain outside, soon, won't she, Janet?" Harry asked, anxiously.

"I hope so," Janet replied. Then, glancing at Billy's scowl, "I expect she will."

"She'd better, for your sake," Billy Maynard growled.

But Mother Maynard, who had seemed so invincible to illness all her life, had caught pneumonia and died suddenly at the end of the week.

"We'll bury her in the wood," the grief stricken Billy Maynard said. His mother was the only person he had ever loved in his life.

"She always said she wanted to be buried there," Harry agreed. "I'll come and help you dig her grave."

"I'd help you," said Ainsworth. "But you bein' her sons, maybe it's best you two pay your last respects."

"Yes, you're right, Jack. Thank you for everythin' you've done," said Harry. Billy gave a curt nod in agreement.

When the Maynard brothers had gone out, Ainsworth said to Janet, "You know Billy will kill you when he comes back, don't you?"

Janet began to sob.

"Hush your noise, maid! Look, I don't why I'm doin' this. I don't owe you no favours but I don't like murder, specially not of women though I've seen it done a few times. I've got a horse waitin' outside and I'll take you as far as Southampton. We'll ride there fast as the wind then we can both make a new life there."

Janet Clark flung her arms about Ainsworth's neck. "Oh Jack, you're a good man, I swear I always thought so."

Impatiently, Ainsworth cast her aside. "We ain't got time for that now. Come on, hurry up. We've no time to lose."

When the Maynard brothers returned to the wagon, they found Ainsworth and Janet Clark had gone missing.

"Probably gone to pinch stuff," said Billy Maynard. "I swear I'll get her when she comes back."

"Don't be too rough if you beat her, Billy," Harry pleaded.

A grim little smile played about Billy Maynard's mouth. He did not tell Harry he fully intended to kill Janet Clark for neglecting his mother's welfare, not just to thrash her.

Aloud, he said. "Come, Harry, we'll burn all Ma's things. That's what she always said she wanted us to do, when she died."

For several years afterwards, a legend circulated around the district about a witch woman with miraculous powers who had two sons who were evildoers.

Their ghosts were supposed to haunt the wood at the back of where the witch's wagon had once stood. Children were frightened to pass the stream at night lest the witch dragged them in. If they could not avoid it, they always ran past it as fast as their short legs could carry them.

*   *   *   *

Two days later another meeting was taking place at the stables when there was a loud hammering on the door.

Hill frowned. "What a din. It's enough to waken the dead." He motioned a man to go to the door. "Go and get rid of whoever that is. Warn them not to do it again."

He was startled when his henchman was thrust bodily back into the stables. "What the Devil!" The next moment, the sheriff with a huge, armed posse including Roland Chivers, burst into the stables. "You're all under arrest in the name of the King!" the sheriff said. A group of his men seized and bound a few of Hill's men.

Pandemonium broke out. Men shouted, swore, screamed and drew weapons as the frightened horses reared, stamped and neighed. Some of Hill's men rushed to the door but found their way barred. Many started to fight the sheriff's men and blood was drawn on both sides.

The Maynard brothers arrived. Hearing the noise emanating from inside, Billy quickly guessed what had happened. "Don't go in there," he said to Harry. "We'll keep out of it. I know a tavern where we can lie low while the others are bein' took."

As Harry hesitated, Billy gave him a push. "You 'eard what I said. Follow me. Run! Quick!"

Hill's men were eventually all overcome due to the superior numbers and weapons of the sheriff's men. Miraculously, nobody had been killed.

The sheriff looked triumphantly at the bound, gagged and now dishevelled Hill.

"I've wanted to catch you for such a long time that it gives me great satisfaction to have done so at last." He turned to Roland. "I cannot thank you enough for your information, Mr Chivers. Very soon, we'll go to the whorehouse to remove the young lady you mentioned."

He ordered his second-in-command to remove the prisoners and to ensure that they were well guarded. Then, the sheriff, Roland and about six others went outside and boarded a waiting carriage.

They drove to Caroline Turner's house. A manservant answered the door.

"I must speak to your mistress," the sheriff said. "I have an important message for her from Mr Samuel Hill."

The manservant looked doubtful; nevertheless he informed Caroline who then came to the door herself.

"You have a message for me from Mr Hill, sir?"

"I do, madam. But it's confidential so I must speak to you inside." Caroline looked suspicious. She wondered why so many men had arrived together in broad daylight. "Who are all these other gentlemen?"

"They've been sent as clients for your girls by Mr Hill." The sheriff's tone was firm. "Please just let the two of us in for now, so that I can give you his message." The sheriff indicated Roland.

Caroline still looked dubious but beckoned them to go in. After they had entered, she slammed the front door shut in the others' faces. She was visibly tense.

"This gentleman has been specially sent by Mr Hill to speak to one of your young ladies by the name of Miss Starella Denny," the sheriff said, pointing his thumb at Roland.

Caroline began to relax. "She's in the parlour with the dancing master. Come this way." After they had been admitted, Starella turned very pale when she saw Roland. "He must speak with her absolutely alone," the sheriff said.

"Signor Calvini, please leave us for a moment," Caroline said.

The Italian dancing master inclined his head and made a graceful exit from the room.

"Madam, I saw two of the paintings in your hall," the sheriff said. "Might I examine them more closely because I think they're very beautiful?"

"Of course, sir."

"Please come with me and point out the details while I look at them."

"I'm at your service, sir."

"Starella," Roland said in a low voice, when they were alone. "I've come to take you away from this place."

"Have you come to help to arrest me?" Her face betrayed no expression but her tone was despairing.

Roland shook his head. "You're shrewd, sweetheart, but no, I have not. Take my arm, walk out with me and say nothing until we're out of doors."

Starella pinched her arm to make sure she was not dreaming; then she took Roland's arm and walked out of the room with him. In the corridor, they passed the sheriff and Caroline.

"Mistress Turner, might I have a quick word with a few of your other girls?" the sheriff asked. "Could we go into this room on the left for a moment?"

Roland led Starella into the street. He tensed when he saw the manservant still standing in the hall but the servant did nothing to stop them. Once they were outside, Roland nodded to the other men still waiting by the front door. They stared at Starella but none of them uttered a word.

"There's a carriage waiting for us around the corner," Roland said. He helped her to mount the steps.

"You're probably wondering where I'm taking you."

Starella nodded, staring at him with wide green eyes.

"To a cottage in the Forest where you'l sleep for a night. Then the day after your guardian and I will ensure you reach Exeter safely this time."

"My guardian. Do you mean the captain?"

"Yes, I do."

"I doubt he will want to have anything to do with me now. I have brought disgrace upon his name."

Roland gave her hand a light squeeze. "You've been through a lot; your name has become known around the Forest. But I know nothing which has happened to you has been your fault because you've been at the mercy of evil men."

"How did you know where to find me?"

"Do you remember seeing me in that tavern?"

"Yes, of course."

"When Jenny Lane spoke to me, she told me as much as she could. I managed to arrange another meeting with her."

"But Hill put a man to work with and watch over Jenny."

"I know he did. He placed them both in an inn but Jenny borrowed a pair of nailed boots from a stable lad there, knocked him out with them when he was nearly asleep and made her escape.

Starella laughed. "She has spirit, that one. I know she hated Hill.'

Roland half smiled. 'She's not the only one with spirit."

Starella looked rueful. "I think if I had stayed longer with Hill and the others, it would all have been scared out of me."

Roland nodded. "I'm sure you're right but fortunately it won't happen now. I informed the sheriff what Jenny had told me about the stables and the times Hill's gang were likely to meet. When I told him all this, the sheriff was delighted as Hill's slipped out of his grasp a few times before. Jenny explained your predicament to me and I asked him if I could have leave to bring you away from the whorehouse. We put our heads together as to how we would do it."

Starella looked anxious. "What will happen to Jenny?"

"She'll give evidence in Court; then the sheriff will help her get away to London or some other large town away from here."

Starella was relieved. "I was afraid she might be charged herself."

"No, her evidence against Hill and the others will be too valuable."

"Caroline Turner didn't ill treat me. In her own way she was kind to me. I don't like to think of her being severely punished for what she does, wrong though it is."

"I'll have a word with the sheriff and Captain Mountjoy. They both know at least two of the magistrates and they'll use their influence to see that her sentence is lenient."

Starella felt as if her heart would burst with gratitude any minute. "Mr Chivers, I cannot thank you enough for what you have done for me. I'm sure I don't deserve it all."

Roland's voice was husky as he looked intently at her. "Yes, you most certainly do. I dread to think what might have happened if we hadn't found you."

"I'm so glad you did," she said, softly. Roland bit his lip and looked out of the window.

*   *   *   *

"Let me have just one more look at that painting," the sheriff said. "Do come with me to view it again." Caroline did not know why she was uneasy. The man had been talking quite amiably to some of her girls but he had not asked her for any particular one.

Perhaps that was it, she decided. Maybe he was asking her to go back to the painting so that he could discreetly ask for one of them. Possibly he was too shy to ask directly in front of them all. But he did not seem to be a bashful sort of fellow.

Caroline wondered why he had such an obsession with a particular painting but in her trade she knew very well that certain men had peculiar fancies. He was once again admiring and discussing it with her.

"Would you like to buy it off me, this nymph painting?" she asked.

"Yes, I think I would. Could we go back into that other room and could you ask your man to take the picture down from the wall and bring it in to me so that I may examine it more closely?"

Caroline did as he asked. When the picture was handed to him, the sheriff examined it more closely. 'My God!' thought Caroline. 'What else can there be to look at?'

Suddenly, he threw the painting to the ground. Caroline looked at him in bewilderment. The next moment he pushed her to one side and deliberately tripped up the manservant with a nearby chair. Some of the girls screamed. Like a lightning flash, the sheriff was outside the heavy oak door and they heard the key being turned in the lock.

He opened the front door to admit the other men. Then he unlocked the door of the room on the left.

"Caroline Turner," the sheriff said. "You are under arrest for keeping a disorderly house." To the others, he said, "You are all free to go."

They all cheered as Caroline began to wail.

*   *   *   *

"Well, you certainly seem to have made an infamous name for yourself, mixing with rogues, villains and vagabonds, both male and female." Mountjoy spoke with a controlled anger. "Mr Chivers told me what he planned to do and asked me to come to this cottage, in the hope we would see each other again. I must say you've come to a pretty pass."

"I realise that but it wasn't my fault. I was abducted, forced to act as a decoy to stop coaches so that they could be robbed. Then I was taken to Samuel Hill who told me he was going to make me a whore. I didn't like becoming notorious but I couldn't help it. How could I fight men twice as strong as me?"

Starella burst into tears. Awkwardly, Charles patted her shoulder.

"I do understand even if I spoke sharply. I've been worried sick about you in case you were murdered, hanged or transported. It's a relief to have you back safe and sound. I've berated myself for letting you travel alone with no escort when you first went to Exeter."

"First went there?—I never even reached it."

"Obviously, you didn't," Charles snapped. "Do you recall my telling you that my cousins are an elderly couple? With everything that's happened to you, you might easily have forgotten."

Starella nodded. "Yes, I had remembered."

"Good. We'd better both retire now before Mrs Robins' candles burn out."

Starella slept much more soundly than she had for a long time but she still managed to rise early the following morning.

Captain Mountjoy's smart new carriage arrived in the bustling city of Exeter with no mishaps. The party called at a coaching inn for refreshment on the way. Starella had little appetite and ate and drank mechanically.

"I've been offered a post as a thief taker in Exeter," Roland said. "The sheriff recommended me to the authorities there because I helped to catch Samuel Hill who he had been after for quite a while." There was a note of pride in his voice.

Charles looked concerned. "Are you going to take it?"

"I'm certainly considering it."

"It's your decision, of course, Mr Chivers. But I think it could be dangerous."

Roland shrugged. "I could also be in danger if I stay in the Forest. I believe a few of Hill's and Marcus Rose's men are still at large. Ainsworth and the Maynard brothers have vanished as if into thin air."

"I'm glad Harry wasn't arrested," Starella said. She had hardly spoken at all on the journey. "He was always kind to me."

Mountjoy frowned. "That part of your life is over and best forgotten, Starella. We've almost finished our journey."

*   *   *   *

In the dusky light, Starella saw that the Travers' house was a timber framed Elizabethan building near the Cathedral, which had been enlarged. She liked the look of it. The coffee house sign outside read "Dolly's Coffee House." It had been closed that evening in honour of Captain Mountjoy's visit although the Travers, especially David, did not really like losing profits.

The elderly couple came to the door. "Come in, my dears, you are most welcome sights," said Margery, small and stout with grey hair and eyes. "You must all be ready for your suppers." Her husband was taller but not very much, bald and although plump, was not as fat as Margery.

"So you are Starella," said David. "I must admit you're not quite what I expected." She felt slightly uncomfortable under his penetrating gaze.

"I'm sure my ward will be a great asset to you in helping to run your coffee house," said Mountjoy.

Starella scowled. The captain was speaking as if she were some sort of scullery maid.

"We'll certainly be glad to have the help of a young, lively person," said Margery.

"Yes. My wife and I aren't so nimble as we used to be," David added.

Inside, their large parlour had been converted to a coffee house with oak panelled rooms and ten mahogany tables. The six tables in the Merchants' Room, as it was unofficially called, were covered by clean, embroidered cloths.

"Come and sit down, all of you," said Margery, as David poured out glasses of wine. She rang a bell and a maid brought in dishes of hot food. "I cooked a lot of this, myself," said Margery.

"You're certainly a good cook," said Roland.

Margery looked pleased. "I don't want you to think I have a conceit of myself but so I've often been told, haven't I, Mr Travers?"

"You have, indeed, dear," her husband agreed.

"My buns are famous." Margery looked as if she were going to expand on this subject when Captain Mountjoy spoke quickly.

"I have brought you some money for Starella's keep. But I should like to know what her duties will be?"

Starella felt both irritated and depressed by the fact that she was being regarded as nothing more than a servant.

"She'll give a hand with the laying of tables and serve the customers," David Travers said. "If she's good enough, she'll go on to serve in the Merchants Room." He said this as if it were a great honour. "She'll have all her meals with us, we'll give her money for clothing and—"

"I think Margery should definitely accompany Starella each time she buys material and such-like," Charles said, firmly. Starella felt even more irritated.

"Very well," said Travers. "Now as to her wages, I think they should be—"

Starella was interested to hear this, determining she would save as hard as she could until such time as she could find alternative employment of some kind. But Roland insisted on drawing her aside to a corner of the room.

"You'll be safe here, Starella. I'm so glad." He touched her hand. She wished he would hold it but he moved back to the table.

Starella reluctantly followed him.

CHAPTER 13

▼

"The mistress says you're to come down to have some breakfast before you start work," the dark haired maid said to Starella. "I expect you'll be tired by the end of the day. She'll make sure you earn your keep."

Starella was dispirited by this information but passed no comment, merely asking the girl what her name was.

"Evelina Dart, but I'm always called Eve. I was an orphan Mr Travers found beggin' by the river so he brought me back 'ere to be their maid. It ain't so bad, really, the food's good. All that's wrong is the mistress always remindin' me how grateful I should be for their charity to me."

"I imagine it must become rather tiresome," Starella sympathised. "How old are you, Eve?"

"Fourteen or thereabouts, I think. I'd better be on my way 'cause I'm so busy."

"Yes, you had," Starella agreed, inwardly amused because Eve did not seem to be in anything of a hurry. She seemed to be more in the mood for a long talk of a confidential nature.

"They don't have many servants. There's another maid what comes in the day and gives 'and with the cookin' but don't live in."

"I believe she served us last night."

"Another woman comes in to do the rough cleanin'. I sometimes wish they had more servants so there wouldn't be so much work. But then again, if they did, I'd probably be bossed about by 'em, too, and I know I wouldn't like that!" She winked. Starella laughed, beginning to feel better.

"Do you want some help to get dressed?" Eve asked, hopefully.

Starella shook her head. "No thank you. I'll manage on my own."

Slightly disappointed, Eve left the room.

After Starella had breakfasted with David and Margery Travers, waited upon by Eve, David went out.

"Right," Margery said to Starella. "I'll take you to the room where you'll start work. I shall be serving in the Merchants' Room, myself."

Starella must have looked disappointed that she was not to work in the Merchants' Room. Margery noticed her expression. "I think you'll be a good worker, Starella. If you are, I shall allow you to serve the merchants."

She announced this favour as if it were a great honour so Starella tried to look as if she were delighted although she was mollified.

*   *   *   *

Margery, Starella and Eve laid the rosewood tables in the Merchants' Room, placing cutlery and jugs on top of the embroidered cloths.

"The merchants come in here from their Exchange," Margery said.

"Their Exchange?" Starella queried.

Margery nodded. "It's a large space railed in near the Cathedral with pleasant walks round it. They meet there twice a day. My dear Mr Travers sometimes speaks about their business to one or two of them. That nice Mr Chivers who the captain said had done you both a great favour, said he'd like to look at the Cathedral with us some time. It's a shame he had to rush away on urgent business last night."

Starella tried to look as if she were indifferent. A short but burly and balding man walked in. "This is Abel Simpson," said Margery. "Abel, Starella has come to help us." Abel Simpson nodded towards her but did not speak.

"Simpson clears the glasses off the tables for us and spreads the newspapers around on them," Margery added.

"He's a bodyguard, too," Eve whispered to Starella. She was rebuked by Margery but did not look particularly crestfallen.

Simpson placed neatly folded copies of the 'Mercury,' the 'Post Boy' and the 'Post Man' newspapers on the tables. He pretended to be reading them but Eve again whispered to Starella, "He can't really read."

"Evelina!" Margery snapped. "That's quite enough. I know you were a beggar girl when dear Mr Travers found you, but we've taught you correct manners out of our charity for you. Please remember this in future."

"Yes, mistress, I will," said Eve, still not looking ashamed. Margery tutted but said nothing further.

*   *   *   *

Starella was fascinated by the mixture of people, all male, who patronised Dolly's Coffee House. She had now been here for three weeks. It was now well into the Autumn. Cascades of leaves were falling from the trees. The rich and the poor, the learned and the unlearned, all mingled here. There was always a lot of noise and bustle. Loud arguments sometimes broke out. Authors found topics and inspiration there and journalists picked up news items. Politics, fashion and marine insurance were also discussed.

Dolly's served wine and gin, chocolate, sherbet, cordials and tea as well as toast and Margery's delicious buns. Many of the men smoked clay pipes which caused a smoky atmosphere. Starella had become quite adept at avoiding the grasping hands of those who had drunk too much.

The following Friday morning, Starella was placing the cloths on the tables in the Merchants Room which Eve had first rubbed beeswax into, before polishing them. She had grumbled to Starella that she did not see the point of this particular task as the tables were only going to be covered in any case.

Margery bustled in with two large plates of buns she had baked very early that day. She handed them to Starella who placed them on the two tables where the most important merchants usually sat.

"The buns you baked the other day, Starella. They were very wholesome," said Margery.

"Thank you for telling me but I still cannot make them taste as delicious as your own."

Margery beamed. "Dear Mr Travers helped me lift them out of the oven before he went to the Exchange."

Starella often wondered what business transactions David Travers carried out with the merchants as he went out frequently and was never forthcoming about his activities. Margery, however, liked to give the impression that her husband was a well-respected tradesman. Starella often wondered if he had a secret mistress although she thought this was unlikely.

"I have a secret for you, today, Starella," Margery said, looking coy. "It concerns a young gentleman."

"Is it important for him to remain a secret?"

"Yes." Margery was disappointed that the girl did not have a more eager expression of anticipation. Starella idly wondered if the Travers' had the idea of introducing her to some worthy young man they considered suitable for her but whom she would not like.

"Our visitor is coming to supper with us, tonight," Margery said.

"Why may I not know who he is?"

"Dear Mr Travers and I thought it best to leave it until tonight for you to find out."

Starella suppressed her inclination to shrug; then Avery Hodgkins, a very prosperous wool merchant, entered. He was considered by the Travers to be their most important patron.

Hodgkins was a tall, well built man in his fifties with a fresh complexion and thick grey hair that showed no signs of thinning.

"I bid you good morning, ladies," he said. "I was speaking with your husband earlier, Mistress Travers. We had a most interesting discussion."

Margery almost curtsied. "Would you care to partake of one of my buns, Mr Hodgkins?" she asked, anxiously.

"I should love to as I'm quite peckish. I should also like some coffee."

Starella picked up one of the plates and held it out to him. She moved aside in order to make his coffee. Margery engaged him in further conversation.

Glancing back over her shoulder, Starella tutted to herself. She thought Margery fawned on this man far too much, important customer or not. She saw him pick up a newspaper and knew that Hodgkins had decided to terminate his conversation with Margery as he now felt he had been pleasant enough.

Unlike many other men who frequented the coffee house, Hodgkins had never tried to touch Starella's body in any way. He had always been polite and had given her generous tips.

But she had never been able to like or trust him without quite knowing why. She sometimes thought that she disliked him more than any other customer, wishing she knew the reason why.

Later that morning, a noisy argument broke out between two of the merchants' sons. It had started with one young man raising his voice enthusiastically upon a particular subject. The other had at first not taken offence but then he had disagreed with a particular point the first had been trying to make. Then, they had began to quarrel about their respective fathers' business transactions, the dispute becoming more and more bitter as each accused the other's parent of unfairness.

Several patrons began to join in with the altercation, taking different sides according to who they liked best. Then, the first young man's servant who had just returned from an errand he had been sent on by his master, entered the room, drawing a knife.

Observing this, Hodgkins sprang to his feet, surprisingly light on them for one of his heavy build and rushed over to the combatants.

"Tell your man to put his weapon away this very minute, Blake!" he thundered in such a loud voice that everybody was momentarily silenced. Simpson ran in to see what was happening. He hovered behind Hodgkins but did not move.

"I believe your father recently had some dealings with Lord Adrian Mallard. Is that correct?" Hodgkins asked.

Blake nodded and motioned his servant to stay his hand.

'Well, Lord Mallard will shortly be coming here. I don't think that you would like him to tell your father you were involved in a coffee house brawl like a common prizefighter."

Blake reluctantly agreed. He ordered his servant to put his weapon away.

"I think you should leave now, Mr Blake, sir," said Simpson, trying to assert his authority.

"That shouldn't be necessary as long as Mr Blake keeps his voice down in future," said Hodgkins.

"I was about to leave anyway," Blake said. "I don't like this place all that much. Come, Whiteley."

Blake turned on his heel and left the room, accompanied by his manservant. A little disappointed, Simpson returned to the other room. Hodgkins went back to his own table and picked up his newspaper again. Some tried to engage him in conversation but he answered in monosyllables so they gave up and other lively discussions began.

Starella went on with her work. Despite her dislike of the man, she admired the calm way in which Hodgkins had handled an explosive situation.

Margery entered with some drinking chocolate an important customer had ordered. "Just fancy, Starella. Mr Hodgkins is bringing a real live lord here."

"He could hardly bring a dead one!" Starella snapped. She frowned as the door opened to admit yet more customers. Rain always brought them flocking into the warmth of the coffee house and everybody demanded attention at once. Starella was tired and irritable.

"Don't be out of sorts, girl. It's not seemly!" Margery bit back. "Dear Mr Travers must have spoken with Mr Hodgkins and that gentleman is doing us a great favour."

"Yes, I suppose he is," Starella said, making a great effort to sound reasonably enthusiastic. She had a headache and her feet were hurting.

*   *   *   *

That evening, after the coffee house had been closed, Margery said, "Our mystery guest has arrived. I'm sure you'll be pleased to see him once again Starella."

"We enjoyed his company the last time we saw him and we thought you would appreciate seeing a young gentleman from your part of the world," her husband remarked.

The new maid ushered Roland Chivers into the parlour. Starella experienced a sudden lifting of her spirits. Her headache disappeared as if by magic, and she forgot that her feet were sore.

CHAPTER 14

▼

"Could I take Miss Starella out for a walk before supper before it grows dark?" Roland asked.

Starella thought she felt her heart leap. She waited with bated breath for him to be given permission to do so.

"Yes. It's a pleasant evening now the rain's stopped," said David. "But don't keep her out too long." Margery did not look very happy but said nothing.

Roland and Starella both thanked him and the latter fetched her cloak. They walked to the Parish Church of St Mary Steps in West Street in order to look at the picturesque clock with its three figures, known as 'Matthew the Miller and his Sons,' embellished with representations of the four seasons.

"How do you find being a thief taker? I imagine it's rather dangerous, sometimes," Starella said, with an anxious frown.

Roland shrugged. "I must admit there are times it becomes, shall we say—a little hair raising. But the sheriff has begun to use me on other duties which aren't quite so risky. I'm not at liberty to say what they are."

Starella guessed he was acting as some kind of a spy and felt as if she had been gently reproached for prying.

"Do you like working in the coffee house?"

"It's hard work. I confess there are times when it tires me but I wouldn't say I dislike it, exactly. It's quite interesting to see all the different folk who eat and drink there."

Roland's voice was husky. I' m glad you're reasonably happy. I only wish—" "What?"

He shook his head. "Oh, no matter."

"I found Exeter a bit over-large and noisy at first. There were so many people rushing here, there, and everywhere. But I've come to like it, even though I still miss the Forest."

"I hope Captain Mountjoy is well."

"He is. He wrote to me recently. I hope he comes to visit us soon, then I'll show him the Cathedral."

"Would you mind if I came, too?"

"Of course not."

Roland suddenly took Starella in his arms. She knew he was about to kiss her. Her arms crept around his neck as she felt his firm hands on her shoulders. "Oh, Starella, I've been longing to see you for such an age!"

Starella laughed nervously. "I haven't been here that long but—" She hesitated. "I know you'll think I'm over-bold for saying this, but I've been living in hope that I would see you again soon."

Roland began to rain passionate kisses upon her making Starella feel as if she had been swept up in a gale. She clung to him for a few moments, staring up at him, letting her instincts rule her actions. Then, she gave a little cry as she pushed him away, gently, trying to resume her customary self-control. Starella looked down at the ground, then back up again. She knew she must clear her mind of tumultuous thoughts that could end in disaster.

"We must go now," she said, reluctantly. "The Travers will start wondering what has become of me."

Roland nodded, his expression resigned. "Yes, you're right. They will think I've abducted you."

Starella gave a slight shudder. "Have you forgotten I was kidnapped once? It was hardly a pleasant experience."

Roland could have bitten his tongue out when he saw her expression and heard her tone. "I was most indiscreet. I do hope you'll be able to forgive me as I didn't mean to offend you."

"I'm not offended now, sir. However, I fear we may be a little late for our supper." Starella's tone was slightly formal.

"I'm not particularly hungry for food," Roland said, wistfully.

Starella did not reply although she had heard the longing in his voice and she desired him strongly. She was afraid to speak in case she betrayed her own feelings and would be unable to control herself again.

Roland offered her his arm. She took it and they strolled back to Dolly's Coffee House in a preoccupied silence.

*   *   *   *

The next day, Roland Chivers paid an unexpected visit to the coffee house. He asked for a private word with the Travers and Starella. Margery sent Simpson to fetch her husband from the Exchange.

"I have a surprise for you all," Roland said, after David had returned. "Excuse me a moment." When he came back, he ushered in two small, shivering Negro boys, both bare-chested and wearing ragged breeches.

Starella and the Travers stared at them.

"Their names are Reuben and Raphael," Chivers said. "Reuben is to be my page. As for Raphael, I am sure you will be able to find him suitable employment here."

"Do I understand you to mean, Mr Chivers, that you are giving us this child, obviously a slave, as … a gift?" David Travers asked in amazement.

Momentarily, Roland looked uncomfortable then he said, "Indeed, I am. I found them both at the market. An Exeter captain had brought them there from the docks and put them up for sale with other adult Negroes. I think they are about nine or ten."

Neither boy had yet spoken. Both looked around the room with great interest, rolled their eyes and exchanged glances. Starella continued to stare at them in fascination. She had previously only seen negro servants at a distance.

"Well," Margery was obviously flustered. "It's a kind thought of yours, I suppose, Mr Chivers. I have quite often seen fine ladies with blackamoor pages and suchlike, but never thought to have one, myself." She turned to her husband. "What do you think, Mr Travers? What work should this slave boy be given?"

"Before they start anything, my love, they should be taken to the kitchen and fed while we discuss this."

Margery sent for the maid who looked just as astonished as her employers. However, she had the sense to keep quiet, escorting the two black lads to the kitchen.

"Well, what tasks shall we set him to, Mr Travers?" Margery repeated, after they had gone.

"H'm, I think he could light the fires when the winter comes and generally help Simpson by placing the newspapers on the tables and so on. He could also help Starella and Eve to serve."

Margery looked relieved. "Yes, a good idea, really. Don't you agree, Mr Chivers?"

"Yes, it is." Starella frowned in annoyance. "Does the boy himself have any choice in what he is to do?" she asked.

Margery gave her a black look. Roland spoke quickly. "I forgot to tell you that I've been told he can play a kind of wooden flute the Negroes have. Your patrons might find this quite diverting."

"Of course he won't understand himself yet what's expected of him," said David Travers. "But I must say it was most helpful of Mr Chivers to have supplied him to us."

"Could I have a private word with Mr Chivers?" Starella asked.

"Very well," David said, reluctantly. "But only for a few minutes."

"I have really offended you this time, have I not, Starella?" Roland said, when they were alone in the corridor.

"Yes, you have. They're human beings and I don't agree with slavery."

Roland sighed. "I know you're not alone in the way you feel. Many others would agree with you. But we have to realise it exists and we cannot stop it on our own."

"But surely we don't have to encourage it! You're not in the West Indies, now."

"My dear, the boys would have been slaves to a chief in Africa, their own country. They were part of a tribe which was captured by another."

"What I completely fail to understand is, if you had to buy them, why have you brought one here to the coffee house?"

"Because Captain Mountjoy's relatives are growing older and you said you tended to get tired on occasion. An extra pair of hands is always useful."

In spite of her disapproval, Starella felt herself begin to soften. She was beginning to relish the prospect of having a youngster she could teach to assist her with the making and serving of various drinks. Hopefully, she would not have so much running around to do."

"Starella," Roland said, a mild note of pleading in his voice. "I know the Travers will treat Raphael fairly and kindly as I shall treat Reuben."

"I'm sure they will," Starella conceded.

"They could have gone to a cruel master and mistress. I bought them because they're still children and I should not have liked this to happen to them."

Starella gave her head a slight shake. "I suppose you're right," she said, in a resigned tone. "I really must get back to my work now, Mr Chivers."

"As you wish," Roland answered, sounding as formal as she did. He moved aside to let her pass. She did so without the backward glance he was hoping for.

Starella bit her lip. She wished she could dislike Roland for what he had done but knew she could not.

*   *   *   *

"The sheriff's right hand man has brought two nigger boys to Dolly's," the Travers' new maid said to Samuel Hill. She and Hill were seated in Avery Hodgkins' luxurious town house, one evening two weeks later. Around the room were various items—swords, pistols, men's brocade suits, women's silk gowns and fans and jewellery. Both men nodded. "I'm going to sell them as soon as we take over," said Hodgkins.

"Starella won't like it," the maid added. "She didn't agree with it."

All three laughed.

"I'm going to have my revenge on that bitch when we own that damned coffee house," Hill said, grimly. "I'm going to have a star sign outside so that people will know what the place's real use is and she can be the whore I always intended her to be."

The young woman looked pleased. "That'll serve her right for thinkin' she's better than me! I don't like havin' to wait on her at table." Hodgkins gestured to the maid. "Come here." He handed her two golden guineas which she bit.

"You've proved your usefulness with the information you've given. But I shan't need you again. Leave us now." With some reluctance, she left.

Hodgkins gestured at the goods lying around the room. "You've done well to bring me this stuff, Sam. It was worth your escape. Tell me how you did it again. I know I've heard it all before but I like the story."

"Marcus Rose, the Smuggling King, who I knew years since, heard about my plight. He used to visit me and bribe the jailers. One night, he had given one particular jailer who he knew to have a particular fondness for liquor, two bottles of brandy. The fool almost drank himself insensible because he couldn't hold his drink."

"A real idiot, I agree," Hodgkins said.

"Rose also brought me food, drink, candles and crooked nails with which to pick my handcuffs. I still had leg irons on but managed to break the links holding them to the staples in the floor. I used a thick iron bar to pull myself up to the chimney. Then, I climbed through it and broke through a wall into a strong room from where I used one of the iron spikes on the wall I managed to get on to an outside wall. I was lucky to be able to climb down this wall with no broken bones, only cuts and bruises."

"I like a good, strong man around me," Hodgkins said, approvingly. He gestured at the items strewn about the room. "I can't sell this lot in England because their owners are too well known. I'd be traced."

"What will you do with them, Avery?"

"I'll send them in my sloop to a Flushing warehouse. They'll be sold there."

"And other stuff brought back, I expect."

"Naturally. I advertise as a trader who can be found at a certain coffee house in the city."

Both men laughed heartily.

"Simpson's our man. He'll co-operate with us for a good reward."

Hill nodded with satisfaction. "I'm about to pluck a new bird I've found. He'll help me get even with the sheriff's interfering crony," he said.

"Who is it?"

"A young, noble gentleman who, stupid bastard, got himself into debts he couldn't handle. I like that kind." Hill was gloating.

Hodgkins made a dismissive gesture. "Yes, yes, but what's his name? I might know him."

"I believe you do. It's Lord Adrian Mallard."

CHAPTER 15

▼

The welcome early Spring had arrived in Exeter along with Captain Mountjoy. The Travers were allowing Starella a few days off from the coffee house to spend some time with him. She was very grateful to them and delighted to see him again.

The morning's weather was fine although containing a slight breeze as they walked to Exeter Cathedral. They looked at the fifteenth century clock in the north transept showing the sun and moon revolving around the earth thereby telling the hour and age of the moon.

Charles was especially interested in the Minstrels Gallery with the angels playing fourteenth century musical instruments including the viol, harp, shawm, timbrel and cymbals.

"Your mother might have been interested in these musical angels as her brothers were sort of primitive musicians," Mountjoy said.

"Yes, I suppose she would." Starella was wishing Roland were with them.

Charles glanced at her sharply but merely said, "We'll leave here now and go to a good inn for refreshment." After their meal, they returned to Dolly's where Charles asked David and Margery if they would like to go to the theatre that evening with himself and Starella, at his expense.

They happily said that they would love to do so as Simpson could be left in charge of the coffee house and Eve was sent to bespeak the tickets.

"I hope we'll be safe there," Margery said, with a delighted shiver of apprehension.

"Why should we not be?" Starella asked, puzzled.

"I'm not sure I should repeat the tale to you, my dear. It's a little unfit for young and delicate ears."

"Starella can be told," David said to his wife, a little impatiently. To Starella, he said, "There's a legend about that theatre in Waterbeer Street where we're going." He leaned forward, looking grave yet eager at the same time. "There was a performance of 'Dr Faustus' in '49 and it was said that the Devil himself appeared beside the actor playing Mephistopheles." Margery gave another shiver.

"Maybe it was only a rumour. We all know what tricks our imaginations can play on us at times," said Charles. "It could have been realistic acting."

Starella nodded. "Probably only a tale."

"Tale or not, it was very widely rumoured," David announced.

"Even so, I'm certain no devils will trouble us tonight," Charles said.

"I believe, myself, that the only devils which might plague us are the blue ones," Starella said. She had earlier experienced a feeling of melancholy she could not quite understand and had tried, unsuccessfully, to shake it off.

David frowned, Margery sighed and Mountjoy spoke, his tone a little sharp. "We shall not be troubled by any devils, blue or otherwise."

"Before it grows dark, I intend to hire a carriage and take Starella to that beautiful village you told me about, David," Charles said. "I believe it's called Ide," he added.

David Travers nodded. "Yes, it is."

Starella began to feel more cheerful. She had been afraid that once they had re-entered the coffee house, she would be expected to resume her duties. She smiled and thanked the captain for his kindness.

Charles and Starella found their visit to the village of Ide nestling in the folds of steep hills with their many streams, very pleasurable. Starella felt closer to her former guardian than she had for a long time and began to wish they could stay together on their own for a longer period of time. She felt almost contented.

"I'm not sure I wouldn't prefer to stay here rather than go to the theatre, tonight," she said.

Charles shook his head. "You would always wonder what you had missed. You've never been to the theatre before in your life, have you?"

"Aunt Catherine didn't believe it was right for me to attend or so she said." She hesitated. "However, I have a confession to make. I have seen strolling players."

Mountjoy smiled. "Have you, indeed?"

"Yes, it was most interesting."

That evening, they took their seats inside the theatre. Margery sat, wide eyed with wonder at its surroundings although she was a little frightened by some of the noisy people in the audience. Starella was delighted, determined to enjoy the performance. But she experienced a slight thrill of fear when she realised the main subject of the play concerned a highwayman.

When the leading actor began to act the scene of a stage coach hold-up, a man sitting near Captain Mountjoy's party shouted out, "I heard of a real life 'old up not long ago where a lady reported the villain. So, afterwards, he cut her tongue out just before he stabbed her!"

Margery shivered again although looking interested. Starella could not repress a shudder. She was relieved that nothing as bad as this had ever happened while she was a decoy. Charles saw her expression.

"Excuse me but I do not really think this is a suitable subject when there are ladies present," he said.

"No, it's not. I beg your pardon," the man said, a little stiffly. He took his leave of them as the next act was about to begin.

At the end of the final act, the well-dressed man wearing a new wig, his face hidden in the shadows by his high shirt frills, quietly said to his companion, "That confounded girl's too well protected for me to grab her tonight. But as for the old couple, you know what you have to do about them, don't you?"

"Yes, Mr Hill," his accomplice replied.

"Do it soon. Simpson will help, if necessary."

*   *   *   *

The following day Captain Mountjoy visited Topsham, the attractive maritime village at the head of the Exe Estuary to do business with a fellow ship builder. The day after he returned to the Forest, pleased with other contacts he had made in Topsham. Starella was sorry to see him go and resumed her duties at the coffee house with some reluctance.

"Starella," David said. "Margery and I have been invited to pay a visit upon an important merchant tomorrow. It's quite an honour so I want to ask a favour from you. We know it's a lot of responsibility but we are trusting you to run Dolly's for us as you've proved yourself to be capable. It's only for one day. Do you think you'll be able to manage it with Simpson's help?"

"I should imagine so." Starella had seen the unspoken plea in David's eyes.

He looked highly relieved. "Thank you so much. We will, of course, let you know the address we'll be at in case anything untoward happens. We'll have to pray it won't."

"Don't worry. I'm sure everything will run smoothly."

David looked grateful. "We'll reward you for this."

"It's a kind thought but I'm sure there's no need."

"No, no, I insist. We'll give you some sort of gift."

Starella was pleased by his comment.

The coffee house was busy the next day but she felt she had coped well and looked forward to receiving her present.

The Travers came back with Roland Chivers.

"We met Mr Chivers on our way home," David said. "We've insisted on bringing him back with us to share a glass or two of wine. You must have some, too, Starella. You deserve it."

Roland inclined his head in Starella's direction.

"You haven't seen him for some time, have you?" Margery asked, coyly.

To her annoyance, Starella felt herself blushing. Embarrassment made her unintentionally abrupt. "No."

"It's a pleasure to see you, Miss Starella," said Roland. "I only wish I could pay calls more often but I'm so busy, I'm afraid it's impossible."

They all shared a bottle of claret washed down with Margery's buns. Roland talked of generalities, only occasionally including Starella in the conversation although he often looked at her. She found herself more tongue tied than usual, knowing it was not only caused by wine and fatigue. She wished she could have made witty, engaging remarks but they eluded her.

"Dear Mr Travers is so glad he's managed to gain some more business," said Margery. "And I must say I'm delighted for him."

"Thank you, my dear."

"I must say," said Roland, "that I think Miss Starella fared very well in running the coffee house as she did. However, if you will forgive me speaking plainly after you've shown hospitality to me, I don't think she should be left on her own again, especially as Captain Mountjoy particularly asked that she be protected at all times."

David frowned and Margery twisted her hands together, nervously, after glancing at his expression. Starella looked down at the floor, biting her lip. She was half irritated that Roland seemed to think she was too irresponsible to be left alone, half flattered that he was concerned for her safety.

"It was only on this one occasion," David said, testily. "And she would have had protection from Simpson had the need arisen."

"I know, and it's fortunate there's been no trouble." Roland gripped his glass as he looked around the room. "Agreeable as Dolly's is, I don't really believe that a young lady like Miss Starella should be left here to run it on her own."

Slightly mollified, David said, "I doubt that she will be, again." His tone indicated that the subject should now be closed.

"I must take my leave of you now," said Roland. He thanked David and Margery for their hospitality. "Sleep well, Miss Starella," he said, as he left.

"I'm sure I shall, Mr Chivers," she said, dryly.

$$*\qquad*\qquad*\qquad*$$

The next morning Avery Hodgkins said to Margery, "My dear Mistress Travers, I believe Lord Mallard is calling here once again this evening."

"Yes, he is, Mr Hodgkins," Margery simpered. "I'm so excited about it. I found him so charming the last time he came. Such a shame he could only stay for a little while."

"Well, Mistress Travers, Lord Mallard would like to take you and your husband out for a ride in his new carriage this afternoon for an hour," Hodgkins said. "I know your husband is at the Exchange but I'm sure he'll be back here in time." He looked around the room which was moderately full but not crowded. "But of course you may feel you're too busy attending to your customers, which you do admirably."

Margery beamed, then cast an anxious look in Starella's direction.

"You go," she said, fingering the opal necklace David had given her. "I'll manage."

"But we really shouldn't leave you on—"

"It's only for an hour," Starella interjected, firmly. "If I managed a whole day by myself, yesterday, then I can surely cope for an hour."

Margery looked highly relieved. "You're a good girl, Starella."

"Yes, you are," said David. "Thank you for helping us."

"I'm sure you'll do me a favour in return some day," Starella replied.

"That we will," David agreed, thinking they had already done the girl a great favour by allowing her a week's free time with Captain Mountjoy.

*   *   *   *

That evening, Hodgkins brought Lord Mallard to Dolly's. "We wish to play a hand of whist, Lord Mallard and I," he said.

David looked worried. "It's not really legal to play cards in coffee houses."

"Surely, Mr Travers," said Margery, laying a pleading hand on her husband's arm. "It wouldn't matter just for once."

Starella glanced at Lord Adrian Mallard who was scowling. He was a tall, handsome young man with blond hair and a fair complexion. Yet she decided, there was a petulant twist to his mouth.

"Did you enjoy your ride with me, Mr and Mrs Travers?" he asked.

"Very much indeed, of course we did," said David.

"Well, then, I really don't see why."

"I'm sure if you allow us to discreetly play just one game, we'll clear the deck away at the first sign of any raid," Hodgkins said, smoothly. "But I'm sure that won't happen."

"Just this once, then," David Travers said, reluctantly. An interested crowd started to gather around Lord Mallard's table.

Several card games were played that night. Lord Mallard began by playing with Hodgkins and winning. Then he challenged other patrons to play with him which they readily agreed to do. But Lord Mallard won each game.

Raphael had been unobtrusively watching every move. When the opportunity arose, he slipped out of Dolly's, running swiftly through the dark streets to Roland Chivers' home.

"Massa Roland, I done see dat Lord Mallard playin' cards at de coffee house. He's a cheat."

Reuben's eyes opened wide. "You sure 'bout dis?"

"Yes, I sure am," Raphael said, contemptuously.

"Thank you for telling me, Raphael, well done," said Roland. "Is Miss Starella all right?"

"Yessir."

Roland breathed a sigh of relief. "Good. Reuben, go and get the carriage and the horses ready. Then I'll drive us back to Dolly's Coffee House."

"Yes, Massa Roland."

"Will you be able to get back in without being seen, Raphael?"

"Sure thing, Massa Roland. I knows way in by de back door."

254 A ROSE AND A STAR

Roland gave Raphael a golden guinea. "You're a wonderful mine of information, Raphael; so is Reuben about other things. I'm lucky to be able to use you both almost as an extra pair of eyes and ears. Hide your money, don't say I gave it to you."

"No, sir."

"Have you played your flute at the coffee house, lately?"

"Yessir, but not tonight. Dey too interested in de cards."

Roland gave a rueful smile. "Yes, they will be."

Reuben came back to announce that the horses were saddled and the carriage was waiting.

Roland halted a street away from Dolly's. "Get down, Raphael, and get back as quick as you can. Watch out for any more games of cards and let me know what happens like you have, tonight. Then there'll be two golden guineas for you. I do hope you don't get into trouble for running out, tonight."

"I won't get in no trouble, Massa Roland, I swears."

"I hope so, for your sake. Watch Miss Starella for me."

"Yessir, I will do dat."

Raphael climbed down from the carriage with a lithe, quick movement. A moment later, he had vanished into the night. Roland sat in his carriage with a thoughtful expression on his face.

*   *   *   *

Raphael returned to the coffee house. Lord Mallard signalled to him to bring a drink over to the table where the card game was becoming noisy. Raphael approached Lord Mallard to take his order.

Lord Mallard looked up from the game. "Send that girl over to me, nigger boy," he said, pointing to Starella who was serving another customer. Raphael was apprehensive but did not know how he could disobey.

Suddenly, a fierce argument broke out. "You've been cheating, Mallard, you're a card sharp!" one of the other players protested. Mallard hotly tried to deny this but many others agreed with his opponent. David tried to stop the altercation but to no avail, as Margery burst into noisy tears. Starella bit her lip.

Raphael seized his opportunity to fetch Roland.

"Please, Lord Mallard, please leave," Starella said. "Many people here tonight aren't enjoying your company and you're abusing the hospitality of our house."

"I don't take orders from serving maids," Mallard protested, bodily thrusting her out of the way. He grinned. "All the same, you'll make a good armful later on."

Starella flushed. She was shaken but managed to object. "No, I most certainly shall not!"

Bottles, cups and glasses started to be knocked off tables and punches were thrown. Fortunately, no-one was seriously hurt even though some were badly bruised and one man sported a black eye. David, Margery and Starella could do nothing but stare in horror. Then, an audible pistol was heard being fired into the air just outside the coffee house door. It startled all those present into silence.

The door swung open and Roland walked in. He gasped in horror as he looked around at the carnage. "What the devil has been going on here?" he asked David.

"Lord Mallard was playing cards but found to be a cheat. We think he should be arrested."

"You're right, I'll summon the constables," Roland agreed, glancing at Starella who, to his relief, did not appear to be physically hurt apart from her obvious distress.

Mallard placed his hand on Roland's sleeve. "Please, sir, I'll pay you some money if you don't go for them."

Roland shook his hand away. "I don't take bribes."

David said, "I've changed my mind, sir. My wife and myself would be much obliged if you would take the money as long as Lord Mallard agrees to leave quietly and never comes back here."

"It's a good idea," Starella said as Roland hesitated.

"You are unhurt, Starella?"

"Yes, though I admit I was scared for a while."

Roland smiled. "I'm not surprised." He turned to Mallard. "I don't want your money, I just want you out of here as quickly as possible."

"I'll go now to satisfy you all," Mallard said, striding quickly out of the door.

"Everyone else should leave now, too." Roland's gaze encompassed the room. Some customers left a little reluctantly but they all went eventually. Roland ordered Reuben and Raphael to make sure Mallard was not in the vicinity.

"I'm going to keep Raphael living with me," Roland said. "I think he'll be safer than if he stayed here."

Starella was delighted. "I am so glad. I'm fond of him and I'd hate anything bad to happen to him."

"He's proved to be of great service tonight."

"I don't know how to thank you for what you've done for us, Mr Chivers," David said to Roland.

"Don't try now," Roland replied. "I think you should all go to bed and get as much sleep as you can before you start tidying up. There'll be a lot of work for you all to do tomorrow."

"That there will," David sighed. "I believe we'd best close the place for a week. I know there'll be a loss of trade but I'd prefer to let things quieten down before we open again."

"I think that's a wise decision on your part," Roland said. He smiled again at Starella, who wondered if she had just imagined that she saw a lovelight in his eyes.

CHAPTER 16

─────────▼─────────

"They're very late coming back," Starella said to Eve with an anxious frown. A week after their previous outing with Hodgkins, the Travers had once again gone for a ride in his carriage. "I thought they would have been back at least half an hour ago. It's already dusk and it will be dark soon. I do hope they haven't had an accident of some kind."

She looked around the room, hoping forlornly that the Travers would suddenly appear.

"I'll go and look for them with Raphael," Eve said.

Starella bit her lip. "I'm not sure that you'd be safe yourself. I'd hate any harm to come to either of you."

Eve tossed her hair back with a contemptuous gesture. "I know how to take care of myself and Raphael's a big, strong lad." There was a note of irritation in her voice but Raphael looked pleased by her compliment.

Starella signalled to him to stop playing his flute. She normally liked its sound but in her present anxious state, it jarred on her nerves. She looked around the room. The coffee house was exceptionally quiet with very few customers.

"Well, I suppose you could maybe—"

"No!" Simpson roared. The other three were shaken by his vehemence. He glared at Starella. "Them two youngsters shouldn't wander about on their own. You should have had more sense than to agree to it."

Starella began to feel ashamed as well as worried.

"I'll go, myself," the man added in a quieter tone. "You'll manage, won't you?"

Starella nodded. "Thank you, Mr Simpson. I'll be really grateful to you if you can find them."

Simpson did not reply. He slammed the door behind him after he went out.

"Normally, I'd love this place being so empty," Starella said to Eve. "We could take things easy for once. "But tonight, I wish it were really busy. If we were fully occupied, it would take our minds off things a little." She wondered if her anxiety was making her babble.

"We'd still be fretted even if we was rushed off our feet." Eve was almost phlegmatic. "Then we'd be no use to no-one if we felt worn out."

"I suppose you're right," Starella agreed. Then, she frowned. "I do hope Simpson manages to find them."

"I'm sure he will," Eve said, reassuringly. "He knows his way about the streets like the back of his hand. He's the right man to bring them back."

"Eve, I've got a terrible feeling something really bad has happened."

Eve sighed. "I understand how you feel, Ella, honest I do. But I'm certain sure they've come to no 'arm. They've probably just bin enjoyin' whatever they've been doin' and lost track of time."

"I wish I could believe that."

Another hour passed without sight or sound of the Travers or Simpson.

"Look, Ella, I wouldn't suggest this usually," Eve said. "But why don't you sit down and I'll bring you a glass of the mistress's brandy. I know where she keeps it."

Normally, Starella would have refused and suggested to Eve that she would be in a lot of trouble if her mistress caught her doing such a thing. But with her nerves on a knife-edge, she merely whispered, "Thank you, that's a good idea."

As Eve brought the glass of brandy to Starella, the front door opened. "They're back, thank goodness!" she said with heartfelt relief as she saw Simpson coming in.

But as Starella looked more closely at the man and woman behind him, she realised that the couple were not the Travers. She recognised the old maid underneath the finery and heavy cosmetics the woman was wearing. "Jane, why have you come back?" she asked in bewilderment. "Do you know anything about David and Margery?"

Jane Montgomery scowled. "No, I don't!" she snapped, returning Eve's glare. She shrugged. "As to why I've come back here, I have my reasons which aren't for you to know."

Starella reddened. "Of course they're for me to know. You can't just walk in here cool as a cucumber without telling me why."

"I can and I have. In fact I mean to—"

The few remaining customers all left. Eve wondered why they had all gone at the same time. She had never liked Jane Montgomery and was resolved to give the woman a piece of her mind.

Eve was forestalled, however, when Jane's male companion stepped forward from the shadows the very next moment. "That's enough! I'm not in the mood for a catfight so hold your noise," he snapped at Jane.

A broad grin spread across his features as he said, "I'm so pleased to be back with you again, Starella" He bowed to her as if they were partners at a ball. The colour drained from Starella's face as she recognised Samuel Hill. She turned to Simpson. "Abel, please remove this man from here. He's nothing but a rogue and a hateful criminal."

Simpson looked at her, coldly. "For your information, Starella, he's my master as well as Jane's. And he now owns this coffee house so he's yours, too, whether you like it or not. I'm shortly going to bring the Travers' bodies back from the river."

Starella and Eve stared at Hill with absolute horror as Jane Montgomery smiled maliciously. Starella wildly hoped she must be in the middle of a nightmare from which she would soon awaken.

"Please," she whispered, "say this isn't true. Let none of this be really happening. You haven't really murdered them!"

"Get out, Jane. I'll send for you when I need you again," Hill commanded.

Reluctantly, she left the coffee house, casting a triumphant look at Starella and Eve.

Raphael also picked his moment to slip into the street before the others noticed.

Simpson smiled, almost pleasantly. "It's as true as I'm standing here. It wasn't me personally as killed them, you understand. I just knowed about it."

"And," Hill drawled, languidly taking a pinch of snuff. "You needn't think you can run off to your bloody, meddling guardian, Starella, because I set men to watch on him. All his movements were secretly observed after we saw you at the theatre. I arranged for his carriage to be held up at a convenient place. The fool tried to fight us back and now he's dead, too, because we had to shoot him."

As Starella fainted, Eve sprang at Hill, trying to claw his face but he shook her slight form aside as if she were an insect, giving her a kick that made her cry out in pain.

He moved to Starella and picked up her inert body. "Show me her bedroom, quickly, girl!" he snapped at Eve. "If you don't do what you're told, it will be a lot easier to kill you than it was the others."

With a look mixed with revulsion and fear, Eve did so. Hill gently laid Starella down on the bed. Outside the door Eve had started to run but Hill caught her.

"Get your filthy hands off me!" she yelled.

He put his hand over her mouth, dragging the struggling girl back to Starella's bedroom, throwing her inside the room. She landed on her knees.

"Look after Starella when she comes round," he said brusquely as he locked the door behind him. Eve began to pound on it and shout for help.

"Nobody will hear you, you silly bitch!" Hill roared. "I told you to look after Starella. And you know what I'll do to you afterwards if you keep up this row. And don't try any tricks like climbing out of the windows on sheets and blankets because I assure you, you'll be seen by those who will inform me."

With a cunning smile, he went back downstairs.

Hill asked Simpson to bring him a bottle of brandy and a glass, then dismissed the other man. Hill managed to drain the bottle to the last drop and as he was licking his lips, the door opened to admit Avery Hodgkins. Hodgkins was grinning.

"Well done, Avery," Hill said.

"I think you should take a lot of the credit," Hodgkins replied. "You've masterminded this affair. I merely carried out part of the practical side."

"Did you manage not to be seen, Avery?"

"I'm sure of it."

"I had to do it in a devil of a hurry," Hodgkins said. "My valet was bribed well to say nothing but the other servants have no suspicions."

"Good, we have to know who we can trust. I've sent Simpson home. He's served his purpose for now but I'll be using him again."

Hodgkins looked around. "Where's Starella?"

"In bed with a silly maid looking after her. Starella was quite upset when she heard the sad news about both her employers and her guardian's dreadful murder. Of course, I'll do my best to make her forget her sorrows."

Hill looked down at the floor, the expression on his face a parody of a grief-stricken mourner. Both men laughed heartily afterwards.

"Shall we get the girls down and have some sport with them?" Hodgkins asked, eagerly.

Hill shook his head. "Not yet. They're distressed at the moment so they wouldn't resist much. It'll be better when they feel a bit better. Then, they'll try to put up a fight and we'll both enjoy overpowering them. I'll relish the feeling of power I'll get, then."

"I suppose you're right," Hodgkins said, reluctantly. "Is there any more brandy in this damned place? My mouth feels as dry as a parrot's cage."

"No, but I know where there's some wine. I've had a good look around as you can imagine." Hill looked around with satisfaction. "I have grand plans for this house. They'll include some of your ideas, Avery. The nigger boy will fetch a good price, I'm sure."

"That's one of the first things I think you should do, Sam."

"Don't worry. I intend to. Come on, I'll show you the wine cellar."

Hill and Hodgkins both drank a considerable amount of wine. Hill closed his eyes as Hodgkins walked to a cupboard on the other side of the room and opened the door. "I'm going to visit an obliging whore of my acquaintance," Hodgkins said, when Hill's eyes opened a few minutes later. "Simpson, you can come too."

Simpson looked pleased.

Hill was puzzled. "But I thought you'd both be staying here with me."

"I did intend us to but I've changed my mind. I'll be back early in the morning. By the way, I found some brandy in a cupboard. You can have it."

Hodgkins withdrew a small bottle of brandy from his pocket and handed it to Hill who looked pleased. Hodgkins and Simpson left the house.

In her bedroom, Starella returned to consciousness. She looked helplessly at Eve who was sitting by the edge of her bed. "Oh, Eve, we're in that evil man's power now. I wish I could kill myself. Three people I love are now dead. I might as well be, myself." She put her head in her hands and wept bitterly.

"That's foolish talk, Ella, and you know it," Eve said, sternly. "We'll get out of this coil, somehow." She sounded a lot braver than she actually felt. She put her hand on Starella's brow. "You must go back to sleep and get your strength up."

Starella laughed but there was no mirth in the sound. "I think I've slept long enough."

"Listen," Eve said. "We'll both sleep now, then we'll creep downstairs when we wake up. We'll put a couple of dolls on the pillows. I know you've got one and the mistress kept one of her old ones, too. I know where it is. That bastard will probably have drunk himself into a stupor; then we can climb out of the kitchen window."

Starella was doubtful about the wisdom of this plan. "I'm not sure that would work and we couldn't do this because—"

"Yes, we can and we will," Eve broke in, with great determination. "I need a sleep myself. You don't mind me gettin' in bed with you, do you?"

"Of course not," said Starella, throwing back the covers. "I think I'd be going completely mad without you." The two girls hugged each other. Eve climbed into the bed and was asleep within minutes.

Starella closed her eyes but did not sleep. Images of the Travers and Captain Mountjoy kept surfacing in her mind. Deliberately, she forced them away, making herself concentrate on ruse after ruse about how they could escape from the coffee house without being noticed. But she dismissed each plan as impractical.

CHAPTER 17

▼

There was a very loud knocking at the door of the coffee house the following morning. When Hill awoke, he still felt drowsy and had a bad headache. A loud, masculine voice shouted: "Come on, Simpson, open the door, damn you! This is Lord Adrian Mallard."

Hill let him in.

"You're not Simpson," Mallard said to Hill, as he entered with Roland Chivers. "No sir, he's been allowed a day off."

Hill looked at Roland and his face darkened. "What's this bastard doing with you? I seem to remember him from when I was arrested."

Mallard looked puzzled. Hill glowered in Roland's direction. Roland's bland expression did not change. "I think you are mistaken, sir. I probably just resemble somebody else you saw in the dark." Roland's tone was smooth. Hill still did not look convinced.

"I assure you, Sam," said Mallard, "I became acquainted with Mr Chivers at a card party. It was held by a notorious whore who is no friend of the authorities. I think you know who I mean."

Hill laughed. "Indeed I do. Her card parties are famous. Did you win her hand, Adrian?"

Mallard grinned. "Indeed, I did and much more of her besides. Mr Chivers and I are going to have another hand of whist. I fancied another game."

Hill said, "Yes, your fondness for the gaming table is well known, my lord. Nobody's yet been able to beat you, have they?"

"No."

Hill grinned, wolfishly. "What are the stakes?"

"Mr Chivers has a plantation in the Indies. If I win, it will become mine. If he wins he—"

A covert look passed between Hill and Mallard. Roland pretended not to notice.

"Yes, if Mr Chivers wins, what does he gain?" Hill asked.

"My estate," said Mallard. "It's in Devon; it's called Barwell."

"A prize worth winning, you must agree, Mr Chivers," said Hill.

"Indeed, I do."

Mallard and Roland sat down at a table. Hill stood around, watching with interest.

Mallard dealt. Roland won one trick and then lost one. Lord Mallard did the same and then Mallard won three tricks. He turned over a card from the bottom of the pack, which Roland glimpsed.

"You are cheating, sir!" he exclaimed, angrily. "The cards at the bottom of the pack are marked. So I should be entitled to take your estate. However, I believe Starella is on these premises. If you bring her to me and let her go, you may keep your estate."

A few moments later, the wildly struggling Starella, held firmly in Hill's iron grip, was carried into the room, followed by a loudly protesting Eve. Hill threw Starella to the ground almost as if she were a sack. Eve helped her to her feet. Still shaky, she could not believe her eyes when she saw Roland.

There was another knock at the door. Hill rushed to it and admitted Hodgkins and Simpson. "Welcome back," Hill said, with an evil grin. "You're going to enjoy what's coming next."

Hill swiftly drew out a dagger, yelling, "I'm going to kill all of you now!"

Starella and Eve both screamed in terror.

Quick as a flash, Roland ducked, avoiding Hill's lunge for his heart. Then, he picked up a brandy glass, hurling it at the window. The glass shattered and the front door was once again thrust open.

The next moment, the figure of what appeared to be a bent old woman entered Starella thought she must surely be in the middle of a terrible nightmare.

Hill turned pale, his face as white as a lily.

"Yes, you're right," the apparition said, in a cracked, old voice. "I'm the old woman what you attacked on the highway. You cut my tongue out and I died soon afterwards. But now I'm a ghost I got my voice back."

Hill, Hodgkins and Simpson all looked horrified. Starella felt as if she were frozen to the spot she stood on while Eve fainted. Only Roland looked unperturbed.

The door opened again to admit the sheriff and a posse of his men. Mallard wildly fired at Roland but the sheriff knocked the gun out of his hand. The bullet, however, backfired and Mallard fell to the ground.

The sheriff beckoned to the old woman who threw back her mob cap with hairy hands to reveal a man's face.

"Well done," said the sheriff. "The best acting this side of Drury Lane. It was a stroke of genius to wear the crone's clothes, the ones she wore when she was robbed. I'll have you put on the boards." He kicked the prone body of Lord Adrian Mallard. "Put another shot in him. Save the hangman a job. He'll have enough with these three." He indicated the still pale Hill, Simpson and Hodgkins.

The shot rang out, fired by the "old woman" who then said, coolly, "I'll go out and change these clothes, now."

Eve recovered from her faint. "Where's the ghost woman?" she whispered, fearfully. "I always thought they was white ladies. That one wasn't. That one was dressed all in black."

"It was no ghost, Eve," Starella said, gently. "And it was a 'he'."

"I must protest, sir," Hodgkins said to the sheriff. "I'm no criminal."

"I have to disagree with you, there, Mr Hodgkins," the sheriff retorted. "We've kept a close watch on your smuggling activities, little though you knew it. We also knew Lord Mallard was Hill's creature because of his gambling debts."

Starella yelled: "He's a murderer! He killed my guardian's cousins."

"Do you have proof of this?" the sheriff asked. Starella bit her lip. "No, I'm afraid not."

"The bodies were recovered, sir," said Roland. "It can't really be proved but the old couple were last seen in Hodgkins' company."

"You have done very well, Mr Chivers," the sheriff said. "I'm really grateful to you."

"In that case, sir, could I ask a favour?"

"Name it, though I swear you'll receive a good reward for this night's work. And I'll have a word with the lawyers to make sure you take charge of Lord Mallard's estate."

Roland shook his head. "No, it's not money or land I'm after. Could I please take these two young ladies to a place of safety where I can keep an eye on them? I think they've already seen enough horrible sights for one night."

"Yes, very well. But come and see me tomorrow morning at ten o'clock sharp."

"Thank you, sir. Come, ladies, I'm taking you to a nearby inn. I would put you up at my house but you both need a good sleep and I have things to do, there."

"I'm sure we won't be able to sleep after everything that's happened tonight," Starella said. "You were so brave, Mr Chivers."

"Yes, you really was," Eve said, equally admiringly.

"You will both sleep," Roland said, firmly. He took hold of both Starella's and Eve's arms, propelling them into his waiting carriage. When they reached the large and comfortable coaching inn, he arranged for them to share a room. "I'd like a private word with you, landlord," he said, once the girls were in the bedroom. "Can you have them well guarded?" He handed the man two golden guineas.

"Certainly, sir. I know the very ostler. A big, strong fellow if ever there was one."

"Good. Tell him to be extra specially vigilant."

"Vigilant?"

Roland nodded, impatiently. "Extra specially careful."

"Of course, sir."

"Your lady wife. I'd like her to prepare them a hot drink before they go to bed. Please also tell her to supply them with a maidservant. Only one trustworthy woman, mind."

"I'll tell my wife to do that, sir."

"Would she also be able to give them both a sleeping draught?"

The landlord was intrigued. Roland handed him another guinea. "Not a word to them or anyone else that she's doing so."

"I promise not one word will pass our lips."

"Good. There'll be another guinea for you tomorrow if your wife arranges for them to breakfast privately at nine thirty or so in the morning. I shall be calling upon them later on."

"I look forward to seeing you then, sir."

$$*\qquad*\qquad*\qquad*$$

Starella and Eve, both of them still slightly drowsy, were served a hearty breakfast the following morning. Eve ate well but Starella picked at her food.

"Just think, Ella," said Eve, with great excitement. "The sheriff and the other men, especially Mr Chivers, saved us from all them horrible men. I include Abel

Simpson when I say this. Him who we thought we knowed right well. He turned out to be just as much a crook and villain as the rest of them."

Starella looked around, fearfully. "Hush Eve, you never know who's listening."

Eve shook her head, stubbornly. "No, don't be frightened. We're quite safe now. Though I has to admit we nearly wasn't. We nearly got murdered like poor Mr and Mrs Travers."

"No, we didn't. Don't exaggerate!" Starella snapped. She felt as if her nerves were really on edge and would be until they left the inn.

"Well, I think we'd have at least been beaten and probably forced to do other vile things into the bargain," Eve said, sulkily.

"I'm sorry I was sharp. It's just that last night was such a nightmare before the sheriff and the others came. I know we were in great danger and I'm as grateful as you are to Mr Chivers for what he did for us. But I'm wondering what he's going to say to us when he arrives."

"More coffee, young mistresses?" the landlady's wife asked, hopefully.

"No thank you," said Starella.

"Yes please," said Eve.

Roland arrived and was served with coffee and pastries. Starella felt as if her heart had leaped but at the same time, she was apprehensive about what he would say about the previous evening.

"I trust you both slept well in spite of your—er—earlier fright?" he asked. Eve nodded.

"Yes, we did, thankfully, Mr Chivers," Starella said. "We're very grateful to you."

Roland gave a wry smile. "I must admit, Starella, you do seem to attract a great deal of attention, wherever you are."

Starella coloured. Noticing, Roland looked away, discreetly.

"How did you know what to do last night, Mr Chivers?" Eve asked, her eyes large.

"The sheriff had been watching Avery Hodgkins for some time and he has a network of informers. It was also our good fortune to net Samuel Hill again. This time, he won't escape. Our game was a little dangerous but fortunately it worked."

"You were very brave," Starella said.

Roland gave a light shrug. "It was a combined effort. But I'm no longer working for the sheriff. He was reluctant to let me go but he has insisted that I'm to have Lord Mallard's old estate. He says I won it fairly and squarely."

"Yes, you did," Eve agreed, hero-worship shining out of her dark eyes.

"I was a bit dubious about my right to it. But the sheriff says he will be having a word with a couple of lawyer friends of his to clear my path. I shall be travelling to the estate today. Will you two young ladies accompany me?"

"I should like to," Starella said. "But I intend to return to my cousins' home as they have now been left without a father."

Roland looked concerned. "He was not killed, the villain told a lie."

Starella felt suffused with joy. "Thank God for that! I think I shall still visit them all."

Roland looked concerned. "Ah, I'm afraid he's gone abroad, to the West Indies. He will be gone for a few months."

Starella looked stricken. "Why did he not tell me? Surely he could have at least sent me a letter."

Roland looked down at the floor. "He has gone with a lady companion, a widow of his acquaintance. He was not sure how you would take this news and asked me to break it to you. He also asked that I would see to your welfare during his absence."

Starella was hurt. "I cannot understand why he thought I would resent this lady. I would have treated her civilly. As for you seeing to my welfare, Mr Chivers, I don't think it's necessary."

Roland raised his eyebrows. "As to that, there is something I could say but I won't."

Starella bit her lip.

"Eve," Roland said, "would you go in search of that landlady and ask her for some more coffee and also ask her to bring a glass of brandy and two glasses of wine. Could you help her pour them?"

Reluctantly, Eve went.

As soon as she had gone, Roland drew a deep breath. "Starella, maybe this is the wrong time to ask this question. But I wondered, will you marry me?"

Starella stared at him. "Did I hear you aright? I didn't dream it?"

Roland smiled, a tender expression on his face. "Yes, I asked you to wed me."

"I should be honoured to become your wife, Roland. But I wouldn't want to marry without Uncle Charles attending the wedding." She scowled. "That is, if he would want to," she added, bitterly.

Roland took hold of her hands. "Of course he will want to. He does love you even if it doesn't seem like it, sometimes. However, I respect your decision to await his return. I'm sure you'll receive a letter from him soon."

"But how can I, if I'm not at Dolly's?"

"I've already written to him myself and I'll make sure he knows of your whereabouts."

Starella smiled. "Thank you, Roland. I don't think I deserve you as a husband." "Of course you do. We need each other." He took her in his arms and kissed her.

CHAPTER 18

▼

The landlady gave a discreet cough as she came into the room. Behind her, Eve was grinning.

After the woman had gone, Roland said, "Eve, Starella has consented to be my wife."

Eve's grin widened even more. "That's wonderful! I'm so pleased for you both."

"Thank you," said Roland, as Starella gave Eve a dazzling smile.

"We're not getting wed for quite a while yet as we're waiting for Captain Mountjoy to return before we have the ceremony. But in the meantime I think we could have a betrothal ball."

"How lovely!" Eve breathed.

"I've given Raphael and Reuben their freedom. I arranged for them to work as servants to two families. I know they'll both be well treated there. The couple Raphael's working for are old but they're not in their dotage. And they've promised to be kind to him."

"Good, I liked him when I got used to him," Eve said.

"Starella will need a personal maid to attend her. Will you undertake this duty, Eve?" Roland asked. He turned to Starella. "You're quite happy about this, aren't you, if Eve agrees?"

"Naturally, I'd love Eve to have this position. If she wants to, of course."

"I'd love to serve you in this way, Ella—sorry—Miss Clayton."

Roland and Starella both laughed. "Go on calling me Ella. I don't mind."

"I'm glad that's settled," said Roland. "Right, let's drink our toast and then we'll go out to my carriage and start our journey to Lord Mallard's old estate."

"Your new one," Eve corrected.

Roland and Starella exchanged smiles. Then she frowned. "But I heard he had a wife and children although he didn't see much of them. He mentioned them once as I recall. What's going to happen to them?"

"Don't worry. I'll see they're well provided for. Barwell Manor will still feed and clothe them."

*   *   *   *

In the late afternoon, Roland's carriage bowled down the tree-lined drive of Barwell Manor. The stables were at the gates of the extensive parkland, the fringes of which stretched into encircling woodland.

Barwell Hall itself was set on a low hill with an approach to water meadows opposite a stone bridge. Near the house was a walled garden with a folly, waterfall and exotic West Indian shrubs.

The Dower House was on the eastern side of the house. It was a rectangular building, larger than Starella had expected. The coachman helped her and Eve to dismount.

Roland offered Starella his arm and escorted her to the front door. A plump, middle-aged woman answered his knock. "We wish to see Lady Mallard. It's important," he said.

The woman looked perplexed as she bobbed a small curtsey. There was open curiosity in the look that she gave the two girls. "I'm Mistress Vale, Lady Mallard's housekeeper," she said. "I'm afraid Lady Mallard is not at home at present. She should be back in about half an hour." The housekeeper sighed. "You'd better come in and I'll have a dish of tea sent in to you."

"My name is Roland Chivers. This is Miss Starella Clayton who is going to become my wife and this is Eve, her lady's maid."

The woman lost interest in looking at Eve but examined Starella closely while pretending she was not. They were admitted to a drawing room.

Lady Mallard entered with her two children, a boy and a girl. She looked to be in her late twenties. She wore a hooped lavender damask gown and a small lace cap over her blonde curls. Her expression was haughty.

"I believe you wished to see me, sir," she said to Roland, completely ignoring Starella and Eve. She indicated her two children. "These two are James, the heir and Cecily, my daughter."

James bowed with confidence and Cecily curtsied, shyly.

Roland took a deep breath. "Lady Mallard, could I speak with you, privately? I'm afraid I bring some bad news."

"Of course, come with me."

Starella smiled at the children while Eve looked around the room in fascinated delight. Starella thought it was unusual for her to be so quiet. "What do you like doing best?" she asked the children.

James' eyebrows rose slightly in surprise. "We like riding our ponies."

"I used to have a pony when I lived in the New Forest."

"What was it called?" James asked.

"It was a mare called Russet. I loved her very much."

"I love my pony, too," said Cecily. "Where do you live now?"

James looked displeased. "Cecily, it's not polite to ask such questions."

"I don't mind at all," Starella said. "I did live in Exeter but I—I'm not quite sure yet where I shall be living now."

Eve looked down at the floor, trying hard not to laugh.

When Roland and Lady Mallard re-entered the room, Starella was engrossed in conversation with Cecily about ponies. James did not look altogether pleased. She guessed he was used to doing most of the talking.

"Children," Lady Mallard said, dabbing at a corner of her eye with a lace handkerchief. Neither Starella nor Eve thought there were genuine tears in her eyes.

"It is my sad duty to tell you that your poor father is dead." Lady Mallard wiped another imaginary tear away. Starella was surprised that neither of the children seemed either distressed or shocked.

"How did it happen?" asked Cecily.

"I can't tell you that, yet, my love. I'll have to explain later."

"Then I will inherit," said James, proudly.

Lady Mallard shook her head. "No," she said, with pursed lips. "You're not old enough and in any case this estate is no longer ours."

James really did look shocked now. "No longer ours! Whatever do you mean, Mamma?"

"Mr Chivers, here—" His mother gave a brief nod in Roland's direction. "He is the new owner. He's shown me the document proving this. We shall be removing to the Dower House."

James and Cecily both gasped. Roland held up his hand.

"Please! I'm sure that's not really necessary, Lady Mallard. There's plenty of room for you and the children here. Starella, Eve and I will not be here forever, just on a temporary basis until Starella and I are married." Eve noticed Lady Mallard very slightly screw up the corner of one eye as she surreptitiously examined Starella.

"Then we shall look for our own house," Roland added. "Forgive me for not having formally introduced you ladies. It was just knowing I had sad news to impart, I forgot my manners."

"I'm sure we can forgive you, Mr Chivers," Lady Mallard said, stiffly. "Nevertheless, I still intend to live in the Dower House with my children. I cannot stay here." She encompassed the manor house with a wave of her hand. "It has such sad memories."

Lady Mallard rang a bell to summon her housekeeper to give instructions for packing her and the children's belongings. Then she added, "Have the two young ladies shown to a bed after they have eaten. Send a maid over to the Dower House with our food because James, Cecily and I will be dining there."

Mrs Vale looked startled, then recovered her customary impassive expression. "Yes, my lady."

"After the young ladies have eaten, have them shown to their rooms. The older one is to have her own, the younger is her lady's maid," Lady Mallard added, with a slight suggestion of a sniff.

Roland frowned. "That's quite right, Mrs Vale. Miss Starella is shortly to become my betrothed." He took hold of Starella's hand and kissed it. "And Eve is her lady's maid but also her friend." Eve bestowed a grateful look upon him. "I hope you will be able to help us plan our betrothal ball."

Mrs Vale looked pleased. She dipped her head. "I'd be more than glad to, sir."

"Come, James, Cecily," Lady Mallard said, crisply, ushering them out of the room without a single backward glance.

*   *   *   *

The next two weeks Roland spent his time in riding around the estate with Lady Mallard and James in order to check on its profits and the health and well being of its workers. James had protested at first that as he was no longer the heir, he could not see the point of his attendance.

"Well," Roland said, firmly, "it's quite likely that you may become the heir again. I intend to see lawyers about it. In any case it's a useful thing to learn, don't you agree, Frances?"

"Yes, it is," Lady Mallard said, her lips slightly pursed.

James looked as if he would like to sulk but he said no more.

In the following two months, Roland looked after the welfare of the villagers on his new estate by sending them extra food and timber from its boundaries. Starella was both pleased and proud that he was so considerate towards them, but Lady Mallard said, "There's surely no need to spoil these oafs so. They're too ignorant to appreciate what you're doing for them. They'll take advantage of you. It's a bad example to set James."

Roland's eyebrows rose. "On the contrary, Frances, James should learn compassion to those less fortunate than himself. The timber will be useful this coming winter."

Frances Mallard looked at Roland with disapproving blue eyes but said nothing more.

Starella spent some of her time reading and meeting the other members of the household staff. She asked Mrs Vale to let her know how the house was run. The housekeeper was a little reluctant at first but Starella was so eager to learn that the older woman's attitude thawed.

Starella and Eve visited the dressmaker in the nearest town where she was kept occupied with fittings for the dress she was to wear for her betrothal ball.

Eve was equally excited. "I love that dress you're going to have, Miss Ella." Starella had decided upon a green flowered lutestring gown trimmed with a rich silk fringe.

"You'll be quite the most beautiful lady in the room," Eve insisted.

Sterella smiled. "Thank you."

"It's true. I swear it!"

✳   ✳   ✳   ✳

On the evening of the ball Roland wore a silver tissue suit. Starella thought she had never seen him look so handsome. He whispered to her while they were dancing, "I love your gown. Its colour matches your beautiful eyes." Starella dimpled with pleasure.

The kaleidoscope of colours of the rich materials the guests wore glittered and swirled in the candlelight but Roland and Starella were only conscious of each other.

Then, an apologetic servant informed Roland that a gentleman outside was insisting upon speaking to him. He resisted the temptation to swear and went out to see who his caller was. To his amazement, he saw that the man was accompanied by a totally black-clad Lady Mallard.

"I believe, sir, you have deprived this poor widow of her estate. Shame on you!"

Roland looked at the other man who was tall but plump. He was well dressed and his voice was cultured.

"It's true that I won Barwell in a card game from her late husband," Roland said, coldly. "But I had no wish to turn Lady Mallard out. It was her own choice to live at the Dower House."

"The poor lady couldn't do much else. She hardly wanted to live in the same house as you and your doxy. I have a good mind to call you out, sir."

Roland controlled his temper with difficulty. "I shouldn't advise it, sir. I am a good shot and if you were not with a lady, I would have flattened you this minute!"

Lady Mallard placed her hand on her companion's arm. "Please, Adam, there's really no need for such unpleasantness. Mr Chivers has been kind to me in his way. This gentleman, Roland, is our neighbour on the next estate, Sir Adam Turner."

"I wish I could say I am pleased to make your acquaintance, Sir Adam. But I cannot when you have just insulted my future bride."

"Maybe I spoke too hastily, Mr Chivers. I hope there will not be bad feeling between us."

Roland gave a very slight inclination of his head and turned on his heel. He overheard Turner say, "A stiff necked fellow, Frances."

"Maybe, but I can well believe him when he said he would knock you out if I weren't present although I appreciate the fact you offered to defend me. I should have been really upset if either of you gentlemen had been hurt. I think we should all be good neighbours." There was a tinge of contempt in Lady Mallard's voice which she could not entirely hide. But the next moment, her tone became placatory.

"Come back with me to the Dower House, Adam, do. I can't attend the ball because I'm a widow, as you know. But I've engaged an excellent fiddler called Silas Incoll. He's the best for miles around. I engaged him before Mr Chivers could do so. Sweet music will soothe our nerves. I also have a fine bottle of claret I'd like you to share with me. I can't drink it all on my own."

Roland found his earlier temper cooling. He smiled as he went back into the ballroom. Immediately he sought out Starella. He signalled to the musicians to stop playing.

Taking Starella's hand in his, Roland announced, "Let's drink a toast to my future bride, Miss Starella Denny."

All the minor gentry and estate workers and the servants watching from the corners of the room, cheered. Roland placed a diamond ring on Starella's finger and kissed her, warmly.

When he escorted her out of the ballroom at her request, in order to take her back to the parlour, the crowd was still shouting hearty congratulations. Eve said, 'It's really been a wonderful night. I expect you're ready for bed, Miss Ella."

Starella looked at Roland and correctly read the expression in his dark eyes. She completely understood his need. "You go on up to bed, Eve," she said, gently. "You must be tired, yourself, by now. I shan't need you, tonight."

After Eve had gone, Roland took Starella's hand and led her upstairs to her bedroom. No words passed between them.

Roland undressed her slowly. "My God, Starella, I cant believe you looked so beautiful tonight.. If you hadn't let me do this, I think I would have gone quite mad. I've waited so long for this moment, I can't describe how I've ached for you."

"You may think I'm too forward but Eve felt exactly the same about you."

There was no need of further words as they took great delight in discovering and exploring each other's bodies. Then, they were both swept away in a passionate blaze of glorious love.

CHAPTER 19

▼

While Roland and Starella had been dancing at the bail, Lady Mallard had been enjoying her conversation with Sir Adam Turner.

'I'll get rid of that impertinent oaf, Chivers, for you, Frances. Then, you can be restored to your rightful place in the Manor House."

Frances shook her head. "No, please Adam. I admit there are times Roland Chivers has annoyed me almost beyond measure. It galls me to see him dancing attendance on that chit, Starella.

"Who is Starella? It's an unusual name."

"Roland Chivers has told me all about her. She's the daughter of a gentle-man—a squire." Frances paused to let her next sentence take effect. "And a gypsy dancer."

Turner's eyebrows rose. He almost whistled.

"That's right. I've been told Starella was born on a full moon night when there were a lot of stars in the sky so her mother took a fancy to give her that name."

"I would not have thought a gypsy slut could be so imaginative."

Lady Mallard frowned. "This stupid ball is being held tonight so that Roland can become betrothed to her."

"He does not mind her birth?"

Frances shook her head. "No, he's no fool in other matters. But anything which concerns Starella, he's smitten beyond reason."

Sir Adam Turner looked as if he could not believe such foolishness. Then he said, "But of course Chivers is no true gentleman himself. You've told me his father is a tradesman, a boat builder?"

"Yes, but in the West Indies."

"No matter, he's still a tradesman's son even if he does act above his station."
Turner laughed but the sound was not pleasant. "I've told you already, I can put
a stop to his wedding."

"No!" Frances almost shouted. "I've told you I don't like him lording it over
our rightful estate. But I certainly don't want him to be murdered in cold blood."

Turner laid his hands over hers and spoke soothingly. "Don't distress yourself
so, my dear. I didn't say I was going to kill him. There are other ways."

"What are they?" Lady Mallard's tone was suspicious.

"I can't tell you in detail. They're too complicated. But trust me to do the
right thing for you, Frances."

"I really hope you can, Adam."

*   *   *   *

"Captain Mountjoy's coming back soon," Roland said to Starella on a cool September night as they were lying in each other's arms.

"I know. He's sent me a letter explaining that he will be marrying himself
when he returns. He apologised profusely for not having informed me that he
was going abroad. She sighed. "He said it was because he thought I might not
approve of his future bride. But I still can't quite forgive him for not telling me he
was going away and so far, too!"

"I do understand how you feel, love. But I should just look forward to his
return. We'll go together to meet him off the ship if you like."

"Yes, I would like that very much. I can't wait for him to come back so that we
can get married."

"I can't wait for the wedding to take place, myself. But at least it won't be long
now. My letter says that the captain has met my father on quite a few occasions."

"I expect you would like to see your father soon, yourself, Roland."

"Yes, I would. My father has had some good fortune. He's inherited a plantation from a second cousin who died without issue recently."

"That's excellent news," Starella said.

"It is, indeed. I should love to show you the islands."

"That would be wonderful!" Starella breathed.

Roland smiled in the darkness. 'I assure you it will be for both of us."

"Do you think Lady Mallard will marry Sir Adam Turner? I know he's been
calling upon her a lot recently."

"I'm not sure," Roland said, pensively. "Men like him are fickle. I daresay he would if she had more money. In the meantime, he's probably quite happy to keep her as his mistress."

"As I am yours."

"Yes, but it won't be long now until you're my wife. After we're wed, I'll have to show you the West Indies."

"I'll probably dream of your islands tonight if I ever go to sleep."

"I'd like to keep you awake all night but I know its not fair!"

They kissed each other, tenderly, before failing asleep with their bodies closely entwined.

*   *   *   *

Early the following morning, Sir Adam Turner surveyed his two hard muscled henchmen. "My servant has acted as a good spy. I persuaded Lady Mallard to send him to help out in the Manor House. Chivers will probably be riding back along the lane in an hour's time. You both know the copse well, I trust."

Turner's henchmen both nodded.

"And I'm glad to see you both have your cloaks, pistols and masks. Put them on now."

As Roland rode to keep his appointment with a violinist he had booked to play at his wedding, later that morning, in the fine weather, whistling a cheerful tune to himself, he came to the most lonely part of his journey across a deserted moor.

The next moment he saw the two masked men jump out of the elegant carriage and advance towards him.

"God above! Highwaymen working in broad daylight!" he exclaimed. "And isn't that Sir Adam Turner's carriage?' he asked himself, suspiciously. Did Turner derive some sort of thrill from disguising himself as a highwayman? But surely it was hardly sensible to use his own carriage? And these two had a slimmer build than Turner. Maybe they had accomplices working in the Turner stables. Roland wondered what he could offer the two men—his watch or his ring?

But the expected demand for money or valuables was not forthcoming. One highwayman knocked him off his horse, giving the animal a blow that sent it flying. While Roland tried to stand up from his sprawling position on the ground, the other felon brought the butt of his pistol down on the back of his head with a ferocious strike which resulted in Roland's becoming unconscious.

The two criminals raced back to the elegant carriage, where they climbed in swiftly. 'Well done, lads,' Turner said with great satisfaction. He then told his coachman to take him to Lady Mallard's house at double-quick speed.

Just before they arrived at the Dower House, Turner ordered his coachman to halt the carriage in a field. "There's nobody working here today, thank God! Right, you two, here's your purses. Now take off your masks, hide your pistols, get out of my carriage and make yourselves scarce. Be off now."

"Will you use us again, sir?" one of the former highwaymen asked.

"Perhaps. I know how to contact you if I do. I'm grateful for what you've done for me today but I want you well away from here now."

"Thank you, sir," said the other former highwayman forestalling his companion's desire to press Sir Adam into a firmer promise. The felons both jumped out of the carriage with an almost athletic grace.

"Frances," said Turner, an hour later after he had been taking tea with Lady Mallard. "Roland Chivers has gone away."

"Where to?" said Frances, looking puzzled.

"My dear, I persuaded him that it would be in his best interests to do so."

"To do what and to go where? You didn't answer my question, Adam."

"I pointed out to him that I have lawyer friends and—"

"He's told me he has them, himself."

"Please, Frances, let me finish. It's not fair that he should act like he's lord of the manor and deprive your son of his inheritance. I have put matters to rights. He agreed to go away, I don't know where to, but surely you agree its a good riddance to us."

Frances gave her lover a sceptical look. "And what about his marriage? Is Starella going away with him?"

Turner looked sly. "Ah, now there he has come to his senses and decided that he does not wish to wed a half-gypsy after all. He's going to send the girl a letter to explain this so she'll also have to leave here and so will her impertinent lady's maid."

"Adam, do you swear you're telling me the truth. You have not bullied him in any way?"

Turner widened his eyes in an effort to make himself look innocent. "I have not threatened him either by word or deed."

Frances looked worried. "I do hope I can believe you, Adam."

Turner took hold of her hands. "My love, I swear that I, myself, have not attacked Chivers." He looked hurt. "I wish you would believe me. I can't bear to think you don't trust me when I love you so much."

"I'm sorry, Adam. I know I should have more faith in your wisdom."

They kissed passionately, then Turner broke away. "I'm sorry, Frances, much as I should like to take you to bed this minute, let's go and break the sad news to Starella."

Lady Mallard smiled. "Yes, we'd better let her know she's not going to be a bride after all."

*   *   *   *

After Starella had offered refreshment to Sir Adam Turner and Lady Mallard which they had both politely declined, Frances said, "I'll come straight to the point about why we've called upon you, Starella. I warn you, you won't like it."

Starella looked wary. "Really?"

Turner cleared his throat. "Miss Denny, Mr Chivers has decided to leave these parts. He has also come to the conclusion that he cannot marry you as he has thought better of being wed to a half-gypsy."

Starella gasped. "Do you have proof of this, sir?"

"Here's a letter he wrote to me, informing me of all his decisions in this matter."

Lady Mallard handed the letter over as Starella examined it in minute detail.

"It does look a bit like his handwriting, only the letters sprawl a bit more and it's untidier than he usually writes." Starella was crestfallen.

"He was most likely sad that he had to impart his news to you in this manner," Turner said, smoothly. "But I believe he must have thought it was better for him not to see you in person in case his resolve weakened."

Starella's face had turned lily white but her voice was steady as she said, "Could you both leave me now, please?"

"Of course we will," Frances said, in a gentler tone than usual. After they had left, Starella began to sob hysterically. Eve came running in.

"Miss Ella, whatever's the matter? You seemed so happy this morning."

"Eve—he—he does not—I am not to—"

Eve put her arms around Starella and rocked her gently. "Get your breath back, then tell me."

*   *   *   *

On the journey back to the Dower House, Frances Mallard said, "I have no love for Starella but I couldn't help feeling sorry for her. I wish I'd never told you I'm good at forging other people's handwriting because I used to copy my husband's so that I could pay bills, myself."

Turner patted her knee. "Don't worry about it. It'll all turn out for the best, you'll see. She'll only have received Chivers' letter early. By the time his real one comes, she'll have gone away."

*   *   *   *

While Turner had been riding to Lady Mallard's, Silas Incoll, a tall, strong man who was also an excellent musician, was walking over the moor where Roland had been left. Silas had been playing the night before but had had rather a lot to drink. He liked walking on the moor at all times but this morning he hoped the fresh air would clear his aching head.

As Silas walked along, he was startled to see the prone body of a man. After checking that the man was alive, not long afterwards he saw a chestnut horse without a rider.

"What a stroke of luck," Silas said to himself. With his great strength, he managed to lift the unconscious man into the saddle while he led the animal to his cottage where he tethered it to a post after summoning his son to help him carry Roland inside.

"It's a good job you're such a skilled herb woman," Silas said to his wife, as she and her son helped to put the unconscious man into a bed. "I found this poor gentleman on the moor. Probably been set upon by footpads."

"Heaven help us all!" Silas's wife said, fervently. "There's such villains about nowadays."

When Roland awoke, his head was throbbing. He looked around the room in amazement. Silas was sitting by his bedside. He explained to Roland how he had found him on the moor.

"I believe I was set upon by fellows hired by Sir Adam Turner," Roland said, bitterly. "I think you, sir, are an angel in disguise especially sent to be my rescuer."

Silas laughed although not unkindly. "I don't have no harp, sir, but I am a fiddler. It's interesting you've said Sir Adam Turner. I played for him and his sweet—er—his friend, Lady Mallard, a few months ago."

"How ironic," said Roland. "I was on my way to see another violinist, George Perry, to confirm I wanted him to play at my forthcoming wedding."

Silas smiled again, more broadly. "George Perry, now, sir, he's my great rival."

Roland sighed. "He'll think I'm not keeping my promise to him."

"Don't you fret about that, sir. Though me and him don't always see eye to eye, I'll send my son to tell him you're not well enough to see him yourself—but do you still want him?"

"Yes, of course. But I was wondering, would you mind playing at the wedding as well?"

Silas grinned. "Would I mind, sir? I'd be more than glad to."

"Good. I'll see you're well paid for it." Roland put a hand to his forehead.

"Thank'ee, sir, thank'ee most kindly. Now you lie back and I'll send my wife in with one of her famous 'erb potions. It'll make you feel better in a trice."

'I'd only feel better if I could see Starella now,' Roland thought, wryly. Aloud, he said, "Thank you so much. I'm really grateful to you all for what you've done for me."

"Think no more of it, sir. We'd do the same for anybody as was hurt bad like you. Though you're lucky to only have cuts and bruises instead of broken bones."

CHAPTER 20

▼

"Wherever am I going to go, Eve?" Starella asked in despair after she had finally stopped crying. "The captain's still away and I definitely don't want to stay here. There's no need for you to stay with me now if you don't want to."

"I'm not leavin' you now, Eve," Eve said, firmly. "We've been through too much together."

Starella was touched. "I cant thank you enough for your loyalty and friendship."

Eve looked pleased. "You're worth it." She wrinkled her brow. "I know you might not agree with me but I think we should go back to Exeter."

"Exeter!" Starella said, almost horrified. "But look at everything that happened to us there. We both have sad memories of the place. I think I'd rather go to London."

"London's a lot further away, Ella. It would cost us more money to get there. I don't know what we'd do once we're there, either."

"There must be some sort of work we could find in such a large city."

Eve shook her head, doubtfully. "I've 'eard tell it can be a wicked city for two innocent young ladies like ourselves."

In spite of her distress, Starella had to smile wryly at this description.

"There's a stagecoach to Exeter in four days time and we can hire ourselves out at the Hirin' Fair. You'll probably be hired as a parlour maid. I know it's a big comedown from what you've been used to lately but you can always leave after a while. And me—" Eve sighed. "I suppose I'll have to be a kitchen maid again."

"Maybe someone will engage you as a parlour maid," said Starella. She had initially been unenthusiastic about Eve's suggestion but she was now wondering if she might possibly be able to find employment at a dressmakers or milliners.

But she would accompany Eve to the Hiring Fair and see her friend settled first.

*   *   *   *

Roland recovered remarkably quickly from his injuries. Silas Incoll shook his head. "I know my wife's skilled with herbs and suchlike but I declare I've never seen anybody in your condition get better and be up and about so quick."

Roland smiled almost grimly. "I owe a lot to your wife's kind attention, I must admit. But I was also determined to recover as soon as possible. I used a lot of willpower."

"That you did, sir," Silas said, with admiration.

"Now, will you come with me to see Sir Adam Turner, this very morning Silas? I hope to catch him at Lady Mallard's house. I have a few things to say to that gentleman."

Silas nodded. "I will, Mr Chivers, and gladly."

*   *   *   *

"There's two men insistin' on seem' you, my lady," Lady Mallard's maid said, nervously, twisting her hands. "One's dressed like a gentleman and the other's Silas Incoll, who was here the other night. They said it's real important they see you."

"How dare Incoll and this other fellow demand to see you, Frances," Turner said, indignantly. "Send them away this minute girl!" he snapped at the servant.

"But sir," she protested, almost in tears. "I've already tried to do this. They won't take no for an answer …"

"That's quite right, we won't, under any circumstances," Roland Chivers said, coolly, as he strode into the drawing room accompanied by Silas Incoll.

"What's the meaning of this outrage?" Turner was indignant.

"Don't act the innocent with me, Sir Adam," Roland said. He spoke quietly but there was menace in his tone. "You set up men disguised as highwaymen to attack me on the moor three days ago. Silas here is my witness."

Turner began to bluster. "Incoll is a musician. What would he know?"

Silas drew himself to his full height and approached the other man with a threatening expression. "I may be only a musician to you, Sir Adam. But I knows what I sees with my own eyes."

"You're bluffing!" Turner said contemptuously.

"No I ain't. I was on the moor the other morning. My eyes are very sharp and I seen your carriage. I also recognised the two chaps you had with you even though they was in disguise." He turned to Roland. "They're well known villains in these parts but they've been lyin' low for a bit."

"Silas is a reliable witness," Roland said, triumphantly. "I suppose a lot of other men would call you out but I shant waste my time doing so. You're not worth the effort."

"I believe you're too much of a coward to do so, Chivers."

Roland flushed. "I assure you I'm not. But I could arrange to see you in Court."

"You have no proof."

"Didn't I just produce a witness?"

Turner's eyebrows rose. "Incoll's word against mine? Do you think that would count for a lot to the magistrates?"

"Don't forget, sir," Roland almost hissed. "I know several magistrates. They would all believe me."

Frances had been watching the men with a horrified expression on her face. She spoke for the first time. "Adam, I can see by your expression and tell by your face that you're guilty of the crime of which you've been accused." She gave a heartbroken sob. "But, villain as you've proved to be, I can't bear to think of you rotting away in prison."

"Don't distress yourself so, Lady Mallard," said Roland. "I have no intention of pressing charges. If Sir Adam agrees to go a long way from here, this matter can now be forgotten."

"I was thinking of moving away from here, anyway," Turner said, haughtily. "It's too small and unamusing for my liking. I'm off to London." He looked at Lady Mallard. "Will you come with me, Frances?"

"I cannot after what you have done. I never want to see you again for as long as I live!"

"As you wish," Sir Adam Turner replied coldly. He stalked out of the room, his face a picture of impotent rage.

As soon as he had gone, Frances burst into tears. Roland put his hand over hers.

"I understand how you feel, Frances. But you're really better off without him."

Frances nodded. 'I know I am. Oh Roland, I've been such a fool. He promised me he wouldn't hurt you and I was taken in by him."

'I'm thankful you didn't want to see me set upon," Roland said, dryly. "You could have desired it after I arrived with my news of your husband's death and announcing that I was taking over your son's rightful place."

"Oh, my son's too young yet as you know. And I have to admit you've done good work on this estate even though I confess I did resent you a little at first. But I've never disliked you however much I've tried." She rang for refreshment.

After he and Silas had finished drinking, Roland said, "I must go and see Starella now."

But when he arrived at the Manor House, the servants informed him that Eve and Starella were gone.

"Do any of you know where?"

"I could be wrong, sir, but if I tell you where I think they might have gone, would it be worth my while?"

"I'll give you half a crown if that's what you're after. Speak up, girl."

"They could have gone to Exeter, sir. I 'eard 'em talkin' about it. Not that I was deliberately listenin', mind. I wouldn't do that. I just couldn't help over-hearin'."

"Here's your coin. I know you wouldn't listen intentionally but I'm very glad you did."

One of Lady Mallard's footmen came running to the kitchen. "Mr Chivers, sir," the man said, trying to catch his breath, "Lady Mallard begs that you see her again, immediately. She says its most urgent, sir."

*   *   *   *

As Starella and Eve were about to join the long lines of male and female servants, Starella suddenly pointed. "Look Eve, there's Raphael. We must speak to him." The two young women approached him. A delighted grin spread all over Raphael's face when he saw them. He was carrying his flute.

"Raphael, what on earth are you doing here? It's wonderful to see you but why have you come to this place?"

"First massa I had after I got my freedom died. I doan like his son so I left him."

A well-dressed farmer who was passing by frowned and said to his companion in a very loud voice, "I'll wager that's no servant but a runaway slave. We might get a handsome reward if we turn him in."

Starella looked around wildly at the crowd—the carter with a piece of whip-cord tied to his leg, the serge makers holding pieces of cloth and the maids carrying brooms and mops. They were all staring at Raphael with great interest.

"The boy's with me!" she shouted in desperation. "My master has sent me with him to hire him out as a musician to gentry for balls and suchlike. Play your flute, Raphael."

Raphael began to play as if his very life depended upon it.

"He can play a strange tune right enough but the maid's tellin' a Banbury tale if ever I 'eard one, you mark my words," said the carter with a snort of derision. "For some wicked reason of her own, she wants to shield the nigger."

"No, she's definitely telling the truth," a deep, cultured masculine voice said.

Starella whirled around in amazement to see Roland Chivers accompanied by Lady Mallard. She wondered if she had been dreaming she was at the Hiring Fair.

"I wish to hire the black boy. Do you want to work for me again, Raphael?"

Raphael beamed. "For certain sure, massa Roland."

"I'll go and inspect the women to find the maid I was looking for," Frances said. She turned on her heel and swiftly left them.

"Good day to you, Mr Chivers," Starella said, coldly. "I seem to have lost Eve so I must go and find her."

She tried to walk past him but he caught her arms in a firm grip and turned her around to face him. "I could shake the life out of you, Starella!" He turned to Raphael. "You go and find Eve but don't bring her back here yet or return yourself until an hour's time. Be off with you now!" He gave the boy a shiny coin.

Raphael ran off to discover Eve deep in conversation with a handsome young shepherd who had a sheep's tail pinned on to his sleeve. Eve chatted to Raphael for a little while, then she also asked him to make himself scarce for a few minutes.

"You're a fine one to talk, sir," Starella said to Roland, angrily. "You pretend you want to marry me. You even go so far as to hold a betrothal ball. Then you decide you don't want me because my mother was a gypsy. You could have let me know a lot earlier than you did if that's how you felt. And it was unpleasant having to be told by others ..." Her voice broke on a half sob.

"I said nothing of the kind, you silly little fool. You didn't have the sense to wait and hear the truth from my own lips. No, you have to believe the lies of others!" Starella stared at him. "The lies—then you didn't say—"

Roland shook his head in exasperation. "I certainly never said I didn't want to marry you." His mouth was set in a grim line. "Turner persuaded Frances to forge my handwriting on that stupid letter you had the foolishness to take heed of."

"But I couldn't have borne to hear it from you!" Starella said in a distressed tone. Roland placed his arm around her shoulders and in a softer voice said, "You shouldn't have had to hear it from anybody. But don't blame Frances, she's contrite."

"I'm sure she is." In spite of her earlier unhappiness, Starella was sarcastic.

"I mean it. She told Turner she wanted nothing further to do with him after he set his fellows upon me."

Starella was horrified. "What happened when you were attacked?"

"It's a long story which I'll tell you later. Frances confessed to me what she had done. She wanted to come to Exeter because she has decided to rent a house here and live with her two children there rather than in the Dower House. We travelled in her carriage."

"But why did you come to the Hiring Fair?"

"Frances thought she would like a new parlour maid. Her other one's leaving to look after her ailing mother. If she hadn't wanted to come here, I wouldn't have found you again. You see, she's done us a great favour."

Starella exchanged his smile with heartfelt relief. "Yes she has. I feel ashamed now that I misjudged you."

"Well, please don't find me guilty of such deception again." He bent his head and kissed her. Then he took hold of her hand. "Frances is staying with a cousin of hers tonight. I think we should now go back to the inn you stayed in before."

"Before we do so, please let me find Eve."

"Very well. She's over there, I saw her earlier on. She's still talking to a shepherd."

When they approached Eve, the girl looked apprehensive. "Master Roland, 'ow did you know we was here?"

"It's an involved tale, Eve. I'll be explaining it to your mistress soon. And I do still want to marry her."

Eve grinned. "I'm so glad for you both."

"I expect you're looking forward to dancing at our wedding."

Eve bit her lip and looked down at the ground. Then she turned to Starella. "A farmer's agreed to take both John here"—she indicated the shepherd—"and myself as a nursemaid for his three children. I'll miss you of course but I'd really like to go with him." She looked at John with longing.

"I can't stop you going," Starella smiled. "You weren't my slave."

"But you're not cross with me for wantin' to?"

"Of course not," Starella said, gently. She smiled a t John. "Take care of her, she deserves a good man. She's been such a friend to me. But I hope we'll see you both again, soon." She kissed Eve's cheek, affectionately.

"Eve," Roland called over his shoulder as he and Starella were walking away arm-in-arm. "Please do me a favour and tell Raphael not to return in an hour. Give him the address of the inn you and Ella stayed at before you left the city. Tell him to report there at eight o'clock sharp tomorrow morning."

Roland escorted Starella to Lady Mallard's carriage and helped her in. "I'm going back to find Frances," he said.

Starella looked out of the window, thinking that if Roland had not seen her when he did, she would now be walking around Exeter's streets, calling at dress-makers and milliners to look for employment. Possibly a fruitless search, she thought, grimly.

She was apprehensive about seeing Lady Mallard again, terrified she would have a blazing row with the other woman and make herself look a shrew in Roland's eyes.

However, when Lady Mallard was seated in her carriage, she spoke first. "Starella, I cannot tell you how sorry I am that I was the cause of Roland losing you. I was tricked by that evil man, Sir Adam Turner. I should not have been so foolish. I do hope you can forgive me."

Starella hesitated for a few minutes before speaking. "I could feel very bitter towards you, Lady Mallard, but fortunately all has ended satisfactorily by an extremely lucky chance. Therefore, I won't bear a grudge against you."

"Thank you."

"We're grateful to you for letting us ride to the inn in your carriage," Roland said. "You ladies might not have liked walking in this drizzle."

"You're more than welcome for the ride," Lady Mallard replied. "I'll go to my cousin's house afterwards."

After Roland and Starella had entered the inn and been served a delicious meal by the landlady who fussed over them both, Roland said, "I hope this won't come as too much of a shock to you, Ella, but Captain Mountjoy's coming here tomorrow with his betrothed. I have been involved in correspondence with him; he always asked after your welfare. And I've seen him once since his return."

Starella turned pale, her feelings mixed. "So I'll see him at last." She clenched her fists. "But you asked me if I wanted to meet him at the port when he came back to England. I said I did. Why didn't you honour that promise?"

"I could say because you have a habit of disappearing," Roland said, almost grimly. Then he relented. "No, it was because he wrote to me, expressly asking that you didn't meet them at the port."

"So he wanted to disown me then?' Starella was hurt.

Roland shook his head. "I'm sure that's not the reason, sweetheart. He does wish to see you but he probably didn't like to think of you being exposed to the rough characters you could see there."

Starella laughed harshly. "After some of the folk, I of all people, have been forced to associate with!" She glared at him. "You're withholding something from me, Roland. Please don't deny it."

Roland sighed. 'I admit I have been sworn to secrecy. I wish I had not but I do understand the reason. All will be revealed tomorrow. For the moment, darling, please let's not speak of it further. Come to bed with me."

He stood up and held out his hand. Despite her earlier anger, Starella took it with a knowing smile and they spent a blissful night in each other's arms.

*   *   *   *

The following morning, after they had breakfasted and Roland had spoken to Raphael and sent him on some errands, the landlady ushered Captain Mountjoy and his future wife into the private parlour. The captain looked tanned and healthy. His intended bride looked much younger than him.

"Mr Chivers, Starella," Charles said, stiffly. "This is my future bride, Miss Belinda Collins."

Starella tried not to stare at the other woman. *So she's black! That's why he didn't want me to meet her at the port.* Aloud, she said, "I am delighted to make your acquaintance, Miss Collins."

Belinda gave her coffee-coloured face a tiny pat before she spoke. "As I am pleased to meet you at last, Miss Denny. I've heard a lot about you and you truly are beautiful."

"You're lissom and comely yourself, Miss Collins, if I may say so," Roland said, with some gallantry but to a certain extent it was true.

"Thank you, sir," Belinda said. She turned to Starella again. "I met your guardian at a supper party at Topsham. Then we travelled back together to the West Indies. Now I've returned to a cold island."

"I hope you weren't too sad to leave the Indies, Miss Collins."

"No, I'm happy to be wherever dear Charles is. I'm going to be blunt now, Miss Denny. You must forgive my plain speaking but this is my manner. Do you mind your adopted uncle marrying a mulatto?"

"I—I should not presume to—" Starella wished she were not stammering.

Belinda held up her hand. "Pplease don't be too embarrassed to say what you really think. A mulatto, Miss Denny, if you don't already know, is a person with mixed black and white blood."

"I do know this, Miss Coffins."

Belinda nodded. "My father was a plantation owner and my mother was originally his slave girl but he married her. He was very rich you see but I was his only child and sole heiress. Both my parents are dead now so I can sympathise with you being an orphan."

Charles broke in. "Starella, I know you have a lot to forgive me for. I know I was a coward not to confide in you that I had met Miss Collins and was sailing away with her. I was wrong not to let you know what I was doing, but I was not sure how you would react if I did tell you."

"I have to admit I was both hurt and surprised by your behaviour, Uncle Charles," Starella said, stiffly.

"I do understand how you felt, believe it or not," Mountjoy said.

"I tried to explain you thought no less of her, Captain Mountjoy," Roland said, awkwardly. "But I couldn't betray your confidence."

"For which I'm grateful," said Mountjoy.

"You're not really happy about your guardian marrying me, are you?" Belinda asked Starella, her voice wistful. "I should have known!"

Starella looked at her and the dark eyes met and held with the green. "On the contrary, Miss Collins, I'm thrilled my uncle has met such a pleasant lady as yourself."

The atmosphere in the room had been very strained but they all now began to relax. Belinda was beaming.

"I am going to be plain spoken now, Miss Collins," Starella said. "Uncle Charles has not always approved of my loose tongue in the past but I must say two things. The first is that some people have looked down on me because my mother was of Romany blood. So who am I to look down on you for your parentage? You could not help it any more than I could. The second is that I think I shall like you better than Uncle Charles' first wife."

Charles looked a little embarrassed but merely said, "Ellie, you'll be pleased to know I met your uncle, your mother's brother, Jacko, in the Indies. He's become prosperous."

"That's marvellous news, Uncle Charles."

"And Roland, your father's new plantation is doing very well indeed."

Roland grinned. "I'm delighted you've come back, captain. You're bringing us all good tidings. After Starella and I are married, we'll be travelling to the West Indies."

Starella looked almost as if she were in a trance. "We'll be going after the snow falls. It will cover the ground with a white blanket and make lace shapes on the trees. When we awake each morning, we'll see frost flower patterns on the windowpanes. Then all the whiteness will go and we'll sail over the blue sea to the golden sunshine where our children will become Caribbean jewels. Lady Mallard's steward will keep up the good work Roland has done on this estate until James is old enough to take over."

"What's all that you're saying, love?" Roland asked, anxiously. "How do you know all this?"

Starella smiled, putting her hand to her brow. "Call it a premonition if you like." She looked at Mountjoy. "Uncle Charles, will you give me a special Christmas present, seeing as you've upset me with your secrecy?"

"Naturally, whatever you like. Name it and I'll see to it."

She hesitated for a few moments while the others all waited for her words with a little of the earlier tension returning to their features.

"My desire," Starella said, in a loud, clear voice, "is for us to have a double wedding at Christmas with much merrymaking."

A loud cheer of joy erupted from all of their throats at exactly the same moment. "A toast to us all. We must have a toast!" Roland exclaimed.

The walls of the room echoed with the sound of their combined happy laughter.

END

978-0-595-47254-3
0-595-47254-0

1/24

Printed in the United Kingdom
by Lightning Source UK Ltd.
124202UK00002B/106-123/A